He raised her . to
"Not everyone ___ to
hurt you. Some___ ou
to trust me, but ___ und
for."

He saw the little ___ ace now. The one who
wanted so desperately to be loved, but was so
afraid of being hurt. He wanted to kiss her, but
feared it would immediately explode into passion
rather than offer reassurance.

A small smile curled her lips. "Lisa said everyone
isn't as persistent as she is."

"I can be just as stubborn as you are. Of course,
mine is tenacity."

"Whereas I'm just stubborn." Her tone was lighter
and life was reanimating her body.

"You wasted a perfectly good week when I was so
conveniently right there in town."

"Clearly you wasted too much time before prying
into my deep, dark secrets and discovering my
magnificent character."

How many of her secrets had she shared? "Oh?"

"Yep."

To his surprise, she reached up and kissed him.
It was more of a promise than an invitation. He
would've responded if she hadn't immediately
leaned back. He kept his hands on her waist,
waiting to see what she'd do next. With the smallest
encouragement, he'd take her home with him. Given
the opportunity, he'd show her exactly how much
he cared.

THE PROFESSOR

CATHY PERKINS

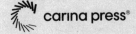

If you purchased this book without a cover you should be aware that this book is stolen property. It was reported as "unsold and destroyed" to the publisher, and neither the author nor the publisher has received any payment for this "stripped book."

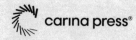

ISBN-13: 978-0-373-00230-6

THE PROFESSOR

Recycling programs
for this product may
not exist in your area.

Copyright © 2012 by Catherine Perkins

All rights reserved. Except for use in any review, the reproduction or utilization of this work in whole or in part in any form by any electronic, mechanical or other means, now known or hereafter invented, including xerography, photocopying and recording, or in any information storage or retrieval system, is forbidden without the written permission of the publisher, Harlequin Enterprises Limited, 225 Duncan Mill Road, Don Mills, Ontario M3B 3K9, Canada.

This is a work of fiction. Names, characters, places and incidents are either the product of the author's imagination or are used fictitiously, and any resemblance to actual persons, living or dead, business establishments, events or locales is entirely coincidental.

This edition published by arrangement with Harlequin Books S.A.

® and TM are trademarks of the publisher. Trademarks indicated with ® are registered in the United States Patent and Trademark Office, the Canadian Trade Marks Office and in other countries.

www.CarinaPress.com

Printed in U.S.A.

Dear Reader,

Welcome to South Carolina! I've found people don't know much about the area, other than hurricanes hit here and we have more than our share of politicians behaving badly. For such a small state, it has so much variety—mountains, lakes and beaches; big cities, small towns, with lots of pine trees and cotton fields in between them. The people are just as diverse.

What does that have to do with a suspense novel? Several years ago, a serial killer terrorized a small town in upstate South Carolina, killing five people over three days before dying in a shoot-out with the police. Once the horror faded, my author brain whispered, "What if...?"

What if instead of a small town where the murders were immediately linked, the killer roamed South Carolina's small college campuses? Could he "get away with it" longer? Would that make him (or her?) more difficult to find? What if the killer's next obsession was Meg Connelly, the hero's new girlfriend?

The Professor grew from those initial musings into state law enforcement agent Mick O'Shaughnessy's race to pull together the puzzle pieces and find the killer before another woman died.

The devastated relatives of the victims worked their way into the story, as well. Ripples of family dynamics drove the characters to make decisions—to keep secrets. Mick's close-knit family provided a source of strength and renewal, while the hypocrisy of Meg's contributed to her poor choices, which she saw as independence. I found I loved this theme and suspect I might have to explore it further.

Enjoy the story and look for more adventures from the cast of *The Professor*. Stop by my website (www.cperkinswrites.com) or find me on Facebook and let me know what you think.

Cathy Perkins

For Chuck, for always believing in me.

THE PROFESSOR

ONE

Wednesday afternoon

THE BODY LAY in dappled shade. Patches of light caught pale flesh—an ankle here, a hip there. Resurrection ferns spread lacy fronds, partially concealing the limbs. Mick wondered if the irony was deliberate.

This deep into the woods, the trees blocked the breeze and the humidity increased as the air sucked moisture from the thick mulch spread across the forest floor. The noxious mixture of smells pressed against him in a cloying layer that was nearly visible amid the shifting patterns cast by the overhead branches. Pausing at the edge of the clearing, he batted at the flies circling his head. He hated flies. He associated them so strongly with death that a fly in his condo drove him crazy.

Two local detectives looked up, acknowledging Mick's presence. His short hair marked him as a cop as much as the holstered pistol and gold badge clipped to his belt. The locals would already know who he was. He hadn't been able to escape the publicity surrounding the murders—the Captain kept putting him in front of television cameras. The Greenville, South Carolina, stations had been particularly relentless in their quest for footage, repeatedly lurking outside the upstate SLED—State Law Enforcement Division—field office.

The medical examiner crouched over the body, obscuring the head and upper torso. He stood when Mick approached, revealing the now familiar pose. Emily Geiger—if the nude corpse was Emily Geiger—lay on her back, arms opened with the hands palm up in a welcoming gesture. Her legs were spread, bent at the knee, a blatantly sexual posture. Frozen in full rigor, the body would have to be photographed and transported in this degrading position.

Until the Newberry police department asked SLED for assistance, Mick had no authority at the scene. He listened as the ME reported his findings to the local detectives. While they talked, he studied the men, looking for the best way to interact with them. Detective Larry Robbins looked like an oak tree, stocky rather than fat—the kind of guy Mick would want on his side in a bar fight. His twenty years of experience showed in his eyes: weary, heard-it-all-before cynicism. Jerry Jordan, on the other hand, was a greenhorn. He was trying to project confidence and experience while keeping his lunch down. The effort sharpened his jaw and squared his shoulders, but he still looked like a kid in over his head.

The ME estimated the time of death as sometime Monday night. "Lividity's fixed. Rigor's just starting to relax, so it's been less than forty-eight hours. I'll be able to narrow it down when I get back to the lab, but she's been here at least twenty-four hours."

"How can you tell?" Robbins asked.

The doctor gestured at the sample he'd collected. "Blowflies. They show up within fifteen minutes of exposure and lay eggs in the natural orifices and open wounds. The egg stage lasts twenty-four hours. These are blowfly larvae."

Jordan looked even more nauseous.

"A dump site." Robbins gave the clearing a disgruntled look.

The ME continued, "Lividity indicates she died lying

faceup, but see the dual pattern on her arms and legs? They were repositioned after the blood pooling started, but before rigor set in."

"What time would you estimate she was moved here?" Mick asked when no one else did.

"Early Tuesday morning, roughly six hours postmortem. I expect he moved her while it was still dark."

"We'll canvass the area," Robbins said. "We have some early risers around here."

Mick nodded, noting the unspoken commentary. *This is our city. We know our people.* Fine, he thought, as long as they tell you something. The locals sometimes resented SLED's involvement, but with a multi-county case like this, the state police's participation was essential.

Greg Lewis, the responding patrol officer, called from the edge of the clearing. "Crime Scene van's here. You ready for them?"

Robbins looked at Mick. "Are you lead, Agent O'Shaughnessy? Or one of us?"

"I'm advisory at this point. But my gut says she's number three."

"Okay." Robbins turned to Lewis. "I'm lead. Send 'em up."

Outdoor crime scenes needed to be processed quickly. Animals carried off evidence. Storms washed away footprints, blood and semen. The wind scattered everything. There were no walls or locked doors to keep out trespassers. It would get dark before they finished, further complicating the search.

Mick and Lewis followed the dirt road toward the cluster of marked and unmarked police cars parked at the entrance to Lynches Woods Park. Rolling hills extended in all directions, covered with pines, oaks, sassafras and poplars. The cooler October nights were turning the poplars yellow, but overall the place still felt like a quiet, green retreat. In a rural area—which included most of Newberry County—a park like this wouldn't draw as many visitors as a similar oasis in a larger city. A murderer would be practically assured of privacy.

"The park's inside the city limits?" Mick asked. Newberry was a small town. He'd expected to find the sheriff's department in charge.

Lewis nodded. "Conservation Corps built the place in the thirties. It's not very big—only a couple hundred acres. We don't have much trouble out here. Used to be, you'd only see one or two cars on a weekday. There's more now that we hooked up with the Palmetto Trail." He gestured at a sign marking the trailhead. "'Course Central Tech backs up to the property. You get some students over here."

"Walk-ins?"

"There's no perimeter fence. They've cut some paths over from the campus."

Mick motioned to the chain blocking access to the park's interior. "That's always there?"

"The maintenance guys have a key, but everybody knows this road's closed. They stay on the main drive to the parking lot."

The dirt roads were well-maintained. The killer wouldn't have needed four-wheel drive. Flags along the road's shoulder marked the car's path. Tire tracks. Mick smiled. Finally, physical evidence to work with. Other flags marked scuffed-over footprints. Several of the prints remained clear enough to cast.

"The guy who found her…"

Lewis consulted his notebook as they approached the parking area. Just beyond them, a dejected-looking man sat on a picnic table with his head in his hands. "His name's Phillip Lyles. He started his ride at noon, did the Main

Loop, then backtracked to the Spur. Picked up the dirt road to ride out as a cooldown. Said the smell about knocked him off his bike."

They glanced at the cyclist who still looked as green as the diamonds decorating his spandex jersey.

"He served in Iraq. He knew exactly what it was. Called nine-one-one from his cell."

"When?"

"The call came in at 12:57 p.m. The time's right if he rode where he said he did."

"Sounds like you ride."

Lewis nodded. "I try to go midweek. The weekends get crowded."

"Did he say whether anybody else was here when he arrived?"

"Had the place to himself. We got here about five minutes after the call came in. I walked in far enough to confirm the body, then backed out and secured the scene."

Lyles glanced up when they ducked under the perimeter tape, as if hoping they could tell him he could finally go home. Mick stored an impression of tired eyes, wiry muscle and sweat-matted hair before the man resumed his inspection of the dirt at his feet.

Mick left Lewis talking to the cyclist. He exchanged his sports coat for a nylon SLED windbreaker and rejoined the Newberry police. By the time the CSU completed its grid search, he was tired, filthy and sick of swatting bugs. They needed a hard freeze to kill the damn things, but they weren't likely to get one for another month. He drove to his motel, stripped and dropped his clothes directly into the laundry bag. The shower washed the stench from his hair and skin, and the warm water loosened the tight muscles in his back.

Emily Geiger had vanished Monday morning. Tonight,

someone, probably her father, would identify her body. At the autopsy tomorrow, the coroner would confirm both the corpse's identity and whether this was victim number three. By tomorrow, his captain would notify him of the Newberry PD's official request for assistance. He wished he had more to offer than frustration and an inability to locate the monster who'd raped and killed three young women.

Wednesday night

THE LIBRARY CLOSED at midnight. Normally, the doors closed at nine, but during midterms, students and faculty had access to the reference materials, space, and quiet for three extra hours. Tucked away in a third-floor carrel reserved for graduate students, Meg Connelly had been grading papers. Occupied with the chore, she hadn't noticed the building gradually empty.

The librarian locked the door after Meg stepped outside. The library's rosy brick facade contrasted with the wireless technology hidden behind the *Gone with the Wind* exterior. A small liberal arts school in a small town in South Carolina, Douglass College had a respectable academic reputation, but at times it seemed as if the second half of the twentieth century had passed unnoticed.

Meg paused at the top of the limestone steps that descended to the quadrangle. Mature oaks and magnolias flourished above the magnificent azaleas lining the brick pathways. A long rectangle, the quad extended east from the library to the Admin Building. Silent, darkened classroom buildings surrounded it. A shorter, north-south corridor crossed midway. The quiet splash of the intersection's fountain murmured beneath the other nocturnal sounds: frogs, insects, and an occasional bird. A gaudier fountain on the northern leg marked the center of Greek housing. Meg's apartment, one of six carved from an old Victorian, stood on a cross street just beyond the sorority houses.

During the day, the quad's lawn formed an outdoor living room for students to read, nap and dream away the afternoon. After dark, it was simply dark. The widely spaced, decorative lampposts left enigmatic pools of shadows that shifted against the thick shrubbery. The leaves whispering in the breeze urged caution.

Meg clutched her messenger bag and surveyed the deserted area. Normally, the dark didn't bother her. After three years, she could walk across campus blindfolded. Douglass was a cocoon of safety, isolated from the violence delivered by television and newspapers. Half the time, people didn't lock the doors. But earlier this week, Emily Geiger had been kidnapped from nearby Windsor College. Only thirty miles separated the schools, and everyone was on edge.

She eyed the shadowy expanse and wished she'd called the campus escort service before leaving the security of the brightly lit reading room. Now the library was closed and Meg couldn't afford a cell phone. She descended the stairs, acutely aware of the thud of her sneakers against the stone, and reached the path that angled northeast across the quad.

"Hey, Connelly!"

She jumped and spun around, then forced her tense muscles to relax as she recognized Tony Baldwin and Dino Famiglio. Both were in her statistics class. For ΣAEs they weren't bad guys. A fifth-year senior, Tony was concentrating on school this fall instead of football. For once, his bulk felt welcome rather than intimidating.

"How come you were at the library?" Tony asked.

"Maybe the better question is, why weren't you?"

He shrugged. "I was earlier. We took a break and went into town for pizza."

And beer, by the smell of it, she noted.

Tony moved closer. "Do we really have to turn in the stat project this week?"

Meg adjusted her messenger bag. "It's been on the syllabus since the beginning of the term."

"I don't suppose I could talk you into helping me? Maybe some private tutoring?"

She rolled her eyes. "Stop by my office if you need help. During regular hours."

He dropped his arm around her shoulders. "I could get ideas from you."

"You already have too many ideas." She laughed and shrugged off his arm. "Remember we talked about boundaries? Me, teacher. You, student."

"Go long," he said to Dino, who obligingly sprinted ahead. Tony faked a football pass and Dino mimed the catch and score.

Tony turned back to Meg. He smiled slyly and pulled the ribbon from her hair. The curly auburn mass tumbled around her face. "You should wear your hair down. You look like a nun with it pulled back."

"Boundaries, Tony, boundaries. Besides, maybe I secretly am a nun." She reached for the band. "Give that back."

He dangled it above her head. "You should listen to my ideas. I have great ideas. Lots of them involve you."

"You say the sweetest things. I can't imagine why girls aren't falling all over you." The problem was girls did fall all over Tony, and he couldn't understand why she didn't. He had been trying all semester, with varying degrees of effort, to get into her pants. She constantly blocked his moves. Sometimes she wanted to suggest indifference as an effective strategy to the girls who struggled to attract his attention.

Meg grabbed the ribbon and followed Dino's path. They caught up to him as he finished his victory dance. Abruptly, Dino stopped and turned his head. "Sounds like a party at the Trev."

Feminine giggles came from the direction of the Greek's fountain. Alumni from some forgotten class had installed an elaborate fountain the students immediately dubbed the Trev. As in the Roman incarnation, Neptune rose amid swirling waters, riding a chariot drawn by winged sea horses. Unlike the original, the Trev sported mermaids around the perimeter. Water gushed in a noisy cascade from the seashells poised in their hands.

A group of women stood next to the fountain. The circle opened, and Meg's mouth sagged open in shock as Didi Hammond, clad only in her Victoria's Secret underwear, lurched toward the wide ledge surrounding the Trev.

"Oh, my God!" Meg turned appalled eyes from Didi to Tony.

"No way," he said with a laugh.

Uptight, über-bitch Didi? Drunk? In her underwear?

Normally the sophomore wrapped her upper-class entitlement so tightly around herself Meg wondered how she could breathe.

Didi climbed over the ledge into the knee-deep pool. Egged on by the cheering women, she turned an unsteady pirouette. Someone added liquid soap, and bubbles exploded under Neptune's steely gaze. Didi giggled and grabbed at the spume. She slipped and landed mid-pool with a wave of foam.

"Go, Didi!" Dino added an enthusiastic male voice to the women's encouragement.

Didi crawled to the nearest mermaid and hauled herself

upright. The self-appointed guardian of virtue cavorted in what were now see-through undergarments, splashing mounds of bubbles at her admiring audience.

Other male voices approached the fountain. Once they reached the surrounding lights, Meg realized the voices belonged to Sigma Nus who were half-carrying Didi's boyfriend, Brad. He was equally drunk, very naked, and obviously very happy to see Didi. He clambered over the ledge, tripped and belly flopped into the fountain, splashing water and bubbles over the growing crowd.

"Hope he didn't break anything important," Tony murmured into Meg's ear. Given the husky note in his voice, he found the scene a turn-on rather than appallingly amusing.

"Maybe it'll keep him from reproducing."

Brad staggered to his feet and caught Didi in a sloppy embrace. Within seconds, his tongue was down her throat and his hands were in her panties. Didi clung to his shoulders and hooked a leg around him.

"Go for it," the guys called.

"You don't think he'll actually…?" Meg tugged on Tony's arm.

"If we're lucky," Dino answered from her other side.

If anyone deserved the chance to make a fool of herself, it was Didi, but drunken sex as a spectator sport went too far. "Do something, Tony."

"Com'on, Teach. They're just doing what comes natural."

More people poured from the surrounding buildings and camera phones flashed.

"We can't let them screw in front of everybody."

"I'm not sure they know or care."

Meg gave him an exasperated glare and shoved past the people closest to the fountain. "Didi," she called as she pulled off her first sneaker.

Tony sighed and followed her. "I'll do it."

He stepped over the ledge and waded toward the oblivious couple. Smacking Brad's shoulder, he knocked him back several feet. Didi lost her balance and fell, landing in a billow of bubbles. Brad gaped drunkenly at Tony. "Wha-a?" He looked around as if he'd lost something, but couldn't quite remember what. "Didi?"

Tony hauled Didi to her feet. "She's right here. You need to get a room, man."

The pair gaped at him, as if their hearing were on a time delay setting. Slowly, Didi's head turned, her eyes squinting at the sea of faces surrounding the fountain. A flurry of activity caught her attention, and a well-dressed brunette emerged from the crowd.

The woman stared, horrified, at the sodden trio. "Oh, my God, Didi. What did they do to you?"

Didi blinked as her friend's words apparently registered. She sank to her knees and crossed her arms over her chest. "They made me do it," she sobbed.

TWO

Thursday, late morning

MICK O'SHAUGHNESSY SAT in his car behind the brick building that housed the county medical examiner's office.
The sun shining through the window felt good against
the morning chill. He cracked the window, savoring the
fresh air, and slumped in the seat, postponing the moment
he had to enter the building.

His empty stomach rumbled—the coffee he'd had at the
Geigers' burned—but he never ate before an autopsy. He
dreaded autopsies—a necessary evil in homicide investi-
gations. He couldn't imagine working with the dead day
in and day out; better Dr. Spindler than him. Technically,
he wasn't required to attend, but he needed to observe. Everything in the field pointed to the killer he'd been tracking for months. If it was the same man, he wanted to learn
it firsthand, not read about the signature detail in a report.

Mick slammed the car door and walked into the building. He'd spent the morning with Emily Geiger's shattered
family. While the crime scene techs processed the girl's
bedroom, he interviewed—or at least tried to interview—
her parents. The victim's family usually talked more, remembered more details, in comfortable surroundings, but
the experience was always surreal: the sunny living room,
family portraits smiling from the walls, the central player
gone forever, the ones left behind slack with shock. Like
the other families, the Geigers lived in an upscale devel-

opment, this one wrapped around a golf course. The lavish appointments hadn't kept tragedy from finding them. This family was as bewildered as the rest, endlessly wondering what they'd done wrong.

Mick had read the statements taken when Emily disappeared, but he'd pressed for details, searching for and finding the pattern of harassment. She'd mentioned the feeling of being watched. Her laptop confirmed at least one harassing e-mail message. If she'd deleted others, the computer jockeys in Columbia could recover them. Her parents had been stunned, then angry. They'd lashed out at Mick, as if his uncovering the information made him responsible for her death.

In the autopsy suite changing room, Mick layered a surgical gown and shoe covers over his clothing and added a paper cap. The cap kept his stray hairs out of the operating field. The rest was because he'd seen what spilled off the table. The stench he'd carry home in his hair and clothes was bad enough. He didn't need to add blood and clumps of tissue. Before donning gloves, he twirled a Q-tip through the vat of VapoRub and dabbed the greasy concoction under his nose. The sharp scent masked at least some of death's pungency.

Squaring his shoulders, he opened the connecting door to the autopsy room. The place was spotless, gleaming tile and polished stainless steel. Jerry Jordan and Larry Robbins were already in place. Jordan stood against the wall, putting as much distance as possible between himself and the table. Robbins apparently still couldn't decide whether he thought SLED was helping or interfering. Arms crossed, jaw jutting stoically, he stood opposite Dr. Spindler. "Wasn't sure you were going to show up."

"The Geigers had a lot on their mind," Mick said mildly. Robbins stared at him a moment, glanced at the draped corpse, then roamed the room for a place to focus his attention. "They took it pretty hard."

"Most parents would."

Dr. Spindler snapped his gloves into place. Mick had arranged for him to autopsy this latest victim, since he'd examined the first ones. His assistant had the body prepped and the instruments in place. He removed the screening drape. Emily's remains lay on the steel table in horrifying contrast to the vibrant photos Mick had endured that morning. No one would call her pretty now.

Under the pitiless glare of the examination lights, she looked in worse shape than she had in the woods. Rigor had broken overnight. At least her limbs lay slack and straight. The greenish skin of her abdomen drew his attention. For a moment, he irrationally imagined the decay arose from the site of her violation rather than the natural action of bacteria. His stomach turned over and he wished he'd skipped the coffee too.

Forcing professional detachment, Mick silently studied the pattern of cuts and bruises. "What kind of knife did he use?"

"A medium-sized chef's knife. The blade was unserrated. See the jags here?" Dr. Spindler pointed to her thigh. "Some initial hesitation on these, but none here." His hand moved to the breast and abdomen.

"He gained confidence as he went," Mick said.

Robbins stood ramrod straight, his gaze locked on the sliced flesh. "Hell of a skill to acquire."

Jordan ventured a quick look. He gagged, lurched to the sink and vomited. He clung to the steel counter a few minutes, then rinsed his mouth and returned to his former position. Two red spots burned on his otherwise pale cheeks.

Keeping his eyes on the corpse, Mick said conversationally, "The first time I saw a dead body, I was fresh out of the Academy, riding shotgun with a patrol sergeant. We were first on the scene for a wreck out on 520. You know the four-lane going into Myrtle Beach?"

He glanced at Jordan. The kid's eyes were still fixed on the floor. "A logging truck spilled its load."

"A log fall on somebody?" Robbins asked from Mick's other side.

An interested expression lifted the man's features. Mick gave him a startled look, then continued his story. "Nope. A kid in a convertible—his license said he was sixteen—must've panicked when the first log came off. There weren't any skid marks."

"He probably hit the gas instead of the brake."

"Probably. He went straight under the trailer." Mick caught the wince that wrinkled Jordan's face. "I walked over to where the car stuck out from under the chassis. The kid's head was lying on the road, looking up at me."

Jordan gagged again.

"When I came to, my sergeant was scraping me off the pavement, while a Highway Patrol officer hovered behind him. Sarge never said another word about it. Just told me to keep my head between my knees until the spinning stopped."

Jordan didn't say anything, but his shoulders dropped an inch as his tension level fell. Message received. Nobody thought less of him for tossing his cookies over a mutilated body.

"The skin's already been taped for hair and fiber," the doctor said into the following silence. "I don't think we'll find much trace evidence. Her dental X-rays are on the light box. Dr. Christopher sent them over last night."

The curse and advantage of living in a small town: the tragedy touched everyone, but they were also quick to help. Mick crossed to the viewer, relieved to move away from the body. He studied the film clipped to the flat box. Teeth like small headstones glowed softly against the black background.

"Silver amalgam filling in number two. And see the short, blunt roots on seventeen through twenty-eight? Orthodontic work."

Orthodonture. Long after the flesh was gone, the teeth distinguished the rich from the poor. Someone struggling to put food on the table didn't worry about the appearance of the teeth that bit it. All three victims were sounding distressingly familiar—young, female, college students. White, pretty, well-to-do. "Confirmed match, then?"

"These are definitely the remains of Emily Geiger. The cap would confirm it, if I had any remaining doubts."

"She's kind of young for caps."

"Number seven." He gestured at his left front tooth. "She probably broke it when she was a kid. The color's a little off. The fill material doesn't stain at the same rate as natural enamel."

Jordan stirred. "She fell off the monkey bars at school."

Ah, shit. Jordan knew her. Probably grew up with her. Mick looked at the X-rays, waiting a beat, until he was fairly confident both of their faces would be calm. Returning to the table, he studied the pattern of bruises around the neck. The discoid bruises were visible even against the underlying postmortem discoloration. "Did you x-ray the neck?"

Dr. Spindler nodded. "There are bilateral thyroid horn fractures, consistent with manual strangulation. So's the petechiae."

Manual strangulation. Dr. Mathews, the forensic psychologist consulting with the task force, called it the most intimate way to kill someone. Face to face; flesh on flesh. Squeezing her throat until he felt her life drain away.

"What's petech-y?" Jordan asked, inching closer.

"Petechiae. Strangulation causes an increase in venous and capillary pressure that damages the inner walls of the capillaries. The result is minute points of bleeding—pinpoint hemorrhages—in the softer tissues." Dr. Spindler rolled the corpse's right eyelid. The pinpoints were visible on both the eye and the inner lid.

Frank Meyers, Mick's partner, pushed through the changing room door. A big, sandy-haired man, he was in his late forties. Fast food and no exercise had padded his body with a spare tire and jowls. With an open face and gentle, brown eyes, the extra weight gave him a teddy-bear approachability, and Mick wished he'd been present for the family interview that morning.

"Sorry," Frank said. "Did I miss much?"

"We're just getting started." Dr. Spindler turned to his assistant. "Let's get her in position."

Mick steeled himself for the worst indignity—the rape exam. He couldn't imagine how a living, breathing, humiliated woman endured it. Not for the first time, he was grateful he was male and excluded from those examination rooms. But he couldn't escape the ritual in the autopsy suite. Rage spurted through his detachment. This murdering bastard not only ended Emily Geiger's life, he threw her away like yesterday's garbage, and brought her to this final degradation. Mick clamped his jaw closed and focused on the table as the assistant spread the corpse's legs.

Frank shifted uncomfortably beside him. Mick suspected he had been late on purpose, hoping to miss this part. The man had three teenage daughters.

"Did you x-ray the pelvis?" Mick asked. He watched Dr. Spindler's hands, feeling like a ghoulish voyeur.

"Definitely a foreign object there."

Dr. Spindler made vaginal and rectal swabs. After rolling a swab across a slide, he added saline and moved to the microscope. He adjusted the machine and examined the first slide. "This is different."

Mick's attention sharpened. "What?"

"We have semen."

He hung over the doctor's shoulder. "Enough to work with? How soon can we get a DNA profile?"

"Whoa, O'Shaughnessy. One step at a time."

Dr. Spindler quickly examined the remaining slides, then returned to the table. Moving his task light, the doctor catalogued the damage to the genitalia in a detached voice. He inserted a speculum and slid forceps into the vaginal opening. Moments later, he extracted a rock and dropped it with a clang into a sterile receptacle.

"What the hell?" Robbins burst out.

"It's him," Mick said flatly. "That's his signature."

The psychiatrists could talk all day about what it meant and why he did it. To Mick, it just confirmed who killed Emily Geiger. But the killer had made a mistake. He'd left behind evidence. If there was any justice, the bastard's DNA was in the Combined Index System. *Just give me a name. I'll hunt him down like the animal he is.*

As far as Mick was concerned, the autopsy was over, but he had to endure the rest of it. Dr. Spindler started the Y-shaped incision, moving from the left shoulder to the sternum, then matching the incision from the right. When he opened the belly, Mick took a step backward, as the stench of decomposing organs hit the air like a polluted wave. "Jeez."

The pathologist looked up, then silently returned to work.

Mick wondered if the man's olfactory system even worked anymore or if it had shut down in self-defense.

Several long hours later, the procedures were finally

finished. Mick removed the protective garments, tossed them in the basket and headed toward his car. He needed to shower and change clothes before the meeting with all the task force detectives. He could remove the source of the stench, but he knew he would smell the residue—he imagined it trapped in his sinuses—all day.

His partner jogged down the hall after him. "Cap'n just paged me. Conference call this afternoon at three o'clock."

Mick glanced at his watch. That didn't leave much time to clean up. "He say what it's about?"

Frank shook his head. "Something over at Douglass College. A girl was kidnapped and assaulted on campus. Some boy broke it up. Cap'n thought it might be related to our case."

Mick frowned. "That doesn't sound like our guy's MO. He's never assaulted a woman in the open."

"I got the impression this came from somewhere up the ladder. Like maybe the Chief told the Cap'n to look into it."

"Great. Just what we need. More pressure and more politics."

"Yeah," Frank sighed. "Guess dinner isn't happening today, either."

"Look at it this way. You may drop some of that weight you bitch about."

Frank patted his belly. "Not my preferred method. I'd rather drop it on a beach, with a sailboat and a big margarita."

"Oh, yeah. That'd work off a lot of pounds."

"The blonde with me might help."

"Swinging from the catamaran's trapeze?" Mick laughed. "Does Marilyn know about this?"

"Yeah, yeah. Rub it in. Guy's gotta have his fantasies. You'll get old someday. I'm gonna laugh when *your* hair starts falling out."

"Ain't gonna happen. My granddad still has all his hair."

"He's your dad's dad. Baldness comes from the mother's side. I always knew women caused it. And I've got four of them at home. Five if you count the dog."

"You're just frustrated. Makes you tear your hair out."

"Something you wouldn't know about."

Being single had its own frustrations, Mick thought. "See you at four."

THE PROFESSOR FOLDED the newspaper neatly and deposited it in the recycle bin. He would have liked to keep it, but if the police ever came calling, he didn't want evidence of his conquests lying around. He'd read enough—studied numerous case histories—to know better. Then again, if they saw the articles, here in his home, it would already be too late. They wouldn't come unless they knew.

Affiliates in the larger cities were covering the story now. He'd been disappointed at first. Mary Baldwin's death was front page in the *Greenville News* for two days before a train derailment pushed the story to the Metro section. The *Spartanburg Herald* ran Ashley Cohen's story longer—it was a smaller town—but the coverage trailed off when no lead appeared to keep the story moving. There'd been a brief flurry of excitement last month when a reporter, finally clued in by SLED joining the investigation, linked the two deaths.

He knew he should be pleased the papers had nothing to report, but he missed the validation of his careful planning. The current newspaper coverage made up for the prior oversight. The headlines were gratifying: "Serial Killer Slays Three" and "Serial Killer Stalks College Campuses."

He liked that one. "Stalk" implied an appreciation of his efforts. "College campus" was riskier. It could reflect the women's student status. It might also provide some insight into the police's hypothesis: he traveled among the colleges seeking women. If so, it was concurrently right and wrong.

He returned to his den, intending to work, but found himself contemplating his current situation instead. All too soon, the coverage of Emily's death would degenerate into a repetition of the same limited facts, followed by more inane commentary from a consulting psychologist. The Professor wasn't sure if he found them an irritation or pompous frauds. Their sloppy research and analysis would never be tolerated in his field. Settling more comfortably in his desk chair, he reviewed their arguments.

They thought he was "afraid" of women; that he had "issues"—who came up with that term anyway? Whatever happened to plain-old problems?—with a domineering mother. After Ashley, they'd debated whether he was using a condom or "failing to maintain an erection." Whether he was a homosexual. Whether he could have normal sexual relations.

He'd laughed over that. How much more normal could you get than using a woman for her sole purpose in life—sex? He didn't use a condom to protect himself from the women or disease. Semen was evidence, so he eliminated it.

None of them—the police, the shrinks, the reporters—understood. The pleasure, the euphoria transcended mere sex. He closed his eyes, sinking into the vivid memory: *He presses his palm against her flank, feeling the liquid warmth of her blood, hotter than her skin. Hot, like the passion that burns inside the human beast. Hot, like the life force that he has claimed.*

He lifts his hand to his nose. The scent is distinctive and metallic. Opening his mouth, he licks the wet slickness. Even the taste is metallic. The ancients ate the flesh of their vanquished. Cut out the heart and consumed the soul, taking their enemy's strength for their own.

Pressing his tongue to his palm, he savors the woman's blood and feels her mystery enter him. It runs through him, triumphantly adding to his mastery. His penis stirs in response. Earlier, he'd climaxed explosively while his hands tightened around her neck. Her fear fed his appetite. Stripped of the veneer of respectability, she'd shown her true nature—a groveling whore. Pleading, desperately begging, offering her body in a pathetic bargain, as women have bargained throughout history. He'd held her destiny in his hands. He alone decided if she lived or died.

He stretches above her crimson-streaked body, displaying his magnificent erection to his silent audience. Leisurely, he takes her again. She is a compliant lover now, tireless and uncomplaining. The way a woman should be. His orgasm crests in a shuddering wave and he collapses in a heap, nearly as lifeless as the body beneath him.

The Professor sighed with remembered pleasure. His relaxed smile faded as he felt the dampness in his lap. His hand still grasped his tumescent penis. He didn't remember unzipping his trousers.

With a spurt of humiliation, he realized the unexpected orgasm soiled his clothing.

His mother's voice echoed in his mind. *You nasty pervert. Look at the mess you made, yanking on that pathetic worm. Clean up those sheets. Right now. Don't let me catch you doing that again.*

He hurried to the bathroom, mortification spoiling the glow he should still be enjoying. His face flamed and he avoided the mirror as he furtively swabbed at the stain.

No woman's ever going to let you put that thing inside her. No one but a slut wants all that nasty mess dripping down her legs.

Emily let him. She let him do it as often as he wanted. She didn't complain.

But she was a slut, like all the other women.

Resentment and bitterness crawled through his belly. He didn't have to listen to his mother. He didn't have to listen to any of them. They were all whores and liars, manipulative bitches. He was too smart for them. He was the one in control. He could do whatever he wanted. He could cum all over them if he wanted to.

He froze as full realization engulfed him. The fact hadn't registered properly before. He hadn't used a condom that last time with Emily. He stared in horror at the traces of ejaculate on his trousers. He'd left semen inside her. He'd lost control.

Why can't you control yourself? You're nothing but a loser. The taunting voice mocked him.

His hands shook. Control was everything.

Hurling the tissue at the toilet, he stripped off his clothing and jammed it in the sink.

"Control," he chanted, until the mantra calmed him.

"Control," he repeated as he hung the slacks to dry.

"Control," he muttered as he donned clean clothing.

His panic receded to a tight, hard knot as his intellect reasserted itself. Most of the semen would have flushed down the toilet with the condoms from the earlier cycles of ejaculate. His body needed time to replenish the swimmers stored in his glands. Most of what he lost that last time was seminal fluid, not sperm.

Besides, his DNA wasn't listed with the sex offender registry. The police had to find him by other means first. And the DNA could still be considered circumstantial. Damningly so, but it wasn't a definitive indicator he'd defeated Emily. He could always claim a consensual liaison earlier in the day—before she met her destiny.

Calm again, he returned to the den and sat, idly twisting the swivel chair. What would he say if they questioned him? Staying as close to the truth as possible was best. That way, the lies wouldn't swing around and contradict each other.

He could say he met Emily earlier this fall, when performing research at Windsor. She was studying and they shared a library table. A check of library records would confirm they were there together, lending credence to his story.

He'd followed her, letting her know she was his chosen one, but the police didn't need to know that detail.

They'd had coffee, he decided. A reasonable fabrication. One thing led to another and they'd begun a secret affair. When he saw her on campus that Monday, he'd intended to end the relationship. She'd seduced him. He wasn't proud of it. He should've shown more restraint, but she was a beautiful young woman and an accomplished lover. He could spin enough stories on that topic to make all of them fantasize for weeks. He smiled, a cruel twist of his lips, imagining the detectives masturbating over his inventions.

They didn't have a clue. It wasn't just the sex or the killing. If all he needed was some hag's death, there were prostitutes and junkies available. No one missed them. The conquest, the intellectual challenge was equally important. Moreover, the target must be of a certain class, someone worthy of his attention. A woman who thought she was the equal of a man. Someone with that special spark, who captivated him until he conquered her. Someone like Alison, the brunette he'd followed to the Depot.

Catching himself before he drifted into another daydream, he acknowledged another point. The police had become an element in his game. Defeating them added to his triumph. He'd bested police departments throughout the state without their realizing it. Now, detectives in three cities knew he was their superior. State investigators had joined the hunt. They were all floundering helplessly in his wake.

This was the ultimate challenge, the quintessential hunt. He executed it better than anyone.

THREE

Thursday, early evening

MEG SLIPPED INTO the crowded Chi Zeta Chapter room. Since she was the faculty advisor, the housemother had asked her to join the sorority sisters, but hadn't said what the meeting was about. She suspected it would cover safety. The news about Emily's murder had swept through the campus with a more deadly chill than the October breeze would ever produce.

Two men, cops by their appearance, stood in front of the fireplace. The older one looked like the type of father she'd always wanted—kind and approachable. Someone she could go to for advice or help. Completely unlike her father. *Don't go there. It is what it is.*

She turned to the younger officer and caught her breath. Black hair, blue eyes. Model-worthy cheekbones, a strong jaw, an unsmiling mouth. And the kind of charisma that was giving every woman in the room whiplash as their heads snapped around for a second look. He was exactly the sort of man she'd spent years avoiding.

He looked up suddenly, as if she'd called his name, his intensity pinning her in place. The tension was immediate, as if a wire stretched between them—with the current turned on. For a second, he looked as stunned as she felt. She wrenched her gaze away and scanned the room. Lisa had saved a seat on the couch for her.

Eyes focused straight ahead, Meg angled across the

room toward her best friend. The cop looked too much like a polished version of Steven, someone she didn't want to think about ever again. Seven long years later, the impact of Steven's betrayal hadn't faded. That man's lies and deceit remained his responsibility, but her reaction to them—her actions—were her choice.

And she chose to ignore the handsome policeman.

She sat beside Lisa, determined to put the past behind her. She felt the policeman's gaze on her. Like a physical touch, it tugged at her, demanding attention. It took every ounce of her considerable willpower not to look at him. She was so close to finishing her master's degree, to walking through the doors it would open, to showing everybody what she could do, all by herself. No way was she going to let a man—especially someone so much like Steven—distract her.

The older man introduced himself. "I'm Agent Meyers. This is Agent O'Shaughnessy. We're part of a task force that's investigating a series of murders. We've been asked to look into the incident that occurred yesterday evening, and we'd appreciate your cooperation."

A ripple ran around the room and everyone braced for news of a murder.

"We understand Deidre Hammond is a member of this sorority."

Didi? What does any of this have to do with her? She'd been conspicuously absent today. Had something happened to her after Marie hustled her back to her room?

"We'll talk with you individually, but can anyone give us background on the events leading up to her kidnapping? Did anyone witness the events surrounding the assault? Was there any harassment or stalking prior to it?"

Jaws dropped around the room, and several people

clamped hands over incipient laughter. "Kidnapping." Someone giggled. "Who assaulted who?"

"Do you know that guy?" Lisa whispered in Meg's ear. "He's staring at you."

She shook her head, dismissing the lingering memories. "Something about him *does* feel familiar."

"Like déjà vu?"

A smile curved Meg's lips. "I don't think that applies to people."

"Well, maybe you knew him in a previous life."

Trust Lisa to say something out-there. "Right. You learned that in a dream?" Meg hid her smile behind her hand.

"He can feature in my dreams any time he wants to."

She risked a glance at him. His black-and-cream tweed sports coat and black slacks showed off his build nicely. "He's too old for you."

"Age and experience, girlfriend. He looks like he has both."

Heads were turning and suddenly both cops were focused on them. "Do you find this amusing?" the older one asked.

Oh well. So much for that setting-a-good-example thing.

Lisa slid onto her lower spine, producing the round-eyed innocence of the Gerber Baby. Meg struggled to put a serious expression on her face and failed completely. "I'm sorry. We were talking about something else. But I don't understand your assault and kidnapping question. What does it have to do with Didi?"

"Our unsub—unidentified subject—may have assaulted other women in addition to those he's killed. If he assaulted Ms. Hammond, one of you may be able to give us valuable information about him."

"Officer, we're all assuming you're talking about the fountain incident. Did something else happen to Didi?"

"Why don't you tell us what you observed last night?" the younger officer interjected.

"If we're talking about events at the Trev, I don't know what you were told, but you're way off base." Meg ignored the whispers and giggles and kept her attention safely focused on the older man. "I missed the first part of the show, but Didi climbed into that fountain under her own power. Brad was so drunk a couple of his frat brothers had to practically carry him over there. And assault?" She shook her head, noting the incredulous expression that came and went on the officer's face. "Didi was as glad to see Brad as he was to see her."

Meg shook her head, letting dismay color her voice. "From your expression, you *are* asking about the incident in the fountain." She swung her gaze around the Chapter room, allowing it to linger on women she remembered seeing with Didi the previous evening. A couple of the women looked like they thought she was selling Didi out, but most looked relieved someone had called the spectacle for what it was—stupidity.

"This is your chance to step up. Apparently, these officers were pulled off a murder investigation to check out a case of public drunkenness. You know how I feel about personal responsibility, but how does that sit with y'all?"

The sorority sisters whispered among themselves. Meg glanced at the policemen. Both were watching her, clearly curious about her role. Quickly, she turned back to the group of women. "If you know anything about the fountain incident, please talk to one of the detectives. The rest of you, don't y'all have exams to study for?"

She risked another glance at the officers. "Unless there's

something else you wanted to discuss—a new development in the murders?"

The older man said, "We're continuing our investigation. We would like to talk to as many of you as possible, though, to clarify yesterday evening's activities and wrap up that part of our inquiry."

The crowd broke into chattering groups. Some moved toward the door while others approached the policemen. Meg noticed a disproportionate number surrounded the younger man. Deliberately turning her back on him, she casually made her way across the room. The sorority president—one of Didi's closest friends—gave Meg a drop-dead scowl. She swept past, flanked by two of her cohorts. Meg mentally shrugged. As the advisor, she was supposed to take a leadership role. If the president wanted to defend Didi or offer another version of events, she should have done it instead of acting like a foiled two-year-old.

As the women trickled out of the room, Meg spoke to most, a word about homecoming planning, a reminder about safety. Without being obvious, she made certain the fountain frolic ringleaders talked to one of the policemen.

And she very carefully avoided making eye contact with the younger cop, who seemed to be looking at her every time she glanced his way.

"I'd stick around, but I have to finish a paper." Lisa slid an arm around Meg's waist. "I want to hear all about Officer Delicious later."

"There won't be anything to tell," Meg said.

Lisa laughed and trotted up the stairs. A grad student and Chi Zeta alumni, she was renting a room in the sorority house. At times, Lisa's decision to live there made Meg's advisor role easier; at others, the logic behind it completely baffled her.

Only a few women remained in the Chapter room. Meg

caught the housemother's attention, raised her hand in a small wave and slipped out the door.

Halfway across the lobby, strong fingers closed around her arm. "Excuse me."

She knew without looking it was the younger cop. He spun her, and she ended up nearly chest-to-chest with him. Her eyes were level with his mouth, which was drawn in a tight line. A shadow underlay the skin on his jaw, and it took a conscious effort not to stroke the plane of his cheek.

Mind over hormones. She refused to be attracted to him, even as her body responded to his warm proximity. She forced her eyes up to meet his. At this distance, she could see the web of darker blue shooting through the iris. His eyes locked onto hers and slowly darkened. Her good intentions fled with the wordless communication.

His hand rose, fingers cupped as if to caress her cheek. They hovered, inches from her face, then abruptly, he blinked, dropped his hand and stepped back. "I have a few more questions."

She blushed, disoriented. "I don't know anything more than I said in there."

"You're telling me this 'assault' was actually consensual groping."

She nodded, struggling to regain her composure. Surely he'd heard a dozen versions of the incident. "Didn't the women tell you?"

He ignored her question.

Trying to distance herself physically as well as emotionally, she stepped back and silently studied him. An expressionless mask covered his face, but she felt his anger behind it.

Taking a slow breath, he widened his stance and crossed his arms over his chest, making him look bigger and more authoritarian. "I was told Ms. Hammond didn't drink.

She's underage. She reported being unable to remember events, blocks of time, which is consistent with a date rape drug's effects."

Meg sighed and crossed her own arms. Relieved he was putting a professional spin on the conversation, she pushed the surge of attraction firmly into its corner. "Not being able to remember is consistent with being drunk, hungover and embarrassed the next day too."

"Was the man—"

"Her boyfriend, Brad." Another prime example of too much money and not enough parental involvement during his formative years.

"—giving her the drinks?"

Meg shoved her exasperation aside and pulled up her teaching tone—calm and even. "I wasn't there when Didi was drinking, but Brad didn't show up until later. After she was already in the fountain. Dancing her little heart out, by the way."

He ignored that. "You didn't observe the transfer to the fountain or the preceding events."

"I was in the library."

"So you don't know if she was coerced or not."

Meg's patience evaporated. She flung open her hands. "Look, I don't know how you got dragged into this, but Didi screwed up and, like always, she's trying to make it someone else's fault."

He looked at her for a long moment. The muscle in his jaw jumped. "I was asked to investigate."

He didn't say by whom. Didi's family was wealthy and well-connected. Her father probably told the police chief his precious baby was attacked, and these guys got stuck coming out to look into it. For half a second, she felt sorry for the detective.

"Can you verify your whereabouts?" He removed a notepad from his jacket pocket.

"Excuse me?" Her sympathy fled.

"Ms. Hammond apparently drank with someone," he said patiently. "I need to know who was there and who *wasn't* involved. You said you were in the library. Can anyone confirm that?"

"Why do I need—" She bit off the rest of the question. *He's just doing his job.* "The people around me. I signed out some reference books. The check-out slip shows I left at midnight, just before the library closed. I walked back over here afterward. That takes about ten minutes."

He frowned. "You walked back alone? That late?"

"I usually do."

"Don't you have an escort service? Especially now?"

"A couple of students caught up with me. We heard the noise at the fountain and went to investigate."

He asked a few more questions about the bacchanal. "Okay. That gives me a clearer picture of events. What's your name and number?"

"Why?"

"What do you mean, 'why?'" His pen hovered over his notepad.

"Why do you need my name? I already told you what I know."

"Investigation? Witness? Statement? Any part of that you missed?"

She rolled her eyes to cover her embarrassment. "You don't think this was a kidnapping and assault any more than I do. Surely you have better things to do."

With a sigh, he lowered his pen. "Sometimes you gotta go through the motions, okay? And yes, I have better things to do. So let's wrap this up, and I'll help Agent Meyers gather the last of these incredibly informative statements."

He fished in his pocket and handed her his card. "Call me if you remember anything relevant. Now, let's try this again. Name?"

"Meg Connelly."

"A good Irish name." His smile lit up his face.

She inhaled sharply. Lord, he was intoxicating.

"Number?"

"Just call the house phone." He didn't need to know she didn't have her own line.

Or how to reach her, period.

FOUR

Thursday night

It was an all-too-familiar sight: a gathering of tired detectives with five o'clock shadows. Files and crime scene photos lay scattered across the conference room table. Discarded fast-food bags added to the general funk in the air. The only good thing about the debacle at Douglass College was that Clinton was centered between Greenville, Spartanburg and Newberry, making this conference with all the task force detectives feasible.

Karen Ward, the Spartanburg detective, dropped the Geiger crime scene photos on the table. She was a no-nonsense brunette wearing slacks and a turtleneck. "It's a complete change in MO. Are we sure it's the same guy?"

"The staging, the rock, the e-mails," Frank said.

Ward slumped in her chair. The violent death and the posing had received extensive press coverage, but the content of the stalking e-mails and the rock were holdbacks, details withheld from the public. Only the killer knew about them.

"It's an escalation, not a change," Mick said. "I've walked all three crime scenes. This guy's methodical. Everything's planned. He chooses his victim, knows when they're alone and he won't be interrupted. He comes to the residences prepared with a murder kit. He leaves almost no trace evidence behind."

"There was semen," Trey Andersen, the Greenville

detective, pointed out. His carefully styled haircut only partially obscured his receding hairline. He propped one cowboy boot—shod foot on an empty chair and smirked.

Whoa, an almost helpful comment, Mick thought. *Maybe he's decided to cooperate for a change.* Initially, Andersen had resented the State Law Enforcement Division's involvement, but as the case dragged on and the body count rose, he was more than willing to let SLED take the heat.

"So he managed to get his rocks off," Robbins said bluntly. "Unless he's a registered offender, it doesn't help us."

"Has anyone checked on the sexual offenders?" Mick asked. "These guys don't start with murder. Somewhere there's a record on him, even if it's just soliciting a hooker."

"He may have juvenile offenses: voyeurism, arson, petty theft," Frank added.

"I've got friends in Vice," Ward said.

"How close a friend?" Andersen asked and blew her a kiss.

She glared at him. "I'll get a list started." She scribbled a note, then turned to Mick and Frank. "Should we bring in a psychologist?"

"He's crazy," Jordan said. "Maybe we should."

"He's not crazy," Mick said. "Not in a legal or medical sense."

"He's just evil," Robbins muttered.

Frank leaned back in his chair and crossed his ankle over his leg. "All a psychologist will tell you is the unsub appears to be a sociopath, but he isn't psychotic."

Appears? Mick thought. *The bastard ruthlessly tortures and kills three women. Oh, yeah, he's definitely not getting the "Citizen of the Year" award from me.*

"He gets off on humiliating women," Frank continued.

"He hates his mother. Maybe he was screwing her as a kid or she kept bringing guys home and taking them to bed. Maybe they took him to bed with them. Something. Anyway, he hates her and he's trying to get back at her by assaulting these nice women."

"You don't care why he's doing it?" Jordan asked.

Mick had been watching Jordan's face as the other detectives talked. Now that there were no dead bodies in the room, the kid was interested, even excited. "Not particularly. We've worked enough of these cases to know most of what the psychologists are going to say. Sometimes the profiles help, but you catch them through police work."

Robbins nodded. "Hard work and a little luck."

Mick glanced around the table. They all were excited, although the older cops hid it better. It was part of the reason they'd chosen law enforcement. Deep down, they all wanted to play cops and robbers, do something more than write speeding tickets and settle domestic disputes. They wanted to catch for-real bad guys, rescue damsels in distress. Mick admitted, at least to himself, it was part of why he'd chosen SLED over a better-paying position at the beach.

"Talk to one of Ward's friends in Vice if you want to know more about these assholes." Frank resumed his lecture. "Now, our killer's started cutting the victims, but it isn't a frenzy or directed at the genitals in a sex substitution. From the traces of lubricant on the victims, we know he's performed normal sexual intercourse with all three women."

"I'd hardly call it normal," Ward objected.

"The penetration is penis into vagina—normal," Mick said. "What's abnormal is the use of pain and terror in the process. It's the power over them that thrills him. He wants ultimate power—life and death."

Mick leaned back in his chair and closed his eyes, deliberately recalling the graphic images from the three crime scenes. "I think the first one was an accident. The drugs started wearing off, she woke up and put up a fight or something. He grabbed her around the neck to shut her up. Maybe he panicked and didn't know when to quit. Maybe he realized it and it turned him on. He intended to kill the next two. Whichever, the violence is increasing."

"And he's getting off on it," Andersen twisted restlessly in his chair.

What's he going to do next?

The unspoken words hung in the air.

"What's with the rock?" Pragmatic Robbins broke the tense silence.

"Only the killer knows." Mick shrugged. "And even he may not be sure. He's done it every time. It's an impulse he can't resist any more than he can quit obsessing over the women."

Ward waved a finger at Mick. "Back up a minute. Why'd you call Geiger an escalation?"

"Get into his head for a minute," Mick said. "The guy's killed twice. Maybe he felt scared after the first one, but when he wasn't caught, the fear left. Instead, he remembered how much he liked it. The next time, it was less frightening. In fact, it was so much fun, he decided to raise the stakes. His third victim lived at home. He may have considered a home invasion."

Robbins didn't look happy. "Killed her while her parents were there?"

"Or killed them too." Mick could tell Robbins had mulled over that possibility. "Instead, he got deeper into his fantasies. He kidnapped the victim, presumably from a public place."

"And kept her longer..."

"The longer he keeps them, the longer he has to hurt them. If he takes another one, the only way she's coming out alive is if we move fast and find them."

Andersen's cowboy boots hit the floor with a thud. "How are we supposed to do that? We haven't gotten anywhere on this."

Mick's gaze took in all the detectives seated around the table before returning to Andersen. "We have to find him before he takes his next one."

Silence followed Mick's quiet comment. They all understood what they were up against.

Jordan sat back with crossed arms. "Greenville-Spartanburg is practically one city. What's he doing down here in Newberry? I don't see where Ms. Geiger fits the pattern."

"It's not that far," Frank replied.

"We don't have a pattern," Mick said. "Outside of pure, dumb luck, the only way we're going to find this guy is through the victims."

"The victims come from similar backgrounds." Ward shuffled the crime scene photos. "But there are differences in height, body type, hair color."

"It may be more subtle. Was it the way she smiled? Walked down the street? We need to concentrate on any overlaps: friends, places, habits in common. It may give us the clue about where he's meeting them." All the detectives had started with the usual suspects—family and friends. They'd covered people who didn't like the women, ex-boyfriends; where they spent their days; what they did outside of class. They'd come up dry on all counts.

"I thought serial killers targeted losers," Andersen recrossed his legs and flicked a speck of dust from his boots. "You know, prostitutes, hitchhikers, people like that. These three were cheerleader types."

"Maybe that's the point," Frank said thoughtfully. "Maybe that's what he always wanted, but couldn't have."

Mick scrubbed his hands over his face. "What do we know about Geiger?" He'd studied her file last night. Robbins and Jordan had to be exhausted. They'd worked practically around the clock for two days, not knowing Emily Geiger was already dead.

"She was a sophomore at Windsor College," Robbins said. "Pretty girl; sweet kid. Always struck me as smart, really confident."

Mick thought about the life cut short. "Sounds like you knew her."

"My wife taught her in Sunday school." Robbins stared glumly at the table. "She was friends with my daughter. Melanie's all torn up."

Mick and Frank exchanged glances. Working a homicide was tough enough without personal involvement. Should they ask Robbins to excuse himself? Wouldn't anybody else in the department have the same problem? Mick flicked a glance at Jordan. The kid wore the same shell-shocked expression in unguarded moments. "So, no theories about where or how he's meeting them?"

Ward shrugged. "All of the victims were in college."

"They're different schools," Jordan objected.

"It's still possible the doer's a student," Andersen said. "Hell, my kid brother's over at Windsor and Prescott as often as he's at Wofford. They're back and forth, going to football games and parties. A student's the only thing that makes sense."

"There was no forced entry at the apartments," Ward said.

"And?" Robbins asked.

"A student could get inside another student's apartment," Andersen said in a tone that added "idiot" and Robbins bristled.

"They've got a point," Mick said. "It's irrational, but most students trust other students. But the profile makes the killer older. He wouldn't fit in as well with a college crowd."

"That college crowd looked ready to accept you tonight," Frank drawled.

Mick stifled the mental flash of Meg Connelly. "Up yours, Meyers," he said. "They wanted you to be their daddy."

"I don't think that's what they had in mind for you." Frank's eyebrows rose suggestively.

The other detectives were looking at them expectantly, the earlier tension forgotten.

"Oh, yeah," Frank continued. "Old Blue Eyes could've had his pick of places to stay tonight."

"Whatever," Mick said. He was too tired for the ribbing he routinely received from other cops. "I don't think a student could improvise the way our killer does. Or plan so meticulously."

Ward propped her chin on her fist. "Isn't that a direct contradiction?"

"The first two assaults were planned. Without knowing Geiger would be at the mall that morning, how could he plan the abduction? If he was following her and saw an opportunity, then he'd have to improvise. There's too much outside his control."

Mick rubbed at the grit in his eyes, trying to think things through. "I wonder if there's some decompensation. Once the killer started, he can't stop, but he's also started thinking he's invincible. To get the same satisfaction, he has to get deeper into his fantasies."

"You mean, take bigger risks."

"And because he thinks he won't get caught, he'll go after the next victim more quickly."

Ward's hand smacked the table. "You're saying he could already have the next one picked out?"

"Probably. You gotta remember, the stalk is an important part of his fantasy. But if he strikes sooner, he won't have as much time to plan beforehand. Maybe he'll make mistakes."

"And that's when he gets caught," Andersen said with satisfaction.

"In the meanwhile, this is the worst kind of killer. He's careful and organized." Frank paused. "He's white, early thirties, neatly groomed. He doesn't stand out in the victims' neighborhoods."

"Someone who fits in there," Jordan said thoughtfully.

"If it was just the apartments, I'd wonder if he was a maintenance guy," Robbins said. "But that doesn't fit with the mall."

"What about a security guard?" Ward suggested.

"What about a teacher?"

Everyone turned to Jordan. He blushed, but met their gaze.

"Why do you say that?" asked Mick.

"Students trust teachers. The age fits the profile better and they're around schools."

"One school," Ward objected.

"Not necessarily," Mick said. "They go to conferences and stuff. Andersen, is anybody teaching at more than one school? Or transferred recently?"

"I'll check." Andersen scribbled in his notebook.

"The academic world, especially if the killer is a researcher, would appeal to a meticulous personality like an obsessive/compulsive," Frank said. "But if he's a professor, it's probably not at the victims' colleges."

Andersen groaned. "Do you have any idea how many schools there are in the Upstate?"

"A woman isn't going to let a teacher she doesn't know into her home any sooner than she would another stranger," Ward said.

"That's right," Robbins agreed. "And I still think it's too far for him to drive down here and stalk Geiger, if it's some guy who's teaching up in Greenville. He's supposed to be in class. He can't cut like a kid can."

"Besides, he knew how to cover his tracks with those e-mails," Andersen said. "Computer geeks are mostly kids."

Ward raised her eyebrow at Mick. "Did you get anything on the latest e-mails?"

"Same as the others. Our computer guys ran trace programs. Like the ones the feds use to go after hackers," he added at their blank reactions. "Don't ask me to explain how they work."

"A professor would know how the mail works at their school, how the names are set up," Jordan said.

Andersen groaned. "Give it up, kid."

For a moment, none of the detectives spoke. They were all tired. "Are we getting anything off the hotline?" Mick finally asked.

"Confessions and sightings." Robbins massaged his temple. "So far, most aren't worth the time it takes to process 'em. We're having more luck with the folks out on Wilson Road."

That was the road in front of the park, Mick remembered. He also remembered the comment: *our city, our people.* "What have you got?"

"Multiple reports of a dark-colored vehicle that morning around five. Big engine, maybe a V8 or a 356. The night clerk at the Holiday Inn said it was a coupe, not a sedan."

"A sports car." Mick rubbed his hand over his cheek,

considering the implications. "Any chance he got a plate? Or a make?"

"She. And God wasn't feeling that benevolent."

"Okay." He smiled tiredly. "It's the first decent lead we've had. Run with it. The lab should have something for us tomorrow on those tire casts. That'll help."

The session had gone longer than anyone expected. "It's late, people. Let's wrap it up." Mick glanced around the table. "Y'all have press contacts. We need to keep the message out there the victims were stalked. Young women, especially college-aged ones, need to be careful."

"See if you can get those Sexual Assault people involved." Andersen rotated a vague hand. "Get them to hand out stuff on campus. Date rape drugs, personal safety, that kind of shit."

"You guys always put the responsibility back on the women," Ward groused.

"We need to get the press off the sensationalism and focused on the women," Frank said.

"Good luck," Robbins muttered.

"The killer will be following the press coverage," Frank said. "He needs his nose rubbed in them being people, not objects he can throw away."

"Everybody use what you can," Mick said. "We just have to keep digging."

Three victims, and they were no closer to finding the killer than the day they started. The detectives packed their files and headed to the parking lot.

"You staying here tonight?" Frank tossed his case onto the backseat.

"Yeah," Mick said. "I can stay at the Days Inn for what it costs me in gas to run up to Greenville and back. You got reasons to go. Say 'hey' to the wife and kids."

"I sleep better in my own bed."

Mick watched Frank lumber away and wished he had someone waiting for him, someone to make him forget about the case and death. To remember there was good in the world: life and laughter and innocence. Meg's face immediately appeared. Of all the women in the sorority house, he'd noticed *her* the moment she walked in the door. Watching her, he'd felt like he already knew her, which made no sense. Obviously, the stress of this case had short-circuited his brain.

Sleep, he decided. He definitely needed sleep.

And to find this murderer.

Two hours later, he rolled over and punched his pillow a few times. The guy upstairs had finally quit pacing around and gone to bed. The motel was silent except for the air conditioner, which cycled at about eight-minute intervals.

Giving up on sleep, Mick rolled to his back, tucked his hands behind his head and stared at the ceiling. What happened to him in that sorority house? He was minding his own business, avoiding eye contact with a couple of women, when Meg walked through the door.

Cold sweat had drenched him. His heart rate had doubled. He'd stared like a sixteen-year-old with his first crush. Then his eyes locked with hers and something hot, raw and primitive passed between them. From the expression on her face, the connection hit her with the same stunning force.

Her refusal to look at him afterward surprised him. Usually he read people easily, but Meg remained a mystery. Watching her giggle with her friend, he'd reminded himself she was young. Then she'd coolly tagged his "investigation" for the political farce it was.

He sorta admired that part.

When she walked out, he'd scrambled, figuring it was his opportunity to interview her.

He snorted. Who was he kidding? He'd wanted to know if that initial reaction was a fluke.

Groaning, he pulled his hands down his face. So what had he done? He'd spun her around, invaded her personal space and got lost in her eyes.

That was totally insane, almost as crazy as the overwhelming urge he'd had to kiss her. Damn, he'd nearly touched her. What had he been thinking? Clearly, he'd lost it. When it came to vics, witnesses and suspects, "Don't touch," might as well be tattooed on a cop's hands. You just didn't do that. Not if you wanted to keep your job.

Meg Connelly was the last person he needed to hook up with. She looked older than the other sorority girls, but damn, she was still a college kid. He didn't need the complication. He ought to keep his focus on finding this killer, on doing the job he loved, rather than chasing a dream woman.

A fantasy.

Abruptly, an impression of tumbling curls, laughing eyes and stunning sensuality slammed through him. Desire roared and he groaned again.

He had to find a way to see her.

FIVE

Friday morning

MEG ROLLED OUT of bed early. Operating on autopilot, she straightened the sheets and fluffed the quilt, then padded over to her tiny kitchenette. As she reached for the coffeepot, she gave a bang-your-head-against-the-wall groan. No coffee.

"Damn it."

Between the ridiculous meeting at the sorority house and letting that cop rattle her so badly, she'd forgotten all about going to the grocery store. She opened the cabinet and shuffled through the contents, hoping to unearth a tea bag. There were a dozen packages of Ramen noodles, five cans of soup, tomatoes, half a jar of peanut butter and random spaghetti sauce spices, but nothing containing caffeine.

She turned from the cabinet with a sigh. When she finally finished graduate school, she was never going to eat Ramen noodles again. Scholarships and a job had covered most of her undergraduate degree, but the student loans she'd needed to make ends meet kicked in as soon as she picked up her diploma. As a lowly associate at Douglass College, her salary barely covered the loan payments and the rent on her apartment.

Glancing at the clock, she did some quick mental calculations. She could walk to the store, buy coffee and bread, fix a sandwich and still make it to class on time. But she absolutely had to restock her cabinets this afternoon.

She pulled on clothes and locked the door behind her. Pausing only to check her mailbox—empty—she dashed across the foyer, opened the outer door and ran smack into Mick O'Shaughnessy.

She felt like a raindrop bouncing off a boulder. He didn't move. She splattered. His hands gripped her arms, steadying her until she recovered her balance.

"Morning, Meg." He smiled at her. "Do I dare say I was hoping to run into you?"

"Very funny." She shook off his hands. Retreating a step, she crossed her arms and glared. She was not going to notice how warm and strong his body was. Or the way his eyes lit up two seconds before she flattened herself against him. "What are you doing here?"

His gaze dropped, just for a second, and she remembered she wasn't wearing a bra. If he hadn't figured it out during the full body contact, he knew it now. She dropped her arms and then wondered what to do with her hands. *Pockets...pockets would be helpful.*

"I'd hoped to catch you before class. You didn't give an actual statement last night."

"No, Detective. I mean what are you doing *here*." Her finger stabbed down, indicating her front porch.

His surprise showed. A faint blush tinted his cheeks. "It's 'Agent.' Actually, I went by the sorority house. They told me your address."

Meg gave him an assessing inspection. His clothes were casual today—khakis, long-sleeved polo shirt and loafers. A leather flight jacket draped his body like it had been custom-formed to his shoulders and chest. No one should have the right to look that good first thing in the morning. Most likely, he'd charmed her address out of whoever was working the desk at the Chi Zeta house. "Remind me to address security and personal privacy at the next Chapter meeting."

He laughed. "Let's try this again. Morning, Meg." He stuck out his hand. "Agent Mick O'Shaughnessy."

Her gaze moved from his hand up his nice solid chest to the smile that was starting to fade, then tripped over his blue eyes. She took his outstretched hand, noticing the warmth that flowed from his fingers. Her brain flashed "danger" signs while her mouth said, "It's not morning until I've had coffee." Her lips turned up in spite of the voice in her head that yelled, *What are you doing?*

"Is that where you're headed?"

She tugged her hand free. "Actually…" If she told him she was going to the store to buy coffee grounds, he'd expect her to invite him in for a cup. No way was she letting him inside her apartment.

"I could use a cup too." His face wore a hopeful expression.

Could she call them or what? "There's a coffee shop over on the Strip."

"What if we head over there?" He paused, looking a little uncertain. "Do you have time? I mean, we can do this later."

She wasn't interested, of course, but the bashful thing was working for her. Her head moved, a rueful shake. If a formal statement helped wrap up this ridiculous Didi incident so Mick could get back to his murder investigation, she might as well get it over with now. "This is fine."

Barracuda's was on Cumberland, the commercial strip about a mile away. They silently walked into the residential area that separated the stores from campus. Meg peeked at him, wondering what he really wanted. Mick looked completely relaxed, hands thrust deep into the pockets of his jacket, but his eyes moved constantly. "Gonna be pretty today."

The weather? He was actually talking about the *weather?*

But it *was* going to be gorgeous. The sun had cleared the tree line, catching the tops of the maples. They glowed with color that graduated from fiery red, through Day-Glo orange to demure yellow. The lower branches still supported green leaves, but they were a muted yellow-green rather than the emerald shade of summer. She squinted against the light. She should've brought sunglasses. She snorted softly—like she'd planned any of this.

Mick glanced at her, raising a questioning eyebrow.

Going for cool self-containment rather than merely cold, she pulled her arms across her chest. She should've brought a coat, but she'd thought she was only dashing to the store. She'd pulled a sweatshirt over her camisole. Her breasts bounced as she walked. Hopefully the bulky sweatshirt hid their movement.

At least she'd brushed her hair. Makeup hadn't been on her agenda. She couldn't bring back a mental picture of the two seconds spent in front of the bathroom mirror while she dragged her brush through the unruly mess. Given the way her luck was going, she probably had raccoon eyes or a giant zit on her face.

What difference did it make? Mick wasn't there to see her. Things were strictly business between them. Twenty more questions so Didi's daddy would get off the police department's collective back.

"Is Meg short for Margaret?"

Her attention snapped back to Mick. "Yeah. And Mick's short for what? Michael?"

"That and the whole Irish thing." He shrugged. "It stuck somewhere along the way."

"Irish? That sounds more Boston or New York than South Carolina. Of course, there were lots of Scotch-Irish settlers in the Upstate—my family settled there in the early 1700s—but most tended to have Anglo names." She stopped, her face flaming with embarrassment. She sounded like a blathering idiot. Or a total dork.

"'Fraid we were more recent immigrants. My grandfather came over after World War II. My family's down in Conway."

"You left the beach to come up here?"

"I worked there for a while, but I wanted more than traffic tickets and drunk-and-disorderly tourists. At SLED, I work cases across the Upstate, usually ones that cross jurisdictional lines."

"Do you like what you do?" she asked with genuine interest.

"Most of the time." A shadow crossed his face before he changed the subject. "So you're a teacher."

"More front desk information?"

A self-satisfied smile tugged at the corner of his mouth. "Is it right?"

"Graduate assistant. I teach some classes." She lifted a shoulder in a half shrug. "Until I finish my master's."

"Seems like my college instructors were ancient experts who spent most of their time somewhere else."

They crossed the street and turned right, past a huge Victorian that had been converted to student apartments. Before he could dig for more information, Meg asked, "Where'd you go to school?"

"North Carolina. Chapel Hill."

Her mouth nearly fell open. "It's hard to get into UNC from out of state." Expensive too. She'd been accepted by the university, but hadn't been able to afford it.

Mick shrugged noncommittally.

She mentally raised his probable IQ a few points. "I didn't know you had to go to college to be a cop."

He quirked an eyebrow. "So you think we's just a bunch of igner't rednecks?"

She blushed and stammered, "Th-that's not what I meant."

He laughed and pulled her into a quick sideways hug. Yesterday's simmering desire surged through her and she stiffened. He'd already dropped his arm, apparently unruffled, but the fine hairs on her body had risen like tiny antennae, tracking this new, dangerous threat. She hugged herself tighter and concentrated on steadying her breathing. She refused to be attracted to the man. She was only here for the coffee. That was it—caffeine. Period. End of sentence. They were almost to Cumberland. Barracuda's was less than five minutes away.

"You have to have a degree to get anywhere, anymore," he said. "Some people are hired with only a high school diploma. You can generally tell which ones at the Academy."

"The Academy?" This was better. Nice, safe conversation put some distance between them. Without looking, she knew he'd put his hands in his pockets and gone back to scanning his surroundings. She wondered if it was a cop thing.

"Criminal Justice Academy. Basic's a nine-week cram course in procedures, rules. Police stuff. Are you cold?" he asked abruptly.

Surely he couldn't see her taut nipples through her sweatshirt. The combination of Mick, the camisole's soft fabric caressing her sensitive skin and more Mick, was driving her wild. She snuck a surreptitious glance at her chest. Her clenched arms, that was what he noticed. She forced herself to relax. "Not really."

He already had his jacket off. Reaching around her, he

draped it over her shoulders. "I should have offered sooner. That sweatshirt can't be warm enough."

His hands lingered on her shoulders. Her traitorous body tingled. She kept her gaze fastened on his chest and tugged at the coat's edges, closing the jacket.

Dropping his hands, he stepped back, took a deep breath and smiled. "Better?"

The coat carried a heady mixture of scents: leather, his aftershave, and the subtle base note that was Mick. She fought the urge to bury her face in the collar. The jacket was still warm from his body, and her stomach gave a funny twist as the warmth spread lower. "I'm fine, really."

She raised her hands, ready to return the coat.

"We're almost there. I don't want you frozen *and* caffeine-deprived."

Barracuda's was just beyond Andy's Deli. Mick held the door, politely waiting for her to enter.

A few students huddled over coffee and their books in the booths at the back. Otherwise, the store was empty. Meg opened her pocketbook, wondering how much cash she had on her, but Mick said, "I got it."

He stepped up to the counter without waiting for her response.

Meg started to argue, but the woman behind the counter tossed her hair and smiled, giving Mick the full treatment. "What can I do for you?" she purred.

He appeared oblivious, which Meg already knew was an act. He was the most *aware* man she'd ever met. "Two lattes, grande, low fat. And two scones."

He turned to Meg. "Uhm." For the first time that morning, he looked truly flustered. "I'm sorry. That just came out, like I already knew what you wanted."

A beat passed as she considered the implications of his statement. "That's exactly right."

Without further comment, she walked to a table near the front plateglass windows. Sunlight bathed the space, warming it. Shrugging off Mick's jacket, she placed it on the chair opposite her. He arrived moments later, carrying their breakfast. She sipped the strong coffee, then closed her eyes and lifted her face to absorb the sunlight.

"What do you teach?"

Ah, the safety of banality. She opened her eyes. "Mostly basic finance courses. Statistics."

"Is that your master's area?"

"Partly."

He folded his arms over his chest. "Care to expand on that?"

"I'm not deliberately being difficult."

"Really?" he drawled. "Could've fooled me."

She felt warmth again climb her cheeks. She hadn't blushed this much since she was seventeen and Steven teased her. She brutally severed that line of thought. She absolutely refused to even think that man's name. "I double-majored in undergrad, history and finance, so I'm taking graduate level courses in both areas. One of the few benefits of teaching is that the college waives my tuition for the classes. Once I graduate, though, I need a real job, a career. That's the finance part. The history's just because I find it interesting."

She felt back in control. Caffeine, wonder drug. She took another hit. "What'd you major in?"

"History," he said dryly.

She couldn't help herself; she giggled. He grinned at her. The giggles turned into a full-belly laugh and he chuckled, as well. Finally, Meg subsided and wiped her eyes. "I don't know why that hit me as being so funny. It really isn't."

"Sure it is. You have a great laugh, by the way."

Meg lifted her cup in a salute and drank deeply. What was her problem? Mick was a nice guy. He was smart and had a sense of humor, both of which she found attractive. And he was no slouch in the looks department. Besides, after today, she'd never see him again. She was an idiot, overreacting like she always did if a guy looked too closely.

He pulled out a notebook. "I actually do need a statement about the fountain incident."

The written statement didn't take long.

Meg swirled the remnants of her latte. "Did you always plan to be a cop?"

"No."

Another shadow crossed his face. She was vaguely surprised he let his emotions show. She'd seen what she called his cop face: wary, closed off, giving nothing away.

"I planned to go to law school."

She heard the wistful note. Dreams deferred. She knew about that. "Why didn't you go on to law school? There are student loans…" She trailed off as his face closed down. Maybe he wasn't accepted, or his folks had a thing about debt. "Never mind. I understand. Things happen."

"I'd been accepted, but my father died unexpectedly. My mom needed help with my brothers and sister and the family land." He stared out the window. The lines around his eyes tightened, and she wondered what time and place he saw. Finally, he sighed, then faced her directly. "He was killed. Mom fell apart."

The words were delivered flatly. Although it had happened years before, the pain still showed. She knew about that hurt, the hole a parent's absence left in your life. Losing her parents had been one of a string of devastating events her final year in high school. Mick had lost his dream on top of his tragedy. She'd never have made it without a dream to hold on to. Instinctively, she reached across the table and rested her hand on his. "I'm sorry," she said softly. "For everything."

Their eyes caught and held. He was attracted to her, but there was something more than lust there. That *something* scared her. She could care about this man. Silently, she retracted her hand. She wasn't good at hiding her emotions, and she felt exposed under his gaze.

"Is everything okay?" Concern was foremost in his posture now.

"Sure." She wedged up the corners of her mouth into a smile. *Keep it light and get away before you get in any deeper.* "I need to head back. I'm going to be late for class."

He crumpled the scone wrappers into the empty cups. "I'll do the dishes," he deadpanned. "Can't expect a sorority girl to pick up after herself."

"Excuse me? I expected better than rampant stereotypical nonsense from a college-educated, experienced detective."

He grinned. "You aren't at all like the sorority girls I knew at Chapel Hill."

"There may be a few with their heads up their butts, but most of the women are great. And you'll note I'm all grown-up and the advisor now."

"Believe me, I noticed." Warmth flickered in his blue eyes. "But I'm still surprised."

She ignored the commentary. "I'll forgive you— maybe—since you don't live here. But your detective skills are open to debate."

He opened his mouth to refute that, but she wagged a finger at him. "In case you didn't notice, this is a small town. There isn't much in the way of a social life outside the college. Most of the social life on-campus revolves around the Houses. Besides—" she grinned like a little girl with a secret, "—by being the advisor, I can use their laundry room instead of the Fluff-and-Fold and they feed me at least once a week."

"Creature comforts." He said it as if he were making notes. "I'll have to remember their importance."

"That's right," she solemnly agreed. "Right up there with chocolate and air."

His face grew still and his expression intent. "I shouldn't do this for a whole bunch of reasons, but I want to get to know you." He glanced at his watch. "We've been together nearly an hour and it feels like it's been five minutes, max. I could sit here all day talking to you."

He laughed self-consciously, then breaking the eye contact, leaned back in his chair. "Okay." One hand rose and scrubbed his face. "That was incredibly stupid. I'll walk you back."

"It's not stupid," she said, before her brain caught up with her mouth. Fear spurted from its hiding place with her words—fear of the desire he generated, fear of letting anyone get close to her again. She stood; the chair legs scraped loudly over the tile floor at the abrupt motion. "I have to go."

She strode to the door.

He grabbed his jacket and scrambled after her. "Meg, wait…"

She ran down the street. She'd nearly reached the Victorian when she heard his footsteps directly behind her. He caught her arm, but this time he didn't release her when he spun her against him. Instead, his hands dropped to her waist, pulling her closer. His heart pounded against hers. His arms imprisoned her, but she made no effort to free herself.

"There are a whole bunch of reasons we shouldn't do this, either," she said.

"There are a lot of reasons we should."

She wanted to shake her head, but she couldn't. His gaze dropped to her mouth. His lips followed. The first contact was gentle—and electric. She could barely breathe for wanting him. Her whole body focused on Mick, attuned to his every move. He shifted experimentally, changing the angle of the kiss. He tasted of coffee and a deeper essence that was him. The pressure increased, and a glow started in her belly that warmed and loosened her limbs.

His tongue traced her lip, cascading sparks of desire. Electricity surged through her body, melting her defenses. With a sigh of longing, she opened to him and he took possession. While his tongue made love to her mouth, her hands slid up his chest and circled his neck, feathering the fine hairs at the nape of his neck.

He moaned low in his throat and maneuvered her closer, deepening the kiss.

Thought vanished. There was only sensation: pleasure and desire. The texture of his hair, the heat of his body. Strength and masculinity surged though his lips and fingers at an elemental level, entangling and binding them. His hands roamed her back, and she arched into his unmistakable physical response.

"Oh, Meg," he groaned.

Some residual spark of sanity stopped them. He tucked her head against his chest, and she clung to him, weak-kneed, listening to his stampeding heart and ragged breathing. "I thought I'd die if I never got to kiss you," he whispered huskily. "I think I just died and went to heaven."

Control over her limbs returned along with her higher brain functions. She straightened, trying to break his embrace, but his arms were inflexible.

"Don't run away. I didn't mean to come on so strong."

She drew in a shuddering breath. *Are you crazy?* demanded the voice of authority in her mind. *What are you doing? You know better.*

His lips brushed her temple, and his hand stroked her back in a tender caress. "It's bizarre," he said slowly. "We just met, but I feel like I already know you. When you tell me something, it's like I'd just forgotten. Like, oh, yeah, I knew that. God knows, I want you, but this is so much more than just that."

He tucked a finger under her chin and gently raised her head. "Don't push me away."

His erection throbbed against her belly in wild counterpoint to his quiet words. For a moment, she feared he'd give her another of those mind-melting kisses, but he shifted position, retreating slightly. He reached between their bodies, made an adjustment, and grimaced. "I'm not sure I can walk, but how about a lap around the block before I take you home? Maybe then I won't make a complete ass of myself this morning."

"Mick." She stepped back and this time he let her go. She studied his face. Even with desire and hope riding the surface, strength and intelligence gave it structure. It would be so easy to lose herself in this man.

"I can't," she whispered.

She turned and fled.

SIX

Friday, midmorning

"WE DON'T HAVE time for this," Mick snapped. He threw his jacket onto the borrowed Newberry Police Department desk and jammed his fists against his hips.

"Don't bite my head off. The family insisted," Frank told him. "He's their personal physician."

"He's a shrink, not a forensic psychologist."

"He's a pain in the ass, but he's our pain. Geiger's folks called their good buddy, the governor, who called the chief, who called the cap'n—"

"Yeah, I get the picture."

"—thereby proving once again that shit does indeed roll downhill."

Mick and Frank joined the men already assembled in the conference room. Jordan and Robbins looked better today. Newberry PD had thrown everything they had at the kidnapping. It was the biggest case they'd had in ages. In the three previous years, they'd had numerous traffic fatalities, but only one murder. A drug-addicted teen killed his grandfather during an argument over money. The case had shocked the community, but it hardly posed a challenge for law enforcement. Currently, the four most wanted criminals in Newberry County included two for passing bad checks, one simple assault, and a woman driving on a suspended license. If those were the county's biggest crime worries, no wonder the Chamber of Commerce considered the area paradise, Mick thought, remembering the literature strategically placed in his motel room.

In spite of his frustration over Meg, he'd arrived at the police department expecting to get something accomplished today. They had leads, tangible physical evidence, to follow. Instead, they had to sit through this ludicrous meeting.

The shrink sat at the head of the table, and Mick wryly wondered if he'd considered the psychological implications of the different positions. Small, neat, with graying hair and wire-rimmed glasses, he looked like a history teacher. As soon as he opened his mouth, however, Mick detected little man syndrome—overcompensating for nominal stature with a superinflated ego. He nearly groaned. He did not need this today.

"I'm happy to be of assistance," Dr. Perrin said, moving around the table, making eye contact with each person. "I do believe understanding the perpetrator will assist you in making an arrest and ending this reign of terror for our communities."

Jesus, spare me, Mick thought behind a bland facade.

With no choice except to cooperate with the guy, the detectives summarized the three cases and handed the doctor the crime scene photos. The shrink blanched. Mick couldn't help but wonder if he'd seen similar graphic depictions of violence before.

He also noticed the man lingered over some of the pictures. He couldn't see which ones from his angle, but he could guess. Over the years, Mick had met cops who showed a little too much interest in the details of sex crimes. They dawdled over the crime scene photos of women with splayed legs, studied the path reports of the injuries. Discuss the details of the case with them and he heard the prurient curiosity in their voices, even as they tried to appear professional.

It angered him, sometimes as much as the loathing he felt toward the rapist. He had no respect for cops like that. If he was ever partnered with one, he'd find a way to switch. Finding the same tendency in this shrink added to his instinctive dislike and distrust of the man.

Finally, Dr. Perrin settled his glasses on his nose and inspected his notepad. "There are four major categories of serial rapists," he began. "Most are simply compensating for their feelings of inadequacy. They force women to have sex with them to enhance their perceptions of personal power and potency. Then there are the exploitative ones—not our perpetrator."

Mick stifled a groan. The guy was quoting FBI briefing materials Mick had reviewed when he chased his first sexual predator—five years ago.

"You're dealing with an anger rapist."

Thank you, Dr. Perrin. We would have never figured that out on our own.

"He's acting out his issues with his mother. In some way only he understands, these women—these innocent college students—remind him of his inadequacies, which his mother fostered in his formative years.

"As a result of this early abuse, he may display aggressive, macho behavior. He is contemptuous of the victim, generally uses foul language and threatens them."

That's a power asserter, Mick thought wearily. *They're different subgroups.* He focused on a spot just over the psychologist's shoulder. How telling, he thought, that this shrink saw the crimes in terms of sexual predator types rather than concentrating on the motivating factors for serial killers.

"The response he wants from the victim is fear and total

submission. He has no sense of the woman as a person. While most anger rapists seek only to purge their anger, some do murder their victims. It's his complete disregard for women that allows him to advance his deep-seated need to dominate to include murder."

What do you know? Mick thought. It was a weird way to get there, but that last sentence summarized their assailant.

"So you see him as a control freak," Robbins said.

"In simplistic, layman's terms, yes. You must understand, deep down, he's afraid of women. Actually, he hates them. Thinking of them as inferior, as objects, empowers him. He probably is incapable of normal sexual relationships. He may even be impotent. Only when he is completely dominant can he achieve sexual satisfaction. His possible use of a condom during the sexual assault could be fear of disease, but I believe it is symbolic. He is denying the reproductive power of women, shaming them further with the societal disgrace of the barren womb."

Say what? Mick carefully kept the incredulous expression off his face. The men surrounding the table, even Jordan the rookie, displayed equally expressionless faces.

"Historically, women who could not produce an heir were shunned, discarded or on occasion, executed. The sexual revolution changed our ideas about pregnancy, but many people continue to view reproduction as a woman's primary purpose. It is objectification—denying the woman's role as a person—but it is undoubtedly consistent with an anger rapist's view of women as property."

"Doctor," Frank said. "This is interesting background, but I think we're getting a little off course."

"It is imperative that you understand his frame of mind, his context."

Mick was relieved they'd withheld the rock information from him. No telling where he'd go with that. And

Mick had the sinking impression this man wouldn't hesitate to call a press conference, standing in as the "family's spokesman."

"This perpetrator displays the narcissistic infantilism typical of the schizophrenic. The emerging pattern fits a pseudo-reactive schizophrenic. His bizarre behavior serves as a cover-up for the hidden psychosis. His emotions swing from intense euphoria to deepest depression. He may attribute the highs to his murders or the attacks may be what drive the ascent to ecstasy. As a result, when he tumbles into the following depressive valley, he will seek the thrill of the stalk and assault to again achieve the pleasurable upswing."

"How low will his depression go?" Jordan asked.

Mick glanced at him. *Was he actually swallowing this psychobabble?*

"Are you asking about suicide? It is certainly a possibility, but his actions are still too carefully orchestrated to indicate that level of personality disorganization."

"You believe he's a schizophrenic rather than a sociopath?" Mick asked. Dr. Mathews, the consulting forensic psychologist, had found no evidence of psychosis.

"The terms are often confused by nonprofessionals. The correct terminology is antisocial personality disorder."

The man droned on. Mick strove to keep a straight face. He couldn't yawn or laugh without later repercussions. The man had some valid points, but even a blind pig found a few acorns.

Mostly the doctor was overreaching, taking points he'd probably researched yesterday and trying to fit the killer— what was with this perpetrator stuff? Too much *Law and Order?*—into a neat box. Thank goodness he wasn't trying to distinguish between a hedonistic serial killer and a power/control one, the sheer pleasure and exhilaration of the first's stalk and kill versus the other's compulsion to hunt.

Mick's mind wandered as the man murmured about the debilitating effects of childhood trauma, poor nutrition and improper parenting skills. He settled on a more intriguing, and baffling, topic. *What was up with Meg? And with him?* He couldn't get the woman out of his head.

He replayed their conversation. After that inane weather comment of his—where had *that* come from?—everything had been going great and then—*boom*. She took off like the hounds of hell were after her. When he caught her, when she was in his arms, it felt so incredibly right.

Kissing her just happened. It was only a kiss. Okay, it was a monster of a kiss with the promise of a lot more, but still...

"Mick." Frank hissed behind his hand and nudged his foot under the table.

Dr. Perrin had finished his monologue and was now looking at him expectantly. *What was he supposed to do? Applaud?* Mick silently sighed, wondering what the man had just said. "Thank you, Dr. Perrin. That was very informative. You've certainly given us some new insights."

"As I said earlier, I'm delighted to be of assistance in these stressful times. Knowledge is power, isn't it?"

At times. Sometimes, connections are far more useful. "We appreciate your meeting with us. And for sharing your accumulated years of experience."

The man nodded gravely, looking pleased. "I'm willing to assist you as you attempt to formulate a profile. I understand that can be quite helpful in developing a list of suspects."

"We appreciate your offer. I'll call you when we get to that point."

Mick stood. The doctor looked startled. "Aren't you going to do that now?"

"We have some physical evidence we need to process today. The courts still weigh that more heavily. We have to give it preference." He lifted his hands and dropped them as if to say, *What can we do with such ignorance?*

Dr. Perrin rose and picked up his briefcase. "In the interim, please keep me informed. I'll be happy to act as the liaison with the family. Perhaps I can provide a buffer, to shield them from more unpleasantness."

Was that a dig at him for yesterday's rancorous session? "Terrific idea. Please let them know this case is our highest priority."

He escorted the shrink through the door and down the hall to the lobby. "Thanks again."

Mick reentered the conference room. Robbins grinned. "Damn, O'Shaughnessy. I knew your Irish bullshit charm would come in handy."

"'You certainly gave us some new insights.'" Jordan dropped his voice into a pompous imitation of Dr. Perrin's. "Between the two of you, I thought we were going to have to break out the shovels to get out of here. How do you do that with a straight face?"

"I didn't say who the insight was about."

Both detectives snorted with laughter.

Frank gathered the photos into a loose pile. "What's this physical evidence we're looking at?"

"The lab called right before this started. Dr. Clark has something he wants to show me with the duct tape."

"Want me to go with you?"

"Nah. Didn't you get a couple of matches on the victim contact lists?"

Frank nodded.

"Head back to Greenville and follow up on that. I have to go through Columbia on my way to the beach anyway."

"Oh? You and Jess make up? Margaritas and sailboats this evening?" Frank grinned.

The guy thinks my life's one big party. Generally, Frank resisted the temptation to live vicariously through what he imagined Mick's single life to include. Lately, he'd been making too many comments. "Jess and I are ancient history. You know 'policeman' wasn't on her approved list of suitable occupations. It's Tricia's birthday. I can't miss the party and expect to go home again."

"Give your sister a kiss. You coming back tomorrow?"

"I'll be here for the funeral. I'll call you from the car."

THE PROFESSOR STARED at the young women arrayed in tiers before him, like a banquet offered for a visiting prince. *I'll have that one,* he thought, *and that one*.

His gaze moved from the blonde to a brunette. Her long, silky tresses cascaded past her shoulders. She noticed him watching her and self-consciously looked away. He continued past her, losing interest. Vapid; an unworthy opponent.

He moved on, ignoring the corpulent ones, fastidious in his taste. Already, he heard the summons inside him. For now, his hunting was leisurely, merely considering possibilities. His mind and body still resonated with Emily's death. He needed time to appreciate her, to review the triumph of his endeavors.

Nevertheless, the craving was there, a faint scratching in his belly. The want, the need, had become more insistent with each success. His eyes swept across the classroom. If his prey wasn't here, there were other venues, numerous colleges where lovely, young women congregated, careless with their lives and their bodies, convinced they were invulnerable and perhaps immortal.

Another woman entered the classroom, late, but unrepentant.

He smiled. He'd been watching this one, studying her. He knew her routine: the library, the sorority house, the businesses she frequented on the Strip. She moved freely about campus, often alone, sure of herself.

Like all women, she was a fool.

No woman was a match for a man, especially one like him.

Silently, he watched her cross the room. Something was different. She always moved with a confident grace. Today, she carried an added glow. Sexuality simmered below the surface. Something had awakened it. His instincts responded. Like fresh blood drew a predator, she enticed his senses.

Others noticed, as well. Cocky young men, testosterone-driven, followed her movements. Her hips rolled in her tight jeans and her breasts jostled softly, unrestrained beneath the sweatshirt. Her hair cascaded in a riot of curls around her face. Usually she confined it, smoothing it back in a braid.

Triumph surged through him. He could always spot the ones with a secret. She'd held herself out as different, demure. But she was a slut like all the other women. She had risen late from her lover's bed to come to him.

She will be mine.

SEVEN

MICK GLANCED AT his watch. He was cutting it close. Dr. Spindler had called just as that ridiculous session with the shrink broke up. The ME narrowed Geiger's time of death to between midnight and three, consistent with the other victims. Mick tapped his hands against the steering wheel and nudged the cruise-control setting higher. With the SLED cruiser, he wasn't likely to be pulled over, but he didn't like abusing the privilege.

His meeting with the captain was in fifteen minutes. SLED occupied a large campus on the northwest side of Columbia. Most of the traffic was commuters streaming out of downtown, heading home to the suburbs, or people traveling to the mountains for the fall weekend. If traffic wasn't backed up too bad around the retail zoo at Harbison, he should make it on time. He'd update his boss on the murders and then figure out a way to tap-dance out of the political minefield around that debacle at Douglass.

Meg Connelly popped into his mind, but he pushed the thought aside. Later. That whole episode was too weird to get into right now. He had enough weirdness with Didi Hammond and her fountain frolic.

An hour later, Mick left the captain's office with relief. Most of the time had been devoted to the Hammonds—both the politically connected family and their delinquent daughter, Didi. An expression that groaned *shit* had crossed his boss's face more than once, but the word never came out of his mouth. And that particular monkey was now on the captain's back rather than his.

The captain had also pointedly told Mick to take some time off. "Good detectives work hard," he said, "but they learn how to stay sane. They know when to go home and have a life. An overstressed, overtired, obsessed agent is no good to anyone."

Mick agreed completely. He just wasn't sure what to do about it.

He pushed open the door to the lab. For someone so meticulous in his work, Dr. Jason Clark's slovenly appearance was always a surprise. Young detectives tended to underestimate him. Maybe it was just his weight, but Clark's clothes fit poorly. The white, short-sleeved polyester shirt strained across his belly and the too-short slacks pinched at the crotch as the specialist perched on his stool behind the microscope.

Clark looked up and dragged a hand through limp, brown hair that needed a trim. "Ah, Mick, you made it. Come on in."

"I was afraid you might've already left."

"I had a few things to wrap up. I didn't mind waiting."

Several lengths of duct tape were spread, adhesive-side up, on trays around his workstation. Even without the microscope, Mick could see short, blond hairs caught in the closest one, pulled from the victim when the tapes were removed.

"I looked at the fibers on her skin first."

Mick nodded, his attention still on the tape.

"I'm afraid I can't help you much there."

He knew Clark's nuances. The scientist had found something on the tape, but they had to finish with the other fibers first.

"They were from a tarp, the kind you can find in any Walmart in the country."

"Nothing distinctive, impossible to trace."

"Pretty much." Clark shifted his bulk and gestured at the trays. "Our unsub used duct tape, another generic commodity, to restrain all three victims."

Mick nodded again. "The first two were bound to their beds. The last one was restrained, but cut loose. The tape was still around her wrists and ankles when we found her."

"Dust, hair and skin cells are visible on the tape under ultraviolet light," Clark said. "I'll isolate those. Probably they're the vic's, but maybe we'll get lucky. This is what I wanted to show you." He pointed to the tape edge.

Mick studied the length of tape. Burgundy fibers, flecked with tan particles, ran along the entire upper edge of the piece. "What is this?"

"It's on all of victim three's pieces. It could be a leftover from the manufacturing process, something misaligned when it was made."

"You obviously don't think so."

"You're right," Clark replied cheerfully. "Think about a roll of tape for a minute." His free hand mimed holding a roll and turning it over. "When you place it on its side, the entire surface picks up traces of whatever it's pressing against."

He gave the scientist a questioning look. "And?"

"The tape from victim one was clean, leading me to think it was a new roll. The unsub probably unwrapped it there. The second set of tapes has leather on the edges."

"Those tan specks?"

"Correct. I figured he carried the tape in a backpack or a satchel. I understand you think your killer may be a student, so that would be consistent. The specks turned out to be belting leather, though, which you rarely see in a book bag."

"Some of the higher-end day packs use it," he said. "And lots of briefcases and suitcases. Not many guys are going to carry a suitcase to a murder, though."

Clark nodded. "These burgundy fibers are nylon. At first, I again thought, book bag. You've seen those packs with a nylon top and leather bottom?"

"Yeah."

"But the denier's completely wrong for that. The density is much higher."

"So what kind of fiber is it?"

"Take a look." Clark placed a slide under the microscope, and Mick peered through the eyepieces. "What do you see?"

"It's smooth, sorta triangle-shaped."

"Correct. The delta shape is characteristic of carpet fibers. Nylon six, six to be exact. This fiber's cross section and light birefringence make it a Dupont fiber commonly used in automobile carpets."

Mick sat back and rubbed his cheek. His fingers rasped against his beard and he dropped his hand. "Not many cars have burgundy interiors. Didn't that go out with the nineties?"

"Try the eighties." Clark moved the slide to a holder and placed it in a file. "He probably dropped the roll in the trunk. The color has faded, but not as much as the floor mats would."

"That doesn't fit. Our profile makes the killer white-collar. He's taking victims from upscale neighborhoods. It's his comfort zone. Someone in those neighborhoods isn't going to drive a twenty-five-year-old beater."

"What about a twenty-five-year-old classic? Say, a Mustang. It'll be a domestic car, not foreign."

"Why?"

"Jaguar used wool carpets. Triumph used a different brand of nylon." He waved his hands expansively to include the remaining universe of automobiles.

Mick considered Clark's words and nodded. "If the guy's in his thirties, his age fits the profile. A hot car from back then could be compensation. I doubt he had one as a teenager."

Clark smiled agreement. "Since the wheels of bureaucracy grind to a screeching halt at five o'clock on Friday afternoons, I already turned in your request to the DMV for a list of all the 1980s cars registered in the Upstate. It's set up to hit your e-mail account as soon as it finishes processing." He grinned. "It should be a monster file."

"Thanks, I think." Between sorting car records and Emily Geiger's funeral, his weekend was going to suck. "Can't wait."

"It gets even better." Clark pulled in his chin as he grinned and crossed his arms. His neck blossomed into multiple rolls that sagged over his collar. "There's a specialty finish on the fibers. It's worn, but I've picked up the chemical formulation. I sent it to the manufacturer about an hour ago. I should hear back early next week. The results should narrow your list."

"You're my hero." Two million cars just dropped to twenty thousand.

"And don't you forget it, glory boy," Clark said. He turned back to his microscope. "Go on, get out of here. It's Friday. It's late. You must have better things to do, a hot date or something."

Why did people keep saying that to him? he wondered as he headed toward his car. People were so quick to make assumptions. He was single and women seemed to find him attractive. Therefore, he must be a party animal with a love life to rival a Hollywood star.

Was he making similar assumptions about this killer? The thought brought a sobering pause. Did he need to seriously consider possibilities other than a student?

He pulled out of the parking lot. Rush-hour traffic had peaked while he was in the lab, and Broad River Road traffic was moving. At I-20, he made a quick decision. Rather than traveling the Interstate, he swung onto Sunset and headed for the southeast side of town. Soon the chaos of new construction along Sumter Highway fell behind, and he settled into the old back-roads route to the beach.

As the miles passed, he unwound from the week's tension and let his mind drift through what they knew about the killer. He'd heard too much about the bleak childhoods of these criminals. Too many people—including the assailant—wanted to justify their behavior as an unavoidable consequence of their childhood. Nearly all serial killers and sexual predators came from abusive or otherwise dysfunctional families. It didn't excuse their actions. Too many other people rose above similar circumstances. There was no correlation that said: given this background, these people must commit violent crimes.

No, it was the ultimate selfishness. These men did what they did because they wanted to. It gave them satisfaction or pleasure they didn't get in any other aspect of their lives. It made them feel good, regardless of the consequences to others. Once they crossed the line and broke a law, they forfeited whatever claim they had to victim status. They became just another criminal.

Lake City came and went with gasoline and fresh coffee. He returned to his musing. How were they going to stop this killer? Where was he hiding? Most human predators hunted in areas where they felt safe. They blended in with the locals. They knew the roads and the traffic patterns, where the cops hung out. They understood the habits of their prey, because they observed them every day as they went about their less-lethal activities.

The first two victims lived in nice apartment complexes with decent security: well-lit and maintained, with good locks on the doors and windows. The bodies' discoveries had prompted immediate hysteria in the surrounding community, followed by the disappearance of children from the sidewalks and yards. Geiger's abduction from the mall had caused a similar evacuation. Although the victims were young adults rather than children, Mick couldn't blame the parents. The instinct to protect was strong. On the other hand, the demands for resolution increased exponentially with each grisly discovery.

More dark miles passed. A car roared up on his bumper, then quickly backed off, assuming he was patrolling. The lights annoyed him, so he eased to the side of the road and let the car pass.

By Kingsburg, his mind was again roaming freely. White-collar neighborhoods. College kids. Leather and twenty-five-year-old carpets. Why not a professor rather than a student? A briefcase and a muscle car. Students would invite a recognized professor into their apartments. If given a plausible story, they'd step outside a mall with one. But how did a professor meet women from three different schools?

When he got the DMV list of cars, he could cross-reference it with the professors from the three colleges. He'd already asked Frank to look at possible connections among the schools, a recent transfer or something.

The first outlines of the killer were starting to form.

Finally.

EIGHT

Friday night

MICK STOPPED IN front of the house where he'd grown up and cut the engine. His sports coat and tie had hit the backseat when he'd stopped for gas outside Lake City. Rolling up his sleeves, he climbed from the car, then stretched to ease his cramped muscles.

The house lay half-hidden beneath a sprawling, ancient oak. A cluster of palmettos, myrtles, and overgrown azaleas obscured the front. Spanish moss, banished when his father was alive, had reclaimed the tree and dangled in a ghostly cloud. Although the lots were large in this neighborhood—nearly an acre each—the house looked smaller every time he saw it. It was hard to believe five kids had grown up in a space not much bigger than his condo. Of course, they'd wandered in and out of their friends' houses in a freewheeling innocence that was unheard of today. Mick figured he'd probably slept more nights in a hammock on the screened porch and at his best friend's house than in the bedroom he'd shared with his brothers.

A gibbous moon hung above the tree line, pearly in the thin bands of clouds that hid the stars. The faint light gleamed on the crushed shell drive. They hadn't needed an outdoor light when they were kids. The oyster shells reflected enough light for them to ease onto the porch, whatever time they straggled home.

He identified the cars in the drive. His mother's sedate Buick was in the carport. Vince and Laurie drove the soccer-mom Suburban. Colin had the BMW instead of his 'Vette. Apparently, he had his son this weekend. The brand-new minivan must belong to Shaun and Maureen. Tricia's ancient Civic was last in line. It stayed all girled up with dangly things on the mirror and assorted bottles of fruity stuff that knocked his head back when he opened the door.

The whole gang was here.

It'd be bedlam inside.

Mick leaned against the hood, listening to the engine tick as it cooled. The ocean was too far away to smell, but the tidal creek and the surrounding swamps lent a pungent tang to the air that said "home." A soft breeze whispering through the pines behind the house lifted his hair. The air was thick with moisture, and he smelled rain riding the breeze.

The front door opened, spilling noise into the yard. A silhouette moved to the screen door. "Michael? Is that you?"

Only his mother called him Michael. "Out here."

The door creaked on hinges that had long ago given up hope of lubrication. She crossed the yard, staying on the path to avoid the sand spurs. "What are you doing?"

He hugged her and kissed her temple. His mother's rich brown hair had streaks of gray now. Years of Carolina sun had weathered her skin to a web of fine lines, but her blue eyes were still as vivid as a girl's. "Enjoying the quiet."

She chuckled. "Not much of that inside."

"It'll be quiet soon enough. Last one's getting ready to fly the coop."

"Tricia? She's not gone yet. Vince and Laurie are just up the block. Don't worry, with their kids, I have plenty to keep me busy." She leaned against the car beside him and studied him in the faint light. "Is it a bad case?"

He gave a small sigh. "Aren't they all?"

For a few minutes, they listened to the night sounds without speaking.

"Mom?" he asked finally. "When you and Dad got married, how did you know he was the right one?"

She took her time before answering. "Marriage isn't all passion and roses, Michael. It's commitment. Sharing goals and beliefs. It's two people loving each other enough to see each other through the bad times. And having someone to share the good times. To create the good times. When you find the person you want to do those things with, you know."

He nodded silently, his eyes fixed on the house.

"Have you found somebody?"

Images of Meg filled his mind: the confident woman who stood up and spoke her mind, the laughing coffee-shop companion, the passionate woman in his arms, and the terrified child who'd run. Which one was the real Meg? All of them? None? "Maybe."

It was one of the things he loved about his mother. She understood without asking a lot of questions. "It's not easy being married to a cop."

"You never did beat around the bush."

She shrugged. "Doesn't do any good."

"I know." Being a cop was one of the reasons he was still single. Not many women could handle not knowing if their husband would come home at the end of his shift. He'd seen what it had done to his mother. A Wildlife officer's duties included tracking down fugitives when they took to the swamps. His father had died while wearing his uniform. With a start, he realized what his mother's collapse said about the depth of his parents' love.

"Let's go in before they send out a search party," she said.

Noise, light and people swirled through the small house. His brothers had ESPN blaring in the cramped living room. The women chattered in the kitchen, oblivious to the children who bounced between the two groups, excited by the presents and the noisy confusion.

"Happy birthday, Squirt." He kissed his sister and looked into her smiling face. She had their mother's chestnut-brown hair and the O'Shaughnessy blue eyes. "Finally legal and you're spending the evening at home with us?"

She grinned. "Did you really think Mom would pass up the opportunity to get y'all over here for a party? I'm going out with my friends tomorrow."

"This is your brother the cop speaking. Two words: designated driver."

She rolled her eyes. "Stay home and you can do it. In fact, there's somebody I'd like you to meet."

He was already shaking his head. "I have to get back tomorrow. This case..." He didn't want to think about death and monsters tonight.

Tricia shuddered. "I don't want to talk about it. How about I call Amy after dinner? We can ditch the kids and go get a drink or something later."

"Don't worry about my love life. I can still find my own dates."

"Yeah, I see all the women you bring home."

Shaun clapped him on the shoulder. "We were getting ready to eat without you. Come help me with the steaks."

His wife drifted by, their baby on her shoulder. "Make the biggest one rare. I'm still eating for two."

Shaun tweaked her full breast, kissed her and stroked the baby's velvety head.

Maybe kids aren't so bad, Mick thought, watching them.

He grabbed the platter of steaks and headed for the backyard grill. As he immersed himself in his family, he wondered if these trips back home were an escape from the harsh reality of his daily life or if this was real and he labored in an endless bad dream.

NINE

Saturday morning

MICK ROLLED OUT of the bunk bed in his old bedroom and tripped over a pile of miniature sports equipment—Vince and Laurie's kids' stuff. His mom took care of the boys during the day, and apparently half their toys had migrated into her house. At four and six, the boys were rowdy and rambunctious, but an assortment of computer games also crowded the shelves above the new computer on his old desk.

Limping on his bruised toe, he entered the hall bathroom. Tricia was still asleep, but her presence pervaded the room. He tested and rejected three bottles of shampoo before finding one that smelled merely citrusy. Frank would give him endless grief if he used one of the flowery ones.

Breakfast smells drew him to the kitchen. Grits bubbled on the back burner and coffee perked in an ancient pot. His mother half-turned from the stove when he entered the room. "Morning. You want your eggs scrambled or fried?"

"You didn't need to get up."

She smiled. "It's nice to have someone to cook for. When Tricia's home, she sleeps until noon and dashes out of here with a bagel."

He filled his coffee mug and settled at the massive oak trestle table. Seating for seven—or a pull-your-elbows-in eight to ten, as often as not—had been a necessity when they were growing up. "Do you feel lonely?"

His mother slid a plate in front of him and sank into her spot at the head of the table. "I drink my coffee on the porch most mornings, watching the sun rise over the creek." She smiled at some private memory. "I've always loved the creek. The swamp took longer to appreciate."

He attacked his eggs. She hadn't answered his question. "I worry about you being here by yourself."

"Are you asking why I didn't date after your father died?"

She could still read his mind. "You're still young, attractive."

"Why aren't you married, Michael? You've dated some lovely young women."

He shrugged, not wanting the conversation to be about him. How did they end up on this topic anyway? "None of them was the right one."

"There's your answer. I met and married my right one."

He quickly finished his breakfast. "I have to run. I'll come back after we catch this guy."

"Soon, I hope." She ran a hand over his hair. "Bring your young lady. It sounds like I need to meet her."

He smiled ruefully. How did mothers just know stuff? "We'll see."

The sun was merely a suggestion in the eastern sky when Mick left Conway. He settled his travel mug in the cup holder and roared up Highway 501. Only an occasional puddle remained as evidence of the overnight rain, but the thick, humid air glazed his windshield. By midday, the sky would be a brilliant blue. It'd be a perfect day to be outside, but by noon the highway would be bumper-to-bumper with tourists thronging the outlet malls instead.

At this early hour, he had the road nearly to himself. He picked up I-20 at Florence, westbound to Columbia. Clearing Malfunction Junction at I-26, he figured it was late enough to call Robbins. "What'd you hear about the tire casts?"

"We may have finally gotten a break. The tire's a specialty, after-market one. A Goodyear Eagle GT14. To be specific, a 225/60 R16. Goodyear's running a list of distributors. I'll contact the local ones as soon as it comes in."

"I'll have the DMV list soon. We can cross the tire list against it," Mick said.

"I talked to the sheriff. He's onboard with manpower to check the cars around here. Ward and Andersen are handling the agencies in their areas. We'll feed the results back to you."

And to think he'd worried about this man wanting to run his own show. "Sounds like a plan. That covers the Upstate. I can get some of my guys to look at the rest of the state."

"I thought we agreed he lives inside the Greenville-Spartanburg-Newberry triangle. He isn't going to drive to Charleston to buy a tire."

"You're right. Good work on the tires, by the way."

"Thanks. I gotta run. We're setting up the cameras at the church and the cemetery right now."

"Remember to be discreet. These guys call the governor the way you call your mom. We don't need any more of his attention."

"No problem."

Mick closed the cell phone. There were always problems when emotions were involved. It was just the way life was.

TiVo WAS A wonderful invention. The Professor knelt in front of his television, adjusting the playback. He started with the Greenville NBC affiliate. He liked the blonde reporter with the pouty lips. He pressed Play and sat back on his heels to watch.

"This is Jennifer Thornton, reporting from Newberry, South Carolina. Emily Geiger, the third victim of the brutal serial killer stalking the Upstate, was laid to rest today by her grieving friends and family."

The scene behind the reporter shifted to the cemetery. "While the police have been unable to produce a single suspect, they were highly visible today, interrupting the ceremony more than once."

A shot of a scuffle between an overzealous reporter and a uniformed officer appeared on the blue screen behind Thornton. The Professor smiled at the stupidity. How could she not see the irony? Her grim, serious expression looked ridiculous on a face designed for carnal pleasure. There was a breathlessness in her voice that was almost sensual, as if she were getting off on the assault. The hunger inside him stirred with interest.

"Ms. Geiger, a rising star in the sophomore class at Windsor College, was tortured, sexually molested and murdered by a man police say is little better than a wild animal."

Wild animal sounded harsh, he thought. It really wasn't appropriate given the planning involved. He retreated to his chair and toyed with the remote, sampling various broadcasts. He'd started to attend the funeral, had actually driven to Newberry. As he approached the church, however, someone—it had to be a cop—stepped out of the door and panned the parking lot with a handheld camera. He'd driven past, averting his face, relieved he'd driven the Honda and not the Camaro.

Finally, the section he was looking for scrolled onto the screen: the press conference. Driving home, he'd heard the radio announcer talking about it. The three police chiefs stood at the podium in front of the Newberry Courthouse, the lead detectives from each involved agency arrayed behind them. The chiefs solemnly pledged to find the murderer, but offered no details. They were terse, straightforward with their comments. The SLED captain stepped forward and made the appropriate political blatherings. When he finished, a forest of hands shot skyward as the talking heads struggled for face time and the print guys tried to create column space that could compete with television's sound bites.

The first questions were almost intelligent. Then another reporter cut off a question with a shout of his own and the whole thing turned into a fiasco. By the end, news photographers were standing on car hoods, firing off shots of the chaos as the TV cameramen jockeyed for position.

The Professor was delighted. This pandemonium showed better than any print coverage just how disorganized and inept the police were. He watched the clip a dozen times, trying to consider every nuance. Were they frustrated? Incompetent? Afraid? He wished he could see the entire press conference, and briefly considered calling the television station to inquire about obtaining a copy of the recording.

He ran the segment again and found himself watching the detectives. They were the ones doing the scut work. They would find him—or not. He considered each man in turn, wondering about his abilities. The woman he dismissed automatically.

Finally, he focused his attention on one figure. "Him," he said, touching his finger to the screen. The SLED agent wore slacks and an expensive-looking sports coat. He stood, relaxed, while the others fidgeted. When bedlam broke loose, he looked almost bored.

Smug, the Professor thought, feeling the familiar anger clutch at his belly. The agent looked like he'd been one of *them* when he was younger. Tall, well-built. He still had the stance—arrogant, cocky. He knew he was good-looking. He probably married the head cheerleader or the homecoming queen. They'd likely spawned two brats just like themselves.

The Professor froze the disk and stared at the flickering image. His hatred grew. The agent was probably related to somebody. Coasting through life, like all the rest of them. Letting the others do the dirty work.

Loathing ran through his body like poison. If he could, he'd find a way to bring down Mr. Smug Law Enforcement Agent. He'd bring them all down, he thought with a vicious streak of vindictiveness. He was smarter than they were. They were fools, bobbing along in his wake, waiting for his next step.

The Professor glared at the SLED agent one last time. "How does it feel, loser? Not to have a clue what to do next?"

Late Saturday afternoon

THE DOWNLOAD FROM the DMV was taking forever. Not a good sign. The file must be massive. Mick was stuck at this borrowed desk at the Newberry PD until it finished.

Frowning, he closed his cell phone. Directory Assistance didn't have a listing for Meg Connelly, Margaret Connelly, M Connelly or any other combination he could think up. Why hadn't he gotten a phone number out of her Thursday evening? He grimaced, annoyed with himself. Because he'd assumed she was a student, another of the Chi Zetas.

He'd tried calling the sorority house. Whoever answered said she'd seen Meg at the library. With Meg's teaching load and midterms, maybe she really was studying or grading papers.

Or maybe she was avoiding him.

He returned the phone to his pocket, sighing with frustration at the ridiculous situation. What was he doing, pursuing a woman who didn't want to be caught? He snorted, knowing he didn't believe that. If she truly wasn't interested, he'd vanish. Delete the sorority house number from his cell phone and Meg's face from his brain. Move on.

But she was as interested as he was, whether she wanted to admit it or not. He was completely intrigued, which made no sense at all. She was a total mystery.

Brooding, he replayed his conversation with his mother. Was that all this infatuation with Meg was about? Was he simply ready for something in his life besides work and an empty condo? Did Meg happen by at the right moment?

He thought about it some more, then slowly shook his head. None of those things had crossed his mind until Meg wandered into his world—and upended it. But how could she have so much impact in such a short time?

He considered that for a moment, his gaze absently roaming the open bay. Shoulder-high partitions carpeted in a gray, synthetic loop divided the room into workstations and separated the desks. Metal bookcases crammed with department manuals and law books competed for space with file cabinets. Normally, the area would be full of noise: phones ringing, metal file drawers banging, murmured conversation, low laughter. The distinctive cop-shop smell remained: cigarettes, greasy take-out chicken and a faint odor of locker-room sweat.

The room felt oddly deserted after the flurry of activity earlier in the day. The funeral had been completely depressing. Overflowing church. Crying girls. Crying parents. Everyone shell-shocked, mouthing the same platitudes. The bright autumn sunshine had made things worse, mocking the somber mood of the ceremony. Resentful of the cops' presence, as if they caused the death of a beloved child, the crowd sullenly shifted from the church to the flower-smothered grave site. The intrusion of the press nearly started more than one fistfight, which the local police also had to manage.

Finally, the family had retreated to the big, black limousine. The crowd dissipated in their wake. Mick had returned to the Newberry PD building, where technicians set up their projection equipment. Hours passed as assorted officers patiently tried to identify every person inside and outside the church.

Gradually the other cops drifted away—other things to do on a Saturday afternoon. For just a moment, Mick resented their leaving, though he knew there was no reason for them to stay. They'd done everything anyone could think of. All they could do was wait. Now only empty desks, silent phones and other people's clutter met his gaze. Even Frank was gone, catching a few precious hours with his family.

Mick's fingers hovered above his computer keyboard. He felt guilty for about a nanosecond as he fed Meg's name into the system. Her DMV picture popped up almost immediately. It was a few years old. Her hair was longer; her eyes a little sadder. Margaret S. Connelly. He wondered briefly what the *S* stood for. Five foot six; one eighteen. Brown and blue. He wouldn't call her hair *brown*. It was honey and fire, caramel touched with copper. Strawberry blond ripening into auburn. Definitely not brown. And her eyes were more green than blue.

He checked her birth date; she was nearly twenty-six. A few years younger than him. Funny, her age seemed irrelevant when they were talking.

And when they were kissing.

He forced his attention back to the data on the screen.

She used the Clinton address. That was interesting. Most college kids kept their parents' home address on their license. Of course, Mom and Dad probably owned the car and paid for the insurance, so keeping their address a little longer made sense. Meg was a graduate student. She was probably on her own, which explained the student ghetto apartment address. Or had Meg's parents moved out of state? A local address would mean less hassle writing checks. He remembered the sympathetic understanding in her eyes when he told her his father died. Were her parents still alive? There was so much he didn't know about her.

She didn't have any moving violations. That wasn't completely surprising. When he worked Patrol, as long as it was just speeding, a pretty girl usually drove away with a warning.

Pushing his luck, he ran her through NCIC. The National Crime Information Center reported no arrests, no warrants. He felt a little guilty—not for checking, but for using the resource for personal reasons.

Mick slumped in his chair, propped his feet on the desk and checked the download status again. Damn, only 62 percent complete. He'd be checking cars for the rest of his life.

He sighed and let his mind return to Meg. Why did she run? Literally. He'd seen fear in her eyes. She was scared of something.

So start with the obvious. She was scared because he was a cop. She knew the "inquiry" with the sorority girl was political bullshit. He could look deeper, ask some questions, but he'd already found out what he needed to know there. Meg wasn't in trouble with the law. There wasn't any reason for her to fear a law enforcement agent.

Was she afraid of him? He'd let things go further than he should've, but whatever scared her was already there.

Was it men in general? She came across too confidently for that, although it could be an act. What would make her so frightened? A bad experience? Of course, he thought. The possibility of sex had scared her.

Why would she be afraid of that? He doubted she was a virgin. Her passion had initially matched his. In his experience, there was only one other reason women feared sex. The thought chilled him and solidified in cold anger at some faceless man. At that moment, he'd have bet his life's savings some bastard had raped Meg Connelly. And she probably didn't report it. Or get counseling. Too few women did—afraid of the trial and the public backlash. He ran her name again, searching for any field: victim, complainant.

Nothing.

Mick cursed himself and the faceless rapist. He'd lost control too.

He shouldn't have let it happen, but it was a kiss they'd both wanted.

Closing his eyes, he deliberately replaced his anger with good thoughts: the walk, their conversation, and finally that mind-blowing kiss. He relived every second of it. She'd responded. God, had she responded. Her body had melted into his. His penis stirred and he knew he should think of safer things, but he retraced each movement of his hands. He could smell her, taste her. He revisited every curve, every soft moan until his erection throbbed painfully against his jeans. He'd wanted to lay her down and explore her supple body. Pleasure her until the last shred of restraint vanished and she screamed his name as she exploded into orgasm.

He took a shuddering breath and packed away his fantasy. It was after they stopped that she panicked, as if she realized what had nearly happened. If they'd been somewhere besides a residential street, it might have. "Ah, Mick, you're a fool," he whispered. "You're too old to think with your little head."

So what if she could sear him with a glance from across the room? If she could send a thousand volts shooting through him with the briefest touch of her fingers. He was supposed to be an adult, dammit!

He prayed he hadn't blown his chance with her.

He had to figure out a way to talk to her again.

But right now, he had a different problem. He needed to either make it to the restroom unobserved and do something he'd never done before at the office, or else think of something disgusting. Something like his upstairs neighbor. Mrs. Wilcox wore too much makeup, too little clothing—two sizes too small—and made her interest more than a little obvious. Definite turnoff.

Or he could get his mind back where it belonged—on this case. Then maybe he could find the bastard.

TEN

Sunday morning

FRANK DROPPED THE *Greenville News* onto the kitchen counter in Mick's condo. "I got your paper."

"Thanks." Mick didn't lift his eyes from the laptop on his dining room table. Normally he worked in the small bedroom he'd converted to an office, but the case files had outgrown the space. He typed in his password and waited for the computer to finish loading.

"Man, does your neighbor always dress like that to get her paper?"

Oh, jeez, Mrs. Wilcox strikes again, he silently groaned. The good mood that sleeping in his own bed and an hour at the gym had produced evaporated. He stared at the computer, urging it to start faster.

"It wasn't so much what she was wearing, as what she wasn't."

He sighed. Frank wasn't going to leave it alone until he responded. "What was she wearing this time?"

His partner rocked on his toes. Enthusiasm lit his voice. "She had on this little-bitty robe over a baby-doll gown. It was that kinda sheer material, you know, where you can see, but not really."

"Hmm." He focused on the laptop and launched the database program.

"That's the best you can do? 'Hmm'? What is *wrong*

with you, O'Shaughnessy? She's hot. I mean, she has these tits…"

He rolled his eyes. Frank was pantomiming cantaloupes or maybe watermelons. "Go for it. She's not my type."

"Your type?" Frank asked, incredulous.

"Yeah. As in Barbie has no brain."

"Who cares?" The man's hands rose and fell in exasperation.

Mick ignored him and opened the car file.

"Christ. Sexy woman throws herself at him and he bitches 'cause she isn't a nuclear scientist." He opened a cabinet, grabbed a mug, and poured coffee. "You're out of sugar again."

"There's Sweet'N Low."

Frank made a face, but emptied several packets into his mug. He moved to the refrigerator and stood in front of the open door.

Mick shot a concerned glance into the kitchen. Frank had been making too many comments like that lately. But what was he supposed to ask? Was everything okay between Marilyn and him? Was he thinking about having an affair? Their relationship didn't work that way. Frank meddled in his life, not the other way around. His partner was supposed to be the solid, married man.

Frank pulled out the milk carton, sniffed and grimaced. "This is pathetic." He examined and replaced a carton of orange juice. "What's this?" He lifted a white container as if it might contain anthrax.

He leaned back so he could see what the guy held. "Probably leftover Thai. You might not want to eat it."

"Do you have anything in here that didn't die last week?"

"I haven't been here. The apples and those little carrots in the bottom drawer are okay." He'd had a handful for breakfast, along with a bagel he found in the freezer. "I need to go to the grocery store this afternoon."

Frank grimaced and closed the refrigerator. He opened cabinets and finally found a box of Triscuits. "You want more coffee?"

He shook his head, his eyes never leaving the DMV records scrolling down the screen. "There are over two hundred thousand lines in this file. I had no idea there were so many old cars around here."

"Half of them are in my neighbor's yard," Frank replied around a mouthful of crackers. He leaned against the counter, scanning the front page while he crunched noisily. "You see this?"

"You just brought the paper in."

Frank held it up and Mick glanced at the headline.

"The Professor, huh?"

"Yeah, he's made the big time. Bastard has a name now. I'm sure he's rejoicing, wherever the asshole is."

"Damn. If the TV people use it on the news tonight, we'll be stuck with it. Anything interesting in the article?"

"Let's see...rehash of the press conference. Wasn't *that* fun? Here we go, unnamed sources...believe he's a professor at one of the local colleges. Is that official now?" Frank looked up, an amused expression on his face. "Where do they get this stuff?"

"Did Terri Blankenship write the article?"

Frank glanced at the paper. "How'd you know?"

"Rumor has it Andersen's sleeping with her."

"Ouch. Talk about sleeping with the enemy."

"No kidding. I wonder what else he's leaking to her. And don't even say what you're thinking."

"Yeah, yeah. I guess we'll find out tomorrow." Frank dropped the newspaper on the counter. "How do you want to tackle the car?"

"All we have are reports of a coupe or sports car and a big engine. No one actually got a real description." Mick's fingers tried to smooth the tension from his forehead. He'd had a headache for days. He propped his elbows on the table, thumbs at the hinge of his jaw, fingers cradling his head. Their one clue was turning into a grain of sand on a wide Carolina beach.

Frank wandered into the dining room and peered over Mick's shoulder.

He angled the screen so Frank could see the information. "Let's see how many we can get rid of. If we ignore the generic Chevy and Ford four-door sedans, that cuts it nearly in half."

"Get rid of all the trucks too," the other agent suggested.

Mick further narrowed the list by excluding the foreign cars. He paged through the remaining records. "Corvettes didn't have big enough trunks to conceal a body."

"Thunderbirds were clubby boats by then," Frank said. "They had big engines, but they weren't cool enough for our guy to be driving one now."

"The clerk did say it was a coupe."

"You were what in the eighties? Two? Three? I was in college. I can't believe that was thirty years ago." Frowning, Frank drummed his fingers on the table. "What were the tough guys driving?"

"British cars were hot when I was in high school." Mick stretched, remembering a time that seemed so simple in retrospect. "Old Triumphs and MGs. Jeeps and Blazers were big. Lots of 4x4's. As far as domestics went, we're talking Mustangs, Camaros or Trans Ams."

"They've been around a long time. Seems like they were big when I was in high school too."

There were thousands of them. He cursed the mild South Carolina climate that didn't turn cars into rusting hulks, eaten away by salt like the cars of the Northeast and Midwest. They'd have to find and investigate the owners of each car.

Frank hung over his shoulder. "It would help if they'd included the exterior color."

Mick's attention caught on the Vehicle Identification Number. "The manufacturer would have everything—including the original body color and interior package. Clark said the fibers were old. They could be the original carpets."

"Good idea," his partner nodded. "It's possible he repainted the car, but we can at least start with the shorter list."

Mick's fingers danced over the keys, sorting the remaining cars by maker, then model, and sent each manufacturer the relevant VIN list, requesting specifications. As much publicity as this case had generated, he knew he'd have no trouble getting the information.

The message list refreshed with the outgoing requests, and the incoming message tone sounded.

"That was quick."

"'File received' confirmations," Mick said. He pointed at the screen. "Who's Kevin Rynd?" The message subject line read, "Investigation."

"Agnes Scott address. Did we talk to him when we interviewed people at the college after Baldwin's murder?"

"I don't think so." Mick opened the message.

Miss Geiger—Emily, since I have been intimate with her—is not young and beautiful any longer. Such is the cost of war. Soldiers die, women break. She is not the first, nor will she be the last.

What the hell was this?

Emily foolishly believed in her own abilities. Women have neither the strength of mind nor body to compete with men. Soon they will recognize this and return to their subservient position—the one they have held throughout history as man's property and indulgence.

"My God," he murmured. "Read this."

He turned the laptop so Frank could see the screen. "The asshole's sending *me* e-mail now."

At the end, Emily's struggles were pathetic, but her fear, her terror, was very real.

Anger clamped Mick's jaw like a vise. The contemptuous bastard.

You understand the exhilaration of wielding authority over others.

What? Was this scumbag trying to draw a comparison with what the police did?

But you can't imagine the bliss, the rapture, of holding the scales of life itself. Will Emily die today? Or tomorrow? Or should I show mercy to the vanquished? Why should I? Emily signed her own fate when she haughtily assumed random, genetically provided features afforded her special compensations.

What about the next one? Shall she die, as well? It is not her decision. It is up to you. It will be on your conscience, not mine.

Don't lay that on me, you asshole. Even as he rejected it, Mick felt the taunt hit home.

How confident are you of your abilities? You stand at the fringes of my battles, my successes, looking manly and proud, but we know it is a charade. You follow my lead, waiting for any bread crumbs I deign to throw your way. I have the upper hand—and I'm laughing at you.

"Jesus," Frank said.
"Amen," Mick answered.

ELEVEN

Monday morning

MICK SETTLED AT his desk in the Greenville field office,
a cup of coffee clutched in his hand. His mood was as
gloomy as the weather outside. He slid the band off the
Greenville News and scanned the morning's article on the
Professor. "Well, damn."

Frank stopped mid-sip. "What?"

His partner's desk abutted his. Mick spun the paper and
poked a finger at the headline. "Bereaved Father Blames
Police." Nathan Geiger had vented his rage to a reporter.

"If the police had told us about the e-mails from this
monster, Emily wouldn't be dead," Frank read aloud.

"Yeah, like she told her parents about anything happening in her life."

"'You wouldn't believe the things this animal said to my
daughter. If she'd known the murderer was saying things
like that, she'd have shown them to us. We could've pro-
tected her. Obviously, the police can't protect anybody.'"
Frank shook his head. "No, we're just sitting over here
eating doughnuts."

The Newberry PD had wisely taken the "not our issue"
position on Mr. Geiger's anger, exonerating themselves
and thereby laying another stink bomb at SLED's doorstep. The SLED spokeswoman had confirmed only that
the victims had received suspicious e-mails, which were
being investigated.

The police had told the press about the stalking and the e-mails, but withheld the contents. The article offered the lurid details. "Let's hear it for sensationalism," Frank said when he finished reading.

Only someone intimately involved in the investigation had that kind of access. "I'm going to wring his stupid neck," Mick said.

"Which one? Geiger or Andersen?"

"Both of them. The press are gonna be all over us. By this afternoon, we'll have all kinds of terrified women forwarding e-mails."

"And a hundred emotionally stunted men will find it amusing to send them."

"We'll have a dozen copycats active by noon," Mick said grimly.

"Come on, O'Shaughnessy. Treat it like any other leak," Frank said with a shrug. "Set up a hotline."

He took a deep breath and shook off his anger. What was done was done. "Benny already set up a mailbox for suspicious e-mails. If the cap'n hasn't called to chew us out in five minutes, I'll ask Lucy to come up with a press release."

"Ninety-nine percent of the messages will be bogus," Frank agreed. "Maybe we'll get lucky with that last one percent. We know his pattern: stalking, increasing possessiveness. We'll recognize his style."

"The problem is, the victims didn't recognize them as a problem at first, so we don't have the earliest ones. They didn't tell their friends until the messages got really creepy. We might miss the initial ones to his next target. Assuming he keeps it up after this. With the publicity, he may change tactics."

"He's not gonna change," Frank said. "Hell, he's sending you e-mail."

"That's true." He threw the paper in the recycle bin, drained the dregs of his coffee and with one last frustrated sigh, turned to the mountains of paperwork that had piled up while he was out.

Three hours later, he logged off the system and rolled a cramp from his shoulders. "I'm going down to Newberry. I want to look at those statements again, maybe go out to the mall. That guy at the Orange Juice stand was the last person to see Geiger. We never identified the second guy the clerk saw her with. Maybe there's something there, something we're missing. You want to come?"

"I have paperwork on those prison guards at Tyger River. I'll catch up with you later."

RAIN-HEAVY CLOUDS loomed ominously over the low-slung brick building that housed the Newberry Police Department. As in many small towns, several emergency services shared the physical space. A HazMat truck was parked in a smaller, second lot beyond the two fire engine bays. A municipal court sign pointed toward doors at the far end of the building.

The same architectural firm that designed the new sheriff's department building must have handled the building's renovation, Mick decided. He recognized the standing seam metal roof and Tinkertoy arch above the double doors.

He parked between a cruiser and a civilian car. A cold, blustery wind pushed a paper cup across the parking lot. Flipping up his coat collar, he hurried toward the front door. He automatically noticed the occupied Mazda Miata parked in the adjacent row, and turned as the driver's door opened.

"Mr. O'Shaughnessy?"

The girl wrapped her unzipped jacket across her chest

and hugged herself from either cold or nerves. He recognized her immediately. The petite blonde was Emily Geiger's younger sister. She was also seventeen and a high school student who should be in class.

"What brings you down here, Ms. Geiger?" Questions, he wondered, or more blame from her family?

She shuffled from one foot to the other, a nervous dance. "Can I talk to you?"

"Sure. What can I do for you?"

"Not here." She peered around uncertainly.

He smiled, hoping to help her relax. "Not at the station or not out here in full view of everybody?"

Blushing, she blurted, "I've never been in a police station before."

"Actually, they're pretty routine. We can use one of the interview rooms, if that'd make you more comfortable."

He led her inside and signed them in, then escorted her into the back. She stared wide-eyed at everything. Other than the uniforms and cop gear, he thought the station's interior looked like any other office space—desks, computers and file cabinets. The posted suspect photos were different, he supposed, but the cartoons were universal.

The interview room contained only a table and two chairs—nothing to distract the person being questioned. "How's your family, Ms. Geiger?"

"Um, call me Susan."

A second later she added, "please," with what sounded like parental-installed politeness.

"Okay, Susan."

She perched on the edge of the chair. "I don't think it's real yet. I keep expecting Emily to walk in the door."

He knew the feeling. "I'm truly sorry for your loss."

Susan continued as if he hadn't spoken. "The press are

such assholes, hanging around. And there are these jerks calling, saying stuff about her."

"Get someone—a friend, one of the people who ask what they can do to help—to screen your calls."

She nodded. "I'll try."

Her tone said her suggestions didn't carry much weight. Given her father's personality, they probably didn't. Mick figured she hadn't come down to complain about the nut cases and related villains. "What's on your mind?"

She fidgeted with her pocketbook, moving it around before carefully tucking it under her chair. Lacing her fingers, she placed them first in her lap, then on the table. Finally, she separated the entwined digits and adjusted one of her silver rings. "I heard you talking to Mama and Daddy, asking about Emily's schedule and all. Um, where she went and stuff."

He deliberately relaxed his posture and waited.

"She always went to the mall before her English class. She didn't tell anybody."

"Every Monday?"

"Every Monday, Wednesday and Friday."

"Always?" No wonder the sales clerks knew her. Robbins and Jordan had focused on that Monday, retracing Emily's steps, rather than looking at the bigger picture. If she had that regular a schedule, they needed to re-interview all the mall witnesses. If the killer was stalking Emily—and the abduction made a lot more sense now—someone at the mall might've seen him.

Susan nodded, still studying her fingers. "For about the last month."

"It's a long way to the mall to go that often."

"She didn't want anyone from around here to see her." Mick kept his face blank.

She hesitated, then confessed, "There's a guy. He works

at Barnes and Noble. She'd meet him during his break. Mama and Daddy didn't know about it."

He held his breath. *Why hadn't anybody gotten this from her during an interview? This guy could be the killer, or at a minimum, he'd know something.*

She risked a quick look at him. "They're pretty…strict." Her eyes dropped to her hands and she picked at her cuticles.

"Tell me about the guy."

He was completely unprepared for her response.

"He's black, African-American. Mama and Daddy freaked when they met him and told Emily she couldn't see him again. They *say* they're open-minded," she burst out. Her chin came up, challenging him. "But not when it comes to *their* precious blonde princesses."

I'll be damned. The OJ guy's unknown male. It made sense now. "What's his name?" She wouldn't be here if she didn't want to tell him.

Her gaze slid away. "Robbie wouldn't hurt Emily."

"I don't think he did either, but he may be able to tell us something. Emily may have confided in him."

Susan considered that possibility. "My parents will freak. How will they hold up their heads at the country club if word gets out their daughter was dating a…" She couldn't bring herself to utter what was undoubtedly a derogatory term.

"They're already freaked. Robbie could help us find out who killed your sister."

She worried her cuticle for another minute. "You won't tell him who told, will you?"

"No."

"I don't want to get him in trouble."

"The only way he's in trouble is if he killed her. And you're sure he didn't."

She thought about that. Finally, she sighed. "Robbie. Robbie Mahaffey."

They talked until he was sure she had nothing else to offer about her sister or the investigation.

"Thank you. You've been a big help." He looked at her and used the same tone of voice he'd use on Tricia. "Aren't you supposed to be in class?"

She blushed. "It's only Spanish, which has got to be the easiest class in the world."

"For you, maybe. I'm trying to learn, but I'm terrible at it."

"That's 'cause it's harder to learn when you're old."

Ouch. Out of the mouth of babies. "Well, don't make a habit of cutting or you could find yourself down here again."

Her mouth made a perfect *O*. She shot to her feet and fumbled with her pocketbook. Edging to the door, she said, "My teachers have been pretty cool about me missing, but maybe I should, you know, get back."

He handed her his card and walked her to the lobby. "Call me or come down—after school—if you think of anything else."

She flashed a smile that so closely resembled her dead sister's pictures that Mick felt his stomach cramp. How must her parents feel each time they looked at her? What they still have, and what they lost, in the same face.

Susan disappeared out the door.

Mick spun around. "Where's Detective Robbins?"

TWELVE

Monday

THE PROFESSOR WATCHED Meg enter his classroom—the long, fluid strides. His eyes tracked her, then slowly blinked into a private vision. *She was gloriously naked, moving smoothly down the central aisle toward his desk. With a beckoning smile, she draped herself over the wooden surface, inviting his exploration. Slowly, he drew his knife the length of her leg before plunging it into her belly.*

Her eyes went wide with terror.

Her scream resonated through his body.

His answering arousal was immediate.

He fumbled with his briefcase, reining in his thoughts, and pulled his lecture notes as a distraction from the fantasy. He quickly sat, hiding the bulging evidence of his need. His hands shook as he realized he'd nearly lost control in front of a classroom full of students.

Control, he silently chanted. *Control is everything.*

He could control anything, he reminded himself. He had control over these students. He gave them a baleful glare. They were swine. What would they do if he let them see his true nature? They'd never understand. They'd merely run screaming with all the other lemmings to the nearest cliff.

Scorn brought his throbbing penis under control. His eyes raked the classroom. He was better than all of them. His gaze caught again on the redhead. Meg sat with the football player who always wore a fraternity jersey. The boy leaned toward her, signaling his interest, but she didn't respond as the oaf expected.

She was flirting, the Professor decided, not with the jock, but with him. He watched her signals, how easily she manipulated the boy.

A faint smile lit his face, anticipating his own confrontation with her. He had no question about the outcome. She wouldn't find him so easily swayed. He would conquer her, dominate her.

The victory would be sweet.

The restless craving was building already. He'd spent the weekend with the newspapers—Greenville, Spartanburg, Newberry and Columbia—rereading all of them. He'd lain on his bed and rerun the memory of Emily dying. By Sunday, however, images of Meg and Allison had begun spinning through his mind. Redhead and raven beauties, they rotated in a Technicolor dream as first one, then the other joined him in his desire. He masturbated, feeding his fantasies, until the new ones' faces replaced Emily's. Endlessly, they cycled in his mind.

Meg and Allison would color his days and fill his nights in the coming weeks. He'd never followed two women at once. It was exhausting and exhilarating. He couldn't have managed it if they weren't on the same campus. Allison facilitated his quest by detailing her life—her public life—in her online journal. Meg was more studious, spending numerous hours in the library. It was a waste, lavishing her time and energy pursuing a field for which her gender made her ultimately unsuited. But it made tracking her movements easy.

He would flaunt his knowledge of their days, showering each chosen woman with a deluge of e-mails. Sharing his erotic visions gave his raging need an outlet, but he knew the women secretly welcomed the attention. And taunting them with his familiarity—showing them how powerless they were—heightened their fear when the time was appropriate.

He'd sent the first message to Meg right before class began. How would she react? Concern? Fear? He imagined terror in her eyes rather than the amusement he currently observed. Or would she respond to his advances?

The tension in his groin again grew painful. "Control," he whispered. "Control it."

Meg rolled her eyes at something the football player said. He liked her dismissing the boy. A private smile crossed his lips. She might be his most delicious opponent yet. He could manage the tension that scratched at him, needing another body, another death. He would savor her, taking his time while he learned her secret.

His instincts were rarely wrong. She had a secret—they all had secrets. He suspected a lover, but he'd found no further evidence. All he had to do was remain patient and she would expose her weakness. They all did eventually. It was a flaw that ultimately doomed them. Their efforts to cover their tracks—to hide their sweet obsession—made them easy targets.

Meg smiled, a brilliant eruption of vitality animating her face. He was captivated. He imagined her sprawled across his bed, her auburn hair fanned over his pillow, sweat glistening her fair skin like morning dew. Tiny drops sparkling like diamonds in a web. She wasn't smiling. She was caught in his web. Like a fly, she fluttered helplessly against her bindings. Her confidence was destroyed, shattered along with her innocence. Panic widened her eyes. Her lips drew back in a scream of agony. Completely submissive now, she did his bidding in a futile grasp at life.

"Professor?" A boy's whiny voice intruded. "It's time to start class."

Startled, he scowled at the scrawny boy for interrupting his fantasy. For one harsh moment, he considered killing him. The thought carried no sexual pleasure, only anger. He should make the weasel watch while he took his pleasure with the next one. He wouldn't interrupt *then*.

What would the insignificant toad do? Would he squirm with impotent rage, or would lust pound through his pathetic body, straining for release?

The surge of power that followed the thought gave the Professor pause.

An interesting possibility, he considered as the boy flinched under his unrelenting stare. An audience, someone to appreciate his superiority.

Or even better, a way to humiliate an enemy.

Turning, the Professor favored his chosen with a final, lingering appraisal. Soon, he'd know her, in every sense of the word, until he possessed her, as completely as he owned the others.

He glanced at the boy and smiled. An audience. Yes, an intriguing possibility. Maybe it was time to raise the stakes again.

THE OJ GUY's employee badge said his name was Tommy Brice. He was maybe seventeen, skinny and had the worst case of acne Mick had ever seen. Putting sympathy and revulsion in the box he reserved for emotions, Mick explained what they needed. "I'm going to show you some photos. I'd like you to see if you recognize the man you saw with Ms. Geiger last Monday."

Brice gnawed a ragged fingernail. "Like they do on *Law and Order?*"

"Same general idea."

"Sweet."

The kid picked at a crusty spot on his cheek, and Mick

turned his attention to the photos in his hands. In addition to Robbie Mahaffey, he'd pulled nine pictures of young black males from the booking photo database. All of them featured the same cropped hair and unsmiling, resentful attitude. He laid the photos in a grid on the counter and Brice leaned over the array, idly fingering a trio of pimples on his chin.

He made a mental note never to eat at the food stand.

"This one," Brice said. He placed his forefinger in the middle of Mahaffey's picture.

"You sure?"

"Yeah. I've seen him around. I just don't, like, know his name."

He pulled out a form and entered the appropriate notations. Sliding the document and photo across the counter, he said, "This says you identified photo number four as the man you saw with Ms. Geiger that Monday."

Brice signed in the designated places. "Do you think he did it?" Curiosity and maybe excitement tinged his voice.

"No." He shook his head. "We just needed to clear up who this guy is."

The kid looked disappointed. "Whatever."

He returned the photos to an envelope, and tucked them into his pocket. He joined Robbins and they wandered across the food court. "I'm going to get some coffee," the Newberry detective said. "Want some?"

"I'm good."

Robbins stepped over to the frozen yogurt stand. He stayed and talked to the clerk awhile. Mick figured he probably knew the teenager. While he waited, he studied the arrangement of the food court, the ebb and flow of foot traffic. The rain wasn't keeping the crowd away from the mall this evening. When Robbins returned, Mick said, "There's no way the guy pulled her out of here without someone noticing, especially if she was wobbling like a drunk."

The tables in the center of the food court were visible to every food stall.

"We don't know how fast the drugs hit her," Robbins said. "Besides, not all of the booths open before lunch, and she was at a table over beside that pillar. She wasn't looking to be noticed when she was with Mahaffey."

"How would you do it?" It was the question every detective asked when they needed a way into a crime scene.

"Me? Dress up like a rent-a-cop. Either she left her lights on or she's parked in a 'no parking' zone. Walk her out and keep going." Robbins nodded at the mall entrance. "If the roofies had already kicked in, I'd make it look like a bust."

"Someone would've seen them come through the food court."

"Maybe he waited until there was a lull or until the guy at the OJ stand was busy." Robbins shrugged. "How would you do it?"

"Out that corridor." He gestured toward the service bay. "There aren't any stores down there, and those food stalls don't open until later in the day. Straight out the back door and keep walking."

"There's an alarm on the door, hotshot."

"I'd be long gone by the time security showed up. If there was no commotion, they'd write it off as kids."

"That might work," Robbins conceded. "It's still hard to believe no one saw her leave."

"One thing I've learned is people have an amazing ability to forget."

"Especially stuff that doesn't involve them personally."

An Hispanic man arrived, pushing a cart loaded with cleaning supplies. He raked a few discarded wrappers into a bag and swiped a cloth over the tables, then pulled the trash can from the central enclosure.

"Good catch on the cup, by the way," Mick said. "What made you look for it?"

"This started as a missing persons case." Robbins shrugged. "Geiger didn't come home Monday night. Nothing pointed to her taking off without telling anybody. After we found her car in the mall parking lot, we treated it like a kidnapping. The same thing you asked nagged at me: how'd he get her out of here without a scene? It was either someone she knew, someone like a security guard that she'd trust, or she was drugged. Soon as I talked to the OJ kid Tuesday morning, I went Dumpster-diving. Collected all the OJ cups, narrowed it down to the ones with that concoction she liked and started testing. Number twenty-six had the roofies. We sent that one off for DNA testing. In about a year, we'll find out if it was hers."

The state lab stayed backlogged. "You think about a private lab?"

Robbins grimaced. "No budget. In the meanwhile, I knew she was doped. That's when the chief called y'all."

Mick nodded, still watching the janitor. "She knew this kid, Mahaffey."

"Funny, her sneaking around like that. I guess the adventure added to his appeal."

"Lewis knew a lot about the kid's background. Why's that?"

"The family's only been here a few months, but Lewis has been out there a good bit."

Patrol didn't make social calls. He wondered why the young officer had been out there, but figured Robbins would get around to it.

"Mahaffey's mother's a local girl. She went to school

up north. One of those 'more' places: Swath-more, Bren-more, something like that. She married a fellow up there."

"What brought them back? Her folks need help?"

"No. Her husband forgot the first rule of motorcycling."

He raised a questioning eyebrow.

"You go up against a car, car's gonna win every time."

He'd seen some nasty motorcycle wrecks when he worked Patrol. "How bad was he hurt?"

"Bad. He's crippled, in a wheelchair, living on disability. He's not your poster child for overcoming the odds."

"Oh?"

"Bitter's a major understatement. The kid's the same way. With his dad not working, money's tight. Instead of going to whatever school accepted him up north, he's down here at Tech, working at the bookstore to help pay his tuition and living at home in a poisoned atmosphere. Lewis has been out there a lot on Domestics."

"Keep talking," Mick said dryly. "You've about convinced me Mahaffey did it. It makes sense, now, why the local kids don't know him. He didn't go to high school with them."

"I checked with Tech. He hasn't made many friends. The ones his mother said he went camping with over the weekend are about it. He was supposed to be back from the mountains last night. She's worried."

"I asked the sheriff's department to check the state parks, but he could be anywhere."

Robbins crossed his arms over his belly and looked sideways at Mick. "He looks good for this, O'Shaughnessy."

"There are a lot of strikes against him. I want to know why he didn't come forward on his own, why he hid the relationship. Mahaffey has a temper?"

He glanced at Robbins for confirmation. The older detective nodded.

"Geiger could've dumped him Monday morning. He had access to her, to the park. That black Trans Am of his isn't helping his case. Any way we can get into the trunk for a carpet sample?"

"Let's see if he volunteers."

"Yeah, he's volunteered so much already. With all these questions, he'd be at the top of my suspect list if we were only looking at Geiger. Without the rock, I'd figure him for a copycat. But there's no way he knew about that detail."

"So you don't think he's the doer?" Robbins asked.

"It doesn't feel right. He was involved with Geiger, but what's his connection with the other two? We know the same guy killed all three of them."

Robbins snorted in agreement.

He watched a girl maneuver a stroller next to a table. She was pretty, blonde and pudgy with residual baby fat. Either he was getting old or she looked about ten years too young to have a child of her own. "Did Ward come up with anything from the sex offenders list?"

"She has a huge list, but until we have a description, nobody can do anything with it."

"That's the bottom line, isn't it?" Mick pursed his lips and blew out a thoughtful breath. He watched a family fill a table with pizza wedges and sodas. Quality family time at the mall. "Where are the earlier victims?" he asked, as the thought slid into his idling mind.

"Huh?"

"The earlier sexual assaults? There have to be some. Maybe we can find one. The victim could identify him."

"I've worked rapes, O'Shaughnessy. You know as well as I do, half the time, they don't get reported unless the woman's vindictive or damned sure she can prove it."

"Shit."

"Yeah."

The early evening crowd was filling the food court. "Where *is* this guy?"

Robbins shrugged. "The boss said Mahaffey called and traded his morning shift for this evening."

He restlessly looked at the stores surrounding the food court. "I'm going to talk to a few of the managers while we wait."

"You're going to go hang out in the Hallmark shop some more, you mean. If the clerk wasn't old enough to be my mother, I'd worry about you. Or maybe that should make me worry more."

MEG WALKED SLOWLY across campus. She'd avoided the sorority house all weekend. Mick had called the House and left a message, asking her to call. The Chi Zetas had teased her, amazed she wasn't excited. Of course, they only looked at the external package while she focused on the man inside.

Not returning his call was a separate issue. Actually, it was amazing he'd called at all, given the way she'd acted. Could that whole episode have been any more embarrassing? Why—beyond the obvious that Mick scared her to death—had she run away? How hard would it have been to say, "I'm attracted to you, but…"

Yeah, that was a major understatement when ten seconds earlier he'd had his tongue performing magic in her mouth and she was plastered to his chest, dying to rip his clothes off.

No, no, no. Do not think about that. She should've calmly told him she wasn't looking for a relationship right now. She didn't have the time or energy to put into one. And she didn't have casual sex.

Not that sex with Mick would've been casual. The electricity between them could fuel the entire campus network. That plus the promise of his kiss said it would've been blow-her-mind-and-her-future-plans-away sex. The sweaty-body, sheets-on-the-floor, last-all-night kind. The kind she wanted with Mick so badly she could tear her hair out.

Absolutely not going to happen, she thought fiercely as she crossed Bellwood. She'd been down that path—and she knew who got burned in the end. She'd worked too hard, sacrificed too much to throw it away. Mick would eventually get the message. So what if she was taking the coward's way out?

She mentally cringed. She never backed away from a fight. She stood on her own two feet.

Then why was she afraid to confront Mick? she asked as she turned onto her apartment's walkway.

Because she wasn't sure what she wanted, whispered the mutinous little voice in her head. She wasn't sure she could tell him "no" to his face. The undeniable connection between them scared her—she felt it just as strongly as he said he did. She wanted to know everything about him: what he was like as a little boy; more on his views on the environment; whether he'd stay a cop or go back to law school. None of which meshed with her plans, so really, she had to stop thinking about him.

She stomped up the front stairs and unlocked the outside door. Fear had nothing to do with it. She couldn't get distracted right now. If things went according to plan, in one and a half semesters, she'd be launched in a new career, finally earning enough to live comfortably. And she'd have done it all by herself. She'd prove to everybody, including her parents, that they were wrong.

She stopped at her mailbox. A square, blue envelope stood out from the bills and junk mail. Her name was neatly printed on the front. An unfamiliar Greenville return address filled the upper corner, but she knew it was from Mick. She slipped the card in her bag and hurried upstairs.

Dropping her messenger bag on her desk, she unpacked her books and opened one. For a full five minutes, she stared at the text, not understanding a word on the page. With an exasperated sigh, she jerked out the envelope and ripped it open. The front of the card read:

The other day, I was standing in a crowded elevator, when all of a sudden, somewhere between the 8th and 9th floors, something made me think of you. I could picture you in my mind, with that intense look you get…
   Then, just as quickly…

Where was this going? Meg wondered. She opened the card.

…the elevator doors opened and the smell dissipated.

She groaned. Gotcha, bathroom humor.

Sorry. Call me, Mick.

Sorry for what? The card? The kiss? For being born?
   She tapped the card against her desk, then tossed it in the trash and started her laptop. The Microsoft logo sprang to life and the machine asked itself if it felt okay. While she waited for the startup diagnostics to finish, her gaze dropped to the card. She plucked it from the wastebasket and placed it on the corner of her desk. It was juvenile. In spite of herself, her lips quirked into a smile.

An hour later, she eased out of the economic theories underlying interbank rate swaps. Rubbing her hands against the small of her back, she stretched and rotated her neck. Her eyes inevitably landed on the card. She reached for it automatically. It *was* funny, the humor offbeat enough to appeal to her.

Lucky guess on his part.

Monday evening

"WHERE *IS* THIS kid?" Robbins had grown impatient as the time for Mahaffey's shift to begin came and went. He bounced on the balls of his feet, restlessly peering around the bookstore.

"He'll turn up," Mick said. "Patrol's looking for him. His boss says he's on the schedule. The only thing we can do is wait."

"You must think he's coming in, since we're still here." Robbins's fingers crept toward a nonexistent pack of cigarettes.

Mick wondered when the guy quit smoking. "I've been trying to put myself in his place," he said. "He thought his world sucked, then he met a girl. They hit it off. Life was looking up. Now, she's dead. His parents and buddies don't seem to know about her. My guess is he's been drowning his sorrow in a bar or he's off somewhere by himself, licking his wounds."

"Makes sense. Getting to work on time isn't going to be his highest priority."

Robbins wandered down the aisle, cataloguing the other patrons rather than the books. Five minutes later, he returned.

"You want to go back to the station, see if the manufacturers have sent the VIN details?"

Mick shook his head. "Let's give him a few more minutes."

Robbins twisted his wrist, checking the time. "Aren't we supposed to talk to Dr. Mathews about those e-mails?"

He shrugged. "I rescheduled. The computer guys are still sourcing them."

The detective sighed and trailed a finger along the books in front of him. "What is it with women and self-help books? They're always trying to fix something— themselves, us, the dog."

"And we're usually happy with things the way they are. You ever look at any of those?" He gestured at the books.

"Who, me?" Robbins looked appalled.

"Maybe our jobs wouldn't be so tough if more men did."

"Getting in touch with your softer side?" Robbins laughed. "Hell, there's always gonna be assholes."

"And we're always going to watch football."

"And hockey and the fights."

"With a few friends."

"And pizza and beer. What's wrong with any of that?"

A patrolman's distorted voice sounding from the radio at Robbins's hip interrupted them. "Subject's on his way in."

Robbins immediately returned to cop mode. "We'll take it from here."

"You need backup?" the voice asked.

Robbins glanced at Mick, who shook his head. "Negative. Tell Dispatch you're clear." He tucked away the radio.

The policemen watched a slender young man enter the store. Robbins adjusted his holster. "Come on. It's showtime. I love being the bad cop."

They intercepted the young man at the door to the employees' lounge. "Mr. Mahaffey?"

"Who wants to know?" Mahaffey had closely trimmed hair, suspiciously red eyes and a major attitude.

Both men opened badge cases. "We'd like to talk to you about Emily Geiger."

"I got nothing to say."

He tried to brush past, but Robbins cut him off. "I think you have plenty to say. We can do this nice, right here, or we can do it at the station."

Mahaffey's hands tightened into fists. "Why you come down here for? You dis'in' me, making me look bad."

"Drop the 'brother' speak," Robbins said. "I've seen your class schedule and your grades. You aren't any more of a gangbanger than I am."

"Then why are you here harassing me?" He thrust forward aggressively.

"Why didn't you come forward on your own?" Robbins got right back in Mahaffey's face. "You knew we'd want to talk to you."

"Talk," he sneered. "Yeah, right. That's why we're *talking* out here in the middle of the store where everybody can see."

"Why don't we sit down," Mick said. "The coffee shop, the employee lounge. Wherever you'd feel comfortable."

"I don't feel comfortable talking to you, period. Especially not that cracker." He jerked a thumb at Robbins. "Whatever you want to *talk* about, *he* already thinks I'm guilty."

"I thought you and Ms. Geiger were friends. I don't understand why you don't want to find out what happened to her. Everybody else volunteered to talk to us," he said.

Mahaffey jammed a card through the reader and pushed open a door marked Employees Only. Mick and Robbins caught the door before it slammed shut and followed him past a pile of boxes to a small, locker-lined area. Mahaffey stuffed his wet jacket into a locker, then turned and crossed his arms over his chest. "What do you want?"

All the men remained on their feet, ignoring the plastic chairs surrounding the break table. "Let's start with where you've been for the past few days," he said.

"Camping. Is that a crime?"

The friends his mother said he'd camped with had denied going. "Where? With who?"

"I don't have to justify myself to you."

"This would go a lot smoother if you'd cooperate."

Mahaffey heaved a gigantic sigh, as if the burden of the world lay beside the huge chip on his shoulder. He spun a story about camping in the mountains, detailing his adventures.

Mick listened to the lies and let them go, letting Mahaffey get them all out there. The guy had a story—he'd probably thought it up over his long, lonely weekend. Along with Robbins, he'd whittle away at it. Once that first story crumbled, the kid would have another version, and they'd go to work on it.

"You were at Pisgah?"

Mahaffey nodded. His shoulders straightened with renewed confidence.

He shook his head sadly. "You sure you got the right place? Pisgah's campground was closed this weekend. Water main's busted."

"Oh, yeah, that's right."

He waited for the next story.

"We *planned* to go there, but it was closed. It was that other one, um, Table Rock."

"I don't think so. It's a fall weekend. Table Rock's been full all month."

"We didn't have like one of those parking places. We went up the trail and found a spot."

He stroked his chin, considering. "By the river? Or up nearer the lake?"

Mahaffey hesitated, as if unsure whether the question was a trick. His eyes wandered toward the door, as if he were considering bolting.

"You headed up to the mountains alone after the funeral?" he asked.

Off guard, Mahaffey was slow on the uptake. "Emily's?" Realizing he'd slipped, he added, "I was camping with friends, not at some funeral."

"We know you were at Ms. Geiger's funeral. We've got you recorded."

"So what? It doesn't mean I killed her." His hands balled into fists.

"Did anybody say you did?"

"Then why are you here? You're trying to hang it on me, aren't you?"

"Did you spend the weekend thinking about her?"

Pain flared across the young man's face. Mick knew he'd scored a direct hit. "You were with her last Monday."

Mahaffey tightened his lips and again looked past Mick toward the door.

"Tell me about your relationship with Ms. Geiger."

"I barely knew her." Back in control, Mahaffey glared at him with cold eyes. Getting no response, the kid looked at Robbins, who'd jammed his hands in his pants pockets. In the process, the detective had pushed back his jacket, revealing his pistol. Robbins apparently ignored Mahaffey, his eyes busy examining the break room and the inventory visible beyond the open doorway.

"But you went to her funeral." Mick reclaimed Mahaffey's attention.

"Well, yeah." The kid was scrambling again, trying to

invent a reason. "She was my age. It sucks when some-one your age dies."

"So you showed up out of respect," he said slowly, as if he believed Mahaffey's statements.

"That's it. Respect." He drew his head and shoulders back, looking down his nose at the detectives.

"What were you talking to her about on Monday?"

"I wasn't talking to her. I told you, I barely knew her."

"We have witnesses who put you together in the food court that morning."

Mahaffey pushed past him. "I have to go to work. You're making me late."

"We know you were involved with her," Mick told his departing back. He shot Robbins a look: *Your turn.*

Mahaffey stopped, apparently unsure how much they knew and how much they were guessing. "I knew who she was. We talked a few times."

Robbins leaned on the door frame, arms crossed over his chest, blocking Mahaffey's path. "What happened?" he asked. "Did she lead you on? Pretty girl like that, what was she doing? Taking a walk on the wild side? Flaunting Mommy and Daddy's rules?"

The kid bristled, but kept his mouth shut.

Robbins's voice was low and taunting. "Rich white girl going slumming? What'd she do that morning, Robbie? Break up with you? Laugh when you said you loved her? Did you smack her around when she didn't come through?"

Mahaffey lunged at the older man, but stopped inches from him.

"Come on." Robbins straightened and held his ground, daring him to attack.

"You are so full of shit. I didn't touch that girl." Anger burned brightly in Mahaffey's eyes. His hands clenched; his whole body went rigid.

The detective kept pushing. "Where'd you go when you left the food court? She left with you, didn't she?"

"I was at work on Monday." Mahaffey was shaking, barely holding his temper in check.

"All day? You didn't find time to slip out to the parking lot for a quickie?"

"Don't talk about her like that. Emily wasn't a slut."

"Somebody was getting some," Robbins taunted. "'Course they weren't real bright. No condom. Lot of 'jac in her."

Mahaffey whirled and slammed his fist into a locker. "Bastard," he whispered. He cradled his hand, using the physical pain as an excuse for the emotion in his face and voice.

"Where'd you go that morning? You take a little ride that ended at the park?"

Still clutching his hand, Mahaffey straightened defiantly. "Back to work. Ask my boss, if you haven't already."

"And after that?"

"To class."

"What class?"

"Accounting. I had a test that day."

"You're a student at Windsor?"

He shook his head. "Tech."

Robbins rocked back on his heels with a knowing look. "That's right behind Lynches Woods."

"You think I don't know that?" Mahaffey's voice was tight. "I drive by that park, and I want to kill the bastard who did that to her."

"Not the smartest thing to say to a cop." Robbins leaned against the door frame, eyeing Mahaffey.

"I don't care." The kid was cracking. "How would you feel if it was your girl? If someone…" He stopped, swallowed and looked away. The muscles in his jaw jumped spastically.

Like killing him.

"I don't know," Robbins said skeptically. "Nine times out of ten, a girl gets killed, her husband or boyfriend did it."

"I love that girl," Mahaffey burst out. "I would never hurt her. Her old man ordered me out of his house like I was some yard nigger. So Emily came to me." He thumped his hand against his chest. "She knew what mattered, what was in our hearts. Not our skin, our *hearts*. We talked about marriage, the future. I'd never hurt her." Tears filled his eyes and he turned away, his lips thinning as he struggled to hold his grief inside.

"We know you're hurting," Mick said. "But you knew her better than anybody else. What'd she tell you?"

Mahaffey shook his head, still working his jaw and blinking his eyes.

"Talk to me, Robbie. I need the truth."

The kid's laugh was harsh. He shot a glare at Robbins. "What do you care about the truth?"

"I care about who killed Ms. Geiger," he said. "I don't think you did it, but you might know who did."

Mahaffey shook his head, sullen now that his anger was spent. "I don't know nothin'."

"You might. Tell me what was happening."

Mick held his breath while the younger man silently debated cooperating. Finally, he crossed his arms and slouched against the locker behind him. "Some guy was stalking her. She said she felt him all the time, following her, but she never saw anybody. She got these weird e-mails."

"She deleted most of them. What did they say?"

"Weird shit." Mahaffey shook his head. "At first, she

said it was creepy. He kinda came on to her, like some pervert. She could tell he was watching her."

"How?"

"Things he said about what she wore, where she went. The longer it went on, the more he sent."

"What do you mean?"

"Toward the end…" Mahaffey's voice cracked and he looked away for a minute. "He was sending them constantly. Emily was scared. She didn't know what to do. I wanted her to tell somebody…" He flicked at glance at Mick that said *somebody* was the cops. "But we thought maybe it was just more…of the crap we put up with."

The couple probably had caught some harassment when they were together in public, Mick thought. "Why didn't you report it?"

"He started going on about Emily's 'secret.'"

"Secret?"

Mahaffey swallowed, his tough shell slipping a little more. "Us. He taunted her, threatened to tell her parents about us. I didn't want her to catch shit from them over me. At the end, the bastard was trash-talking bad. Said he'd do to her what we were doing, but we weren't…you know." He stopped and bit his lip.

Protecting her to the end.

Tears brightened Mahaffey's eyes. "The bastard made her miserable, and then he killed her." Ducking his head, he stabbed his fingers across his face.

"We'll find him. We'll make him pay."

"Sure." Mahaffey pushed away from the locker. "Like you found him after the first two."

The stinging comeback had its intended effect. Mick gritted his teeth. "We'll find him."

THIRTEEN

Early Tuesday morning

Mick stopped at the Holiday Inn's office to check out rather than simply leaving the key card in the room. The night clerk confirmed the details in Robbins's written report. The woman had a clear view of the highway from her seat at the counter. She'd been watching the road the morning Emily Geiger's body was found, waiting for her boyfriend to bring her a forgotten textbook. The twenty-four-hour gas station to the left had done a sporadic business, but only one car drove past from the right—the direction of Lynches Woods.

Mick pulled out of the motel parking lot, then made a quick left onto Broad Street. Two-story, gingerbread-trimmed, wooden structures built in the twenties, lined the road. Newberry had prospered as a rail center before the Depression wiped out the economy. The outer fringes of the downtown business district looked like they'd never recovered. The buildings seemed tired, in need of both paint and customers.

As he approached the town square, evidence of recent prosperity appeared. Awnings fluttered above freshly washed windows. An air of genteel affluence permeated the atmosphere. Most of the buildings were classic revival structures from the 1900s or Victorians built a quarter-century earlier.

The courthouse anchored the square. Doric columns

rose two stories to a pediment above massive double doors. A bas-relief filled the triangle created by the pediment. Added after the Civil War, it showed the American eagle grasping an uprooted palmetto tree. A defiant gamecock at one end of the tree balanced an olive-branch-bearing dove at the other. Given the number of people he'd met who resented the federal government, he wasn't sure the scale should be in balance.

He turned right at the intersection. Various businesses, most of them catering to tourists, surrounded the shady memorial square behind the courthouse. A man sweeping the sidewalk in front of Martin's Grille looked up and waved as Mick drove past.

People here moved slower than they did in Greenville or Columbia. The town reminded him of the way Conway used to be. Small, neighborly; everyone knew everyone else. They were quick to gossip, quick to help. As a kid, news of his exploits had occasionally beaten him home. After his father died, though, the house was buried in casseroles and home-baked cookies, as neighbors stuck to the Southern adage, if you love them, feed them.

The Newberry PD building was maybe a mile from the courthouse. He parked beside a cruiser and went inside. He was stirring sweetener into his coffee when Robbins wandered in, yawning. Pointing to the photo hanging above the coffeepot, Mick said, "Y'all have too much time on your hands."

Someone had carefully altered the logo on the side of a Newberry County sheriff's unit to read: *We'll kick your asses... And eat your doughnuts too.*

Robbins glanced at the picture as he dumped three packets of sugar into his mug. "There are worse things."

He couldn't disagree.

After spreading his files on a training room table, he

sipped coffee and studied the car list. It didn't make sense to work the list without the VIN information. There were simply too many cars. He slumped in his chair and stared at the large-scale map on the opposite wall.

The interview with Mahaffey had produced a big fat zero, simply confirming things they already knew.

Robbins, trailed by Jordan, wandered into the room. The older detective tossed a stack of papers onto the table. "For what it's worth, here are the local tire dealers."

"What's the problem?"

"Jordan talked to them yesterday while we were interviewing the black kid."

"And?"

The rookie sighed. "They keep records by customer, not car. They played with their inventory records and pulled out who bought Goodyear Eagle GT14s. We can run them against the car list, match the owners, but a lot of the sales were just cash sales."

"No customer listed?"

"Right."

"Well, maybe we'll get lucky."

"We could use a break," Jordan said as he handed over the CD.

"I've been reading everything I can about serial killers," Robbins said, his eyes on the map. "We need to figure out his home territory."

Mick rose and stood beside the map. "Greenville, Spartanburg, Newberry." His finger followed the lopsided triangle. Color-coded pins marked each victim's sphere: where they lived, their schools and friends; the mall, Lynches Woods. Nothing overlapped. "It's got to be somewhere in the middle."

His eyes drifted over the map, moving to the center of the triangle. Clinton.

And Meg.

He immediately separated the two. There could be no intersection there. To think it made it possible. That was unacceptable.

"Somewhere in there." Robbins slurped some coffee. "If they're part of the landscape, like everybody says, we're gonna look stupid when he turns up right under our noses."

"So what are we missing?"

"If I knew that, would we be standing here?"

"Have I told you recently what a tremendous help you are?"

Robbins grinned behind his coffee mug. "I hear you're getting e-mail."

He nodded at his laptop. "Today's is open, on top."

Robbins moved and read over Jordan's shoulder. "Sick little fucker."

"He's enjoying rubbing our noses in it."

"What's he trying to do, convert you to the dark side?" Robbins asked.

"Who knows? I wonder if this is how he starts with the women, trying to pull them in."

"You show these to that shrink? Not the asshole, the other one."

"Dr. Mathews? Yeah, I sent him copies. I'm sure he'll have something to say about them." He sighed and began packing his briefcase and laptop. "Thanks for the tire customer list. E-mail the rest as they come in. We'll see what we get. I ought to get back to Greenville."

"We were about to give you your own desk," Robbins said.

"There could be worse things." He paused. "I'm going by the mall one more time. Want to come along?"

"Sure. I'm not getting anything done here."

Thirty minutes later, Robbins followed him into the

food court. "What is it you think you're gonna find that you didn't get yesterday? And don't tell me you need another greeting card."

Mick allowed himself one flash of Meg. He'd sent the card, lobbing the ball into her court, but he knew it'd take more effort than that to break through the barriers surrounding her. "I'm going to make one more sweep through the stores around the food court. Maybe we missed somebody yesterday."

The health food store and the athletic shoe place yielded nothing new. They entered the The Boutique next, one of the few non-chain outlets. Midmorning on a Tuesday, traffic was low. Only one woman browsed the upscale woman's store. A salesperson hovered at her elbow. Mick recognized some of designer brands as ones Jess, his ex-girlfriend, wore. He wondered who bought clothing like this in Newberry.

The manager was shuffling papers at the register. She looked up as the men approached. He caught her double take and silently cursed the genetics that had built his face. At times, he used it to his advantage. Other times, it was a pain in the ass.

The woman was in her late thirties and attractive more from grooming than nature. Her carefully highlighted brown hair feathered away from her face, pulling attention from the softening jawline and the creases beside her eyes and mouth. Her suit was expensive and well-cut, subtly balancing her heavy hips by emphasizing an otherwise modest bust. The color flattered her deeply tanned skin. Striking a pose, she offered a brilliant smile. "May I help you gentlemen?"

She hadn't even glanced at Robbins.

"I'm Agent O'Shaughnessy," he said. "This is Detective Robbins."

"Nancy Henry," she replied, extending her hand. She held his a beat too long after barely pressing Robbins's fingers.

"Detectives Robbins and Jordan interviewed the store managers last week, when Ms. Geiger disappeared. I don't remember seeing your name."

It was as natural as breathing. The subtle emphasis on certain words—"*your* name"—to convey meaning. *I would've remembered you.*

She smiled, a discreet gleam lighting her eyes. "I was out of town last week. I left Monday afternoon for a week in Vegas."

Subtext: *I'm a party girl. I like to have a good time.*

"That explains the tan." He watched her turn up the voltage. Damn, he was going to have to charm her if he hoped to get anything useful. He knew from long experience the actual words didn't matter. It was his attitude, the confidence, the knowledge he had the elusive "it." Most of the time, it was effortless. Today, it felt overwhelming. He mustered a smile. "It doesn't look like the tanning bed variety."

"I tan *au naturel.*"

He raised an eyebrow. "Pretty risky."

She smiled appreciatively. "You don't strike me as risk-adverse."

"I might surprise you." He gave her just the right amount of a smile. "We have a few questions."

"Come on back to my office. You know, I meant to call you this morning, the police, that is," she said over her shoulder.

She was putting everything she had into her walk. He glanced at Robbins. The older cop's eyes were on her undulating hips. His face wore an approving smile.

Mick controlled the impulse to roll his eyes.

"When I got home last night, I heard about Emily Geiger," Ms. Henry continued. "I'd hoped she'd be found. Alive, I mean."

Her office was small, but tastefully decorated with a mahogany desk and two visitors' chairs. She paused just inside the door. "Please, sit down."

She brushed against Mick as he passed. He figured it was deliberate. "Do you have some information about Ms. Geiger?" he asked as she settled at her desk.

"I don't know if this will help or not, but I saw her that morning when I was opening the store. Emily looked like she didn't feel well. An older man was with her. I think he was helping her to the restroom. I guess she left after that."

He controlled his exterior physical reaction, but his heart rate jumped. "Can you describe the man?"

"The man? I don't know. I only saw him for a minute. You know, he wasn't that old now that I think about it."

She was trying to make eye contact. He knew without looking that Robbins had a stupid grin on his face. "That was your first impression?"

"Well, yes. Maybe it was his attitude. You know, *concerned*. Not like he was *interested,* if you know what I mean."

Oh, I know exactly what you mean. "Your store, your appearance, both say you handle high-end fashion."

She smiled, self-deprecating, but clearly pleased he'd noticed.

"You pick up details, probably without realizing you do it. I'll bet you saw more than you give yourself credit. Go back for a minute, and walk me through that day."

She ran through her regular morning routine, ending with raising the storefront grate.

"What time do you open?"

"Ten." She tossed her hair and smiled. "It gives me time to recover from the previous night."

"Or for a leisurely morning," he replied with a slow smile.

Her eyes registered the possibility. "Normally, I like to take it slow and easy, but I was a little rushed that morning. I was leaving town that afternoon. I had everything in overdrive."

"I bet you're something when you get going."

"Oh, you'd be surprised." She was clearly enjoying herself. "Anyway, I opened the grate about five 'til and did a quick scope to get a feel for the traffic. The mall walkers were already gone."

Mall walkers? Had anybody talked to them? "You mean, those people who do laps?"

"Yeah. The oldies and the moldies—ninety-two or two-ninety-two."

Age and weight. "With sensible shoes," he added, eyeing her heels.

She rotated her ankle and pointed her toe, emphasizing her calves. "Somebody'd have to shoot me to make me wear a pair of those things."

"We try not to shoot people," he said with faux seriousness.

"I bet you have a big gun." She smoothed her hands over her thighs, ostensibly removing a wrinkle from her skirt.

"State secret." He smiled. "I can't even show you my department-issued one."

She pretended to pout.

"So you checked the mall traffic. How was it that morning?"

Ms. Henry propped her elbow on the desk and rested her chin on her hand. Her nails were manicured. Rings just this side of flashy decorated several fingers. "Typical Monday. A few moms with strollers at Penney's. Some teenagers at Claire's. Emily was at a table in the food court. The man—I thought it was her father at first—had his back to me, but he was standing beside her table."

She'd seen the man who was probably the killer. "What happened next?"

"I was turning to go back inside when something caught my eye. You know how movement at the edge gets you?" She considered her setup line a second, then added, "Some unexpected move."

"Subtle things catch my attention too."

She did the eye thing again, but she toned it down. "Emily sorta swayed and grabbed at the table. I looked back—that woman instinct, you know—to see if she needed help, but the man leaned over and steadied her. She stood there a second, like she might throw up or something."

"She looked ill?" Sometimes roofies initially made the victim feel terribly drunk. In some people, the physical symptoms included nausea and dizziness.

"Maybe she had morning sickness."

"What?" he asked, startled. Had anybody considered that? Dr. Spindler hadn't mentioned it in the autopsy. What if she'd terminated the pregnancy? Would it show up postmortem? If the women were pregnant, maybe they'd sought counseling or went to the same clinic. It was the kind of thing they'd hide from their parents. It could be the point where it all intersected.

"It happens," Ms. Henry said dryly. "I'd seen her in the mall before with her boyfriend. There wasn't massive PDA, but they were pretty snuggly."

Public displays of affection, he translated. Mahaffey claimed they weren't intimate. "Tell me about the man."

"I didn't pay much attention to him. He was just *there,* you know?"

One of the invisible people. His crimes said he was raging against that designation. Was he using his colorless persona as protective coloring, like a chameleon? "Just an average guy, huh?"

"Yeah, nothing memorable." *Not like you,* she projected.

"Let's cover the basics. What race was he?"

"White."

"Did you see his eyes, by any chance?"

"No." She shook her head. "But if they were as blue as yours, I'm sure I'd remember."

He stifled a groan. "What about hair color?"

"Brown." She waved her hands vaguely. "Medium color. Short, like yours, but without the curl. Not as thick."

Her posture said she wouldn't mind running her hands through his hair. Jeez, he didn't need this. "More like Detective Robbins?"

She blinked, as if just remembering Robbins was in the room. She studied his chocolate-brown hair and deep-set, spaniel eyes. His jaw already carried a shadow. A sardonic smile lifted one corner of Robbins's mouth as he followed her slow inspection. Ms. Henry's gaze tracked across his shoulders, dismissing his polyester clothing. She lingered on his muscular chest, considering, then dropped to where the table cut off her view. "Same texture, lighter brown, not as much gray," she announced.

"You specialize in clothing. What did you notice there?"

She automatically checked Mick's jacket—a Harris Tweed. Her eyes registered approval. "Department store," she said. "It pinched across the shoulders and the break wasn't right."

"A jacket?"

She nodded. "Standard business gear: khakis and a sports coat."

"How tall was he?"

"Gosh, I'm not good at that."

"Think in relative terms. Was he taller than Ms. Geiger?"

Ms. Henry closed her eyes, concentrating. "Her head came up just above his shoulder. And he had an average build." She opened her eyes, obviously checking his pecs and shoulders.

Robbins was openly smirking, and he already regretted the flirting. He'd hear about it for the rest of the week.

"Ms. Geiger was five foot three, so that makes him about five foot nine or ten."

They talked a few more minutes. "I can't remember anything else," she said finally.

"Let's stage it and see if we can bring anything else back."

She looked confused. He stood and gestured for her to rise. "Come out to the food court for a minute."

They reached the table Geiger had used. "You were about here." He glanced behind Ms. Henry at her storefront, then touched her elbow, shifting her a few feet to the left. "Detective Robbins is Ms. Geiger, facing you. I'm the guy. My back's to you until Ms. Geiger stands." His fingers waved the other detective to his feet. "What'd I do? Step around behind her?"

"No. He stepped forward when she stood, put out his hand. It was concern, not like a cuddle or grabbing."

"Like this?" He pressed Robbins's arm and she nodded. "Then what?"

"He put his hand, you know how guys do? Sorta on the small of your back so you can lean on them if you want to?"

He let that one go by. "Emily stood and he moved beside her, touched her back."

The men followed her directions.

"They walked that way." She pointed to the right. "Toward the restrooms."

"Crossed in front of the table?" The men moved away from the food court.

"They must have. The light flashed off his glasses when they walked under the skylight."

"Glasses?"

"I'd forgotten that completely. That must be why I couldn't see his eyes. The glasses were tinted. The kind that gets dark in sunlight."

"Do you remember the shape? Or the frame?"

She shook her head. "Sorry."

"Ms. Henry, could you spend a few minutes with our sketch artist? You may be the only person who can give us a description."

"Oh, I don't know."

She was retreating. The excitement had worn off. She'd realized Mick wasn't really interested in her. The gossip value—"I saw him! I'm helping the police!"—was crashing up against recognition of the time commitment. Like jury duty, becoming a witness suddenly seemed more like a nuisance than anything else.

"We really need your help. With a picture, we could get it on TV, in the papers. Catch him before he hurts someone else." What other hook could he use? "We could mention the boutique. It'd be great free advertising."

She still looked uncertain.

He touched her arm. "Come on. I'll take you over, make sure you're comfortable."

She hesitated. "Well, I can't be gone for long."

He made the necessary small talk as they drove to the

sheriff's department. The larger agency had a Faces computer program for building composite drawings. As he delivered her to the technician, Mick flashed his best smile. "You've been a huge help. Here's my card, in case you remember anything else."

Ms. Henry took the card and briefly examined the assorted contact numbers. "No home number?" she asked, giving him one last flirtatious smile.

"My fiancée made me take it off my cards," he said with a straight face.

"Oh." Ms. Henry deflated, then rallied. "Congratulations. Lucky lady."

"Thanks. We're both lucky to have found each other." He shook her hand. "Thanks again. We couldn't do this without you."

"Yeah, yeah," she said, acknowledging she'd been played. "I'll do what I can."

FOURTEEN

THE PROFESSOR FINGERED the flint knife. The glossy surfaces and wicked edge were as lethal today as they were when an illiterate hunter drew on patience and finesse to flake the beautiful weapon from a core of rock. The ancients had a clearer view of life and warfare. They realized the goal wasn't just to win the conflict, but to destroy their enemy. The early Central American tribes aggressively displayed their prowess, flaunting their trophies—scalps, horses, women—seeking to intimidate as well as prove their manhood. They took everything from their enemies, effectively destroying any future rebellion in the process.

He turned to the treasures he displayed from his study trips into Central America. These early civilizations fully understood the concept. They called it worship rather than torture, offering sacrifices to their gods. Rip the beating heart from your enemy and claim his power as your own. Lift your bloodied hands atop a pyramid-shaped temple and call on the gods for their favor. These tribes embraced their nature rather than hiding it behind false facades.

Modern man still had the same inherent desire to rape and pillage. Today, he used computers and finance and called it civilized. He operated within the rules he created, then bent them when it suited his purposes. Wall Street pretended the lust for power didn't dominate its every move. Trickery and manipulation served modern men as creatively as the Trojans used their horse to destroy the Greeks.

Seldom does history record the place women play in these battles. Literature attempted to define it, but it lacked the courage to be specific. General Zaroff waged the Most Dangerous Game. The ultimate hunter, he stalked the only intelligent prey. Zaroff understood that all manifestations of power, sex and fulfillment were inseparably intertwined in the recesses of the mind. But even he hedged behind the facade of "love."

The Professor needed no ambiguity and shaded no meanings. It was not love, but sex, with all its inherent pleasures. Power, domination and control were the ultimate aphrodisiacs.

Throughout the ages, warriors recognized sex made a powerful weapon, a two-edged sword. It brought pleasure to the wielder, but could be devastatingly effective in destroying not just the targeted woman, but also her partner, family and community. The conqueror who accepted that duality, and used the knowledge accordingly, was unstoppable.

The Professor had learned to take his pleasure with the women denied him by an inbred and decadent ruling class. Foolish despots, unaware their time had passed, still strutted impotently upon an empty stage.

The first women were silent conquests, taken in secret. True triumph, however, required acknowledgment. The fallen must know they had been defeated, or the battle had no meaning.

The conquests of Mary and Ashley were delicious. They were foolish women, betrayed by weakness and forbidden pleasures. The victory over Emily was even more gratifying. The risk was amply rewarded by her exquisite terror before she gave everything over to him. He closed his eyes, remembering every detail: her face, her eyes, her screams as he drew the knife up her body. The trails of liquid fire decorated her body in silent celebration of his mastery. Then came the moment he knew he held her life in the balance. His triumphant explosion of orgasmic release as he took her life transcended any he'd previously known.

He sat at his desk in the gathering dusk. To think it all started right here. He caressed the golden oak desk surface as if it were a lover. The first woman came to him here. Ursula Weiss sashayed into his office late one afternoon, expecting to bat her eyelashes and convert a D on her midterm into an acceptable grade. She fluttered through his classroom, blatantly decreeing that her swarm of acolytes smooth her path through life.

He'd silently watched her routine, the coy gestures, the hollow promises, as if from a distance. Hating her, as he'd hated and desired all the women just like her who'd rejected him. The smug, self-confident in crowd who'd laughed at his efforts to join them. Just as Ursula was attempting now, they'd used him when they wanted something: homework, test answers or to move an illegal keg in his ancient truck. Any suggestion he join their party was met with the ridicule he now recognized as the posturing of empty buffoons.

The same anger he'd felt then built as he listened to Ursula's pretentiousness.

He hadn't planned it. The roofies were in his desk. He'd heard about them, surreptitiously purchased some and fantasized wildly, but he hadn't risked using them. He didn't even know how much to use. Watching Ursula's smug face, he wondered, *What if?*

The thoughts that followed were electric. He saw the scene play out in fast-forward and knew he could do it.

She'd implied she'd trade sex for a grade. Fine, she offered sex. He accepted. He opened his grade book, screening his other hand while he retrieved the pill. He offered her a soda while they discussed her grades and class participation. Convinced of her superiority and invincibility, she accepted the drink without question.

Tasteless and fast-acting, the Rohypnol incapacitated her. He'd bent Ursula over the desk, like the drunken whore she was, and taken her, thrusting and grunting while she drooled on the blotter. Alternating between elation and terror, he'd waited for the knock on his door, for discovery.

Getting rid of her afterward had caused him a moment of panic. A quick glance out his office door revealed a clear coast. He'd hustled her down the hall to the stairs, half-carrying her, his arm around her, giving the impression of solicitous help in case anyone walked into the corridor. He left her in the women's bathroom on another floor. No telling when she woke, unsure what had happened, much less with whom.

For days, he'd lived on an adrenaline high.

The boldness of the action thrilled him. He couldn't believe he'd actually done it. He'd outwitted her and taken what he wanted.

But he'd also waited for Security, the police, her father, someone to pound on his door and demand retribution. He'd relived every moment, detailed every mistake, and devised a superior strategy. By the end of the week, there were still no rumors whispering through the department. He knew he'd won.

The ease of the attack emboldened him. No one suspected. Other encounters followed. He varied his clothes, his glasses and his hunting grounds. There were a dozen colleges within an hour's drive. The only variables were the number of bars and the quality of the bands. He practiced and refined his approach, careful not to frequent the same establishment too often.

The thrill soon proved insufficient. It was too easy and

the women offered only blurry incomprehension in response to his sexual attentions. The challenge lay in the stalk and the capture. As much as that excited him, there needed to be more.

Her acknowledgment of his mastery.

His domination of her.

Her fear in response to his power.

The Professor fantasized about how the act should be played out. He'd taken the next women in their homes. He stripped and tied them to their beds. Their confused terror was like a drug mainlining euphoria into his veins.

With each new woman, he found better ways to enhance their fear. Groveling, begging, screaming with pain, each response drove him to unimagined heights. He soared far beyond mere sexual release. Control over another human being was the supreme high. The ability to create terror, to bring about the slow disintegration of another, was true power.

He wielded it like a scalpel.

MICK AND ROBBINS stood in the service corridor at the mall. Beyond the restrooms, there was a small loading dock and a storeroom for janitorial supplies. A standard emergency exit was located beside the roll-up, overhead door. A large red sign provided the usual alarm warning.

Instead of waiting for the technician to arrive from Greenville, Mick handed the manager of the mall computer store a pair of latex gloves.

"This wire right here," she said, pointing. "He looped it, so the alarm wouldn't go off when he broke the contact." She sent a disapproving look at the mall security agent who hovered in the background. "It's a really crummy system."

The man shrugged. "Most of the kids who shoplift aren't gonna know how to do that. We catch 'em trying to take merch into the restroom on that." He pointed at the camera positioned in the entry passage.

"Do you record that? Or just monitor it?" Mick asked.

Hope died with a glance at the man's face.

"Normally, both. We had a little technical difficulty with the camera…"

"…that Monday," Mick finished for him. "Damn."

He turned to Robbins. "Let's secure the area, anyway. The lab techs can go through the motions. Maybe something will break our way."

Snorting with frustration, he punched the number into his phone. The killer's prints wouldn't be on the exit door. The wire would be the generic stuff available at any Lowes or Home Depot. Once again the killer was a step ahead of the cops, undoubtedly laughing at them over his shoulder.

"You like barbeque?" Robbins asked.

"Does a bear shit in the woods?"

A smile creased the Newberry detective's face. "I know just the place."

Robbins drove a series of back roads, then turned into a rutted, gravel parking lot. Cars ranging from big Beemers and Jags to a spring-shot pickup held together with Bondo filled the lot. Only the best barbeque places drew a crowd that diverse. At the far edge of the lot, a white-painted, cinder-block building sat in the shelter of a huge sycamore.

Robbins found a place to park. Mick opened the car door and breathed in the sweet aroma of hickory smoke and peppery-sharp sauce. He hadn't seen or smelled a place like this since he left the beach.

"Leave your jacket in the car," Robbins advised. "This is definitely a shirtsleeve place."

He hesitated, thinking about his pistol.

Robbins tossed his sports coat on the backseat and

popped open the trunk. "I have a box. "'Course half the guys in here will be carrying."

He shook his head ruefully. Only the cops had to put theirs away. "How many actually have concealed-carry permits?"

"All the good guys and most of the crooks."

He folded his jacket and laid it across the backseat. Shrugging out of his shoulder harness, he joined Robbins at the rear of the gray Ford, then waited while Robbins closed and locked the gun safe.

"I've thought about a shoulder rig," Robbins said. "How do you keep your jacket from bunching under your arm?"

"A tailor alters them. He cuts the shoulder larger on that side."

"Tailor, huh?"

He shrugged. "It doesn't cost that much. I like a shoulder harness better than one on my hip."

They started toward the restaurant. "What about when you don't wear a jacket?"

Mick motioned behind him. "Small of my back. A shirt covers it."

"I don't know." Robbins rubbed his chin. "I've worn mine on my hip so long, I'm not sure I could walk straight with it anywhere else." He opened the door, and the counter cook greeted him by name. "Prepare yourself for the best barbeque you ever ate."

A row of booths lined the front of the building. Formica-topped tables crowded the floor between the booths and the counter, where the take-out stand was doing a brisk business. A faint tinge of old cigarette smoke underlay the pungent odor of savory pork. Most of the barbeque in the Midlands was mustard-based. The owner must've moved in from the eastern part of the state, bringing this vinegar-based version with him.

On the way to their booth, five people looked Mick over, then asked Robbins, "You catch that bastard yet?"

"Workin' on it," was Robbins's stock answer.

As soon as they were seated, the waitress brought tea so strong and sweet it made Mick's teeth ache. A few minutes later, she deposited two platters buried in food. Chunks of tender pork spilled from a massive bun nearly hidden under a load of hush puppies, slaw and onion rings. They were the real thing—thick slices of Vidalia onion, separated in circles, lightly breaded and flash-fried.

He pulled a handful of paper napkins from the dispenser and dug in. For a time, there was silence as both men gave the barbeque the undivided attention it deserved.

Robbins took a long pull of iced tea and leaned back against the faded aqua leatherette bench. "Fiancé, huh?"

He gave Mick a "you dog" grin.

Gossip flies in a police station.

"Since when?" The older man reached forward, loaded an onion ring with ketchup and folded it into his mouth.

"Since never." He shrugged. "More effective than a wife. Don't need a ring and they assume you're still in love rather than ready to stray."

Robbins laughed. "You're something else."

"You married?"

"Divorced. We get along okay. She just didn't like being married to a cop."

He nodded. "It happens."

They compared jobs, pay and benefits while they finished their sandwiches. Finally, Mick licked sauce off his thumb and said, "I thought you might have a problem with me coming in on this case."

"Not me." Robbins shook his head. "We needed the help."

"What about Jordan?"

Robbins thought about it for a minute, picking at a piece of meat stuck between his teeth. "Maybe at first. He was pumped up on the way to the park. You know, his first big case and all. Then he saw the blood and the body and about hurled. Me, I can smell a shit storm brewing. Asshole gets another one around here and we can all kiss our jobs goodbye."

"It bothers me that this last one was so different. Without the rock connecting it to the other two…" He picked up his glass and drained the rest of the iced tea.

"Yeah."

Silence.

"Man, I would love a smoke."

"When'd you quit?"

"Thirty-eight days—" Robbins checked his watch, "—and four hours ago."

"That recently? I'd never have guessed."

"Asshole." Robbins straightened and stretched. "I'll get Lewis to keep an eye on Mahaffey. See if he can deflect some of that rage."

"Good idea."

More silence.

"You think maybe the killer's changing them up on purpose? To keep us off balance?"

"I hadn't thought about it like that, but it's possible. It's hard to find a pattern when there isn't one." Mick ate the last hush puppy and wiped his hands on a paper napkin. "Good 'que."

"Best around."

They rose and headed to the car.

"How many opticians sell those glasses that change to sunglasses?"

Robbins snorted dismissively. "All of them. That won't work. HIPAA put the nail in that coffin. You know it takes a specific court order to look at medical records. We can't go fishing for everybody that wears prescription sunglasses."

"Yeah," he sighed. After a moment, he asked, "Did you catch that morning sickness comment?"

"I was wondering about that."

"Can you get Geiger's health records?"

"You think that's it? They were all pregnant?"

"We can't afford to pass up an opportunity."

"Like Ms. Henry?"

"Jeez," he muttered. "Give me a break."

He retrieved his pistol and his car and headed to Greenville. The meal sat heavy in his stomach. Combined with the sun shining through the window, he felt warm and sleepy. A quiet lassitude dragged at his eyelids. He pulled himself straighter in the seat. He shouldn't have eaten so much. No wonder Robbins was built like a tree stump.

Robbins was okay. Not long ago, he'd have considered the detective's job beyond boring. But getting settled somewhere wouldn't be so bad. Learning a town, knowing his neighbors actually sounded rather appealing. Other than Mrs. Wilcox, he rarely saw the other people in his building.

Fighting sleep, he opened his cell phone. For a moment, he indulged the fantasy that Meg had called, breathless to see him again. Laughing at himself, he clicked through to his voice mail. But during the tiny pause before another cop or a snitch started talking, his heart gave a hopeful lift.

The last message—the prison contraband informant he'd been chasing—finished. Meg hadn't called. It had only been two days. He'd decided not to count Saturday or Sunday, since she wouldn't have received the card until Monday.

He made a few calls, then returned the phone to his pocket. Why was he so hung up on Meg? He'd never felt this way about a woman. Was it just the thrill of the chase? Normally, it was the other way around. Women pursued him. He'd never had to chase a woman. He wasn't completely sure how to do it. Surely, that wasn't the attraction. He'd quit being that shallow in college.

There was more than sexual attraction. He gave in to a moment of male mental vision. Meg, naked, sprawled across his bed. Her head arched back, half an inch from orgasm. Her eyes opened and locked on to his. There was bliss, love and an awareness of him that blew him away. He blinked and sighed.

Yeah, she definitely tripped his trigger.

But it was more than that. In spite of everything—the mixed signals she gave off, whatever had her so uptight— he felt an unexpected ease when he was with her. She picked up on his meanings practically before he opened his mouth. He couldn't believe some of the things he'd said; telling her about his dad, admitting how deeply she affected him. But in return, he'd received understanding, a feeling of coming home.

A few minutes later, he negotiated the road construction maze around the I-85/385 interchange and followed 385 downtown. Leaving the unmarked cruiser in the parking garage, he took the stairs to the sidewalk. The Greenville field office barely resembled a cop-shop. Only its strategic location near the courthouse and the bulletproof glass in the lobby distinguished it.

Fortified with coffee, Mick checked his e-mail. Finally—thank you, Ford Motor Company—the first VIN list was in. He sorted the data by exterior color: black, dark blue. Would the maroon ones look dark at night? There were still hundreds of cars to investigate.

Chevrolet's contribution landed in his mailbox an hour later. Mick opened the file of professors Jordan had accumulated and ran a match query against the sports car database. Thirty-four professors owned 1980s-era sports cars. He pulled up first Ford's and then Chevy's VIN information.

Damn. He crossed off the last one. Of course, it wasn't going to be that easy.

None of the professors owned a black car.

Tuesday night

MEG FOCUSED HER attention on the Mesoamerican civilizations. At their peak, long before Columbus and the Spaniards arrived, the Mayans and Aztecs dominated much of what is now Mexico and Central America.

Growing up amidst dozen of Revolutionary and Civil War sites, she'd developed and nurtured a love of history and an appreciation for its continuing impact on society. A course in Latin America history, taken as a whim, had opened her eyes to hundreds of years of pre-Columbian culture that was virtually ignored except for the ruins touted as tourist attractions.

This graduate course concentrated on the Classical Period, when artistic endeavors and construction of palaces and temples peaked. Her primary interest with this paper was the long-distance trading between the Mayan city-state of Palenque and Teotihuacan. She searched for references to the economic impact of the alliances as she examined the books scattered across the library table. She could use most of the analysis for her International Trade class, as well as this history assignment.

She scanned the crowded library as she rolled her shoulders, easing the cramped muscles. Usually she avoided it this time of day, but the reference books she needed weren't available online. Thankfully, the students sharing her table weren't texting or talking. The baby-faced boy across from her—he had to be a freshman—had stacks of history books she remembered using for papers on World War II. Wearing a frustrated scowl, he laboriously transferred bits of information to his laptop.

Two students passed, deeply engrossed in conversation. One bumped the table and the books the boy had stacked nearest the edge shifted. He lunged for the stack, but the uppermost volumes slid to the floor. She winced as they landed with a crash.

Heads turned, some irritated, some amused. Cursing, the boy began collecting the scattered texts. She picked up the closest book and absently smoothed a photograph on the rumpled page. A cluster of soldiers, RAF by their uniforms, lounged with studied nonchalance against their Airco single-seat biplanes. They were so young, but responsibility tugged at them. A face caught her eye. The pilot was Black Irish: dark hair, blue eyes, an engaging grin. He could've been Mick O'Shaughnessy's grandfather.

She caught her breath as the memory of Mick's kiss seared through her. A flush climbed her cheeks, then warmth flooded her chest as she remembered her wanton response. Desire flamed so intensely, she nearly turned around to see if Mick stood behind her.

Brutally, she forced the images and feelings away. Mick was the kind of man who'd had a lot of experience, far more than she'd had.

And she wasn't just thinking about in bed.

He was the type women made fools of themselves over. She wasn't going to join the parade. He was simply another version of Tony. The only reason Mick was interested was because she'd said no.

"Can I have my book?"

The boy's voice intruded, and her cheeks burned hotter. She closed the book, wishing she could close off her feelings as easily, and handed over the text.

Resolutely, she returned to her own material, but thoughts of Mick wouldn't go away. He probably dated every woman deemed dateable in both high school and college, she thought as she searched for her place in her notes. She, on the completely opposite other hand, had become a two-and-a-half-date woman. Everyone knew you had sex on the third date, so she quit at two and a half. Her reputation accompanied her through college and into graduate school. Most guys didn't bother to ask. Only Tony—and apparently Mick—who couldn't resist a challenge, still dogged her tracks.

Why did Mick have to be so smart and funny? It would be easier to ignore him if he didn't intrigue her.

Of course, she absolutely did *not* want anything more to do with him.

She flicked a glance at the stack of WWII reference books. The photograph tugged at her. Family connections—any family's connections—drew her irresistibly. No matter how hard she tried, a real family always seemed out of reach—an impossible dream.

She pulled up the image of the airmen, idly tracing the pilot's smile. Mick had the same generous curve to his lips, the same sparkle.

From Mick's comments, his family was close. She tried to imagine what a loving family would be like. Even before everything went wrong, she'd never felt accepted by her parents, much less received unconditional love. Her mother saw nothing beyond the aura cast by her father. He was always so busy being a pillar of the church and community, he couldn't see anybody but himself. The hypocrisy of the impossible standard he held everyone else to ignited the old bitterness.

Unshed tears filled her eyes. Why had they abandoned her? Had anything she'd done really been that terrible?

Did they ever think about her? Did they know she graduated at the top of her class? Did they know she was voted Best Young Professor by her students? Did they care?

Blinking, she straightened and closed her book.

Her parents didn't want her.

Fine.

She didn't need them, just like she did not need Agent Michael J. O'Shaughnessy. The world lay right beyond her fingertips. Everything was possible. She wouldn't throw it away. Not for anyone or anything.

MICK WALKED OUT of the bathroom, briskly rubbing a towel over his hair. Four miles on the treadmill and half an hour with the Nautilus had banished part of the fog in his head. Something had occurred to him while he was in the shower. The killer knew Geiger hid a forbidden lover. He'd discovered Mahaffey while he was stalking her. Geiger had hidden the relationship and made herself vulnerable in the process. Did the other victims also have secrets? Secrets the Professor used against them? A mirthless smile twisted his lips. "The Professor." Even he had picked up the moniker.

Mick wrapped the towel around his waist and pulled out the files. Mary Baldwin died at the beginning of the school year, in mid-August. She'd gone to summer school, picking up a class she'd dropped during spring term, along with an introductory anthropology course. Mick automatically added the names of the instructors to those he'd run against the car list.

Why did Baldwin drop the course during spring term? He drew a circle around the instructor's name. Had he threatened her in some way? Come on to her? An exposed affair would damage him, not the women. Had she cheated on a test? Mick couldn't think of any other academic threat. He made a note to follow up with the school and turned to the autopsy report.

Baldwin was a healthy twenty-year-old. He skimmed the medical histories; mostly routine checkups. The most recent report was dated only weeks before her murder. The gynecologist's final note read, "cleared to resume sexual relations." Mick nearly missed the significance of the word.

Resume. Why would sex be suspended on a doctor's orders? Disease or pregnancy termination were the only things he could think of. He flipped through the file, but found nothing else from the doctor.

Nancy Henry implied Geiger could be pregnant. None of the women were pregnant when they died. Again, he considered the possibility of a terminated pregnancy. He'd have to ask Dr. Spindler if it was possible to detect one during an autopsy.

Baldwin's parents were as straitlaced and strict as Geiger's were. He'd seen other sheltered kids go wild when they got away from their parents' control. If Baldwin was pregnant or had contracted an STD, she could've gone to a clinic for either medicine or an abortion. If she paid cash, her parents would be none the wiser.

Mick felt the adrenaline rush that said he was on to something. This could be Baldwin's secret: a terminated pregnancy. There weren't many clinics left—most had been put out of business by the Religious Right. Not many private physicians performed the procedure. A few keystrokes gave Mick the names of the clinics in the Upstate. He opened another form on his computer and started the wording for search warrants at the clinics for Ms. Baldwin's medical records. After a moment, he added Ashley Cohen and Emily Geiger's names to the warrants, as well.

FIFTEEN

Wednesday morning

WARM SUNSHINE AFTER two days of clouds had drawn a crowd to the plaza outside the Student Center. The Professor sat at a table, his laptop open before him. He scrolled slowly through the latest analysis of his activities. All the top news outlets were featuring articles about him now. A self-satisfied smile lit his features. He relished the stories, fascinated by the thoroughness. Murderer, monster; all the labels weaker men used to distance themselves from their own desires.

He switched to the *State* newspaper's web site to get the local interpretation. The site was freshly updated. He stared, dumbfounded, at the sketch displayed on his computer screen. Where had this come from? He checked the heading. The document had posted only minutes previously.

He switched to CNN and refreshed the page. The sketch wasn't there, only the articles he'd already read. He returned to the *State* site and quickly read the accompanying article. Someone from the mall had described him. He ran a brief mental review of the food court that morning. No one had paid attention to them. He'd planned it out too carefully. So who gave the description? And why had they waited so long to come forward?

Casting surreptitious glances at the nearest students, the Professor carefully examined the sketch. Other than a vague resemblance to any thirty-year-old white male, the picture didn't resemble him. He straightened, suddenly aware he'd hunched over the computer, his nose barely inches from the screen. The drawing wasn't anything to worry about. The police had nothing.

He rotated his head, stretching the tight muscles in his upper back. Students clustered at several of the tables around him, laughing and eating. Their laptops were open, streaming music, taking advantage of the campus-wide wireless network. Competing stations underlay the babble of voices.

Would they be so casual if they knew who he was? Not the bland, everyday public persona, but his true identity. Dismissing the sketch, he closed the Internet browser, ending his traceable activity on the web. With practiced ease, he selected and hijacked a student's identity. If by some miracle the police traced his incursions, all they'd find was some schmuck who didn't know how to shield his computer. Masking his computer's Mac address, he tapped keys and entered Prescott College's server via the backdoor he'd set up. He smiled, a cruel twist of his lips. The college still hadn't changed the administrator's pass codes. He moved to the mail server and logged in as Tom Evans.

It was time to jerk the smug SLED agent's chain again. The Professor flexed his fingers, opened an e-mail form and typed:

We are not so different, you and I. We are both hunters, not of deer or pheasant, but of a more intelligent prey. Yet we diverge from the would-be warriors, who don orange-studded vests, denying they respond to the same primitive urge to dominate their surroundings. Never will they admit the instinctive hunger—quickly buried and denied, but there just the same—to hunt another hunter.

The Professor paused, no longer seeing the courtyard around him. He delved deeper into the black well of his fantasies.

Our masks are not the cautious scream of orange. You hide behind a badge. What veneer do I use? Ah, but telling would give unfair advantage.

Have you looked at what lurks beneath your facade? We create our own reality, drawing our visions of the world as we wish it to be. Why should your vision be truer than mine?

Your version is based on the law, you say? A duplicitous construction, built and paid for by the unseeing masses, its sole purpose is to reinforce the status quo. It is routinely abused and disregarded by men powerful enough to flaunt it. I am not bound by such hypocrisy.

I am honest about my desires. Are you? Have you never wished to dominate someone in your custody? Has that whispered confession never triggered a desire to know what it feels like?

The pleasure. The power.

You lie to yourself if you deny it.

MICK POURED A cup of coffee and checked the new cartoons posted on SLED's break room bulletin board. He took a sip and grimaced as his stomach spasmed in protest. He was drinking too much coffee.

Frank wandered in, looking grumpy, and poured a cup.

"I got something that ought to cheer you up," Mick said. "We finally nailed down that dope ring over at the Tyger River prison."

He gave Frank the highlights of his early morning session with an informant. Frank examined the available doughnut selections and chose a jelly-filled one. By the time Mick finished, Frank was smiling. "I knew that peck-erwood was up to his ass in it," he said.

They left the break room, headed for their desks. "It'll be nice to have a success to hand the cap'n," Mick said. "You see today's paper yet?"

Frank nodded. "Makes it sound like we actually have something on the murders. That sketch should generate some traffic."

"Cap'n shook some manpower out of Greenville PD to cover the tip line."

"Thank God for small miracles. You should hear Benny bitching about the e-mail." Frank grinned. "Of course, he's forwarding the ones he rates highest for creativity."

"How'd I get left off his distribution list?"

"We figured you're getting your entertainment in a more personal format. Speaking of which, what's hap-pening with the Fountain Frolic?" Frank asked. "Any ac-tion there?"

"Cap'n's handling that stink bomb, thank God."

"I meant the cutie-pie."

"Excuse me?"

Frank wore a shit-eating grin. "Jordan's brother's a Clin-ton cop. He saw you at Barracuda's the next morning with one of those sweet things from the sorority house."

"Damn, why does everyone see everything except the killer?"

"You don't cover your tracks as well. What's the story?" Frank nudged his shoulder. "He said that's one little hot-tie. So, what about it? You rubbing the old blarney stone?"

Don't overreact, he told himself, even as his temper spiked. "Meg's a nice woman. It's not like that."

"Ah, Meg, is it? That's why you stayed in Clinton that night. Jumping on that opportunity. Which one is she? The leggy blonde? No." He snapped his fingers. "The redhead who stood up. I saw the look on your face when she strolled in."

"Back off, Meyers."

He ignored the warning tone. "Robbing the cradle, aren't you? Is it true what they say about young flesh rejuvenating old men?"

He slammed his hand into Frank's shoulder, pinning him to the wall. "Don't talk about her like that."

Frank's face was a study in stunned surprise.

He dropped his arm and stepped back. "Shit," he muttered and turned away. "Sorry."

"Damn, Mick. I was just raggin' you."

"Well, don't."

"I didn't know you actually liked the girl—woman."

"Drop it," he said through clenched teeth. "I'm just tired."

His pager beeped, saving him from what could've become an embarrassing detour through the wonders of Meg Connelly. He mashed the number into his cell phone.

"Fiber Lab. Clark."

"You paged me?"

"Yeah. I have some results for you."

"Go." He pushed Meg and Frank to the back of his mind.

"I've got more info on those fibers. They're part of a nylon cut pile, constructed from Dupont Antron nylon BCF yarn. And I quote: it's tufted on a 1/8-gauge machine with fourteen ounces of yarn per square yard, unquote. Anyhoo, specific chemicals, which yours truly found present in our sample, were added after the dying process to reduce fading. The manufacturer just verified the formulation." He paused dramatically.

"You're killing me, Clark."

"To be precise, the fibers are a color known as Dark

Carmine Red. It was only used in Chevy Camaros from 1985 to 1989."

"You're a genius."

"Yeah, yeah. Tell my boss about it at performance review time."

He closed his cell.

"Something good?" Frank asked, clearly looking to put the Meg incident behind them.

He repeated the news on the fibers. "That has to narrow down the car list."

Wednesday afternoon

MEG SCANNED THE list of new e-mail. She deleted some spam and read a finance department announcement. There was a Panhellenic meeting Sunday afternoon. She could skip that, thank God. The next sender surprised her: fred.perrin@douglass.edu. She'd taken a class from him as an undergrad. She'd heard he was on sabbatical somewhere. What did he want? She opened the message.

I dream about you, the same way I fantasized about you during class. I lie in bed and remember the way you cross your legs, hiking your short skirts, displaying yourself while I stand at the podium. I savor the intimacy of you sharing yourself, without anyone else in the room realizing it. The thrill of it.

I stroke myself, as I never could in class and imagine you joining me.

What? She reread the words as if the meaning might change. None of that happened.

She stopped, trying to remember his class. Did she ever wear a skirt? Could he see up it? If he could, did he really think she did it on purpose? How creepy that he was getting off on it now, years later.

Disgusted, she started to delete the message. Her fingers rocked the mouse back and forth over the Delete button. She wasn't immune to the rumors swirling through campus. The Professor stalked his victims through e-mails. She'd also heard about all the copycats. That was what this was, wasn't it? Somebody's sick idea of a joke? She scanned the rest of the message and shuddered, as if he'd reached out of the computer and touched her.

For a long moment, she stared at the screen. If nothing came of it, she could always delete the message later. But if it was something to worry about, maybe she shouldn't erase it. Feeling slightly foolish, she saved the e-mail to a folder and closed the program.

Wednesday evening

MICK DRUMMED HIS pen against the dining room table. There had to be something, some detail that could get him inside the Professor's head. They'd nearly exhausted the car list and struck out with the tires. Ms. Henry's sketch was too generic. The detectives had shown it to the victim's friends and family to no avail. The e-mails provided insight into the bastard's personality, but he couldn't see how to use them to find the guy.

The latest message from the Professor was open on his laptop. He was finding it harder to keep his professional detachment. The guy was getting under his skin. He scanned the message, lingering over the final paragraph.

I lie awake at night, wondering who will be next, shuffling my list of candidates. Maybe she will be the beautiful blonde who loves lattes and foolishly cuts through the dark alley at seven each evening. Or perhaps she will be the sloe-eyed brunette that said no when I asked her to dance. Perhaps the auburn-haired beauty who until now has hidden her sexuality. Maybe it will be all of them, since you make no moves to stop me.

Don't make it so easy. If the fight is one-sided, then the victory is cheap.

Bastard.

The computer jockeys had recovered additional deleted e-mails from the victims' computers. Mick opened Mary Baldwin's mail and read the increasingly perverse messages. No wonder she deleted them. He reread the fourth one. *"I know your secret."*

Was the threat a complete shot in the dark, or did the Professor know something? Everybody had something they'd prefer other people didn't know. The killer had threatened Geiger with disclosure of a forbidden lover. What was Baldwin hiding?

He wasn't getting anywhere with the pregnancy possibility. Her friends said she was a sweet girl. Was that the normal, clean-up-the-image-after-they're-dead tendency? She wasn't an angel. She'd had a fake ID for one purpose: getting into bars. He flipped pages in the file, but found no mention of which bars.

Bars.

Drinking.

Dancing.

The word snagged his attention.

He clicked through his own e-mail. *"The girl that said no when I asked her to dance."*

Was there a connection?

He glanced at the clock. It wasn't that late. He pulled out Mary Baldwin's contact list and dialed the first name.

The first two denied everything. The next one was cautious. "I'm over twenty-one, but Mary wasn't," she admitted. "Am I going to get in trouble if I tell you this?"

"We're trying to find a murderer. I'm not going to arrest you for contributing to the delinquency of a dead woman."

In the following silence, he could almost hear her indecisively chewing her lip.

"I need your help." He put his tone somewhere between encouragement and desperation.

"Sometimes a group of us would go out to a club," she said finally.

"Where'd you go?"

She named a popular spot near the college.

"Did Ms. Baldwin ever hook up?"

"Oh, no. It wasn't like that. We just went to dance. I mean, occasionally a guy'd buy us a drink, but that was it."

They talked a few more minutes, until he was sure she had nothing else to offer. "A Spartanburg police officer, Detective Ward, will come by tomorrow and show you some pictures. We'd like to know if you recognize anybody."

"Do you think that's it? The Professor picked them up at bars?"

"We're considering multiple possibilities. But if you go out with your friends, watch out for each other. Make sure y'all leave together. And pay attention to your drinks."

He left her a little scared and hopefully, a little wiser.

He hit pay dirt with the fifth friend.

"Ms. Baldwin liked to go clubbing." He said it like it was a given, not a question. "I've got a line on a couple of the places she liked to go, but we're trying to figure out the rest of them, to find the overlap."

He paused, waiting to see how she'd respond.

"Do you have the Squirrel?" Cheryl asked.

Interesting. Squirrel's had a reputation as a serious pickup spot, with an older crowd than the bars the other women had mentioned. "No. I don't have that one."

"Some of the guys come on strong, but Mary liked to dance, and it has the best floor and sound system."

"How often did you go?"

"Once or twice. She'd call sometimes on Wednesdays, usually last-minute, and ask if I wanted to go."

"What was special about Wednesday?" Other than the fact that Mary Baldwin had been killed on a Wednesday night.

"Ladies night." She said it like *Duh? What planet do you live on?* "No cover and drinks are half price."

Great. Pack in a bunch of women, get them drunk and offer them up to the local predators. He kept that out of his voice. "What happened if you had plans? Did Mary go with someone else?"

Cheryl was quiet for a moment. "I'm not sure. She may have gone alone. She knew some people who hung out there. I didn't know them. I mean, she introduced them…. All I can remember is one's named Jack. They called another one Morp."

"Morp?"

"Yeah, it stuck in my head since it's kinda weird."

"Would you recognize them if you saw them?"

"Gee, I don't know." She was backing away, not wanting to get involved in this part of the investigation. "Do you think one of them might've done it?"

"I'd just like to talk to them. See what they know."

"I only met them that one time, and that was a while ago."

"You remembered their names," he said. "All you'd have to do is point them out to me."

"Point them out?" she asked, incredulous. "You mean, like, go over there with you?"

Why not? "That'd be great," he said, as if she were volunteering. "You wouldn't have to stay long. You could leave after showing me who they are."

"I don't even know you."

"If I remember correctly, there's a Waffle House on the corner near the Squirrel. I could meet you there. That way you'd have your own car. We'd talk to the bouncer for a minute. You'd take a quick look inside for the guys, and that'd be it."

"No way. Look, Jack's got that blond surfer hair. He spikes it. He thinks he's hot, but it's all in his mind. Morp's quieter. His hair's dark, about shoulder-length. He's sexy, like a laid-back musician."

"It wouldn't take but a minute for you to point them out."

"Ask the bouncer. His name's Bruce. He knows them." And she hung up.

SIXTEEN

Wednesday night

MICK CHANGED INTO tight, black jeans and an Egyptian-cotton shirt. When was the last time he'd gone to a club? Other than a few setups he hadn't been able to dodge, he hadn't gone out since he and Jess broke up.

He wondered if Meg liked dancing, then blew out a disgusted breath. It had been three days. She hadn't called. Why couldn't he just let it go?

That was easy to answer, even if it made no sense. He wanted to understand what was going on. One more try, he decided, and then he was giving up.

As Cheryl had predicted, the Squirrel was packed. The parking lot was full, and he left his BMW in a quasi-legal spot. He scanned the area with professional interest. The surrounding businesses were dark, but the club owners had halfheartedly tried to make the exterior attractive. Crepe myrtles and low bushes separated the sidewalk from the blank outside wall. Soft up-lighting turned them into sculptures and minimized shadows. The parking lot was well-lit, with no overgrown hedges or obstacles to hide an assailant. The Squirrel might be a hookup joint, but management appeared concerned that their patrons find only trouble they'd created themselves.

A couple entered the bar and sound blasted through the opening. The bouncer closed the door behind them, then turned and scanned his domain. He locked onto Mick and watched his approach.

"Hey, are you Bruce?" Mick asked when he was closer.

"Last time I checked."

"Maybe you can help me. I'm looking for a girl."

"You're in the right place."

He smiled. "A specific girl."

Bruce shifted. It was subtle, but he was wary now. "We don't want any trouble."

He flashed his badge. "Me, either. Janet's friends said she came in on Wednesday nights." He pulled out a picture of Mary Baldwin. "Recognize her?"

The bouncer studied the photo. "She looks like a girl who used to come in here, but…"

"Just look at the face. Maybe she dressed different."

Bruce partly covered the photo, then nodded. "Yeah, it's the hair. And she wore more makeup. She used to come in a lot, but I haven't seen her for a while."

No kidding. Read the papers often, buddy? "What about these?" He pulled out Ashley Cohen and Emily Geiger's pictures.

After a moment of silent study, Bruce shook his head. "Never saw these two."

"But Janet was here."

"Nearly every Wednesday, all summer. She hasn't been in since mid-August. She must have gone back to school."

"Did you ever see her with this guy?" He pulled out the sketch of the suspect.

"A guy like that…" The bouncer shook his head. "He may come in, but nobody's going to give him the time of day."

"What about other men? Anyone in particular hang around Janet?"

Bruce pursed his lips and returned the sketch. "I can't say for sure. There's a lot of people through here."

"She was a regular. It's important."

Bruce glanced at him, considering, and then dropped his gaze to the photos. "Now that I think about it, she left with a guy sometimes."

"Same one? Different?"

He shrugged. "She'd sometimes hook up. That's all I know. That's what most of these people are here to do. Dance, get drunk, get laid. My job's to keep out the underage kids and toss the drunks before they cause problems, not be their dad."

"Janet's ID looked good?"

The bouncer hesitated, as if sensing a trick question. "She matched the picture and the date's right. You know something I don't?"

"Somebody's supplying phony IDs." He handed the guy "Janet's" ID. "Her real name's Mary Baldwin."

He watched the bouncer process the name. "Where have I heard that?"

"The papers. TV. She's dead."

For a second, Bruce lost his *I'm-too-cool* composure. Just as quickly, his facade was back in place. "Didn't happen here."

"She was murdered on a Wednesday night, in mid-August."

The bouncer played with the ID, rotating it between his fingers. "I don't remember anybody in particular being with her. As for this…" He handed back the fake license. "I haven't heard anything about a market for fakes. Management got stung a few years ago with a bunch of underage kids. We target an older crowd—more your age. They still want to party and meet people, but they know they have to get up and go to work in the morning. Some of the chicks are younger, but guys go for that."

"She hung with a couple of guys, Jack and Morp. You know them? I'd like to talk to them."

"They're here tonight. They usually come in right after happy hour."

Hoping the women are drunk enough not to be picky?

Bruce waved him to the door. "See those guys by the back bar? Jack's the blond with the green shirt. Morp's sitting beside him with the Mexican chick."

SEVENTEEN

Thursday morning

MICK LOOKED UP from the report he was typing when Frank strolled through the office door.

"Cap'n have any interesting insights?" Frank asked around his morning doughnut.

"He just wanted a status report. And for us to catch this asshole so the Governor'll get off his back."

"Oh, well, when you put it like that, I may put some effort into it today."

He leaned back in his chair and laughed. "Pep talks aren't his forte."

"Where are we?" Frank dropped into his seat.

"The guy those morons at the Squirrel remembered didn't match Ms. Henry's sketch." He stretched, loosening his shoulders. "They were focused on the hair and clothes, though."

"They saw Baldwin leave with a guy?"

"Yeah. They didn't know who he was. Said he was mid-thirties, brown hair, gold tips, expensive clothes. He didn't say much, just flashed some cash. They said a couple of girls latched on like white on rice, but he brushed them off. He sat back and watched the more confident women."

"That doesn't sound like Ms. Henry's guy." Frank finished his doughnut and wiped his fingers.

"Maybe. The height and age are right. The other stuff's easy to change. I asked Buzz to redo the sketch with gelled

hair and no glasses." He shrugged. "See if that gets us anywhere. Greenville and Spartanburg PDs are going to run
the pictures—the victims and the mystery guy—around
to all the clubs. I wish that sketch Ms. Henry did was less
generic."

"How is the lovely Ms. Henry?"

"I wouldn't know."

"You're no fun anymore since you've become celibate."

"Tough. I don't have time for a going-nowhere relationship."

"That doesn't mean you have to give up sex," Frank
grumbled.

Mick looked at him sharply. He started to say something, like *stay out of my private life,* but Frank had picked
up the printout Jordan had developed of professors from
the three colleges.

"Do we still want to work this? If the killer's picking
them up at clubs, he could be anybody."

*Let it go. He doesn't mean anything by it. Maybe he's
having a midlife crisis.* "It makes sense to follow up on
the professors. Maybe he spots them at school and then
follows them to the clubs."

"Maybe. You get anything from the abortion clinics?"

"Their lawyers are talking to ours. That may not be the
key, but I think it's definitely going to be Baldwin's 'secret.'
Until we find something else, college is the only thing the
women have in common. You're gonna hate me—I'm gonna
hate myself—but when I updated the cap'n, we talked about
getting all the professors in the Upstate on the list."

Frank groaned. "Between the tip line, the bars, and
the car list, we already have people running everywhere.
Who's got time to do that?"

"We need a professor to turn up on the car list or at
more than one school."

"It sounds like another wild-goose chase."

"Right now, we've got a better chance of catching the goose than this killer."

"Okay," Frank grumbled. "Let's get the kid, Jordan, to work on the teachers."

Ten minutes later, Mick looked up from the car list. He tapped his pen against his desk. "How'd he get home?

"What?"

"If he picked them up at a club, slipped something into their drinks, how'd they get home? The vics' cars were in their apartment parking lots. If she was too drunk, drugged, whatever, he would've driven her car from the club to the apartment. How'd he get back to his car?"

A slow smile spread over Frank's face. "A cab. Hand me the phone book."

MEG CLOSED THE word processing program. She wasn't getting a thing accomplished. Her hands rested on her desk, but her fingers were drawn into tight fists. She stared unseeing at the calendar on her office wall. Her tension had nothing to do with midterms, her teaching schedule or even Mick O'Shaughnessy. With an irritated snort, she punched in the pass code for her e-mail, not sure she wanted to know what the pervert would say next.

She scanned the list of unread mail, zeroing in on the new messages. He'd switched identities, using a different Prescott College account, but she knew it was him. She could sense it, the way she'd felt his eyes on her every time she'd left her apartment, office or classroom today.

I get so jealous when you flirt with other students. This afternoon, you were sitting at the student center. Those jocks are so crude, staring at your breasts.

This was his fourth message. In twenty-four hours, the e-mails had gone from weird to creepy. She'd started looking around, watching people, but she hadn't seen him. Or if she had, she didn't know it was *him*.

Why do you wear such sexy clothes? That green sweater clings to your curves, caressing your skin the way I want to. It makes me think you're just a prick tease. That's such an ugly term, so vulgar, but devastatingly accurate.

He sounded so possessive. And how dare he call her names?

I have to hide my anger and remind myself, those boys—mere children—are no threat to my property.

Property? She recoiled, staring at the message. That was as disturbing as his fantasies about a relationship.

Of course, I can't publicly respond to their challenge. You never follow through with them. I realize you're merely teasing them. You let me play voyeur. Do you get off on it the way I do?

What did he think he saw her doing? That was disgusting. Reluctantly, she opened the next message.

I never realized you were such an exhibitionist. I watch you through your window and imagine touching you, as you touch yourself.

Her head whipped around before she could remind herself she was in the office and not her apartment. There were no windows in her tiny work space and the windows of her second-floor apartment had curtains. No one could see anything through those drapes, could they? Besides, she didn't parade around naked.

My excitement rises. Soon, my temptress, soon we will be together in fulfillment of our destiny.

Destiny? What part of outer space was this guy living in? The rest of the paragraph detailed what he wanted to do to her. Embarrassed and revolted, she couldn't stop reading.

That's my little secret, Meg. We all have them, don't we? You like to appear to be so virtuous, but we both know better. I know your secret.

Her breath caught in a gasp. He couldn't possibly know.

She reread the line. He was bluffing, hoping to scare her. The whole message was creepy and disgusting, but the threat was vague. She slouched in her chair, staring at the screen, uncertain about what to do with the message. The obvious person to talk to was Mick, but she didn't want to tell him. She didn't want to give him a reason to come to Clinton.

Maybe she should tell someone else. Maybe Lisa.

No, she decided. It was time to call the police. She might not be the only person getting these weird e-mails, but the cops would know whether it was the killer or some copycat jerk.

She switched to the *State's* web site, scrolled to the end of the special report on the Professor, and found the link for the hotline. Before she lost her nerve, she picked up the office phone and dialed the listed number. "I've been getting strange e-mails," she told the person who answered.

"Can I get your name and contact information?"

She provided the details and a summary of the messages.

"An officer will contact you to take your statement and review the e-mails."

"Is there anything I should do in the meanwhile?"

"Don't delete any suspicious e-mail. And you should take precautions." He rattled off a litany of safety measures any woman should be aware of, potential serial killer or not.

A few minutes later, she dropped the handset onto the base. Her gaze drifted to the open computer. The message seemed to taunt her from the screen: *Is that the best you can do?*

Sitting back and waiting for someone else to do something wasn't her style. There were additional things she could do until the officer arrived. She filed the message with the others and added the teacher's name to the Block Sender list. Opening the Internet browser, she moved to the yellow pages web site and looked up the phone number for Prescott College.

MICK DROPPED THE phone back into the cradle and crossed off another car record. This was the part they never showed on television. The boring grind. Endless telephone conversations. Massive piles of paperwork. For days, city and sheriff's officers had checked Camaros with Dark Carmine Red carpet. Cars owned and driven by women, old men, Hispanics. Cars that no longer ran. Cars whose male owners had solid alibis.

None of the owners was the killer.

"Damn." He stared at the database table. Most of the original list had been processed. Discouragement hovered like a dark cloud. He could feel the case slipping away.

How many clues had they missed? Was someone else going to die while they were stumbling around?

He recognized the self-defeatist attitude. Recognizing it and pulling out of it were two different things. He had to stay focused—catch the killer—but their leads kept wandering into mazes full of blank walls and dead ends.

Frank threw his pen onto his desk and stretched. "What do we do now?"

"The damn car has to be somewhere. We'll go back to the DMV and get all the Camaros in the state."

"I was afraid you were going to say that."

He scrubbed his hands over his face. The case was settling into one of those inevitable lulls. Waiting mode: waiting on paperwork, DNA results, car reports, bar interviews. After the new Camaro list arrived, he'd have to wait on VIN details. He'd be happy for something credible off the tip line.

Basically, he was waiting for a break that might never come.

He pushed the pessimism aside. He wanted to be out in the field rather than the one everybody fed information. Information that so far didn't amount to a hill of beans.

He shoved his chair away from his desk. "I've got to get out of here for a while."

EIGHTEEN

Thursday night

Meg climbed the stairs to her apartment, clutching the latest envelope bearing Mick's now familiar handwriting. He hadn't tried to call after Sunday. He didn't call the sorority house. He never tried to reach her at the finance office, apparently respecting the professional/personal boundary.

Instead, there was a card on Tuesday and another the next day. Dilbert wandered through voice mail hell on the front of one card, until the inside text advised that calling Mick was an alternative. The next card announced he wanted only two things: world peace and for her to call. Inside the card, he concluded world peace was vastly overrated.

She dumped her books and computer on the table and ripped open the envelope. Today's card added a twist. Instead of just saying sorry, Mick added a line. "I'd like to talk to you."

Yeah, right. Talk, not suck her soul through his lips. Talk, not melt her reserve and body, then blow their brains with mad, passionate sex. Parts of her body she'd thought atrophied clenched, and she swallowed dryly.

Talk.

Sure.

She tossed the card in the trash and pulled up the document for her Mesoamerican history class. It needed one more round of polishing before she turned it in.

Five minutes later, she pulled the card from the waste-basket. She held it, casually rotating it. She was hiding and realized it. It made her angry—with herself and with Mick. Between Mick and the e-mail pervert, the only time she'd left her apartment this week was for class or work. Walking onto campus each morning felt like a test of her nerve.

She'd brace herself for Mick's presence, and then feel foolish—and vaguely disappointed—when he wasn't there.

The weirdo was another matter entirely.

But the daily cards said Mick wasn't going away and she steeled herself for the inevitable confrontation. For a wild minute, she'd even wondered if the e-mails were from Mick, before admitting he wasn't creepy, just dangerous.

But she'd have to tell him to leave her alone.

Sick of her own company and the isolation of her apartment, she dropped the card on her desk, grabbed her coat and keys and headed for the Chi Zeta house. Tossing a wave to Marsha, the sister working the front desk, Meg climbed the stairs to Lisa's room.

"Hey, girlfriend. Are you through hibernating?" Lisa sprawled across her unmade bed. Shoving her glasses on top of her head, she pushed aside a pile of fashion magazines and patted the mattress in invitation.

"Hibernating? I'm not that bad." She tossed a pile of clothes in the direction of Lisa's laundry basket and sat down. "I'm just trying to survive midterms."

"That's what you get for making up such hard tests. You have to grade them."

"It's not just the classes I'm teaching, it's the papers for my grad classes and everything else." She propped a pillow behind her. "You know, sometimes I wonder why I put myself through it. I can't remember the last time I fixed a real meal or got a full night's sleep, much less, God forbid, simply had fun."

Lisa made a show of putting her glasses back on. "Who are you and what have you done with my overachiever best friend?"

"She went on vacation and she didn't take me."

"I want to go on vacation." Lisa flopped against her pillows, her arms flung wide to embrace the world. "There's a concert at the Pit tomorrow. Wanna go?"

Meg kicked off her shoes and tucked up her feet. "Who's playing?"

"Who cares?"

"It's something to do." She lifted a shoulder in a half-hearted shrug.

"There's a party at the ΣAE's tonight."

"I'm too old for that and I'm not in the mood to put up with Tony."

"What is it with that guy?" Lisa hugged her ancient teddy bear against her chest.

"I guess he thinks no means 'playing hard to get.' After a few beers…" She rolled her hand in a vague encompassing gesture.

"He gets thoroughly obnoxious," Lisa finished. "As opposed to Mr. GQ."

"Excuse me?"

"Good-looking; about thirty. Lit up like the Christmas tree at Rockefeller Plaza when you walked in the Chapter room. And Meggy, you were the star on top."

"You've never been to Rockefeller Plaza."

"I've seen pictures, and you're avoiding the question." Lisa pushed to a sitting position and propped the bear beside her.

"Was there a question in there?"

"I saw the card from him you left on your office desk. You really should lock your office, by the way. You went somewhere with him Friday morning and came back all hot and bothered."

Her jaw sagged open. "How...?"

Lisa laughed. "Duh? This is the ultimate small town."

"I'm not interested in him."

"Right."

"He's too old for me."

"Who are you trying to convince? You or me? He's only a few years older than you."

"Lisa," she said in a warning tone.

"Go out with him and find out if you like him. Your instincts are usually pretty good."

"When it comes to my personal life, they suck and you know it."

"You can't spend the rest of your life beating yourself up for something that happened years ago. And it's not like you to avoid the issue. You don't have any problem telling guys like Tony you aren't interested. That ought to tell you something right there."

"I'm not ready to talk about this." She stood up and paced across the room.

"Gosh, that's such a surprise." Lisa rearranged her pillows and rolled onto her side. "Haven't we gotten past the Mysterious-Meg-Who-Must-Carry-All-Burdens-Alone stage? It only took you, what? Three years to finally open up with me."

She fiddled with the owl statuette on Lisa's desk. "It's not like that. I don't have time for a relationship."

"You don't have to marry him. When was the last time you went on a date that wasn't a group thing?"

She put down the figurine. "There's no sense starting anything with him. It never works out for me."

I always end up hurt and alone.

Lisa picked up her worn teddy bear and danced him

across her tummy. "Okay, Mr. Bear. She won't date Mr. Wonderful. She doesn't want to talk. How do we get Meggy to have a life?" She held the bear to her ear. "We go downstairs and watch *Charmed?*"

Lisa bounced to her feet and grabbed Meg's hand. "Excellent idea." She tossed the bear on the bed and dragged her from the room.

Five minutes later they joined the women sprawled on the common room floor, watching as Paige, Piper and Phoebe kicked demon butt, created and solved their romantic issues and looked terrific doing it.

Maybe she needed a scriptwriter for her life, Meg thought.

"Why are you always here?" a voice asked from the doorway.

Both Lisa and Meg turned at the interruption. Didi stood a step inside the room. Meg didn't know the name of the designer of the woman's clothes, but she recognized the sneer on her face.

"Because I asked her," Lisa said before Meg could open her mouth.

"Well, I get so tired of lazy, poor people expecting other people to pay for everything they use."

Meg figured the line was a direct quote from Didi's father. She really wanted to point out that her father paid for everything the woman had or did, but that would mean lowering herself to Didi's level.

"Get over it," Lisa said and turned her attention back to the television.

Didi heaved a dismissing huff and stomped out of the room.

Meg watched her departing back. "What's her problem with me?"

Lisa twisted her mouth to the side. "Maybe your having your shit together emphasizes how much she doesn't."

"I'm the least 'together' person I know."

"Bullshit," Lisa coughed into her hand.

"I just wish Didi would grow up and get off my case."

The commercial ended and the distinctive opening notes for *Law and Order* blasted from the television. Detective Curtis's classy outfit made Meg think of Mick, a far nicer subject to think about than Didi Hammond. She rolled over, stretching her arms over her head and wondered what Mick did in the evenings. Did he sit around watching TV and drinking beer? Cruise bars? Or was he still at work?

"Meg?" Marsha, the sister with front desk duty, stood at the door. "That cop's here to see you."

"Finally." She'd been waiting all day for someone from the Clinton police department to contact her about the e-mails.

"Why's a cop here?" Lisa pulled her attention from the television screen. "Or is it Mr. GQ?"

"No, I called about something else."

"Everything okay? Or is this part of being advisor-ish?" She propped on her elbows.

Meg wondered again about telling her friend about the weirdo. "It's complicated."

"When is your life simple?"

"Oh, please." She climbed to her feet. "I work and I study. What's complicated about that?"

Lisa waved her comment away and turned back to the television.

"DID HE SAY whether I should get my computer?" Meg made it one step into the lobby before coming to an abrupt halt. Mick leaned against the counter. A flat, take-out box rested on the ledge beside him. He straightened when she entered the room. He looked as good as the pizza smelled. Faded jeans hugged his hips. The creamy Irish-knit sweater complimented his skin and emphasized his dark hair and vivid blue eyes. The leather jacket added a sexy, bad-boy element—as if he needed any help in that area.

Her second set of impressions was more subtle. He was beyond exhausted, but his eyes brightened when he saw her, as if she was a tonic that rejuvenated him.

Marsha watched them openly, her head swiveling from one side of the room to the other, attuned to the electric atmosphere. Meg forced her mouth and legs to function. "Hello, Detective."

Acutely aware of him, she caught the tiny shift in his shoulders as his tension dropped a notch. So, he was nervous too. He wasn't sure what she was going to do or say. The knowledge made her feel better. She wasn't the only one floundering in uncharted waters.

"Agent," he said. A grin lit his face and her stomach double-clutched.

"I thought you might need a study break." He gestured at the pizza. "Brain food. All the major food groups are covered."

"Sodium, fat and cholesterol?" She moved closer and felt her body start to tingle. Damn, was he like plutonium? The closer you got, the stronger the effect?

"Actually, I figured you were more the vegetable and extra cheese type, rather than the Meat Lovers Deluxe sort."

She stopped just beyond his reach. "You could be wrong."

"I'm not, though," he said smugly. "It's these vast powers of detection."

He glanced at Marsha, who was listening with unabashed interest. "Is there somewhere we can go? To eat," he added quickly. "I went by your apartment. Your neighbor told me you were probably over here."

Meg hesitated. No way was she taking him back to her place. She looked over her shoulder at the common room. She didn't especially want to talk to Mick under the curious gaze of half a dozen sorority women. She wasn't completely sure she wanted to talk to him at all.

"It's warm enough to sit on the back porch," Marsha blurted.

Both of them turned to her, startled. She blushed and bent her head over her book.

Mick raised an eyebrow. "Lead on."

He followed her down the hall, waiting as she detoured into the kitchen for plates, utensils and napkins. His eyes moved casually, systematically cataloguing the rooms and hall. She pushed open the back door and flicked on the porch lights.

"Your security stinks," he said unexpectedly.

She looked at him as if he were speaking Greek.

"There's no keypad back here, just the card slide. Simple contacts on the door. Nothing on the windows. No motion detectors."

She shrugged. "This door's locked at ten. There's a dead bolt. The women use the front door after that."

"How often does it get reopened so people can sneak in?" He laughed at her expression. "Jeez, Meg, I didn't graduate that long ago."

He placed the pizza on the table and gestured for her to sit down. "It's a lousy system. Y'all need better protection. Sorry. I can't stop being a cop."

"Occupational hazard?" She opened the box and the mingled odors of basil, oregano and melted cheese filled the air. Vague shapes hid under a thick blanket of mozzarella, just the way she liked it. *Damn him, how did he know that?*

She transferred wedges to the plates. Long strings of cheese trailed to the box, and she automatically pulled them free. As she licked the sauce and cheese from her fingers, she heard Mick swallow hard. Sexual tension bubbled closer to the surface. She leaned away from the table, deliberately putting distance between them.

For a moment, there was silence as they ate.

She flicked a glance at him. Should she tell him about the e-mails? She'd feel foolish if it turned out to be one of her students playing a stupid trick. Given the graphic content, it would be easier—if anything about the situation could be labeled easy—to tell an objective person. If something was actually wrong, the police officer would take care of it.

Mick wiped his mouth, then reached for another slice. "Jerry Jordan told me about this place. I didn't expect to find a pizza this good in Newberry."

"You don't live in Newberry?"

He shook his head. "It's a nice town. It wouldn't be a bad place to live. The Opera House is great. Have you been there?"

"A couple of times. I went to see Groove Lily right before school started."

"Really? I saw them too." He took another bite of pizza.

Is he dating someone else? she couldn't stop herself from wondering.

The awkward silence eased as they talked about music.

"Does Douglass have a college radio station?" he asked.

She rocked her hand. "It's pretty lame. I mostly listen to stations I stream on the computer. There are a couple of places to go if you like local bands."

"I used to go hear them," he said. "But…"

He stopped. His face had the expression he wore when he was trying to decide whether to tell her something. She wondered if he realized he was being so transparent.

"Jess, the woman I used to date, didn't like anything but pop, so I got out of the habit of going."

"Pop? Like Britney Spears?" Hmm, the woman he *used* to date. How long ago? What happened?

He groaned. "Jess loved her. Who're you listening to these days?"

"Let's see." He'd changed the subject, she noticed, but he got bonus points for not bad-mouthing Jess. "Two local bands you might like are Jump Little Children and Seven Nations. I can see where they're playing if you'd like."

"Do that. We'll go hear them. Unless you already have plans, that is," he added.

Did she just ask him out or was he asking her? "Usually a group of us goes."

He had that look again, but his eyes were locked on his pizza. "So you aren't dating anyone right now?"

This is your chance. It's the perfect opening to tell him you're involved with someone else. "Nobody in particular."

Brain-mouth filter, she thought as he nodded. The damn thing quit working whenever she was around him. She could see the smile on his lips behind the slice of pizza. He was going to keep calling and sending cards. "The cards were funny."

She gave up on controlling what emerged from her mouth. "How long did it take you to pick them out?"

"Truthfully?"

"The truth is usually a good idea."

"I read every single card on the rack. I think the clerk wanted to call the cops."

"Let's see, that would be you."

He grinned. "Yeah. I could see me trying to explain this."

She blinked, but he hurried on. "I figured the 'I miss you desperately' ones would freak you out and I couldn't stomach the long, gushy 'I'm sorry' ones. There was one about a cell phone set to vibrate with a plea—call me, call me—that made me laugh."

"I did wonder about the potty humor." She took a bite from her third slice of pizza.

"It seemed safer than politics."

She dropped the wedge on her plate and groaned.

"You don't like politics?"

"The groan was 'cause I'm going to explode if I eat another bite. That was wonderful."

Mick leaned back into his chair with a satisfied sigh. "Only thing missing was a beer." He cocked an eyebrow. "Can you have one?"

"You know, for a detective you aren't very observant."

His grin crinkled the skin around his eyes. "On campus? Legally? Someone could end up in a fountain."

Her chin rose a notch. "Questioning me, Detective?"

"Agent," he corrected with a smile.

"Technically, the houses aren't even part of the campus. And I'm not a child."

"No, you're not."

She'd have paid money to know what he was thinking, but he'd closed off his face. She studied the man sitting opposite her. The overhead light emphasized the shadows under his eyes, but he'd shaved. His hair was freshly washed. He looked like a man on a date. She dropped her gaze to her fingers, which were restlessly twisting her napkin. She forced her hands open and smoothed the cloth over her knee. "What'd you want to talk about, Mick?"

He knew exactly what she was referring to. "Just talk,

Meg. Like we've been doing tonight. You're an attractive, intelligent woman who intrigues me. No plots. No ulterior motives. I want to get to know you. Slowly, the way most people approach a relationship."

Not spontaneous combustion, the way they had. "Is that what we're doing? Starting a relationship?"

"I don't know about you, but I'm conducting an investigation. Surveillance of the scene of the crime. Observing the hotbed of revolutionaries who live there."

He took another look around the back porch. She tried to see it through his eyes. The ceiling fans were stationary. The tables and chairs looked like they hadn't been used recently. They were nice, a combination of cast aluminum and fabric, a step up from the wooden picnic tables the frats used, but they were hardly deluxe.

"You know," he said, "I had more of a rich-bitch image of sorority girls."

"There you go with that easy, stereotype problem of yours. I thought detectives were supposed to be more open-minded."

"The good ones are."

"And are you one of the good ones?"

"I'm very good," he said solemnly.

The innuendo was there, just below the surface. Her eyes dropped to his mouth. Yes, he was very good. She forced her gaze away.

"At my job. I'm good at my job."

Lighten up, woman. But her mouth had disconnected from her brain filter again. "You said you shouldn't do… what you did, for a whole bunch of reasons. What are they?"

Mick had clearly replayed their conversation as often as she had. "I'm a cop. I met you during an investigation."

She rolled her eyes and he grinned. "A bogus one, but dating suspects is officially frowned upon."

"A suspect? *Moi?*" She gave him an exaggerated blameless face and he laughed.

"You admitted being at the scene of the crime."

"An innocent bystander."

He crossed one ankle over his knee. "You see. All sorts of reasons."

Meg reached for his plate and stacked both dishes on the box. So, he wasn't willing to acknowledge the incredible chemistry either. Why? His restraint this evening had been admirable. Maybe she'd underestimated him. Or maybe he was afraid he'd scare her off permanently if he let that passion out of its box again.

Maybe it scared him too.

Night noises filled the following silence. A car passed on the road behind the screening trees at the rear of the property. It reached the intersection and turned away from the college. The engine noise faded into the background nocturnal sounds.

Meg roused herself. "I have to teach a class at nine. I don't even know when you work."

"Until this case is finished, I work all the time."

The murders. "Is it as bad as it feels? You seem so... sad."

Her question appeared to surprise him as much as it did her. It was an intimate observation when she was so busy keeping him at arm's distance.

"At times I feel useless," he said. "I'm running after leads that go nowhere, while he's out ahead of us, laughing." Weariness showed plainly in his eyes. "I've—*enjoyed* is too mild a word, but I can't think of a better one—this time with you. I need to remember it isn't futile. We will catch him."

"I know you will."

He studied her face, and she felt warmth climb her cheeks.

"I'm not asking for anything you aren't ready to give. I understand you don't know what you want. From me. From yourself. I can wait." He shrugged, self-consciously. "You remind me there's life and laughter. That what I do matters."

Oh, she could so fall in love with him. "It matters. You matter."

Had those words come out of her mouth? She rose, retreating rapidly. Mick stood, as well. She carefully kept the table between them. "Would you like to take that home?" She gestured at the pizza remnants.

"I'll get fat."

The gleam in his eye belied the serious tone. Her stomach clenched again. He knew he'd scared her just now and was making it easy for her. "Better you than me," she replied, equally serious.

"Palm it off on your sisters."

In one fluid move, Mick rounded the table and took her arms. Lowering his head, he carefully, gently, kissed her. Meg locked her elbows and fisted her hands to keep from reaching for him, but her lips followed their own desires. They softened under his mouth and kissed him back. His hand lifted to the side of her neck. His thumb caressed her cheek, leaving a trail of fire. With just that brief contact, her heart moved into overdrive. Who was she kidding? She so wanted this man. Everything about him attracted her.

Mick stepped back. His face was tightly controlled, but his gaze roamed her face. She waited, suspended.

"I'll call you. Maybe we can have lunch tomorrow." His voice was husky and he cleared his throat.

"I'll leave this way." He edged to the screen door. "Good night."

Meg stood looking into the darkness that shrouded him. Slowly, her pounding heart returned to normal. She didn't want to like Mick O'Shaughnessy, but she did.

She'd be a fool to keep seeing him, but she knew she'd do it anyway.

She was playing with fire.

She prayed she wasn't going to get burned.

NINETEEN

Friday morning

MICK SAT IN his car outside the SLED field office. His boss's words echoed in his mind. *Take some time for yourself. Don't burn out.*

He stared straight ahead, not seeing the morning rush hour traffic on North Street. Two double-shot lattes were barely holding his eyes open. He'd been up half the night, too wired to sleep. Was that what he was doing? Burning out?

He couldn't keep going like this. Between Meg and the killer, he wasn't sleeping. He barely remembered to eat.

He was losing his mind. That was the only explanation.

He'd always been able to step back and see the bigger picture. The key to being a good cop was flexibility. When he was on patrol, one minute he'd be both comforting an old lady who'd been burglarized and taking her report. The next minute, there'd be a call to break up a bar fight. After that, there might be a car wreck, which meant someone could be hurt or killed. In order to do his job, he'd quickly learned to suppress his feelings. Keep the compassion, the older cops taught him, but restrain the emotion.

Controlling his emotions was a rule he'd lived by for nearly ten years. He did it with work. Why couldn't he do that with Meg? If he was only looking for some balance, he should keep moving and not complicate Meg's apparently screwed-up life.

He sighed and gathered the energy to get out of the car. He unbuckled his seat belt, then sank back against the leather.

Leaving, giving up, wasn't an option. He wanted to know everything about Meg, including the hurts she wasn't ready to discuss. He wanted to soothe each one away with a kiss. He wanted to take her to bed and love her until she exploded with pleasure. He wanted to introduce her to his family, the swamps, and all the things in his life that were beautiful.

He just wanted to be with her.

His head sagged forward until it rested against the steering wheel.

He was losing his mind.

"I DON'T KNOW if this club thing's gonna pan out." Andersen's voice grated across Mick's ear. "It's time-consuming as hell. You can't just walk in, flash a badge and a picture and expect instant results."

"I realize that."

Andersen kept talking. "The bartender or waitress you need to see might not be working. They quit over nothing. They change shifts. Hell, half the time they flat just don't want to get involved. I've got five guys making the rounds. So far we got a big zero to show for it."

"We can put both the killer and Baldwin at the Squirrel," Mick reminded him. "Ward found him at the Ramblin' Rose. Cohen was going to Speakeasy—another hookup joint. We need to find them together at enough places to move it out of the coincidence column."

"I still think it's a waste of time."

"You want to check cars instead? The new VIN info files just came in."

Unexpectedly, Andersen laughed. "All of a sudden, checking out clubs sounds real attractive."

"Asshole," he muttered, hanging up the phone. Thank God, there were plenty of uniforms eager to earn some overtime or a few brownie points. There was always a risk they'd miss something, but it got the cars processed.

The phone rang again. He sighed. When this was over, he was taking a vacation someplace where there were no phones.

"I made a list of every teacher in the Upstate," Jordan began. "I've been going back, cross-referencing them. There are some who used to teach at one of the target schools."

Jordan's enthusiasm was contagious. "Why'd they move?" he asked. "Was there any bad blood?"

"Most were brand-new grads looking for a foothold. Two of them weren't going to get tenure, so they moved on their own. There's one guy the Music Department was evasive about. Detective Ward's going to talk to him."

He heard pages rustle.

"This might be more interesting."

"What?"

"Lots of the teachers take the summer off. Some use the time for research. They need to publish to get ahead. Anyway, it looks like about twenty were guest teaching at the target schools this past summer."

"Hang on a minute. Do you mean there's someone who taught at all three schools?"

"Not at all three, but it proves my point that one guy could meet girls from three different schools, either teaching a class or doing research."

"Did any of the victims take a class from a guest professor?"

"I'll ask."

He opened the closest file and flipped through the background reports. "I thought I remembered this. Ms. Baldwin went to summer school." He read off the instructors' names. "See what you can find out."

MEG IGNORED THE incoming-message chime. The constant barrage of e-mails was getting to her. The police officer had taken her statement and forwarded the e-mail, but no one else had contacted her and the e-mails just kept coming.

She'd been distracted since the messages started, re-reading incomprehensible texts, putting the wrong dates on assignments, making mistakes in front of her class. Any time she stepped outside the office or her apartment, this phantom responded with a running commentary. She was constantly watching her back, waiting for some guy to tap her on the shoulder.

Or hit her over the head.

No, she rebelled. Scratch that. Obviously the police didn't think this was the killer. This was just some creep getting off on trying to upset her. She wasn't going to give in to another bully. They never left you alone if you showed them you were afraid. Defiantly, she switched to her mailbox and opened the message.

You think you can conquer the world. Outwardly, you appear so confident—secure and pure. I know the truth, however. I know your secret.

What was wrong with this guy? He couldn't possibly know anything about her.

Your true nature reveals itself in your work: a waitress, a servant. In my daydreams, I see you on your knees, serving me. On your back, receiving my seed. But you will not carry my child. We both know you are unworthy of that.

Meg caught her breath. This guy was vile. Sure, she'd taken a second job to make ends meet, but that hardly made her some kind of servant. And those other comments. Was that what he really thought of women? And what was this "unworthy" stuff?

What would your "sisters" say if they knew your secret? Would they despise you too?

He kept saying he knew, but he couldn't, could he?

She chewed her lip uncertainly. What *would* her sisters say? The other associates and professors in her department? Her students? Would it matter to any of them?

Or did it only matter to her?

"O'SHAUGHNESSY." MICK tucked the phone between his ear and shoulder, his eyes on his computer screen.

Frank looked up, his own phone clasped to his ear.

"This is Greg Pollard. I'm with the Greer PD."

He shook his head at Frank—not a cab dispatcher calling back. He flipped open the roster he kept of the Upstate police departments. There was a Greg Pollard with the Greer police department, but he'd never met him. The press wasn't above impersonating a cop. "What can I do for you?"

"Well, I've been reading about these murders, and something's been bugging me. We had a sexual assault earlier this summer. The hospital contacted us, otherwise I don't think the vic would've reported it."

"Why not?"

"It was sorta strange. I felt bad about it—she was definitely assaulted—but there was nothing to work with."

He bit back an impatient reply. Was there a point to this? "You implied there was a connection to the murders."

"The vic was drugged. Rohypnol. The doer tied her to her bed with duct tape. The asshole left her that way. It happened on a Friday night. It could've been days before anybody found her."

The callous cruelty of it fit their killer. Mick bit back his urge to yell, *Why didn't you call sooner?* and let the guy tell his story.

"There was one weird detail. I don't know if you're using this as a holdback. We would."

"What?"

Pollard hesitated. "Doc said there was a rock in there. The doer shoved it in after he finished."

He sat a moment in stunned silence. "Can you fax the report over?"

"Sure." Pollard correctly read his silence. "We'll keep sitting on that detail."

"Thanks."

Mick hung up the phone and turned to Frank. "You aren't going to believe this."

An hour later, he called Pollard back. "The crime scene report isn't in the file."

"Yeah." Pollard sighed heavily. "Her roommate cut her loose and took her to the hospital. Girl was hysterical. She'd been tied up all night. The roommate got home late and went straight to bed. She wandered in about noon on Saturday to see if the vic wanted to go to the mall."

He winced as he guessed what was coming and found himself nodding as the detective continued. "Another friend cleaned up the room, thinking it'd upset her to come back to the mess. We got the sheets before she washed them, but the tape was hopeless and all the trace evidence was gone."

"The medical report says there was penetration, but no ejaculate."

"That's right."

"No hair?"

"We couldn't find anything. I hear those pervs shave down there."

"Yeah, we caught one once who was bare-assed as a baboon. So, nothing on the sheets?"

"An old peter print—turned out to be her boyfriend."

"Let me guess, solid alibi?"

"Bingo. Like I said, we had nothing. She couldn't remember shit. She started coming around during the assault, vaguely remembers a guy being there, but those drugs totally screwed her memory. With no trace evidence and no witness—" Mick imagined the shrug, "—there wasn't anything we could do."

"We didn't pick this up off VICAP."

"We didn't add it to the database," Pollard said. "That's why I called. Hope it helps."

He replaced the receiver and relayed the story to Frank. He rested his chin on his palm, considering the implications. "It confirms what we suspected. He was raping before he killed Baldwin."

Frank closed the file he'd been working on. "We should use the press on this."

He raised a questioning eyebrow.

"Let's send another request around to all the law enforcement agencies for any reports involving either date-rape drugs or bondage that didn't get processed. If he attacked one, there might be others. If we get the press to run it—that he raped some women, but the assaults never got reported—maybe someone else will come forward."

TWENTY

Friday evening

THE NEED HAD him by the throat. The Professor couldn't wait on Meg. With the rain, she'd get a ride home from the restaurant. It would have to be Allison. He'd watched her slip out of her apartment and steal away. She must be headed to the Depot. She hadn't been there since Emily died. Her need must be gnawing at her, as well.

He grinned, a wolfish twist of lips. The intersection of their desires was an inevitable confrontation. He had something special planned for Allison—a new fantasy he'd harbored all week. He imagined the police's reaction when they found her. Anticipation quickened his step.

He strode down the corridor toward his office, his smile fading. The battle of wills with the police was exhilarating, but he'd allowed it to distract him. This unacceptable trip onto campus was an obvious example of his forgetfulness. Normally, leaving his supplies secreted in his desk was a prudent strategy. He'd never forgotten them before. Late on a Friday, there was little chance someone would see him in his clubbing outfit, but it was an unnecessary risk.

What would he say if someone saw him? A party of some sort? A disguise? He smirked and straightened his cuffs. "Always tell the truth," he murmured.

Lights in the building burned brightly. The cleaning crew must not have finished. His eyes scanned the classrooms opening off the corridor ahead, alert for activity.

He could hear the buffer on an upper floor, but the janitor could be removing trash from any room. He reached the history department office unobserved. A strip of fluorescents lit the central lobby. The dim light reflected off the individual office doors. Breathing easier, he fished for his keys.

"Tim?"

He froze. His keys slipped from his fingers with a jangling clatter. Forcing his shoulders down, he glanced over his shoulder. "Paula. What are you doing here?"

The department secretary stood in the head's doorway, an incredulous expression on her face. The lamp on the head's desk backlit her shape.

Slowly, she took in his outfit. The slacks and shirt were expensive, well-cut and subtly flashy. His hair, which usually hung in a limp fringe, was gelled and spiked. A smile lifted the corners of Paula's mouth and the same calculating assessment he'd seen on countless other women flickered in her eyes. "Wow. You look completely different. You have a hot date?"

Pulling out his glasses, he turned to face her. Fear and anger, fraternal twins, rippled along his nerves. He stooped, stalling as he groped for his keys, frantically trying to decide what to do. His intellect pushed through the panic. *Control it. Act normal.*

Normal; his lips curled around the word. *By whose standards? Hers?*

The thoughts steadied him. *Act like the worm she's used to seeing.* Shrugging his shoulders, he tried to look sheepish. "Well, I don't know about 'hot.' But I left her phone number on my desk."

"You look good."

Her gaze crawled down his face to his chest, and his

lips curled in distaste. He turned and unlocked his door, hiding his reaction.

"Who's the lucky lady?"

"You don't know her. She lives in Spartanburg." He edged into his office, wondering what to do next. This was too unexpected. He hadn't made a plan. He couldn't keep improvising. What if he made a mistake? "I don't mean to be rude—"

"But you need to run. Okay. Have fun." She looked at the pile of papers on the department head's desk and sighed. "This is pathetic," she mumbled. "Everybody has a social life except me. Damn. It's Friday night and I'm doing *paperwork*."

She turned toward the office, still grumbling.

Tim quickly entered his office, and sent an assessing glance after Paula. She'd paused in the doorway.

She was looking at him. Studying him.

A hot fist of rage tightened around his throat. She would remember him dressed like this. She was going to ruin everything, all his carefully laid plans. It had taken him years to learn this disguise, this method.

Shit, shit, *shit*. He dropped into the chair behind his desk. *Assess your position. Control the damage.* He searched for a way to turn the encounter to his advantage.

Responding to instinct, he rose and quietly approached the door. Paula sat hunched over the computer on her desk, typing. He recognized the e-mail program. He *knew* it.

The rage in his chest burned hotter. She was telling someone about him. He couldn't allow that.

The marble bookend was right beside him. It was fated—this was supposed to happen. The cool marble fit perfectly into his hand. The polished oval arced smoothly as he raised it. It made a satisfying thud as it connected with the back of Paula's head.

She sprawled across the keyboard, as graceless as a used tissue. He stared at her limp form until his pulse slowed. Now what?

He gave the secretary another irritated glare. He couldn't leave her here. Killing her here wasn't an option. There'd be too much mess to clean up.

Savagely, he kicked her sprawled leg. This was all her fault.

He shot an angry glower around the departmental lobby. His gaze settled on Tucker's office door. The guy never locked up anything.

Tucker was a complete slob—his research methodology was unacceptable—but he'd returned from a field study two weeks ago. His gear was probably still in the corner where he dumped it.

The Professor crossed the lobby and returned with Tucker's duffel. With rough, irritated movements, he stuffed Paula into it. She groaned softly. Without hesitating, he slammed the bookend against her temple. Her head lolled in the tight confines of the duffel. Satisfied, he dropped the bookend inside and zipped the heavy, canvas bag.

Quickly, he returned to his office and opened his desk drawer. Reaching into the back, he removed a Rohypnol tablet and dropped it into his pocket.

The Professor left his office, carefully locking the door behind him. The janitor was on this floor now, but around the corner in the front hallway. Fear batted at his stomach, but excitement surged through his veins. This was as good as his fantasies. He could control everything. He was growing, stretching himself, handling emergencies. All he had to do was pay attention and use his superior intellect.

He grasped the handles of the duffel and heaved it to his shoulder. The bitch weighed a ton, but he didn't dare drag the bag. The janitor might hear it over his polishing machine and investigate.

Sweating and swearing silently, he made it to the stairwell. With a sigh, he dropped the load and rested until his pounding heart settled. Dragging the bag, less worried about noise, he thudded down the stairs to the rear loading dock, where he'd left the Camaro.

Straining, he lifted the duffel and dumped it into the trunk. He turned and examined both the small parking area and the darkness beyond it. He saw no one, heard only muted traffic in the distance. Easing open the duffel, he applied a strip of tape to Paula's mouth and bound her wrists. That should hold her.

Settling into the driver's seat, he cranked the engine and felt the powerful machine come to life. Buffed to a high gloss, the Camaro looked distinctive in a well-lit parking lot, but the low, black shadow was nearly invisible in the dark. He eased onto the side road behind the college.

What to do with Paula? His fingers played across the steering wheel. He could drop her in the lake, but what if she didn't drown? *No. There was too much risk in that. The roads across the lake were too heavily traveled. Even if no one saw him dump her, someone might see the duffel if it floated for a while.*

He glanced at his watch. He really didn't have time to deal with Paula tonight, not if he wanted to make his rendezvous with Allison.

Allison. He caught himself before he drifted into fantasy. *Damn Paula for interfering.* She deserved whatever he decided to do with her. He straightened in the seat as an idea took hold. He could leave her at the cabin. He could even make her watch when he brought Allison there.

He considered the possibility. Allison wouldn't get to the Depot until ten at the earliest. If he hurried he could drive through Spartanburg, stop at Rumors and make sure the bouncer saw him for an alibi, before moving on. If everything went according to plan, Allison would share a drink with him before midnight. By then, the bar would be throbbing with alcohol, lust and music as the hunters and the hunted circled each other. One more drunken couple slipping out to indulge their hormones in mindless rutting would pass unremarked.

Allison would spend the last days of her life lashed to a bed at his cottage. The experience with Emily had shown him the advantage of drawing out the process. And Paula would be his terrified audience.

He slid a CD into the player and cranked the bass. The first surge of anticipation lit a glow in his belly. Allison was ripe, skittish. Trolling the bars for action was her dirty, little secret. She acted prim and proper in Clinton, but she cut loose in the Greenville bars, slamming shots, dirty dancing, prick-teasing until she selected the night's lucky winner.

Adrenaline kicked his heart rate up another notch.

He'd be the winner tonight.

"I AM SORRY to take so much time to return your telephone call." The cab dispatcher had the lilting, singsong tone of an Indian transplant. "It is after all Friday evening and our most busiest time. Please excuse me."

Mick was suddenly listening to dead air as the dispatcher routed another cab before continuing.

"You wish to know about our services provided on Monday, October the third?"

"That's right." He named the apartment complex.

"We had one request, very late that night. It was not to that specific location, but rather to a convenience store. Would that be of interest?"

"Where?"

"The facility was less than two blocks away from the apartment location."

"Where did you take the passenger?"

The dispatcher read the address—the Waffle House near the Squirrel.

"Could we talk to the driver?"

"I am sorry to report that may prove rather complicated."

He tensed. *Working? Fired? Moved?*

"He is not scheduled to work this particular weekend. I believe he planned to go away for relaxation."

"Do you have a number where we can reach him?"

"I am afraid I do not have that information. He is, however, scheduled to work on Monday. Please excuse me."

When the dispatcher returned, Mick obtained the driver's personal information. "I will ensure the driver makes contact with you when he returns."

"Thanks," he said into the abruptly dead phone. The dispatcher was already gone.

WHERE WAS SHE? The Professor circled the bar twice and finally asked the bartender. The man shook his head. "Allison hasn't been in tonight."

The Professor hid his frustration. How dare she disappoint him? It was after eleven. If she was coming, she'd be here.

The need was choking him. He glared at the other women. They were drunken cows, bitches in heat, useless for his purposes.

He stalked from the bar to his car.

Damn Allison! Where was she? He swept down 385, rage pushing the accelerator. He rounded a curve. Lights pulsed on the shoulder up ahead. Smokey Bear had some schmuck pulled over. He glanced down. His speedometer read eighty-five. Cursing, he slowed to seventy. He didn't need a ticket to cap this fucked-up night. At least he didn't have Paula in the trunk anymore. Wouldn't *that* have been a bitch to explain?

A few minutes later, he took the Clinton exit, heading toward the cluster of student apartments bordering the campus. Slowing to a crawl, he cruised past Allison's building. Several of the old houses on the street were ablaze with lights and music. Friday night parties were still going strong.

Allison's windows were dark. Her car wasn't in the small parking lot. Where in the hell was she?

He prowled the surrounding streets. Cruising the bars that were still open would be futile. She wouldn't be there. She saved her wanton behavior for the venues far from Clinton.

Nearly blind with anger and need, he turned toward the apartment on the north side of campus. Meg's second-floor windows were dark, but he knew she was there.

He envisioned her asleep in her bed, saw the tumbled curls, the rise and fall of her chest. He closed his eyes, playing a silent, private movie. *The window, already raised a few inches, silently yielded to his insistent pressure. The sash opened, obligingly providing entry. The drapes billowed in the breeze, but she didn't stir. A dark figure slipped through the window and approached her sleeping form…*

He smiled as the fantasy unwound. It would hold the need at bay, while he made his plans. He knew exactly where Meg would be Saturday night. His smile widened.

And where she'd be Sunday morning.

In the meanwhile, there was Paula.

TWENTY-ONE

Saturday morning

WEAR SOMETHING CASUAL. *What does that mean?* Meg adjusted the mirror mounted on her bedroom door and studied her reflection. Was Mick going to show up in jeans or slacks and another gorgeous sports coat? She'd split the difference with a pair of black jeans—the ones that made her butt look nice, instead of huge—a thin silk turtleneck, and a sapphire blue sweater that showed off her hair.

"You look great," Lisa said.

She smiled. "Compared to how you look, that's not saying much."

Lisa sprawled across Meg's bed, wearing fuchsia toe socks, ratty sweatpants, an old Mickey Mouse T-shirt and the dorky glasses she reserved for late nights and weekend mornings. She punched the pillows into a more comfortable nest. "I can't believe you're dating a cop."

She rolled her eyes. "I don't think he's going to arrest me if I burp or get food stuck in my teeth. Besides, aren't you the one who keeps telling me to go out with him?"

"He *is* hot. Why is it the cops who pull me over are like forty, with a big gut?"

She tugged at the sweater. "Is this too clingy? Maybe I should wear something looser." She slid the closet door open.

"Don't change again," Lisa groaned. "That's the third outfit you've tried on."

"I don't know what to wear."

"If you didn't like him, you wouldn't care," Lisa pointed out. "I've never seen you do the girly indecision routine."

She closed the closet door and picked up her brush, smoothing the flyaway hairs the sweater had displaced. With a sigh, she said. "I do like him. It's scary."

Lisa patted the bed beside her and Meg slid onto it. "You can't keep pushing everybody away if they try to get close. Not everybody's as persistent as me."

"I know," she said. "It's just spooky. I mean, there's this connection between us. It's like I can see right into his brain and tell what he's thinking and feeling."

"That's called being in love, sweetie."

"But I barely know him. Besides, he can go into cop mode and, *wham,* everything closes."

"It's what he does. It's part of the package. Can you handle it?"

"I don't know." She made a face. "'Course the other piece of it is, he can see into me. And I can't block him."

"It's not like you have any deep, dark secrets."

Meg looked away, nervously twirling a lock of hair around her finger. "Everybody has secrets, things they don't want anybody to know."

"Some guy dumping on you doesn't count. I mean, it's not like, a crime. You didn't rob a bank to pay for school, did you?"

"Only my piggy bank." It was so much more than Steven dumping on her. Deep down, part of her still believed all the things her parents said when her world fell apart. She'd never told Lisa the whole story. Or how severely the betrayal had scarred her.

"Well, there you go. You'll get, what? Ten years for that? Maybe he'll let you out early for good behavior."

Meg smiled and released her hair. "I don't think Mick does that part."

"Then you don't have anything to worry about."

If you only knew. She rose and fiddled with her hairbrush, wondering if she should say more. The intercom buzzer saved her. She crossed the room and pressed the Talk button. "Yes?"

"It's Mick."

"Be right down."

"Just have fun," Lisa said. "Remember, you don't have to marry him."

"WELL, PAULA, WHAT am I going to do with you?"

The secretary flailed against the bindings securing her to the bed. Her eyes bulged above the piece of tape covering her mouth.

"Nothing to say? You usually have an opinion on everything."

The Professor stared at the woman, faintly repulsed. There was nothing sexually attractive about her, but he enjoyed her fear. She'd always been a little contemptuous of him. And because of her, he didn't have Allison or Meg.

Slowly, he smiled. He'd have Meg by this evening, though. For a moment, he transposed her luscious body over Paula's. Auburn curls, milky skin; the fantasy took him until he throbbed with need.

Noise intruded.

His eyes fluttered open and focused on Paula rather than Meg. For a moment, he blinked, confused by Paula's presence. Then a cruel smile twisted his features. He needed release and she was here. It was her fault he was in this predicament.

Casually, he reached over and picked up his knife. Twisting it, letting the light glitter up and down its haft, he watched Paula's eyes dart from the blade to his face. Violently shaking her head, she jerked at her bonds.

Carefully, aiming for the straightest possible line, he ran the knife down the front of her blouse. The fabric separated and a thin line of red appeared on her chest. "Why, Paula," he said. "I never realized you had such nice breasts. Let's see what else you have."

She cringed, trying to evade his knife as tears slid down her face. The power of his control over her was affecting him, adding to his thundering need. He flicked a glance at her face, easily transferring Meg's features. "You wanted me. You've wanted me all along. You're mine now, to do with as I please."

He had new ideas, things he planned to do with Allison and Meg.

He spent the rest of the day testing them with Paula, and found they were very good ideas.

THE TREES ON Greenville's Main Street had just started changing color, Meg noticed. Occasionally, a leaf let go and spun lazily toward the wide brick sidewalk. The downtown shops and cafés were doing a brisk business. She and Mick strolled past couples clad in urban chic, dawdling over coffee.

Mick had been holding her hand since he opened the BMW's door. His fingers were warm, his grip tight enough to send constant reminders of his proximity pinging through her nerves. She hadn't let anyone touch her like this in years. It made her vaguely self-conscious. The other strollers weren't paying any attention to them, though. And Mick had apparently decided to ignore her reaction as long as she didn't retract her hand.

"These guys do the best brunch." He steered her into

Tronco's and after a short conversation, the hostess seated them at a small table on the patio.

"When did they do all this?" Her glance included the shops and the streetscape.

Mick looked at her, surprised. "Years ago. The whole West End's been redone."

"I don't come to Greenville often. If we drive up from Douglass, it's to go to a concert or the mall. How did you know this was here?"

"I live here."

She laughed, even as a blush warmed her cheeks. "You know, I hadn't thought about that—where you live. You're always down in Clinton or talking about Newberry. I thought you were a local."

"You practically got my life history out of me on the drive up. How'd we miss that detail? But you're right, I have spent a lot of time in Newberry recently."

"Do you travel a lot with your job?"

"It depends. Sometimes I feel like I live in my car. Other cases are one big paper chase. I'm mostly in the office on those." He shrugged. His eyes moved, clicking through the other patrons and the street traffic.

She took in the sudden tension in his shoulders. Work wasn't a good topic today, she concluded. "What are we doing after lunch?"

He turned back and grinned, the tension gone as quickly as it had arrived. "It's a surprise." Mischief lit his eyes.

"You were hell on wheels when you were a kid, weren't you?"

"Let's just say I appreciated my parents' tolerant attitude."

She tried to keep her reaction off her face. She couldn't imagine tolerant parents. "Lucky you," she said lightly. "What kind of trouble did you get into?"

He reached across the table and took her hand in silent empathy. *Damn him for being so observant.*

His gaze turned inward, lost in memory. He idly caressed her hand, tracing her fingers. The featherlight touches sent shivers through her, to other sensitive spots. To her surprise, she didn't want him to stop. Her eyes half-closed as she gave herself over to the sensation.

"We used to take a canoe out on the creek or the river. My folks didn't mind if we went fishing or crabbing, but we were always testing the limits."

Meg blinked, tuning back in to his words.

"Our farm's about four hundred acres of swamp and forest. We knew all the trails and roads in the woods—we grew up there—and we thought we knew the swamp. To a certain extent, we did."

His focus remained internal. "It's beautiful there. There's a wild feeling to it, that anything's possible. It's so fertile, you can *feel* things growing. Water's everywhere, of course. You can barely tell it's moving. You have to know how to read the swamp. Where the current is, the ridges."

He really loved it, she realized.

"They're called blackwater swamps. It's not dirty. The tannins in the leaves stain the water. That's from the oak trees, upstream. Down where we live, there's a lot of cypress. Those trees that grow in the water with the knees sticking up around them."

His hand closed over hers, interlacing their fingers. "There's so much wildlife deep in the swamps. Not just deer. I've seen bobcats. And turtles laying eggs."

"And snakes and alligators."

"They aren't so bad." He smiled, leaving his pensive mood. "What you have to look out for are the pigs."

"Pigs? Is this a bad cop joke?"

"No." He sat back and grinned. "Feral hogs. Meanest

mothers you ever saw. It's why we weren't supposed to go into the swamp by ourselves. Most of the time, it was no big deal. But once, I guess I was about twelve, Vince and I snuck back there. Vince is my younger brother. We were goofing off, when a big boar charged us. He ripped a hole in the side of the canoe." Mick shook his head. "Vince and I spent the night in a tree while that hog tore up everything in a thirty-foot circle around us. He was still there the next morning, trying to figure out now to shake us out of that tree, when Dad and two game wardens finally found us."

"They went searching for you?"

"Well, yeah." He seemed startled by the question. "We didn't come home, so Dad brought out the troops. I never could figure out how they knew when and where to start looking. In the summertime, as long as we were home before they went to bed, it was okay if we stayed out late."

"Didn't they get mad when you were late for dinner?"

"We were pretty good about letting them know where we were." Mick shrugged. "They'd ask around. See whose house we were at. That's probably what made them look for us. Nobody had seen us."

Leaning back in his chair, he stretched out his legs and ran his thumb over her fingers. "Usually, some combination of us and our friends eventually showed up at our house. We slept on the porch. We didn't even have to open the back door. But they always seemed to know what time we got in."

"What happened if you were late?"

He frowned. "I don't remember exactly. It didn't happen often. They made us do some nasty chore, like cleaning out the gutters. After the hog incident, we had to work at the fish hatchery until we paid back the overtime for the guys who looked for us."

"That's it?"

"Well, yeah. I mean, we weren't saints, but they cut us some slack, and we didn't take advantage of it. Mom grounded Tricia a few times when she was in high school. I can't see her on a ladder with a scraper, cleaning the gutters. Why? What did your parents do when you misbehaved?"

Beat the crap out of me. "Tricia's your sister?"

He looked at her, just for a minute, and Meg remembered he was a detective. He'd notice she didn't answer his question. *Don't ask,* she silently urged. *Let it go.*

The rest of lunch passed quickly, with Mick telling her more about his family. Meg listened, hungry for the details, as he described the family she'd always longed for.

"Enough about me. I don't know anything about you. Where'd you grow up?"

"Charleston," she answered, surprising herself. She usually made up something and changed the subject when people asked. "Actually, I was born in Summerville, but we moved out to a development on the Stono River when I was eight."

"Stono Ferry?" A startled expression crossed his face.

"You've heard of it?" she asked, a little nervous. It was an exclusive neighborhood of multimillion-dollar homes along the Intercoastal Waterway.

"I worked a case down there a couple of years ago. A security firm was moonlighting with a little breaking and entering."

"I heard about it. I wasn't there that summer." What was she doing? She'd never told anyone about her parents—or why she didn't see them anymore. Dropping her eyes to the table, she fiddled with her fork, pushing the remnants of her lunch around her plate. She felt his gaze, studying her.

Instead of pursuing it, he asked, "Doing what?"

"Working with a private equity firm in Charlotte," she

said with a small sigh of relief. "It was far from glamorous. I was the grunt who tracked their trading efforts. What paid off, what didn't."

"Hmm, exciting stuff."

"Yee-haw." She set the fork aside. "But I got to see how the analysts worked with my boss, mapping their market and working out strategies."

"Is that what you want to do when you graduate? Or are you planning to keep teaching?"

She looked at him, then away. There were all kinds of answers she could give him, but something made her tell the truth. "I don't know anymore. For the longest time, I wanted to be somebody. Somebody who got noticed." *Somebody too special to toss aside.*

"People notice you, Meg." He captured her hand and tugged, trying to get her to look at him. "Not just your looks. It's obvious you're intelligent, self-confident and... aware. The lights are on inside. Somebody's home."

"Thanks. I wasn't fishing." She sat back, pulling her hand free. "Now I just want a job where I get paid enough to live on."

"But... You said..."

She glanced up and smiled ruefully. "You sure you're a detective?"

"I haven't investigated you. Should I?" he asked lightly.

Something went still inside her. He could, if he wanted to. He could ask enough questions and it would all come out. And then he'd probably never speak to her again. He'd leave just like everyone else who said they cared about her.

The cold thing inside her stomach twisted. She kept insisting she didn't want a relationship with him, so what difference did it make?

In a private corner of her mind, a very small voice admitted his opinion mattered.

A lot.

"What's wrong?"

His voice was gentle. She felt tears prick her eyes. Her jaw tightened and she swallowed, trying to blink the tears away. She fought to keep her voice level. "Nothing."

"Talk to me. Let me in."

She sat with her head bowed. *Stop being perfect. Stop being everything I can't have.*

Mick stood up. "Come on, beautiful. We have places to go, things to see."

He grabbed her hand and pulled her to her feet. She gaped at him, trying to catch up to

another of his mercurial mood changes. "I'll give you a hint," he said. "Your surprise is outdoors."

Mick clasped Meg's hand as they strolled down the sidewalk. She'd slipped her fingers through his—a sign he interpreted as progress.

"I haven't been to the zoo since I was six," Meg said. "I didn't know Greenville had one."

Mick glanced at her, briefly admired her shining curls and smiling lips. "It's not as big as the one in Columbia. Let's cut through here." He pulled her toward the flagstone path leading into the Reedy River Park. "This is faster than going around."

"It has a waterfall," she said, delighted. "Right here in the middle of town."

She wiggled her fingers free and stepped onto the platform overlooking the river. He followed at a slower pace, enjoying her obvious happiness. It had been a great day. Meg's imitations of the animals had made him roll with laughter. She'd been fun and relaxed, even if she didn't say much. It was strange to be the one doing most of the talking. Every other woman he'd dated could carry on both sides of any given conversation. Eventually, he ended up half-tuning them out. That was usually the point he'd realized that particular relationship wasn't working.

Flagstones stepped down the hillside and ended in a meadow still lush with grass and fall wildflowers. Trees along the bank blazed with fall color, drawing them deeper into the park. The sun sparkled across the surface of the river. The water splashed musically as it tumbled around granite boulders. Meg climbed on the largest one and waved to him. "Come on."

He shook his head.

"Chicken."

"You're going to fall in."

"Not me." She leapt from rock to rock, sure-footed.

He kept pace from the shore. The streamside trail was littered with leaves that crunched underfoot. "I should've worn my hiking boots instead of these loafers. I'd be on my butt if I tried that in these shoes."

She smiled and jumped over a wide gap in the rocks. "I can't see you being clumsy."

He watched her scramble over another boulder. "I bet you were a tomboy when you were little."

Meg laughed. "I tried. You'd never have known it by looking at me though."

"Oh?"

She hopped to the ground, joining him. The path veered away from the bank as the river curved under a footbridge. They climbed the slope to the bridge. Sturdy stonework spanned the stream, creating a wide ledge that invited lingering. Meg sat on the wall, pulled up her feet and propped her chin on her knees. "I looked like a little priss when I was a kid. These curls." She made a disparaging face. "Imagine a kid having to sit still for that."

He wrapped a lock of hair around his finger. The silky

soft strand clung and he longed to run his hands through the entire mass.

"Mother made my sister and me wear these dresses. Looking back, they were lovely, but at the time, I thought they were a colossal pain. Inevitably, I'd tear mine or get it dirty. Mother'd get so angry. She had it down to a science. First, there was the disappointed sigh." She heaved dramatically. "Then, 'Margaret, how could you? Just look at yourself. You're disgusting, absolutely filthy.'"

Her gaze turned inward. "Me," she added softly. "Not the dress."

He moved in front of her. "You know you weren't." He dropped his hands onto her legs, wanting to hug and re-assure her.

She looked up, startled. "Worthless? Yeah, now. Intel-lectually. That's a pretty sophisticated concept for a five-year-old who just wants her mommy to love her."

She said the words casually, but her eyes were bright.

"Who puts a dress on a five-year-old and tells them to go play? What did she expect?"

Meg's smile quivered. "I was supposed to play *nicely*. Have tea parties or something." She blinked and looked away. "The dresses *were* beautiful. I remember a few. They were hand-smocked with tons of soft, fine cloth."

Her smile was easier now, blurred with memory. "They stood out around me when I twirled—like a bell. One had pencils embroidered like a marching band across the yoke. A line came from the point of the first one." Her finger traced it in the air. "It spelled my name like a banner. I wore that dress the very first day of school."

He put his reactions to her parents aside and concen-trated on Meg.

"My teacher was wonderful. She had an old-fashioned bathtub—the kind with the claw feet—filled with pillows.

If you finished your work, you could get a book, climb in, and escape into a story."

Escape. When you're six. "What kind of stories?"

Meg's face had changed, clouded over again. "Hmm? Oh, the *Boxcar Children*. Fairy tales." The words emerged offhand, as if her thoughts were somewhere else.

She remained silent a long time. Finally, he asked, "What is it?"

She blinked, refocusing.

"Something made you sad. Want to tell me about it?" *C'mon, Meg. Get it out so you can get past it.*

She stood and walked across the stone railing of the bridge. At the far end, she stood poised like a diver, looking down into the water. Or like someone peering over the edge of a scary cliff. He stood beside her, ready to grab her if she misstepped.

"Those damn dresses did me in."

She'd been quiet so long, her voice startled him. It took a moment for the words to register. "Your teacher saw something."

Meg's tone emerged completely flat. "Bruises. Spare the rod and spoil the child."

His hands tightened into fists. The signs were all there. He'd missed them. He forced his hands open and kept his voice level. "She reported it."

"My father tried to get her fired. They moved me to another school. And my punishment changed. It didn't leave bruises…"

Her words trailed off. *Not bruises you could see.* He reached up and rested his hands on her waist. She tensed, but turned under his gentle pressure. He tugged her forward and she jumped lightly from the railing, landing directly in front of him. Her gaze dropped to somewhere around his navel.

"Meg." He lifted a hand and caressed her cheek. "You were a child. None if it—the clothes, the beatings, your teacher—none of it was your fault. What your parents did was wrong."

She turned her head, still silent. Her gaze restlessly roamed the landscape beyond him.

"It's part of who you are. It brought out good things in you too."

Her body went completely still.

"You have an iron will. Maybe that's what I picked up that first night—the strength of your character. Your innate sense of responsibility, of right and wrong. I think you've been standing on your own two feet for a long time. And doing very well."

He raised her chin. Her eyes lifted on their own. "Not everyone who says they love you is going to hurt you. Something tells me it'll take time for you to trust me, but I think you're worth sticking around for."

He saw the little girl in her face, now. The one who wanted so desperately to be loved, but was so afraid of being hurt. He wanted to kiss her, but feared it would immediately explode into passion rather than offer reassurance.

A small smile curled her lips. "Lisa said everyone isn't as persistent as she is."

"I can be just as stubborn as you are. Of course, mine is tenacity."

"Whereas I'm just stubborn." Her tone was lighter and life was reanimating her body.

"You wasted a perfectly good week when I was so conveniently right there in town."

"Clearly you wasted too much time before prying into my deep, dark secrets and discovering my magnificent character."

How many of her secrets had she shared? "Oh?"

"Yep."

To his surprise, she reached up and kissed him. It was more of a promise than an invitation. He would've responded if she hadn't immediately leaned back. He kept his hands on her waist, waiting to see what she'd do next. With the smallest encouragement, he'd take her home with him. Given the opportunity, he'd show her exactly how much he cared.

"We have to leave now. I have to get back to Clinton," she said.

That wasn't what he expected, but he understood. It was as far as she could go today.

"Okay."

He took her hand and headed back to the car. The simmering sexuality remained, but it had taken on a new depth. Meg had taken the first tentative step out of her emotional shell. With the right encouragement, the damaged child would grow up to match the rest of the confident woman.

The woman he suspected he wanted to spend the rest of his life with.

TWENTY-TWO

MICK ACCELERATED ONTO Interstate 385, the wind slip-streaming over the car. He ran through the gears, reveling in the smooth power of the convertible. From the corner of his eye, he saw Meg twist her hair into a knot. "Do you want me to put the top up?"

"No. I love it. I should've known you'd have a cute sports car."

"A BMW Z4 isn't 'cute'. It's a finely tuned piece of precision machinery."

Meg laughed. "It's a chick magnet."

"Is it working?"

"Yep, that's it. I only went out with you for the car."

"You didn't even know I had a car until today."

"I knew you'd have a hot car," she said. "I should be a detective. I have these vast powers of deduction."

He laughed. *Oh, God, she remembered that.* "Why is it I'm taking you home?"

"I have to work tonight."

He threw her a startled look. "You teach a class on Saturday night?"

"I work two jobs."

"Why? Grad school and a day job aren't enough of a challenge?"

"I enjoy eating." She closed her arms defensively. "Is that a problem for you?"

"No, of course not. I just didn't know… Where do you work?"

"At a restaurant on the Strip."

"Near where we went for coffee?" He briefly wondered if she already regretted telling him about her childhood.

She shook her head. The wind caught her hair and whipped it around her face. "Farther up Cumberland," she said as she recaptured the strands.

Mick glanced at his watch. "What time are you supposed to be there?"

"Five. I have to help set up."

"We're going to cut it close. What me to drop you at your apartment or near your car?"

She loosened her arms, relaxing her posture. It looked deliberate to him. "My apartment, please. I don't have a car."

"How do you get to work?"

She gave him the "well, duh" look. "I walk."

"I can wait while you change and drop you off."

He watched her silent debate. "Meg, it's not that big a deal. Put on whatever you wear to work. I'll give you a ride, so you aren't late."

She flashed a brilliant smile, and he was captivated all over again.

"I'm sorry," she said. "In case you haven't noticed, I can be terribly independent."

He dropped an arm around her shoulders and leaned in her direction. "I can live with that."

All too soon, he made the turn onto campus, drove past the street lined with Greek housing and pulled into the driveway beside Meg's building. "My superior driving means you have eight minutes to change and comb the knots out of your hair."

He turned off the ignition and leaned toward her, wanting to kiss her. She reached for the door handle, then stopped. She looked at him shyly. "I had a really good time today."

"I did too."

He raised his hand to her neck and caressed the smooth skin. Ever so gently, he pulled her forward, until her mouth met his. Just a goodbye kiss, he told himself.

Her lips were warm. A thousand nerve endings bypassed his brain and delivered their message straight to his libido.

Everything vanished except Meg: the softness of her skin, her taste, her scent. His fingers threaded into her hair. He caressed the curls, her neck.

She gave a quiet moan. He pulled her closer and felt the barrier of the central console. Damn. He was too old to make out in a car. Reluctantly lifting his lips from hers, his fingers remained tangled in her luxuriant hair. Her face, mere inches from his, was flushed. Her eyes and mouth were soft and welcoming. "Do you really have to work tonight?" he whispered.

She visibly retreated. He'd have bitten back the words if he could.

"Don't…"

"Question retracted. You better hurry."

As soon as the building's door closed behind her, he mentally kicked himself.

Twice.

As a distraction, he slid his phone from his pocket, and checked the missed call list. Eighteen numbers, multiple calls from several of them. He didn't want to think about how many voice mails awaited him. He hesitated, eyeing the front door, and decided he had time for one quick call. The dance clubs were their best lead, and Andersen had called repeatedly.

Andersen answered on the second ring. "About time you called me back."

"I had some other stuff going on."

"We covered over half the bars last night. Baldwin and her girlfriends hit a couple of them, but never hooked up. Nobody's biting on either version of our asshole, though."

"Keep looking. We don't know where he's meeting them, but he's picking women up at these bars."

"You sound awfully sure about that."

"It's my gut feel. We need the evidence to back it up."

"God forbid your gut makes a mistake."

"Come on, Andersen, you never use instinct?"

"Only with women." And he was gone.

Meg returned in less than five minutes, wearing standard waitress garb—slim black slacks and a fitted white shirt. Her hair was drawn into a twist, an elegant style that emphasized her beautiful green eyes and slender neck. Mick's eyes caught on her mouth. Her lips looked delicious, soft and full. With a mental shake, he turned over the ignition. "We can still get you there on time."

He pulled out of the drive and headed toward Cumberland.

"Thanks. I appreciate the lift."

"How are you getting home?"

She shrugged. "Sometimes I catch a ride. Otherwise I walk."

He gave her a stunned look. "Meg, the restaurant must close around midnight. Between the Professor and your average, garden-variety degenerate, you have absolutely no business walking home that late by yourself."

"This is Clinton, not New York. It's not that big a deal. I've been doing it for years." She held up a hand to stop his next comment. "I'm not an idiot. Someone will give me a ride home."

Mick slammed the car into third and slid through a yellow light, gritting his teeth. "I'm staying. I'll be here when you finish."

"You don't have to…"

"I know I don't have to," he interrupted. "I want to."

"Maybe I don't want you to."

"Tough."

"You'd be wasting your time."

"I'll decide about that."

She was getting angry. "I am perfectly capable of taking care of myself."

"Good. Then you'll make it easy for me." He glanced at her. Her jaw muscles were bunched stubbornly. She stared straight ahead. "Look, I have to make about a million phone calls. I have to eat. I can do that just as easily here as I can in Greenville. Better, since I won't be worrying about you the whole time."

She didn't move.

"Indulge me?"

She sighed, but didn't move her head. "You're going to do what you want to, anyway. Just don't eat at Chez Pierre's, okay? That would be too weird."

"Okay."

"I'll call you when we're done."

Mick pulled to the curb in front of Chez Pierre's. She opened the car door and paused. "You really don't have to."

"I know."

She gave him a sad, sweet smile. "I'm glad you care, but don't ever try to tell me what to do."

TWENTY-THREE

Saturday night

CHEZ PIERRE'S FRONTED on Cumberland, at the end of the commercial strip. One of the few chic restaurants in town, it did a brisk weekend business. Anniversaries, engagements and breakups were celebrated there regularly. It was the prelude to many a sexual encounter, the participants lubricated with good food and wine.

The Professor turned off Cumberland onto Twelfth and parked in the deep shadow beyond the restaurant. The cops rarely patrolled these side streets. They cruised Cumberland and returned on Cherokee, looking for easy prey—someone who'd had an extra drink after dinner, or too many beers at one of the bars. For the cops, it was shooting fish in a barrel. Unless Dispatch called them away, they never varied their routine.

He opened the car window a few inches. Night noises entered on the cool, evening breeze. Car sounds from Cumberland were loudest, but he gradually separated the lesser noises: stray snatches of music as a bar door opened and closed, the chink and rattle of glasses and pans through an open kitchen window.

He pondered that for a moment. Meg mustn't be allowed to scream. No one would notice in the noisy bars. The residences were too far away. But someone in the restaurant kitchen might hear her.

Slumping in the seat, he lowered his head below the

headrest. If someone drove past, they wouldn't notice him waiting in the car. From this position, he could see the rear of Chez Pierre's and the parking lot beyond it. The last few patrons straggled out the front entrance and meandered down the sidewalk to the parking lot. A group—two couples—lingered between their cars, chatting. *Go home,* he silently urged. *Leave.*

He'd fantasized and rehearsed each step of Meg's capture—and the events that would follow. Paula had entertained him, but instead of releasing the pressure, his desire kept building. His hand moved to his lap. He fingered his erection through his trousers. "Soon," he whispered.

Anticipation dripped adrenaline into his bloodstream. His senses moved into a higher awareness. He smelled the residual sweetness of onions caramelizing on the grill, heard the hum of the mercury lamp by the restaurant's rear entrance.

The couples turned as one when the restaurant rear door creaked open and slammed. The servers were leaving. First one, then two more emerged. One of the diners laughed, drawing the Professor's attention. The couples separated and entered their cars. They exited onto Crabtree, leaving in a quiet purr of expensive, well-tuned motors.

He turned back to the restaurant. Meg was on the porch. He recognized the way she moved before he saw her features. Her head turned, as if she were talking to someone behind her.

He tensed. This was the moment.

Everything hung in the balance.

She had to walk back to her apartment. His plan depended on it.

The need gnawed at him like an alcoholic craving a drink. It clawed at the edges of his mind, the compulsion ferocious.

The first tendrils of fantasy intruded, plucked at him. He pushed them away. Time for them later, when he had her under his control. He needed to concentrate.

Her head shook no. For a second, the motion distracted him. He wanted her hair loose. His mind's eye added the shake and tumble of auburn curls. He wanted to plunge his hands into it. Knot his fingers in its lush depths. Tighten and pull, arching her neck, baring her milky throat to him. Distort her face with a gathering scream.

He caught himself and jerked away from the vision. *Later.*

Tonight was the night. Meg was walking rather than getting a ride with another server.

He opened the car door, fluid as an athlete prepared for the big game. The interior dome light was switched off; the doors well-oiled. Silently, he eased the door closed and stood still, listening. There was a murmur of voices. Meg was still on the porch, talking to someone in the kitchen.

Timing. Concentrate on the timing.

Meg would cross Twelfth Street to get to Bellwood, the safe route through the neighborhood to campus. His meeting her had to look accidental, as if he happened to be leaving one of the bars. All he had to do was walk farther up Twelfth and wait in the shadows. When she started across the street, he could call to her. Once he approached her, once she recognized him, he could talk her into his car. But he needed to intercept her here, on Twelfth.

He'd taken ten steps away from the car when a light flashed behind him. A faint click cracked like a gunshot in the quiet. The Professor jumped and whirled. He bit his lip to keep from shrieking.

Soft footfalls sounded against the sidewalk. He froze, probing the night. Something moved just beyond the circle of light cast by the parking lot security lamp. Who? A mugger? How ironic would it be if a petty criminal foiled him?

Footsteps clicked closer. On the opposite sidewalk, a man turned the corner from Crabtree and ambled up Twelfth toward him. There was no urgency or secrecy in the stranger's movements, but the Professor felt an alertness. The man's head was aimed directly at his position. The Professor's heart rate accelerated. Could the intruder see him? Tension dug claws into his stomach. Stay still? Keep walking? Which way?

Do something.

The stranger continued up the sidewalk, but now his attention had turned to the restaurant.

How had he missed him? The man had to have been sitting in a car when he arrived. Nothing had moved on the street except the departing patrons.

The Professor's hands shook. The intruder had seen him arrive. Seen him exit his car. He pushed at the panic, driving it back. He'd gone over this a hundred times, planning, anticipating. Here at the critical moment, he'd forgotten the most basic point. He hadn't checked for witnesses.

"Control," he whispered. He eased toward his car. Watching. Ready to run.

The man turned into the parking lot behind Chez Pierre's. The Professor waited, making sure he was headed for the restaurant's rear entrance, rather than doubling back to the road. Silently pivoting, the Professor strained to see in the dark. Was the man alone? Nothing else moved, but he no longer trusted his instincts.

The Professor reached his car and slid into the driver's seat. The man was halfway across the parking lot. He fumbled with the ignition key. "Control," he chanted.

He had to stay in control.

How could he have forgotten something so critical?

The excitement of the hunt had gotten to him. The details had gotten away. This was how other people were caught. They were careless. They made mistakes. He'd never thought it would happen to him. He was too smart. He planned every detail. Now he saw how it could sneak up and bite him.

The intruder approached the building and the Professor switched his attention to the person coming down the stairs to meet him.

His heart stopped. Breathing ceased.

It was Meg.

The man turned when he reached her. The porch light flashed across his profile and the Professor fought the paralyzing stillness. There was something familiar about the man's face. Something distinctive.

The man's hand moved and touched Meg's cheek. Possessive. He brushed a strand of hair behind her ear. She looked up at him, touched his forearm. Little signs of awareness. His head tilted back. Laughter. His hand slid confidently to the small of her back.

This is wrong. It couldn't be. Meg shunned men, didn't allow them these small intimacies. Only he should be allowed to touch her, to explore her body.

They were walking now. She spoke. The man bent his head closer. His hand circled her waist, tucking her against him.

Bile rose in the Professor's throat. Meg was his, *his!* This man had no right to touch her.

The light from the porch was behind them, but they were moving into the circle of illumination in the parking lot.

A feral screech threatened to burst from his mouth.

The tableaux etched into his mind. Agent Michael O'Shaughnessy. With *his* woman.

Touching his woman.

Leading her to a car.

Leading Meg to his bed.

It wasn't possible.

A dull roaring sounded in the Professor's ears. He opened his mouth, gulped air, and time restarted. His eyes clicked over to Meg and rage tore through him. In the time it had taken the policeman to caress her back, everything had changed. She glowed. Light from the overhead lantern gathered on her skin and cast a luminescent sphere about her.

Hatred threatened to swamp his reason. He clenched the steering wheel to keep from throwing open the door and charging the pair.

Meg coiled her arm around O'Shaughnessy's waist and dropped her head on his shoulder.

She was no different from the rest.

"Whore." The word dripped rage through his clenched teeth. She was a lying bitch, like every other woman.

The Professor watched the pair move, unaware of his presence, his fury. That would change. They would never overlook him, never forget him again. Meg slid into O'Shaughnessy's car. *Slut. Going home to fuck him.*

Well, he would have her too, one way or another.

And she would be both trophy and tool.

With one woman—one delicious kill—he would destroy not just Meg, but also the bastard who symbolized every man the Professor had ever despised.

He would ruin Michael O'Shaughnessy.

TWENTY-FOUR

Early Sunday morning

THE SOUND THREADED through Mick's dream. The bell for class became a fire alarm. He tossed in his sleep, hunting for either the fire or the Klaxon. The sound changed again.

The phone.

Heart pounding, he fought the dream's paralysis. He thrashed in the darkness, fumbling for the receiver. "Yeah?"

His free hand groped for the bedside lamp.

"I found him!" yelled a voice.

Mick jerked the phone a foot from his ear. Music blasted from the earpiece. He maneuvered the speaker end closer. "Andersen? You need backup?"

"What? No." The tone changed. "He's not here now." *You idiot,* was added implicitly.

"Can you go outside? I can't hear you over the music."

There was a muffled curse and various crowd sounds. "Hang on."

Blessed silence; Mick squinted at the clock. Damn. 2:47. After taking Meg home and driving back to Greenville, it'd been nearly two when he fell into bed.

Andersen was back. "I'm at the Depot. He was here last night. A waitress recognized that gelled version you had Buzz draw. She said it looked like he expected someone to be here. He cruised the bar awhile, looked pissed off and left."

"Did she catch his name?"

"He ordered at the bar and paid cash."

"What about the bartender?"

"He's not working tonight. Listen. The guy's obviously hunting. And it sounds like he has a target. We're running out of time."

"What exactly do you want me to do at—" he glanced at the clock "—two forty-nine?"

"I thought you wanted to know."

"Why don't we talk about this when it's daylight?" Mick asked through clenched teeth.

He hung up and flopped onto the pillow, cursing Andersen. The asshole was probably saying equally choice things about him.

He was wide awake now. His options for what to do next were equally unappealing. He could lie there and brood about the case or he could think about Meg and get horny and frustrated.

God *damn* Andersen for waking him up.

MEG WOKE SLOWLY. She stretched, then burrowed into the pillows. A private smile crossed her face. If she'd wanted to, she could've woken up in Mick's bed this morning.

She'd considered that possibility while she was working last night—debating the pros and cons behind a smiling facade. At some point during the evening, she'd decided there were definitely worse things than a boyfriend who wanted to protect her—even if she could stand up for herself. A frown creased her brow. The relationship with Mick really was too much, too fast.

Still...

She suspected her go-slow style frustrated Mick. Instead of being a jerk about it, he actually seemed to respect her for it. His kisses left no doubt about how he felt, but he never pushed it. She hugged herself and reveled in the pleasure of feeling desire without having to act on it. The power to say no was nearly as intoxicating as Mick.

There were wonderful dimensions to him, beyond the physical attraction. She loved watching his face and hands when he told a story. The way his eyes lit up when he saw her. The ease of being with him—laughing over lunch, at the zoo. The concern in his touch. His acceptance of what she'd lived with for too many years.

Part of her couldn't believe she'd told him anything about her childhood. Another part felt such relief at sharing the burden. She realized she wouldn't have told him any of it if she didn't instinctively trust him.

In spite of herself, she did trust him.

She rolled out of bed and stood in front of her mirror. What did he see when he looked at her?

She picked up her brush and slowly stroked the curls. What did she see in Mick? The exterior package or the man inside? The physical magic was wonderful, but it was the intelligence, the humor, the inner core she was falling in love with.

She sighed and stretched. Love or not, she had work to do. She pulled on a sweatshirt and powered on her computer. On autopilot, she opened her mailbox and breathed a sigh of relief when no strange teachers' names appeared. In spite of what the police officer had said—and not said— she wondered if she ought to tell Mick about the e-mail too.

There were a couple of messages from RadConKing@ hotmail.com. Didn't Randy Caruthers use that ID? She hadn't heard from him since he graduated. She wondered if he was still designing computer games. She clicked the message open. It shouted in bold capital letters:

Don't block me again. When I talk, you listen.

She recoiled, as if he stood in her bedroom, shouting. He'd been weird and perverse, but this...

She hesitated before opening the second message.

The compulsion to know overrode her concern.

She clicked on the message. Anger sparked from the words.

Don't try to leave me. You're mine.
I decide when this is over.

For the first time, she felt fear.

"O'SHAUGHNESSY? MAN, you wake up cranky." Andersen's cell phone sputtered, then cleared. "Chicks don't like that."

Mick ignored the commentary. "What'd you find out about the guy?"

"I tracked down the bartender. He says the guy's a regular. Doesn't say much, usually just watches women dance. Sometimes he gets lucky—leaves with a girl."

"Any chance we can find one of those women?"

"They aren't big on last names in this place. Anyway, the bartender said the guy asked about Allison last night."

"Allison?"

"Yeah. Real hottie. Bartender said she comes in occasionally. Said she hasn't been in for a while. Not since this Professor stuff started getting a lot of press."

"What about the guy? Did you run his sheet?"

"That's where it gets interesting. The guy always uses cash at the club."

"We don't have a name?"

"Yes and no."

"What does that mean?" Mick asked testily. He was too tired to play twenty questions.

"After he turned into a regular, the bartender asked his name. I ran the name he gave. That guy's clean."

"*That* guy?"

"Yeah." Andersen was clearly enjoying himself. "*That* guy is a professor at Furman. He's on sabbatical—in Greece. He's also six foot two, and about two hundred sixty pounds."

Mick swore creatively. "So we don't have any idea who this guy is?"

"We're working on it. Every agency around here's handing the sketches to the uniforms. Highway Patrol's making it a priority. The press has it."

Meaning Terri Blankenship, Mick thought uncharitably. "Good."

Something had occurred to him while he wasn't sleeping at 3:00 a.m. "Even if this guy is picking up his targets at bars, he may still be meeting them through the schools. Fax both versions of the sketch to the head of Human Resources at every college in the Upstate. Jordan has the names and numbers. Ask them to send it around to the department heads. Somebody has to know who this asshole is."

"Good idea. Shouldn't take more than a day or so to ID him. I'll let you know if we find anything."

THE PROFESSOR LOWERED the carefully wrapped vase into the packing box. Swirls of ebony climbing the crimson sides of the Codex-style ceramic peeked through the padding. He'd found the artifact on one of his earliest exploratory missions.

He reached for the basal flange bowl. All four legs still supported the bulbous vessel. A stylized bird's head formed the knob on the lid. Graceful wings spread across the lid and flowed down the bowl's sides. It was a prize, one of the few he'd seen intact. Smuggling it out of Mexico had presented a challenge. Tearing another length of bubble wrap from the roll, he swaddled the artifact in a double layer of protection.

The knife was next. The Professor carefully placed it on his desk next to his coffee mug. He lifted the mug and sipped, glancing around his office. What else should he secure besides his treasures? He'd copied all his research files onto thumb drives. Moving the hardbound text and reference books would be too obvious a sign of departure—both transporting them and the gaps left on his bookshelves. Floating a story about lending the artifacts to a colleague at New Mexico State was already pushing the credibility envelope.

Faraday. He snorted his disdain. The little prick might head the department at New Mexico, but he'd been stealing his ideas for years. Publishing and taking credit that should have been *his*. Farady grabbed all the funding—and all the attention. It was part of why he was stuck at this second-tier school instead of taking his rightful place at a leading university. And now he had to give up even that position. It wasn't fair.

Staying wasn't an option. After he saw this morning's newspaper, Plan B—running at some indefinite time in the future—had become Plan A. He'd nearly thrown up on his breakfast table when he saw the picture on the front page.

He retrieved the newspaper and scowled at the article. The picture looked uncomfortably like him in his clubbing outfit. How had the police obtained it? How had they ever connected him to the bars in the first place? He'd taken such pains to ensure nothing connected the women to either him or the pickup spots.

The article hadn't provided nearly enough information for him to make these important decisions. Leaving his position here meant relinquishing years of research. If he went somewhere else, he'd have to choose a new specialty to ensure he didn't inadvertently meet a former colleague.

It wasn't fair that he had to abandon so much.

Maybe he was acting too precipitously. He dropped the newspaper and took another sip of coffee. If you cut through the histrionics, the article simply alluded to the presence of an unidentified man at several nightclubs. The police wanted him identified—and to talk to him.

Right, he snorted derisively. Talk to him. They wanted to manipulate him into revealing information they could use against him.

He picked up the obsidian blade and absently rotated it. They hadn't discovered his identity. And they only had the club disguise, not his everyday persona. At least Paula wasn't around to connect the dots for them. He'd sent the department head an e-mail from her account, fabricating a family emergency. No one else was likely to miss the nosy bitch.

Still, the risk was escalating. He should run, now, today. His eyes dropped to the object in his hand. Self-preservation led his priorities. Disappearing was the most prudent course of action.

Meg. Her image floated on the lustrous black surface of the blade. Her smile turned to a taunting sneer. *"Loser,"* she whispered. *"You couldn't touch either of us."*

She stretched, flaunting her deliciously ripe body. *"Think about me with Michael—him touching me, enjoying me—the way you never will. He gets the girls like me."*

The Professor felt his rage building. *The slut.*

His hatred expanded, reaching outward. That damn agent. He'd outwitted him for weeks—O'Shaughnessy was nothing. But the smug bastard still got the girl—*his* girl, the one *he* wanted.

Pain—physical pain—flooded his awareness. A trickle of blood ran through his clenched fingers. He'd grasped the knife so tightly, it had sliced his palm. He opened his fingers and stared at the smear of crimson against the glittering black stone. Slowly, he relaxed his grip. "Perfect," he whispered.

He would stay, just a few more days. He wouldn't let Meg—or that fucking agent—win. It would be a fitting tribute and a final metaphor for the shrinks to ponder. He would use the obsidian implement when he claimed Meg's life. Sacrifice her as the ancients did. Remove her still-beating heart. Maybe he'd send it to O'Shaughnessy.

Smiling, the Professor placed the knife aside and lifted his hand to his nose. The coppery sharpness smelled as heady as a woman's musk. He touched his tongue to his palm. The bite of fresh blood sent a shudder through him that was purely sexual. Too long denied, the need roared through his veins. He needed one more—no, he *deserved*—one more conquest.

He wouldn't leave without Meg.

TWENTY-FIVE

Sunday night

MEG CLOSED THE e-mail program with trembling hands. Whatever this guy thought he was doing, it had gone too far.

She rose and roamed her living room. Her apartment had always felt like a refuge, a safe haven. But this pervert threatened that security. Tonight, the furnishings looked tired and worn instead of comfortable. The doors and windows old, rather than charming. She crossed to the alcove seat in the bay window and carefully adjusted the drapes, sealing the small gaps between the panels.

Restless, she paced the floor, stopping to peer at books, inspect the contents of her refrigerator and adjust the volume of her music. She had a lecture to prepare, her own homework projects to complete, but the laptop and its sickening messages repulsed her. Hands curled into fists, she glared at the computer, as if it were the source of her frustration.

Still staring at the machine, she made her decision. No one from the Clinton police department had followed up after she talked to the patrol officer. They might not be concerned, but even if it was a copycat, it was time to talk to someone else. With a glance at her watch, she grabbed her keys and headed for the Chi Zeta house. Lisa would still be awake. She could use her friend's phone, or just talk it through with her.

"Hi, Donna," Meg greeted the woman seated behind the front desk.

She climbed the stairs, knocked once on Lisa's door and turned the knob. To her surprise, the door didn't open. She knocked again. "Lisa?"

The door across the hall opened and two women, dressed to go out, emerged. "I think Lisa's at the Pit. We're headed over there if you want to go."

Meg hesitated, and then shook her head. "Thanks for asking, but I have to teach in the morning." She kept her tone light. "I have to stay awake even if y'all don't."

The women smiled politely and headed for the stairs, Meg and Lisa most likely forgotten before they reached the first floor.

Meg jotted *Come find me* on Lisa's whiteboard.

Slowly, she descended the stairs. There wasn't anyone else in the Chi Zeta house she'd consider confiding in, but she was so angry and frustrated. She could call the finance department head, but not at ten o'clock on a Sunday night.

She couldn't put it off any longer. The obvious person to tell was Mick.

But telling him made the threat very real and very frightening.

She stiffened her spine. *Suck it up and do it.*

"I need to use the phone," she told Donna when she reached the lobby.

"Sure." Donna shrugged and returned to her book.

Meg punched in Mick's number and waited.

"Hello?" He answered before she could change her mind or chicken out.

She tightened her grip on the receiver. "Hi, Mick. It's Meg." From the corner of her eye, she saw Donna look up.

"I'm dreaming, right? Meg Connelly called me." He had the sexiest voice. Warm and intimate, it crept from the phone and curled around her. "I'm definitely coming up in the world."

Meg felt both the smile and blush on her face and half-turned from the counter. "Don't get too sure of yourself. We both know how shaky your detective skills are."

"Just shows what you know. A detective's best tools are patience and intuition. Obviously, I have tons of both."

Movement at the other end of the counter distracted her. Donna wasn't even pretending to read. Meg straightened and dropped the playful tone. "We have to talk," she said grimly.

Even over the phone, she felt the surprise and hurt at her abrupt statement and cool intonation.

His voice changed too. "I just got in from work." It was his cop voice, polite and impersonal. "It's late. Is this something we need to discuss tonight? Or would tomorrow in the office be better?"

Meg's heart ached with his reaction. "Mick," she said softly. "I'm sorry to call so late." She chewed her lip. *Coward,* her internal monitor chided. She dragged the phone to the far end of the counter. Mick was silent, waiting her out. "It's just…I'm in the lobby at the Chi Zeta house, at the front desk."

"Oh."

That syllable said so much. *I understand; you have an audience. I'm relieved; you do want to talk to me. I'm happy; you are interested in me.*

"Why are you calling me from there? Is everything okay?"

"I don't have a phone." For some reason, the admission embarrassed her.

"We'll have to do something about that."

What did that mean? "I can't tie up the desk phone, but there's something I need to tell you—"

A hand reached around her and disconnected the call. "I should've known who would have the phone tied up so we couldn't get through."

"Hey!" Meg turned around to Didi's belligerent face. "What do you think you're doing?"

Didi ignored her question and looked at her smirking companion. "If we didn't have to put up with these charity cases, we wouldn't have this problem."

"Just because I'm not living off my father's money doesn't mean I'm a charity case."

"At least my father supports me, unlike *some* people. You think you're so wonderful, but I found out all about you this past week."

"You don't know anything about me," she said.

"You'd be surprised what I know. My parents told me about your high school ad-*ven*-tures. But fill us in. What's your version? Why *did* your parents throw you out of the house?"

Meg went rigid with anger. Didi had no right to invade her private life. That hurt was too personal to be used for petty insult. "It's none of your business."

"You didn't have any problem standing up and putting your two cents' worth into my business. And since you're fucking the detective assigned to my case, I'd say that makes it my business there too."

"That's a lie." Meg's hand rose instinctively. The instant before it flashed across Didi's cheek, another emotion froze her. *Hitting?* an incredulous voice asked. *You were thinking about hitting her?*

Didi's eyes narrowed with spite. "Does that detective know about your nasty past? Or is that what he's interested in? All your experience ought to be good for something."

"There was one man. My fiancé."

"You were engaged?" Lisa's voice. When had she gotten back?

This wasn't so hard, the calm voice in Meg's head observed. *You're not like your father. You can control yourself.*

"Fiancé," Didi hooted. "That's not what I heard."

"How would you know anything but gossip?" Lisa snapped. "Oh, wait, that would require actually thinking, wouldn't it? And we all know where you are with that."

"I heard you were the high school whore," Didi taunted, ignoring Lisa. "That's why your parents disowned you. And as far as that detective goes, maybe he can figure out who the father of your baby was. Nobody else could."

Meg heard the collective gasp from the group gathered behind them. Her hands were shaking with anger. Didi had no right to announce her most vulnerable secret to the world and rip the scabs off unhealed wounds. "You—"

"I think we should call a council meeting." Didi overrode her. "I don't think our *advisor* should be someone with such low morals. I bet you even got arrested. Is that how you paid for school? Prostitution?"

"I was wrong about you," Meg said coldly. "You aren't just stupid. You're a vicious, vindictive bitch."

She turned and pushed her way past the shocked faces of her sorority sisters. *Sisters, what a joke.* They were no more her family than the jerks who'd given birth to her.

"Go on," Didi called. "No one wants you here anyway."

Lisa hurried after her. "Meg, wait. Why didn't you tell me? Fiancé? Baby? What happened?"

"Leave me alone." Meg hurried down the front steps. She wasn't about to explain herself or her actions from years ago. At the same time, the irony of again being driven from her home wasn't lost on her.

She walked into the dark. The parallels to the long-ago

day mocked her. The excruciating details remained permanently etched into her memory.

She'd thrown up at school—again—and the gossip mill was working overtime. Steven had vanished from her life once she'd confided in him. To make matters worse, she'd heard he was claiming he intended to wait to have sex until he was married, as preached by their church. That Meg had fooled him and was running around behind his back.

If it had been anyone else, no one would've really cared. Teenaged girls having babies, with and without husbands, hardly rated as scandalous. But with her parents—or rather her father, the über-righteous pillar of the church and upholder of all things visibly moral—the gossip was irresistible.

As the day progressed, the rumors grew wilder. By lunch, Meg discovered she was apparently having sex with half the senior class.

She knew she couldn't put off telling her parents any longer. The only thing worse than confessing would be their hearing about it at church or the country club. Vaguely, she wondered which venue would bother them more.

Hoping for help and understanding, she approached her mother first. Her prayer that for once her parents would be supportive was answered in a dismally familiar fashion. Her mother did what she always did—deferred to her father. Futilely, Meg wished he'd pay attention to his WWJD tie clasp and actually do what Jesus would do: forgive her.

Instead, he reacted equally characteristically. He pulled out his belt and his makeshift pulpit and beat her with both. "You harlot! You daughter of Gomorrah! You've humiliated us. We didn't raise you to be a whore."

Not once did he ask about the father of the child.

"You're an abomination in the eyes of the Lord," he thundered. "In the early Church, Jezebels were cast out. Stoned. We're more compassionate. We trust in God's judgment. But the community will judge us for your sins. It's our duty to punish you. To restore our family's honor. To force you to accept responsibility."

She knew the futility of arguing with him. It only further enraged him. She tried anyway. "I do accept responsibil—"

"Silence!"

The belt slammed across her bruised shoulders. She couldn't suppress the cry of pain. He hadn't beaten her like this in years. A muffled sound came from her mother. She snuck a peek at her through eyes that already felt puffy. The woman's anguished expression confirmed her expectation. Whatever additional punishment her father planned, it was going to be bad.

Part of her wanted to defy him. To stand up and denounce him.

But he was her father.

She forced her head to bow, at least giving the appearance of submission. She heard his heavy breathing while he watched and waited. Finally satisfied by her demeanor, he passed judgment. "We'll allow you to pack a suitcase. Then you will leave this house. You will not contaminate your family by contacting any of us, especially your sister. You will not tarnish us with the brush of your sins."

Her head jerked up. She stared at him, stunned. "What?"

"You are no longer our daughter."

Her parents turned their backs.

"Mother?" Her voice trembled. "It's your grandchild."

"That abomination is not my flesh." The man who used to be her father led the woman away. *"You have thirty minutes."*

Hollow-eyed with pain and shock, Meg stumbled to her room. She turned in a circle, absorbing the vestiges of her childhood. Did he really mean it? That she had to leave? That they were rejecting both her and the baby?

She didn't know where to begin to plan for such an enormous upheaval. What should she take? What would she need besides everything?

Numbly, she placed clothes in a suitcase and books in her backpack. She tucked her teddy bear into the top of the satchel and fought the rising tears.

Her sister, Lauren, slipped into the room. *"Where will you go?"*

"I'll figure out something." She glanced at the door. *"I don't want you to get in trouble for being in here."*

"I don't care," Lauren replied with a bravado they both knew was false. Meg had always been the defiant one, the one who took the brunt of their father's anger. What would happen to Lauren when she wasn't there to protect her? A tear escaped and she bit back a sob. This wasn't supposed to happen.

Lauren pulled her into a fierce hug. *"I'll find a way to see you."*

Her sister dipped into her pocket. *"It's all I have,"* she said apologetically, as she pressed the crumpled bills into Meg's hand.

"You might need it."

"You need it more. I love you."

Meg's tears fell faster.

Her father's form filled the door. His wrath reignited in the small room. *"I told you to stay away from her."*

He clutched Lauren's shoulder and jerked her back-ward. "I'll deal with you later."

Scowling, he turned back to Meg. "I knew you couldn't be trusted." His eyes narrowed. "Get your things and get out."

"WHO IS THIS?" Mick demanded, when someone finally answered the sorority house phone. He could barely hear over the yelling in the background.

"Lisa. I'm Meg's best friend." The phone was suddenly partially muffled. "Shut up, you bitch!"

Lisa came back on the line, sounding harrassed. "Is this Mick?"

"What's going on? Where's Meg?"

"I don't know. Didi was being her usual awful self. She said some hateful things and Meg left. She, Meg, that is, was really upset. I tried to stop her, but she blew me off."

He finished the conversation and took an impatient turn around his living room. Didi must have taken payback for Meg's comments at the sorority meeting to an ugly low. Concerned, he glanced at his watch. As late as it was, where had Meg gone? To her apartment? Lisa would've looked there, first thing, wouldn't she? Why in the *hell* didn't Meg have a phone?

He paced some more. Where was she? Her closest friend lived in the sorority house. The library would be closed. The thought of her walking to the Strip in the dark raised his anxiety several more notches. Unsure what he was doing, he got in his car and headed for Clinton.

The silent drive did little to ease his worries. Lisa was supposed to call him back if Meg returned. A small corner of his heart hoped she would reach out to him.

What could Didi have said to upset Meg so much? It had to be something about her past. Mick tapped his fingers across the steering wheel and gave the phone another glance.

Why wasn't anyone looking for her? Forget about the Professor. There were plenty of assholes who thought nothing about taking advantage of a vulnerable woman. With that depressing observation, he pushed harder on the accelerator.

FOR A LONG time, Meg roamed the campus. Eventually, she found herself on the Quad with no memory of how she arrived there. Although she hadn't seen her in years, she wished she could talk to Julie. Her best friend's family had taken her in when her parents disowned her. Julie had stood beside her, even when the gossip crested in a nasty wave.

Sinking onto a bench, Meg gave in to the misery and let the memories trample her.

She'd tried to obey the rules. Steven had sworn he loved her. His kisses had grown deeper, his furtive hands bolder, introducing her to the pleasures of her body. She'd always stopped at a carefully drawn line—until the night Steven dropped to one knee and asked her to marry him. Passion had exploded with the wonders of sexuality. In the days that followed, they couldn't get enough of each other. Steven repeatedly pledged his love and devotion. Only once— that first time—was the sex unprotected.

Then the day her period should have begun came and went. She attributed its absence to stress. More weeks passed. She knew she was pregnant. Steven disappeared, taking his worthless promises with him. And her parents evicted her from their life.

For the first month of exile, she held up her head and maintained her silence. But as her pregnancy progressed, it became nearly impossible to endure the comments and the stares, as people she thought were her friends deserted her. Morning sickness racked her body and fatigue nearly leveled her. Fighting to stay awake in class and at her after-school job drained her dwindling resources. She lost rather than gained weight. Circles like bruises darkened her eyes.

Finally, Mrs. Hamilton took her hand and led her into the family room. "What are you going to do?" she asked.

Meg looked at her uncertainly, unsure what she was asking. Fear trickled in like freezing water. Until that moment, the Hamiltons hadn't asked any questions, not even whether she was actually pregnant. Was Mrs. Hamilton saying she needed to make other arrangements? That she couldn't live with them anymore? Was even her best friend going to abandon her?

"About the baby, honey. If you plan to have an abortion, you're running out of time. If you want to give it up for adoption, you need to see a doctor. A lawyer will find a couple who will be overjoyed to raise it. But you can't continue the way you're going."

Relief and panic arrived together. She could stay, but she had to voice another of the enormous truths that kept her awake at night. Stalling, she chewed her lip. Finally, in a small voice, she said, "I want to keep it."

"Honey." Mrs. Hamilton took both her hands. "I understand, but that's not realistic. Don't you want to go to college?"

Meg nodded. She'd talked to Chapel Hill about the change in her status to emancipated minor. The admissions office personnel were sympathetic, but they couldn't change her grant package at this point. Money was already committed to other students. Student loans were available. If she wanted to defer and try again the following year, they offered, maybe additional funding could be arranged. The message was the same at all the other schools, except Whitman. Whitman's alumni fund allowed them the flexibility to offer her a full scholarship.

"How will you do that with a baby?" Mrs. Hamilton asked. "I'm guessing on your due date, but it'll be sometime next fall. Taking care of a baby alone will make studying nearly impossible. How will you pay for the birth? Or afford the baby? Its doctor, clothes, diapers."

"I don't know," she whispered.

"Have you talked to the father?"

Tears sprang to her eyes.

"I take it that means yes. And he was a jerk about it."

Meg dropped her head so her hair swung forward, hiding her face. "He doesn't want anything to do with it. He's telling everyone the baby isn't his."

Mrs. Hamilton bristled with anger. "We can fix his little wagon. I made an appointment for you with my ob-gyn. You think about it some more, Meg. Think about the life you want for your child, what's best for it. It's your decision. If you decide to have it, something will work out. You don't have to marry him—" *she clearly knew Steven was the father,* "—but a paternity test will force him to help support it."

"Her," *she said softly.* "I hope it's a girl." *She pressed her hands against the tiny life inside her.* "I'll love her."

She wanted the child so much—someone to love who would truly love her in return.

"Oh, honey. I know you will." *Mrs. Hamilton hugged her. She wanted to stay there the rest of her life. In the days that followed, Mrs. Hamilton became the mother she'd dreamed of having. She managed Meg's diet, and the morning sickness eased. Together, they read books about pregnancy and fetal development. She acted as if Meg were having her grandchild.*

As graduation neared and her pregnancy approached the end of the fourth month, a small bulge appeared in her slender abdomen. Two days before the end of school, she woke to wrenching cramps. Three hours later, Mrs. Hamilton held her hand as she bled onto a hospital examination table and miscarried the child she so desperately wanted.

TWENTY-SIX

A DARK FORM appeared on the Quad, but Meg barely noticed. She was still in a hospital room, where part of her was dying. The form moved closer and became a man. She tried to rouse herself. "Who's there?"

The man came toward her.

She shouldn't be out here, alone. It could be dangerous. She tried to care, but couldn't shake the lethargy from the evening's emotional firestorm.

"Meg?"

The voice registered. Warm hands settled on her shoulders and gently kneaded the knots. "Lisa said she thought you might be out here."

She waited, not trusting her voice.

"She was kinda excited when I called. Actually, she was screaming at some girl. I got the impression it concerned you."

Again, she didn't answer.

"Want to talk about it?" Mick asked.

Meg shook her head. Lisa had stuck up for her. Her eyes filled with tears. Mick came looking for her. Maybe she wasn't alone after all.

He moved around the bench, and sat beside her. "I'm a good listener."

"I can't." Tears thickened her voice and her mouth trembled. She covered it with a hand. *Don't think about it,* she told herself. *Put it back in its cage and close the door.*

"Whatever it is, it'll be okay." His arm moved around her shoulders.

Nothing will ever be okay. She'd reached out once to what she thought was love. She knew now it was simply an attempt to flee an abusive home. She'd mistaken lust for love, an escape route for a relationship. She'd merely traded one abusive man for another. One betrayal for another. In the process, she'd been damaged beyond repair. Mick deserved someone who had something to offer him. There was nothing behind her facade he could possibly want.

He kissed her temple. "I'm not going anywhere."

At his words, her tears overflowed.

There in Mick's arms, she cried for the devastating abandonment and losses—of innocence, of love, and of the child she might have had—until she had no more tears. Finally, she sniffed and ran her forearm over her cheeks, blotting her eyes with her sweatshirt. Exhausted, she buried her face in his shoulder.

He pushed back the tumbled curls and gently pressed his lips to her skin. "Sh-h," he murmured. He slowly rocked her, like a small boat riding the swells in a sheltered harbor while a storm raged beyond the breakwater.

Gradually she became aware of the solid warmth that was Mick. At some point, he'd pulled her into his lap. His arms surrounded her, shutting out the world. There was only Mick. She felt safe and warm and cherished. Taking a deep breath, she inhaled his scent. It flew straight past her brain and lodged in her heart.

Silently, they watched stars twinkle, an occasional jet and a leaf falling from a tree. Eventually, he stirred. "Better?"

She thought for a moment, then shook her head. It was done. There was no changing the past. But it would never be better.

"It might get better if you talked about it."

She blinked back fresh tears. "Having you think less of me won't make it better."

All this crying was nearly as humiliating as the conversation he thought he wanted to have. "Mick," she looked up at him. "Trust me. You don't want to get involved with me."

His face was inches from hers. "Too late," he whispered. "I'm here. I'm not leaving."

The words echoed in the vast emptiness inside her. *I'm not leaving.*

Her fingers touched his face, hesitantly exploring the plane of his cheek, the arch of his brow. He was so handsome. So strong. And he loved her. It made no sense, but she knew it as surely as if he'd planted sparklers spelling the words in the sky above them.

Her mouth lifted to his and kissed him, and then there was only need. She was lost in it. Needed his love. Wanted his love. Hungered for him. Her body was on fire and Mick was the fuel. She wanted him to break through the fortress of her will. His arms tightened around her.

She couldn't get close enough. Her fingers slid across his shoulders and twined into his hair.

More. She wanted more.

She pressed her body against his. He was so strong, so real.

No, no, no, yelled the censors in her head. *You can't do this.*

She tried to ignore them. Mick. Mick was who she wanted. Loving him, kissing him, sharing with him was the right thing to do. Her heart pounded in her chest. She felt his answering need.

Stop, shrieked her defenses. *You. Can't. Do. This.*

TWENTY-SEVEN

MEG WRENCHED OUT of Mick's embrace. "Stop."

She buried her face in her hands. "I can't. I can't." A shudder spasmed through her.

"Meg." His voice was thick, and he swallowed, trying to clear it. He needed a minute to restart his brain, but he wasn't going to get it. He closed a hand over hers, pulling them from her face. "It's okay."

"I shouldn't have done that."

She tried to twist away, but he moved, holding her close. "You didn't do anything wrong," he said. "It's not your fault."

"I shouldn't have kissed you."

"I wanted you to. God, I'm thrilled you did. But it's okay that you needed to stop. I understand."

She quit struggling, but didn't turn to face him. "You deserve better than this. I didn't mean to lead you on. I'm not one of those women who gets an ego lift from being a tease."

He wasn't surprised when guilt laced her voice. Guessing correctly didn't make him happy. "Is that what he said?" He couldn't contain the surge of anger.

She cautiously examined him from the corner of her eye. "What? Who?"

He took a deep breath, trying to regain control, and softened his approach. "Did he try to blame you? Meg, sweetheart, no matter what the circumstances, you always have the right to say no."

Wearing a bewildered expression, she twisted in his lap. "What are you talking about?"

He reached for her hands, but she shook them loose. "I understand if you don't feel comfortable talking to me, but I wish you'd talk to someone."

She silently waited for him to explain.

He focused on the shrubbery behind her, willing himself to stay calm. *Damn.* He hoped he was making the right decision. Finally, he looked directly at her. "Were you sexually assaulted?"

For a moment, she stared, incredulous. Then she scrambled off his lap. "You think I was raped?"

She gaped at him, appalled. "Is that why it isn't my fault? Just cry 'rape' and that makes it okay? Oh, God, Mick, I'm not Didi. I take full responsibility for what I did. And if I hadn't done it, none of the rest would've happened."

He surged to his feet. "Then tell me why you're so afraid."

"Afraid?" Backing away, she shook her head. "What do you know about fear?"

He followed her. "Explain it to me."

"You don't get anything about me, do you?" Her fingers were on her head, as if trying to keep it from exploding. "God, I'm such a fool, thinking you were different."

"You aren't making sense."

She whirled to face him, her hands flung out to the sides. "Is this plain enough? I don't want to talk about it. I don't want to remember it. Just leave me alone."

He moved closer. "I care too much about you."

"How can you say that? You don't know anything about me."

"We can change that. Let me know you. What could

possibly be so awful you can't tell me? I love you. Nothing's going to change that."

"Love?" She threw the word at him. "Don't confuse lust with love. I did once. I won't make that mistake again."

He was handling this all wrong. He needed to calm her down. Cautiously, he approached her, as if she were a cornered wild animal. "Talk to me, Meg."

She backed away, hands extended in front, as if to ward him off. "Is that your answer to everything? 'Talk to me.' And then what? What happens when you're done exploring the mystery of Meg and you walk away?"

"I won't."

"Don't say things you don't mean, make promises you can't keep." A tear rolled down her cheek.

"I keep my word, I always have." He moved closer, but she stepped back.

"Is that all this is to you? A challenge? A big mystery? Another chance to save the day?"

"Of course not." *Where is all this coming from?*

The tear reached her chin and she swiped at it angrily. "I'll walk away if you don't. I won't let you screw up my life any more than it already is. I won't screw up yours."

"You're not screwing up anything." He reached for her, but she retreated again. "Don't shut me out. I can't change the past…"

"Don't." She turned away from him.

"Meg…"

"Leave me alone, Mick," she sobbed, and kept walking. "Just leave me alone."

Mick stared after her, appalled. What had he been thinking? He knew better than to confront a victim.

Meg's stubborn back retreated into the dark.

He threw up his hands in frustration. "Dammit."

He'd just screwed up royally. Not only did he have *no*

idea what was going on, he'd driven Meg even *further* away. He took a step, then stopped. She was too upset to be rational right now. He'd give her thirty—no, make that fifteen—minutes to cool down, but then they were *going* to talk this through.

Twenty minutes later, he stood in front of Meg's building, tired, worried and out of ideas. He'd followed her, at a discreet distance, just to be sure she was okay, so he knew she was inside.

For all the good it did him.

The apartment house was quiet. Only a few lights shone from the upper windows. How had he managed to foul things up so badly? And what set her off in the first place? Wringing the answers out of her wouldn't solve anything, but he was desperate enough to try.

He crossed the lawn, climbed the stairs and pressed her buzzer beside the outer door.

Nothing happened.

He waited. A minute crawled past.

"Dammit." He knew she was home. She knew he knew it. He pressed her buzzer again.

The door didn't release. The intercom didn't squawk.

Starting at the top, he methodically pressed each of the six buzzers. Someone, he didn't know or care who, pressed the door release. Mick jerked open the front door and stalked into the foyer.

At the foot of the stairs, he stopped. What was he going to do? Pound on her door? Yell through the keyhole? That wouldn't solve anything. It certainly wasn't the way to get her to open up and trust him. And given the way his day was going, the neighbors would call the local police department and he'd never climb out of the resulting hole.

Blowing out a disgusted breath, he slumped against the

foyer wall. Whatever was going on, he couldn't fix it to-night, but dammit, Meg was *going* to talk to him.

Soon.

And in depth.

He glanced up the stairwell. He'd find her tomorrow if he had to camp outside her office or her classroom.

He could leave a message, though. He pulled out his notebook and stared at the blank page. What could he say that would get through to her, but wouldn't embarrass her further if anyone else read it? Something she said kept echoing in his head. *Don't confuse love with lust.* Some-how that was the key to whatever was bothering her.

He thought another minute, then wrote: *I know the difference. Love, Mick.*

He crossed the foyer and tried to slip the note into her mailbox. The box fit flush against the metal plate. He wanted to bang his head against the wall. This wasn't sup-posed to be this difficult.

Another idea occurred to him. He left Meg's building, crossed the street and parking lot, and walked into the Chi Zeta house.

The desk attendant looked up when he entered. "I'm sorry, sir. It's after-hours."

He recognized her from earlier that evening and clearly, she knew who he was. She sounded anything but sorry. If fact, she seemed to be enjoying the drama.

He gritted his teeth and lifted the folded note. "Do you have an envelope?"

The young woman pulled one from under the counter. "Will this do?"

"Thanks. I'd like to leave this for Meg Connolly. Please make sure she gets it."

TWENTY-EIGHT

Monday morning

MICK STOOD IN the break room, staring out the window, thinking the same thing he'd debated in the shower, while he was shaving and during the drive to the office. There was more to Meg's story. She'd sobbed with a desolation that still shook him. There were pieces he didn't know about, but he had to stop making assumptions. He dealt in facts. Why was he apparently incapable of doing that in his personal life?

He casually greeted two other agents who wandered in and poured mugs of coffee, but he continued staring out the window, discouraging conversation. He'd made a huge mistake with the rape thing. Thank God, he'd kept his mouth shut about the abuse.

If he wanted a real relationship, Meg had to trust him. This weekend, she'd opened the door a crack. From the incident she'd let slip on Saturday, her childhood had been less than ideal. Abuse was so personal, the results as varied as the individual. The one thing he was sure about in this whole mess was Meg's strength. Once she trusted someone and opened up, she could come to terms with whatever happened and move on with her life. For reasons he didn't fully understand, he wanted to be that person.

That surprised him. He knew his personality. He wanted to catch bad guys, uphold justice and all that, but he'd never had a superman complex. He never felt he had to save the world. He felt inexorably entangled with Meg, though, and he hoped he'd wedged his foot far enough into the opening to keep her from slamming the door shut again.

"Morning, Mick." Frank ambled into the break room. "Good weekend?"

"Interesting."

Frank poured sugar and cream into his coffee and poked through the box of pastries on the counter. "I shouldn't eat this junk." He turned and looked Mick over. "If I didn't know better, I'd say you had woman trouble."

"What?" Mick threw him a startled glance.

"Only a woman can make you brood that way. Who is she?"

"You don't know her. And everything's fine."

Frank slurped his coffee. "Well, whatever it is, get over it. We've got the morning report with the cap'n in about two minutes and another session with Dr. Mathews after that."

"Yeah, yeah."

"At least Mathews knows what he's doing," Frank said.

"I don't think I could take another round with that idiot the Geiger family pulled in." Mick poured out his cold coffee and turned to face another day.

THE CONFERENCE CALL included detectives from Greenville, Spartanburg and Newberry. Agents who were helping with the legwork crowded the SLED conference room. Mick suspected all three police department phones were similarly surrounded.

They covered the cars, the photos and the nightclubs. Theories were debated and discarded. Assignments followed. Identifying the suspect held the highest priority. Some of the agents drifted away, ready to begin the search.

Dr. Mathews, the forensic psychologist, joined the call

at eleven. "It's fascinating," he said. "Let's start with the tangible—the car. Simply owning it is a peek at this killer's alter ego. While he's driving it, he becomes the man he sees himself being. Not proper and respectable, but recklessly heroic. The James Dean loner women fantasize about, as he fantasizes about the coeds who rejected him when he was a teenager."

"He's killing women 'cause he couldn't get a date?" An incredulous, anonymous voice sounded from the speaker.

"It has more to do with his victim selection than his motivation. Sexual sadists vent deeply rooted urges on carefully chosen targets. You're familiar with the parental issues."

"So we're talking about how he chooses the victims?" The voice sounded like Robbins's.

"Partially. Consistently, sexual sadists have abnormal relationships with women. He's lonely, afraid of women, laughed at, rejected. He hates them and dreams about them. Dreams of bringing them down, humiliating them the way he was humiliated. Destroying them. As a result, a sadist will turn to violent rape or necrophilia."

"Necrophilia?" someone asked.

"Sex with dead bodies."

That produced shudders around the table. Mick heard a few agents whisper, "Gross."

"The second consistent for the sadist is the need for power over the sexual object," Dr. Mathews continued. "He achieves it through violence, restraint and intimidation."

"Where does the e-mail fit into that?" Frank asked.

"They're mind games. He sends messages to let the victim know he can walk in and out of her life at will. As often as he wants, he can remind her of his presence. She doesn't know when he'll appear or what direction the attack will come from. But she knows it's coming. He'll wear her down. Stalk her. Incapacitate her before he moves in for the kill."

"What about the ones he's sending Agent O'Shaughnessy?"

"Taunting the police is typical for this type of killer. In earlier times, it was letters. E-mail is so prevalent, it's not surprising he uses that conduit. Understanding the computer systems well enough to cover his tracks is consistent with the intelligent, loner personality. He'd be drawn to the impersonal method."

"Can you tell anything about him from the messages?"

"The ones to the victims are consistent with dehumanizing them. Note he refers to the women as 'property.' He makes them objects that can't reject him. Items he can control."

"And the ones to the police?" The voice was female. Mick thought it might be Ward.

"It could go two ways. He could be trying to co-opt you. It's part of his fascination with the police. Or it could simply be additional posturing. I think it was Kemper who said at his trial, 'It was a triumphant-type thing. Like taking the head of a deer or an elk would be to a hunter.' Our killer is the hunter and the victims are his trophies."

"He's used that—the hunter reference," Mick said.

"He's overreaching, pushing the military and historical connections. Perhaps he's drawn to the charisma of the military figure—masculine, aggressive, commanding. He's seeking to draw those attributes to himself.

"He definitely wants to be important," the doctor continued. "It's reflected in his word choice—multi-syllable when a simpler word would suffice. The usage is stiff, however, unlike the natural speech rhythms of someone who actually uses the language that way."

"Wouldn't a professor—like maybe a history teacher—use big words and military references?" Anderson asked.

"He may be a professor, but his academic career has likely languished. He feels he isn't getting the respect he deserves."

"So this is a way to get attention?" Anderson persisted.

"Possibly, but I think that's too simple. It's part of his fantasy world. How he sees himself versus how the outside world views him. Most likely, he appears isolated and socially withdrawn. He lives a secret life and shows the world a mask of contentment, pleasantness and ordinariness."

"A wolf in sheep's clothing?"

"I'm not sure it's that deliberate a choice."

"It seems like he has issues with attractive people," someone said. "Like they get unwarranted privileges."

"He's right. Studies have proved it. Attractive people are perceived as smarter and nicer. They get preferential treatment."

"Not all them take advantage of it," Mick protested. "Plenty of unattractive people get ahead. Look at Ross Perot, Donald Trump."

"Yes, but it's telling that he chose *you,* Agent O'Shaughnessy, to receive his messages. It's personal for him."

"Yeah, he's definitely making it personal." Mick muttered.

"It's part of the power and control—dominating not just the women, but you. He knows he's raising the risk level, but it's enormously thrilling when he succeeds."

"What do you mean by 'succeeds'?" he asked.

The psychologist didn't answer the question. "Are you married, Agent O'Shaughnessy?"

Mick took a quick look around the room. The other agents were watching him. "No."

"Involved?"

Damn, this is embarrassing. "I don't see that this is relevant."

"It is. You're an alpha male. He wants to be one."

"I'm not—"

"You are," Dr. Mathews interrupted. "In high school, did you date much?"

He shrugged, although the doctor couldn't see him. "Sure."

"Pretty girls? The cheerleaders and class president?"

He avoided looking at the other agents. "Well, yeah."

"Even then, our killer hated you—or someone like you. The one who got the girls. The popular guy."

"This isn't about me." He was starting to get annoyed.

"Indirectly, it is. You represent the adversary in the subject's private war. He hated the men as much as he hated the women he couldn't have. The rest of us remember those days. There was the popular crowd and the losers. Most of us were somewhere in between. Insecure. Hormones raging. Add an element of mental instability, and you have a recipe for a sexual offender."

High school was a good memory, Mick thought defensively. A group of friends, his father still alive. School was a blur, but he remembered the time outside it. Glorious falls and springs, before the tourists descended. Hot summer days, and hotter nights. Dancing at the Magic Carpet. Drinking beer in the dunes; the fumbling sex that followed.

Had he noticed the guys at the fringe of his group, guys who wanted to be part of it? If he had, he'd dismissed them. A pall of shame abruptly tarnished the memories, and he resented the psychologist for polluting them.

"He knows he's increasing the risk by engaging you," Dr. Mathews continued. "But his fantasies control him just as he seeks to control his victims. With the women, he's all-powerful. But if he can dominate *you,* the reward will be beyond description. He's taunting you already, relishing each small victory. Therefore, I'll ask the question again. Are you involved with someone?"

He hesitated. "Yes."

Frank didn't react, but Mick knew he'd get the third degree later.

"She's at risk," Dr. Mathews said flatly. "His fantasies are growing now, almost beyond his restraint. In them, he sees his enemy defeated and helpless. He does what victorious warriors have done since the beginning of time. He claims his prize."

He listened with a numb horror to the danger he might have put Meg in. *The Professor doesn't know about her,* he thought frantically. *No one knows. She's a secret.*

A secret. The words drained the blood from his face. *Oh, God, what have I done?*

"If the Professor finds out about her, if he finds her, the compulsion to take *your* woman will be overwhelming. It's more than sexual aggression. It's a display of masculine power. The only thing that could make it better for him would be if he could somehow rub your nose in it—taunt you, make you watch—while he violates her. He'd have conquered you completely."

Rage burned inside Mick at the psychologist's words. To have that sadistic pervert touch Meg would hurt him horribly. An assault would send him on a maniacal rampage of his own.

To be forced to watch, helpless, while it was carried out would destroy him.

TWENTY-NINE

Monday afternoon

MICK TUNED OUT the noise from the surrounding desks. He'd already left messages for Meg at her office and the sorority house. Why in the hell didn't she have a cell phone? He was almost ready to call the Clinton PD and ask them to check on her.

He concentrated on the report in front of him. The Professor case had entered another lull, as he waited for one of a hundred threads to lead somewhere. This morning, the captain had pointedly reminded him he had other cases ongoing. He wanted a status report by the end of the day.

The phone rang and he grabbed it, hoping it was Meg. The static nearly drowned out Detective Ward's voice. "O'Shaughnessy?" Her cell phone sputtered, then cleared. "Can you hear me?"

"Yeah, that's better. What were you saying? Something about a sexual assault?"

"You were right," she said. "I talked to the Sex Crimes guys here and at the sheriff's departments about unusual rapes that never got past the initial report. I've found one case already and a guy from Simpsonville's supposed to call me back. A woman called him after reading the *Greenville News* article this weekend. Both cases sound related—bondage and roofies."

"Any suspects for the one you found?" He set the report aside and moved a pad of paper closer.

"None. All they had was the initial report from the patrol officer who responded at the hospital. The victim didn't want to report it. Apparently, she was uncooperative."

"Why?" He scribbled *earlier assault?* on the notepad.

"It could've been anything. The system isn't kind to rape victims. The important thing is, the hospital report's in the file. The rock was there."

"It was?" Mick asked. He underlined the words and added *Spartanburg sheriff's*.

"Yeah. It's our asshole. I've already called the victim and she's agreed to talk to me."

"I'm in Greenville. Want me to meet you?"

Ward hesitated. "Let me talk to her alone. She's down on men. She might do better with just me."

"Okay. Let us know what she says."

He disconnected, tried Meg again and then returned to the paperwork—anything to drown his concern. He'd finished the report on the prison contraband and was deep into the suspected informant inside the Taylors PD when he sensed Frank's presence.

"Cap'n called. Said we might have another victim."

Mick grabbed his jacket as he stood. "Let's go."

"I'll drive."

Frank flipped on the emergency flasher when they left downtown Greenville and merged onto I-385. Other drivers dropped their gaze to the speedometers and eased into the right-hand lane. Frank ignored them as they swept past the slower vehicles. When they passed the I-85 exchange, Mick asked, "Where are we going?"

"Clinton."

Clinton; where Meg lived. His heart skipped a beat before his brain took over. *The odds of that are miniscule.*

Don't think it. Don't connect her to the Professor, even in your thoughts. "What do we know?"

"Not much. Clinton PD called it in to Headquarters. It has all the right elements. White, college girl, stalking e-mails from a professor. Columbia didn't say anything else. Just said to get down there."

He felt the fist of fear ease. "No body?"

Frank shook his head. "This one's still alive. Sounds like we got lucky, got to his target before he did."

"Could be another false alarm." Hundreds of young women, terrified by the murder coverage and the reports of stalking e-mails, had flooded police stations through-out the state with copies of messages.

"Maybe. It could be he's made a mistake. Didn't Dr. Mathews say the perv would start screwing up?" Frank frowned. "There must be something for the cap'n to send us down there."

Mick took an easier breath. No dead woman waited for them. It might even be the break they were looking for.

None of this involved Meg. He'd find her when he fin-ished this—whatever this was—and make her tell him what was going on. Her pain washed over him. He closed his eyes and concentrated on breathing slowly. *Meg, sweet-heart. Nothing's that bad.*

"About this woman you're involved with," Frank began.

Mick's eyes popped open. He did not want to discuss Meg with Frank. A chirping noise interrupted them. "Hold on."

He fished his cell phone out of his pocket, grateful for someone's timing. He spent the rest of the trip on the phone getting updates from dozens of detectives now sorting through various haystacks. Nothing from the cabdriver. He left another message for the cab dispatcher. The calls effectively prevented Frank from asking questions about his new girlfriend.

As he talked, he watched the land flashing past the car window. They cleared the industrial campuses south of Greenville and the sprawling new subdivisions planted in former farmland. An occasional mature tree, spared the developer's blade, poked its head above the rooflines. The developments looked raw and new, both the over-sized McMansions and the cheaply built, starter ranches. Finally, a stretch of woods turned the roadside the rich green of pines. Sumac flamed at the edges, and an occa-sional hardwood thrust sunward in a miniature clearing, glowing with autumn color. It was only a matter of time before they were strip-mined for more sprawl. The thought did nothing to improve his dark mood.

Frank took the Clinton exit, and fear again nibbled at the edges of Mick's conscience. It took a firmer bite when his partner swung onto the perimeter road around Doug-lass College and approached the string of Greek houses on the north side of the campus. A CPD cruiser and a cam-pus security car splashed patterns of blue and red lights over the walls, the trees and the growing crowd outside the apartment building across the street.

This is why doctors don't operate on their families, the rational part of Mick's brain commented. *And why cops don't get involved with witnesses and victims.* Fear had the rest of him by the throat.

Frank parked behind the Clinton patrol car and climbed out. Mick opened his door, but just sat, staring at the build-ing.

"You coming?"

It couldn't be Meg. How many women lived in the build-ing? Women he didn't know. Women he didn't love.

Frank looked at him, then glanced at the building. "Ah

shit, Mick," he said, as he finally understood the silence. "You want me to handle it?"

"No." Whatever spell had rendered him motionless faded. "I'll do it."

The agents moved past the cluster of students at the door. The sidewalk and lawn were filled with students, buzzing in either frightened or curious tones. The campus security guard recognized the two agents and started in their direction. Sidestepping a group of girls, Mick left Frank to deal with the security guy and bounded up the stairs.

On the second floor, he heard voices from the right and turned in that direction. Meg's apartment was on that side, at the front of the building. A group of girls, apparently neighbors, some in jeans and one in a bathrobe, peered through Meg's open door. Over their excited murmurs, he heard Meg's voice. "You can't take my computer."

The words were reasonable, but the note of hysteria under it made him push harder through the crowd.

A uniformed officer faced Meg. In a glance, Mick absorbed the space. Small and neat, a sofa and chairs stood before a bay window. A table separated the sitting area from the kitchenette in the far corner. A desk and shelves were built into the wall on the left. A door near the kitchen probably led to the bedroom. Few personal items were visible—books, candids of friends, but no family photos. A calendar hung above the desk. It was marked with dates for tests and papers, sorority functions and school events. Saturday said simply, *Mick,* he noticed.

"I have to take it in." The patrolman was becoming irritated with Meg's obstinacy. "It's evidence."

"Of what?" Mick asked calmly.

The patrolman swung around. His name tag said *Tolliver.* "I'm sorry, sir. You'll have to wait downstairs."

Mick's attention was on Meg. She looked trapped, standing defiantly in front of her desk. He reached into his jacket, absently noticed the cop's hand dropping to his pistol and unsnapping the holster. Mick extended his badge case. "Agent O'Shaughnessy, SLED."

Tolliver's hand relaxed, but he didn't move. "We're taking the computer in for analysis."

"But I have to have my computer for school," Meg protested. Her tone provided the subtext: how many times do I have to say this? She glanced at Mick, reddened and looked away.

He walked past the uniform and gently moved Meg aside.

"Mick." Her voice carried warnings on multiple levels.

"It's okay." He opened the lid to the laptop. Even at a distance, he could feel her faint trembling. It rumbled below the surface like the quivers of the old Cooper River Bridge when a truck crossed it. He looked up and met her eyes. *I'll take care of you,* he telegraphed. "Show me."

She reached past him, carefully not touching him, and typed in her password. The routine task of restarting the laptop gave her a moment to regain her composure. Behind them, the Clinton officer shifted his weight, clearly not happy with the direction events were taking. From the corner of his eye, he saw the patrolman look from him to Meg and back again, as he tried to decipher the emotional dynamics roiling the room.

Let me know when you figure it out, he thought wryly, before returning his attention to Meg.

She opened Outlook and the screen filled with incoming messages. Moving the cursor to the left panel, she clinked on a folder labeled "Weirdo."

How appropriate. The text of the latest message filled the screen. Mick read quickly, steeling his face into an expressionless mask. *The language, the tone. Dear God, it was him.*

He reached for the mouse. "May I?"

She nodded and one by one, he forwarded the messages to both the computer jockeys in Columbia and his own work e-mail address. "Is this all of them?"

"Yes."

The last message cleared the outgoing folder. "Done," he said calmly and closed the program. "I need you to back up your hard drive."

"You aren't listening. I have to have my computer for school."

"I can arrange a loaner." He'd give her his personal computer if it came to that.

"But…"

"Meg, we need to analyze the messages and establish a chain of custody."

He watched the muscle in her jaw flex as she struggled to maintain her composure. By focusing on holding on to her computer, she'd managed to avoid the awful truth— the messages were from a killer.

"Back up your computer." He nudged her to get her moving.

Wordlessly, she connected an external drive and keyed the program. All three silently watched the program complete its task, then Meg turned off the machine.

Mick handed the computer to Tolliver. "Will you wait for me downstairs? We want someone out front tonight. It's already been cleared with your captain."

He closed the door on the curious crowd in the hall and returned to Meg. Now that the immediate crisis was past, reaction was setting in. She was losing it. Eyes squeezed shut, jaw locked, she was shaking with the effort not to cry. Her white-knuckled fingers dug into the tender flesh of her upper arms as she fought for control.

Oh, Meg. He watched helplessly as she curled into herself. He wanted to take her in his arms, but feared she'd break down completely if he did. As he watched, she forced her hands to her sides. Her chin rose and she momentarily met his gaze. "Do you need something else?"

You. For you to trust me. Why didn't you tell me about this? None of that was the right thing to say. "How are you doing?" *Oh, jeez, that was even more stupid.*

"I'm fine, Detective. Just peachy." There was a defiant edge to her brittle voice. Her eyes darted to the desk, the door, anywhere but him.

"Agent."

Her lip trembled. "Don't, Mick."

He took a step closer and she retreated to the kitchen.

"Is there anyone you can call? Someone you can stay with tonight?"

She turned her back and fiddled with something on the counter. "I'll be fine."

He wanted to take her home with him, but knew better than to even think about it. "You shouldn't be alone. What about your parents?"

"No." Her voice was emotionless.

"Have you called them?"

"Why?" Bitterness seeped through.

Why? He blinked in surprise. "I gather you don't have a great relationship with your parents. But they have to be worried." His sister was across the state at the College of Charleston. He'd called her repeatedly, checking up on her.

"They haven't worried about me in seven years. Why should they start now?"

Her voice was calm, but her hands trembled as she picked up a mug, then abruptly set it back down.

"Why…"

"I don't want to talk about it." The emotional content in her voice was off the scale again—pain, anger, fear.

Whatever had happened—the things he didn't know anything about—had destroyed her already fragile relationship with her parents. Another piece of the puzzle dropped into place—her frantic need to push others away before they left her. In a time of need, her parents abandoned her. Anger surged at the people who'd deserted her. No matter what had happened, they were her *parents*. You don't walk out on family. And whatever the thing was, it was still an open, bleeding wound, not an old scar.

At that moment, he felt completely helpless. Until she let him in, he couldn't change anything. He couldn't even give her the emotional support she so desperately needed. He had to say something. He couldn't just stand there, staring at her. "There'll be a patrol car outside. You'll be fine."

"Oh, yeah, Mick. I'll be just *fine*." She twirled around, anger uppermost now.

"Meg." He took a step closer.

"What am I supposed to do tomorrow, *Detective?* And the day after that? Or the day someone blinks and he makes me disappear? He's chosen *me*. He's told me I'm next."

"Not necessarily."

"There *is* no Professor Dunnavant at Prescott. Or any of the other names he used. I checked. Isn't that how he works? He creates a bogus e-mail account."

"And everyone who reads the newspapers knows it."

She turned and stared out the window. Her eyes blinked rapidly.

"Why didn't you tell someone?"

"I did. I called the police last week."

Last week? And they're just now following up? He bit down the anger. The last thing she needed was more emotional turmoil. "Is this what you started to tell me on the phone last night?"

She nodded. "I was going to…"

"But other things got in the way."

"Yes," she whispered. Her composure wavered and her chin wobbled. Her hands rose and covered her mouth. "Make it stop," she whispered. "Please, make it stop."

It was the opening he'd ached for. He closed the two steps that separated them and wrapped his arms around her.

"I'm so scared."

Her body vibrated with fear. He felt the stifled sobs beneath the shuddering breaths and drew her closer. "It'll be okay," he crooned.

Lean on me, he said silently through his body. *Let me share your burden, ease your hurt.*

Slowly, her tremors eased.

"I meant what I said in my note last night."

Meg shifted, but spoke into his shoulder instead of pulling away. "What note?"

He didn't answer right away. Part of his mind vowed to find the girl working the desk last night. "I know the difference between love and lust."

Meg went completely still.

"I wish we had more time. To do things the way everybody else does. Dinners, movies, and hours of talking to each other about what's important. I don't want to rush you, but I need you to trust me." He tightened his grip. "Anything I said last night that I shouldn't, I'm sorry."

Meg tensed. Finally, she sighed. "It's not you. It's me."

He waited.

"It happened a long time ago." Her forehead rolled against his shoulder. "His name was Steven. He said he loved me, that he wanted to marry me, but all he wanted was sex."

He ignored the double stabs of jealousy and anger. *Damn, worse than a stranger, some punk kid did a number on her.* He forced himself into his professional mode. "If you want to talk about it, now, anytime, I want to listen."

Again, she hesitated.

He slowly stroked her back. *Come on, Meg. Talk to me. I don't know how much time we have before Frank walks through that door. Come on, sweetheart.*

"I'm so tangled up right now. You. That." She waved a vague hand at the door her computer and the officer had vanished through. Her head tilted, her gaze briefly meeting his. "That's not why, you know."

"I didn't think it was."

Her cheek rested against his shoulder. He dropped his lips to her hair, pressed a kiss against her temple. He could stand here forever if the other cops and the bad guys would just go away and leave them alone.

"I'm trying so hard to let go of the past. But I can't go through it again. I lost everything. All I had left was my self-respect. If I let you use this passion against me, I won't even have that."

"I'm not trying to use you. This passion is amazing—it's something to celebrate—but it's only part of what I feel."

Time passed. Mick felt the urgency with each ticking second. He might not get another chance at this if she didn't open up. "What happened, Meg?"

Her spine straightened. Her head rose and she looked into his eyes. He kept his face still, but he wanted to smile. His Meg was back, standing up and taking responsibility. Handling it.

"I got pregnant, and Steven decided he didn't love me after all. My parents announced they didn't want me or my baby. So, you see, Mick, my experience with people who claim to love me isn't very good."

"Not everyone," he said softly. "Lisa was over at the house last night defending you against God knows what. And I'm right in front of you, telling you how I feel."

"I want to trust you, but I don't know how." She gave a wobbly smile. "Saying I trust you is harder for me than saying I could fall in love with you."

Before he could say anything—*I love you. Trust me. Anything*—someone rapped sharply on the door and opened it. Meg leapt away. Within seconds, her shell was back in place. A man stopped just inside the door. His pistol and badge marked him as a Clinton detective. He looked from Meg to Mick and frowned. "Is this a bad time?"

"No. What can I do for you, Detective?"

"Jack Martin. We need you downstairs when you finish here." Martin gave Meg an appraising glance.

"Be right with you." He turned to Meg. "Keep your windows closed and locked. Don't leave the building alone for any reason."

She nodded, her face empty of expression.

He reached in his pocket. "Take this." He extended a cell phone in her direction.

She shook her head. "I can't accept that."

He waved the phone. *Damn Martin for showing up now.* He'd needed more time alone with her. With Martin in the room, he had to be a cop. "Department policy. It's a pre-paid phone. We issue them to people in a crisis situation. Let me know if you run low on minutes."

"The police do this?"

"All the time. Call somebody," he added in a low tone. "I don't want you alone."

"They'll all be in here the second you leave." She waved

at the surrounding building, including her neighbors and the Chi Zetas.

"I'm not talking about people in here being curious. I mean somebody for support."

For an instant, her mask slipped, and a frightened kid looked at him. *There is no one,* those eyes said. Then it was gone. "Thank you for coming," she said formally, and extended her hand. "You said there'll be a patrol car out front?"

He looked at the fingers thrust in his direction as if she'd lost her mind, then closed his own around them. "Absolutely. An officer will escort you to work in the morning."

"Well, then. I'll be fine."

It was either the bravest or the dumbest thing he'd ever heard.

"You have my card. Feel free to call me, anytime, for any reason."

"Thank you, Detective."

"Agent," he whispered and she gave him the ghost of a smile.

Martin made no effort to hide his disapproval as they clattered down the stairs. Mick really didn't care what the man thought.

One sharp look expressed Frank's opinion, but Meg's feelings mattered more. A part of him was still upstairs with her, keeping the monsters at bay. His partner needed him focused, not distracted by personal issues, but Frank also clearly thought Mick was a fool for putting himself in a dicey position in the first place.

The students had been evicted from the foyer, but the patrol officers were talking to a group on the front lawn. Martin turned as Mick joined the men standing beside the front door. Frank had the impatient posture that said he wanted to leave. A smirk crossed Martin's face. Before the detective could utter a word, Mick spoke. "Why in the hell did it take you a week to follow up on those e-mails? You better be damn glad nothing happened to her."

"A week?" Frank asked in a startled tone.

"She called and reported the e-mails." Mick glared at the local detective.

Martin shifted, on the defensive now. "A patrol officer came out and got her statement the next day. There was some confusion over the weekend."

The Clinton detective lifted a shoulder like he was downplaying the mistake. "The patrol officer wrote it up as a routine complaint. I already chewed his ass. The girl called back today. Said she'd gotten more messages that scared her. We got over here as soon as we knew." Martin caught Mick's eye. "'Course, you move pretty fast too."

Mick returned the glare, still seething over the screwup.

Frank broke the tense silence. "We need to hit the road."

"Why?" The problem was here, now.

"We got a lead. When we didn't find the Camaro in the car database—" Frank glanced at Martin, giving him the two-second back story, "—I set up a DMV watch on new registrations."

Frank refocused on Mick. "Your hunch paid off. A guy from the DMV just called. A professor in Spartanburg just registered his car—a black '88 Chevy Camaro. The North Carolina tag expired."

"What else do we know?" Mick asked.

"Guy's been at Agnes Scot a little over a year. Detective Ward called the school he moved from. The department head tap-danced, but finally admitted there'd been rumors about involvement with some students."

"Involvement?"

"That's all he'd say. Ward put in a call to the local PD to see if anybody filed charges."

"And?"

"She hasn't heard back."

"Everything squared away here?" Mick's question included Martin and the security guard hovering just beyond them. "Patrol car's set up for the night?"

"Tolliver will stay here until the next shift relieves him," Martin said. "We'll put somebody behind the building too. I'll follow up on her statement unless you plan to handle that too."

Mick ignored the implied criticism. "We have the e-mails. She didn't mention any other stalking. Ask her about that when you take her statement. The loaner computer has a tracking program on it."

At Martin's questioning expression, he added, "We actually want this asshole to contact her—with us monitoring it, so we know what he's up to."

"I've heard about those programs."

"If this is our guy—" he nodded at Frank, meaning the Spartanburg teacher, "—maybe we can wrap this whole thing up tonight."

"What do you want us to do?" the security guard said.

Don't fuck things up, almost came out of Mick's mouth.

"Do your regular patrol," Martin said. "Chief Norris will have all the units swing through campus tonight."

"We'll be in touch," Frank said to Martin.

Frank followed Mick down the stairs to the car. The trip up I-26 was silent until they reached the Walnut Grove exit. Picking up US 221, they angled cross-country to enter Spartanburg from the south.

"What's going on, Mick?"

Frank's question was neutral, but he tensed anyway. If he admitted he was involved with Meg, procedure could force him off the case. "What do you mean?"

A minute passed. They barreled through the dark countryside. Traffic was light. Only an occasional security lamp above the entrance to a plumbing distributor or body shop broke the blackness. Frank sighed. "I've waited four years to see you more than casually interested in someone. Now this."

"I'm not doing anything wrong."

"She's too young for you. Damn, it's like you dating Jennifer." Frank scowled through the windshield, refusing to look at him.

"Your daughter is a senior in high school. Meg's a college instructor."

"She's still young. And you met her during the investigation."

He rolled his eyes. "That fountain thing was total bullshit and you know it. What is your problem?"

"How you met is not the point," Frank said flatly. "Your relationship with Meg Connelly is the problem. I'm not blind."

"What is it you think you see?" He was starting to get angry. Except for Martin walking in and seeing Meg in his arms, he'd been discreet. She was scared. What was he supposed to do? Stand there like a stone?

"I see a cop who's losing his objectivity." Frank paused. "I see a friend who's going to get hurt."

"Then you're seeing things."

"Shit, Mick. Nobody can be in the same room with you two and believe that. A switch turns on. You light up like a football field on Friday night. It's not just me knowing you so well. First thing, Tolliver asked about it when he came downstairs."

Mick said nothing. They flashed through the crumbling collection of buildings that formed Roebuck.

"You need some separation from this case. Damn it!" Frank's fist pounded the steering wheel. "You *know* it's inappropriate. I was there that night. I saw you get hit by lightning. And she wouldn't give you the time of day. But things have changed. She's the target now. Right now, she needs to feel safe, and you're conveniently right there."

"It's not like that." *Meg isn't using me. And I'm sure as hell not just using her.*

"Then tell me how it is. We've both seen it happen to other guys. Y'all get all hot and heavy. Everything's just peachy. Then one of you wakes up one morning and it's over. Either she's hurt or you're hurt and everybody's sorry it happened."

"It's not like that," he stubbornly insisted.

"Christ," Frank muttered.

They passed in silence through the blue-collar neighborhoods on the south side of Spartanburg.

"Have you said anything?" he finally asked.

"Not yet. I wanted to give you a chance to get your head screwed on straight. But you have to end it. You can't be objective when it's personal. You can't do your job."

He said nothing. What could he say? He'd fallen in love? He already knew his judgment was cloudy when it came to Meg. But that didn't impact his ability to find the Professor.

"If it gets out, you know the shit'll hit the fan. It'll embarrass the team. Cap'n will pull you off the investigation."

That was Mick's one fear. "I get the message," he snapped.

US 221 became Church Street and Frank hung a right on West Henry. The houses moved upscale as they entered Converse Heights, the downtown residential area bordering the college. Frank slowed and parked in front of a stone-trimmed cottage. He stared through the windshield for a moment. "I need you, partner. You need your head clear. The Professor's building up to something. If this is him, he isn't going to roll over."

"Then let's stop the bastard before he does it." Mick said in a voice that defied any further discussion.

THE SPARTANBURG PROFESSOR was ready to lawyer up. He'd answered the first questions when Ward and her partner showed up at his house. Yes, he taught at Agnes Scot and yes, that gave him privileges at other schools. Yes, he owned a black 1988 Camaro with a red interior.

His suspicions already aroused, the arrival of two more detectives spun him into orbit. Frank was the closest to his age, so he smoothly took the lead. "May we have a look at the car, Mr. Manus?"

Manus sat behind a mahogany desk, distancing himself from the police with the wooden barrier. His fingers drummed the surface. Periodically, he realized it and flattened his palms against the leather blotter. "Why?"

"A similar car was involved in an incident. We're looking at all the Camaros in the area."

"It takes four of you?" He waved his hands dramatically at the group.

Mick had mostly bottled his outrage before leaving the car. He studied the man who might've terrorized Meg. He met the general physical description the witnesses had provided, but so did a good percentage of the men in the state. Owning the right kind of car and being a college teacher made him a big suspect in a small pool. It was all Mick could do not to grab the bastard by the throat and shake a confession out of him.

"If we could just have a quick look at the car," Frank said.

Manus's eyes darted from face to face and his nervous drumming resumed. "It couldn't have been involved in 'an incident.' It hasn't even been driven lately."

"Then you won't mind if we take a look."

"I do mind." Manus was growing indignant, as the shock of multiple policemen appearing on his doorstep receded. "You can't just barge in here. I have rights."

Everybody watches Law and Order *and thinks they know everything about the law.*

"We can get a search warrant," Ward said patiently. "But we'd prefer not to. We'd rather keep this low-key."

"Am I a suspect or something?" Manus was getting louder, more aggressive.

Bad move, fellow, if you have nothing to hide, Mick thought. All the little signs were there—the hunch of his shoulders, the jut of his jaw and the squint of his eyes. Manus was lying about something.

He'd never realized hatred could be quite so tangible. He watched the man's restless fingers. His hands looked strong; his forearms were well-developed. The guy would have the strength to squeeze the life from a woman's throat. Mick wanted to break each and every digit.

"Calm down, sir. We just want to look at the car and ask a few questions." Frank spoke soothingly, the way you would to a frightened child or a spooked animal.

"I want you to leave."

"Mr. Manus, we can ask you these questions here or we can all go down to the station. We're trying to make this as painless as possible for you."

"You're arresting me?" The professor's voice rose.

"No, we just have—"

"I heard you." Manus cut him off. "Some questions. I haven't done anything wrong." His face was getting redder.

This wasn't working; they were losing him. Maybe a quick change of pace would trip him, Mick thought. If Manus was clear, then they were out of here. If not… Well, Frank and Ward would keep him from killing the bastard on the spot. "Where were you, Monday, October third?"

"What?" Manus swung his head toward Mick. The question clearly caught him off guard. His gaze darted around the room, pinballing off the detectives, looking for a sympathetic face and finding none.

"Monday. Two weeks ago—" the day Emily Geiger was snatched from the mall, "—where were you during the day? And that evening." He pulled out his notebook and opened it to a clean page. His hands were shaking. He ignored that, along with the other cops' partially concealed, startled looks.

Manus took a breath, visibly pulling himself together. "I teach."

The words were accompanied by the face thrust and raised eyebrows that said he thought Mick was an idiot. "I was in my classroom. I don't remember what we did that evening, but I'm sure my wife will know."

The wife who was noticeably absent on this Monday evening.

"Can anyone verify that?" His pen poised above the paper. His fingers were white, but the pen was steady.

Manus shot to his feet. "That's it. I'm not saying anything else without a lawyer. You're trying to trick me into saying something. Well, it's not going to work." He stalked toward the front door and pointed dramatically. "You can all leave now."

"Sir, that's not necessary," Ward began.

Manus crossed his arms and glared.

"Okay, you can call your attorney from here or from the station." Ward rose to her feet and gestured for Manus to precede her. "Start the paperwork," she said to her partner. "Get a search warrant."

For a moment, Manus looked shocked, then belligerence returned. Trailed by Ward, he stomped to his desk and picked up the phone. "Do you mind?" he snapped.

"Not at all," Ward replied easily. She crossed her arms and rocked back in a waiting posture.

Manus spoke into the phone, then turned. "He'll meet us at the station," he said coldly.

"What do you think?" Mick asked Frank as they piled into the car and followed Ward away from the house.

"I don't know. Too defensive. More than liberal knee-jerking about Gestapo cops. He's hiding something."

"We won't get anything else from him tonight," Mick predicted.

THIRTY

Tuesday morning

MICK AND FRANK left the Spartanburg Police Department, where Detective Ward was finishing paperwork for a search warrant for Manus's car. The teacher had refused to talk with the detectives this morning—completely lawyered up.

"Let's go over to the college," Mick said. "See what we can find out from the staff and his students."

"Sounds like a plan," Frank said. "Want to stop for coffee on the way?"

They were both going out of their way to be agreeable this morning. Frank probably felt sorry for him. Mick didn't need a mirror to know he looked like hell. There were dark, baggy circles under his eyes. The polished suit he wore wouldn't fool Frank or Ward, but he felt a little better for having made the effort.

Frank hadn't mentioned Meg on the drive from Greenville. Mick saw no reason to tell him he'd talked to her early that morning. She'd sounded exhausted, and he doubted she'd gotten any more sleep than he had. He'd tossed and turned, drifting into nightmares that mirrored all three of the grisly murder cases. Nightmares that ended with a knife-wielding Professor standing over Meg, who screamed in terror while Mick frantically ran down endless, blind hallways that echoed with taunting laugher.

He'd wake, drenched in sweat, only to repeat the cycle an hour later.

As early as he thought Meg might be awake, he'd called, mostly to reassure himself. He'd extracted her promise to stay in the house. He'd told her he loved her. He hadn't told her his fears about what the Professor could do to her.

The music department secretary was less than helpful. She stood behind the long counter in the office, crossed her arms and gave Mick a chilly look. Her light brown hair was pulled back sharply from her face. The style emphasized the dark roots along the part. Mick suspected she was probably a nice person, but the scowl on her face made her look mean. Watching her, he halfheartedly wondered why she disliked him and wished she'd offer them a cup of the coffee brewing behind her. After the initial introductions, she'd pointedly ignored him, focusing instead on Frank. "Dr. Manus is a wonderful teacher."

"I'm sure he is," Frank said. "This is all routine. We're trying to tie down where a few people were last Monday, that's all. His Monday classes are at what times?"

She wasn't buying his reassurances. "Do you have a warrant or something?"

"We don't want to look at his records or his personnel file. We'd just like to know his class schedule."

A few graduate students drifted through the outer office and checked their mail slots. They glanced curiously at the two SLED agents. Dark suits plus short hair spelled cops, and a few quickly headed to the door. Mick smiled tiredly. He could smell residual pot on their hair and clothes from where he stood at the counter. This morning, he could care less.

"My professors used to post their schedules on their office door," Mick said, smothering a yawn. "Let's just stroll down there."

"His first class is at nine," the secretary abruptly conceded.

Mick wondered why.

"The second's at eleven," she said. "He doesn't have afternoon classes on Mondays and Fridays."

"Thank you," Frank said. "Now, is there a way to tell if he was actually in class that day?"

"Not really. College isn't like high school, with the professors playing Big Brother."

Her tone implied neither of them were college graduates, Mick thought with a silent sigh.

"Especially this department," she continued. "Everyone's so creative, we try to be more flexible."

Good thing the rest of us stick to rules and routines. Once you start thinking the rules don't apply to you is when you get into trouble. He mentally winced. He wasn't breaking the law with Meg, he reminded himself. Or even violating department policy. She didn't become a target until *after* they were involved.

"The teachers generally conform to a schedule." She said it like conforming was a bad thing. "Sometimes they cancel a class or reschedule it if there's a conflict. The professors occasionally cover each others' lower division classes, but Dr. Manus's classes are so specialized, getting a substitute is pointless."

Manus as irreplaceable genius. Yeah, I can see the man buying in to that myth. And what's with this "Doctor" crap? He'd checked the man's credentials. The guy didn't have a doctorate.

"Perhaps we could talk to the students in his Monday classes," Frank said. "They may remember."

Whatever cooperative spirit the secretary had harbored vanished. "I can't give out that information."

That was the last thing they got from her. Frank and Mick trudged across campus to the administrative offices, where a more cooperative staff provided both Manus's class rosters and the relevant students' schedules. Manus's Monday classes were upper division ones, specifically for music majors. Unless they were cutting class, all the students would be somewhere in the music building today.

"Campuses were smaller when I was in college," Frank groused as they walked back to the music building.

"That's because you went in the Dark Ages."

They passed a chattering group of what had to be freshmen. "I swear they're letting children in these days," Frank muttered.

"I don't know. They look like they're about your daughter's age."

"Jeez, don't remind me. Jennifer starts next fall."

Mick wanted to change the subject away from college girls before Frank started thinking, much less talking, about Meg again. Frank's family, however, was usually a safe topic. "Where does Jennifer want to go?"

"Carolina—the real one. Not that Tarheel place you went. We told her to look in-state or start applying for scholarships."

"Has she looked at College of Charleston? Tricia loves it there."

"I'm not sure Jennifer has the grades to get in."

They talked about colleges until they reached the modern brick building they'd left an hour earlier. The admin secretary had photocopied the students' IDs as well as their schedules. Mick flipped through the pages as he and Frank clattered down the stairs. Several of Manus's students should be in a seminar taught in a small recital auditorium.

The session ended as the agents reached the auditorium.

"Excuse me." Frank showed his badge and made the introductions. The students paused in their packing-up-the-satchel routine and looked them over. Several of the women, and to Mick's discomfort, a few of the men, openly checked him out.

"We'd like to talk to those of you in Music 308." Mick consulted the list and called out seven names.

The group divided, some heading out the door, the rest circling the detectives. "We need to know whether that class met on the third. That'd be Monday, two weeks ago," Mick added when he received mostly blank looks.

How could they not remember? He knew exactly what he'd done that day. Unaware the Professor was kidnapping Emily Geiger at that moment, he'd been interviewing classmates of Mary Baldwin, who attended *this school*. He'd tried to find any clue as to why she was dead.

What about Mary Baldwin—or Emily Geiger or Ashley Cohen for that matter—had attracted the Professor's attention? What behavior or activity made him select *her* from all the available women?

The next question was intrusive and disturbing. What about Meg had attracted the killer? Geiger's e-mails had revealed the Professor knew about her forbidden lover. Baldwin picked up forbidden lovers at a nightclub. Guilt and fear twined up Mick's spine, freezing him in place. Was he Meg's forbidden lover? Did the Professor know that? The killer's e-mails to Meg made only vague references to a secret.

"I'm doing good to remember yesterday," laughed one of the young men.

Mick forced his attention back to the students around him. Several others shook their heads. "I don't remember. Sorry. I have another class." They edged away.

Thank God for the anal-retentive. One of the women had her organizer out and was tapping the buttons. She shook her head. "Class was cancelled. Dr. Manus told us on Friday he had a scheduling conflict for that Monday. I can't remember if he told us specifically what it was. I'm sure I would've written it down. Anyway, I hope that answers your question."

He got her name and number. "I'll need a formal statement."

"Oh, you can call me." She gave him an inviting smile. "Anytime."

Frank was grinning when he turned. "Women everywhere, Mick. The haunted *Hamlet* look works for you."

But the woman wasn't Meg, and he wasn't interested.

Further checking confirmed the eleven o'clock class had also been cancelled on October third. Manus had lied about his alibi.

We've got you now, you bastard. A hair, blood, a speck of that sandy soil from Lynches Woods, and Professor Manus was theirs.

He opened his cell phone and called Ward, relaying the information. "How soon can we have the warrant?"

"Judge just signed it," Ward replied. "It keeps getting better. Manus held a music series at Westside Baptist this summer."

"And?"

"That's Cohen's church. She helped with the youth program."

"You're awesome." He looked up and caught Frank's curious gaze. "Manus teaches at Baldwin's school. Did the music program at Cohen's church. Lied about his alibi for Geiger's murder…"

Frank grinned appreciatively and rubbed his hands together. "Let's go get him."

They left the classroom. They'd pick up Ward and the warrant on the way to Manus's house. As they crossed the sun-drenched lobby, they heard running footsteps behind them.

"Excuse me. Officers?" A young woman, her long, dark hair floating behind her, hurried across the marble-tiled space. "Could I talk to you?"

She looked around quickly. Several students stood next to the plateglass windows. Another impatiently brushed past them. "Privately."

Mick and Frank exchanged looks. "Sure. Where do you suggest?"

She looked over her shoulder, considering. "In here."

She led them to the main auditorium. Banks of padded seats descended to the curtain-draped stage. Lights and clear acoustical panels shaped like waves hung from the ceiling. For a concert, the room would be alive with light and sound. Today, it was quiet, dim and empty. They stood in the rear, waiting for the woman to speak.

"What's your name?" he finally asked.

The question provoked an interesting amount of anxiety. "Celeste," she said finally.

Celeste—with no last name. Now that she had their undivided attention, she didn't seem to know what to do with it. She fidgeted with her messenger satchel and instrument case, then slid both into a seat at the end of an aisle. "I heard you were asking questions about Steve, um, Dr. Manus."

Steve, huh? "Is there some information you can share with us?" he asked.

She leaned across the back of the seat and adjusted the strap of her bag. "That Monday. The day he wasn't in class."

He waited, depression slumping onto his shoulders. He had a fairly good idea where this was going.

"He was with me."

Tension and adrenaline slowly drained away. Exhaustion replaced them. "All day?"

She nodded, her eyes fixed on her satchel. "We went to the mountains on Sunday and stayed over. He told people he was going to a seminar at Brevard."

"Did you know he's married?"

Celeste nodded miserably "He says he isn't happy. He's going to leave her."

Oh, God, the oldest line in the book. He rubbed his forehead, then slowly worked circles into his temples. *Is Celeste No-Last-Name covering for him?* "Can anyone verify your weekend away?"

She thought for a moment. He watched the emotions play over her clear skin and eyes. She was so young. She looked about sixteen. Manus might not be a murderer, but he was a predator just the same.

"My roommate knew we were going," Celeste said. "She didn't approve. She said she'd heard things about him, but I don't believe her."

"Where'd you go?"

"He has a cabin near Boone."

Great. Leave no trail of evidence. No rental receipt, no desk clerk. How many young women has he taken up there over the years? He looked at Frank, whose expression probably mirrored his—*what a slimy bastard.* "Let's go see the roommate and then have another chat with Mr. Manus."

"But this clears him, doesn't it?" She gripped the seat back and swiveled her head between the two agents.

"Maybe. You understand why we can't just take your word for it, don't you?" Mick softened his voice. "Celeste, he's never going to leave his wife. He's using you. You deserve better."

"You don't know him." Her rosebud lips trembled.

Mick sighed and shook his head. Who was he to be giving love advice?

Manus's defiance folded when presented with evidence of his infidelity. He let them see the car. He'd taken it to the mountains that weekend. He'd feared the incident the police spoke of had occurred near Boone, a location where he couldn't justify his presence to his wife.

Don't you think she knows? Neither the question—or the man—was worth wasting his breath.

Frank and Mick loaded into Frank's car, headed back to their office. He dropped his head against the seat back. "God, I'm tired. I thought we had him."

"It's coming together. Another day or two should do it," Frank said.

He watched the scenery. He wondered if he could sleep for the next fifteen minutes before deciding he'd probably feel worse if he did. Sighing, he called the Clinton PD. Dispatch put him through to the cop in front of the apartment building. "How's it going?"

"If it wasn't for the girls across the street, this would be the most boring thing I've ever done."

Any excitement the patrol cops might've felt over possibly catching a serial killer was long gone. "Keep your eyes open. This guy's not stupid."

Frank turned into the parking garage. "Tucked away all safe and sound?"

Sarcasm sounded weird coming from Frank. "Bite me, Meyers. Just doing my job," he said tiredly. "I'm walking over to Main for an espresso. You want anything?"

"No, thanks. I'll see you inside."

Mick waited until he reached the sidewalk to call Meg. She sounded tense and withdrawn. Twenty-four hours of cops watching her every move was telling on her. "I don't know which is worse," she said. "Everyone staring because these guys take me everywhere, or wondering what'll happen if they leave."

The IT guys said she hadn't received any e-mail that

morning. Of course, if the Professor was watching her, he knew the cops had her computer.

"Why don't you take a few days off? Go stay with a friend, your family?" He hesitated, then added, "Me?"

"I can't miss class. I'll never catch up."

He covered his disappointment she'd sidestepped his invitation. "I understand the routine helps, but let's talk about priorities here. Keeping you alive is mine." He dodged a woman who gave him a strange look.

Meg was silent. Then, abruptly: "Is it true?"

"What?"

"One of the cops said you weren't supposed to be involved with me. He said you'd get fired. Like it was my fault."

"No! I mean, yeah, it kinda is. I mean, we aren't supposed to get involved with victims. Or suspects. Remember? I told you that on Thursday night."

"So you're leaving," she interrupted flatly. "Is this the brush-off call?"

He stopped and rubbed his free hand over his face. This wasn't a conversation he wanted to have over the phone. Especially since it tapped straight into her biggest fear—abandonment. "Meg, I'm not leaving."

"I won't jeopardize your job."

"We were already involved when the e-mail started. That's different. If the cap'n asks, I'll let someone else lead the investigation. But I'm not leaving, and I won't get fired."

"Really?"

Her relief flooded through him like a benediction.

He made a mental note to have the bigmouthed cop reassigned.

MICK STIFLED A yawn and answered his office phone, aware his hand was shaking. "Gotta cut back on the caffeine," he muttered. He was starting to fantasize about an island with a large hammock for two and no phone service. "O'Shaughnessy."

"Vijay—the dispatcher—said you wanted to talk to me." The cabdriver had finally returned Mick's call. "He held on to that picture from Sunday's newspaper. He showed it to me this morning. That's him. That's the guy I picked up that night."

The ID was probably shot for trial purposes, but he figured that was the DA's problem.

"Can you tell me anything else about him?"

"He was jazzed up. Couldn't sit still. I was afraid he was on something, but he never said anything 'cept where he wanted me to take him."

"Did you see where he went after he got out of the cab?"

There was a pause as the cabbie apparently searched his memory. "No," he said slowly. "I sat there a few minutes, updating my log. I didn't pay much attention. I was just glad to get rid of him. To top it off, he was a lousy tipper. But I noticed he walked down the sidewalk instead of going into the restaurant. I thought that was strange. Why didn't he have me take him to wherever he was going?"

"Which direction did he go?"

"East."

Toward the Squirrel. "Thanks, you've been a big help."

THIRTY-ONE

Tuesday midday

"O'SHAUGHNESSY?" WARD sounded excited. "I'm adding you to a call. If I screw up and lose you, call me right back."

With a lead-in like that, Mick's curiosity was definitely piqued.

"You still there?"

"Yeah."

"Go ahead, Detective."

A male voice spoke. "This is Detective Waits. I'm with the Simpsonville PD. I spoke with a female victim this morning. She called yesterday afternoon after seeing the newspaper article about the Professor's earlier attacks. She was sexually assaulted, midsummer. The victim was drugged, but she started coming around during the assault. She can only remember pieces of it. That's how those drugs work—they leave gaps in the victim's memory."

"I know." Mick tried to control his impatience.

"Anyway, she came to and found herself tied to the bed. Once she got loose, she went to her gynecologist instead of the hospital. The doctor found a rock wedged up inside her. Detective Ward says that's your doer's signature."

"The victim never reported the assault?"

"She had a long list of reasons why she didn't. Bottom line, she didn't think she had a good enough case to convict. She didn't want to put herself through it."

"So the scene wasn't processed. All that evidence was lost."

"Bingo."

"Damn."

"On the upside…" He paused.

"Yeah?"

"She's pretty sure she recognized the guy. Says his name is Tim Bradley."

"You've got shit, O'Shaughnessy." His captain wasn't buying the rationale for a search warrant. "He's got no record. You've got nothing tying him to the crimes."

"He was a suspect in an assault two years ago," Mick argued.

"He was released. No evidence."

"We've got him at the same clubs as two of the victims. Another witness puts him with the third victim at the mall. The cabdriver picked him up near a victim's apartment the night she died. A woman identified him in an assault with the same MO. She says he matches the suspect sketch."

"She won't press charges. That ought to tell you something about your lack of evidence. The guy doesn't even own a Camaro. So far, nothing ties him directly to the murders. Everything you have is circumstantial. Get something definite and we'll go after him."

Mick frowned at the phone in frustration. His boss was right, but it didn't change the gut instinct that said, *This is the guy.* He'd spent most of the afternoon trying to link Bradley directly to the three murder victims. There were bits and pieces but nothing concrete. They just had to find the right string to follow.

He looked across his desk. Frank's nose was buried in the file the detectives were rapidly accumulating on Tim Bradley.

"How about if you call your buddy, Jack Martin, down at the Clinton PD?"

Frank quirked an eyebrow at him. "You figure he'll blow smoke at anything you suggest?"

"For some reason, the man doesn't like me."

"When's the last time you talked to her?"

Frank's face said he already knew. "Today," Mick said.

"Great job of breaking things off."

He raised one shoulder. Neither a denial nor an explanation would do any good at this point. "Aren't they watching Bradley? Can they drive by his house? See if he's home? He left school this morning. Maybe Martin could ask a few questions over there."

"Bradley left?" Frank stared at him. "And what were you doing calling him?"

"I called the history department, nothing official, just asked if he was in. Clinton PD isn't telling me a thing, and I wanted to know where the guy was. Figured we needed to talk to him as soon as we got everything lined up. The secretary said Bradley left before lunch, took a personal day."

Frank pursed his lips. "It could be nothing—a doctor's appointment or something."

"That's why I'm here and not there. I don't want to spook him." After the Manus circus, he was working hard to keep his emotions under control. Meg was safe. The pieces were coming together. They just had to finish building the case against Bradley.

"Martin asked the school president for background on Bradley." Frank pulled at his lower lip. "You think he got wind of it and he's running?"

"He might be. I'd sure like to know where he is."

Frank picked up the phone and dialed. Mick listened to him bullshit and then pass along the request. A few minutes later, Martin reported Bradley's Honda visible in his driveway. Frank listened awhile longer, then hung up. "They'll keep an eye on the house until we figure out a way to get a warrant."

He nodded. "As long as we know where he is…"

Frank finished his thought. "He can't hurt anybody."

A little later, the president of Douglass College was on the phone. "I spoke with the history department head. Bradley didn't report for class this afternoon." The man was commanding and to the point. "The department secretary is on vacation, but the temporary mentioned bare shelves in Bradley's office. According to his colleagues, Bradley apparently packed his artifacts Sunday afternoon. He told them he was lending the items to a Dr. Faraday at New Mexico State. I spoke with Faraday. He's never heard of Tim Bradley."

"Can you think of any other reason he'd pack those things?" Mick asked. "Or perhaps the other instructors got the name wrong."

"No, Faraday's the expert out there. I can't think of any another reason Bradley would pack up items he held in such high regard."

"Did you see the pair of composites we circulated to your HR department?"

"Hold on."

The president was back. He sounded grim. "I didn't see the resemblance to the sketch in Sunday's paper, but now that I see the drawings side-by-side, I do. Your suspect could very well be Tim Bradley. If he's running, he has nearly a half day's head start."

"Do you have a recent picture?"

"Give me an e-mail address. I'll send the one from his faculty identification card."

Thirty minutes later, Frank's phone rang. Bradley's picture had already gone to the Highway Patrol in Georgia,

North Carolina and South Carolina. Clinton PD and Laurens' sheriff's department were also alerted.

"He isn't?" Frank looked over and mouthed, "Bradley's gone." He listened some more and then asked sharply, "What kind of sports car?"

Mick sat on the edge of his chair, knee jiggling, waiting for Frank to tell him what was happening. Frank rang off and flipped several pages in the file on his desk.

"Well?" Mick asked.

Frank didn't look up from the file when he spoke. "Bradley's neighbor said he left this afternoon. He drove the car he keeps in the garage, rather than the Honda."

He fought to stay as outwardly emotionless as Frank. The guy had to be worried about his reaction. "What car? He only has one registered, the beige Honda Civic." *Where did Bradley go?* His fingers itched to grab the phone and confirm Meg's safety.

Frank shook his head. "The neighbor said it's a black sports car."

"Okay," Mick breathed. Now they knew. The car could be the all-important link. That meant Bradley could be the Professor—and he was running.

Or hunting.

Mick willed himself not to sweat.

But if Bradley owned a Camaro, they could have a warrant in minutes. Mick clicked over to the DMV database and ran "Bradley" as an owner query. He quickly scrolled through the results. "Timothy S. One car, the Honda."

He slumped in his chair and drummed his fingers on his desk, thinking. The bastard was a planner. He'd have distanced himself from the car.

An idea sparked. "Where'd he go to school?"

"College?" Frank asked, not following Mick's thoughts.

"High school," Mick said impatiently. "Dr. Mathews said these guys' crises hit in puberty, in high school."

Frank turned pages in Bradley's file. "Walterboro."

Mick re-sorted the Camaro database. "There are two cars registered in Walterboro. Johnson and Stoddard."

Frank flipped more pages. A smile broke over his face. "We always say these guys have strange relationships with their mothers. Guess what Bradley's mom's name is."

Mick took in Frank's expression. "Johnson or Stoddard?"

"Stoddard. She remarried when Timmy was twelve. Guess the new guy never adopted him."

The phone interrupted them.

"O'Shaughnessy?" Jordan was excited. Paper chases hadn't burnt him out yet. "I've been investigating Bradley, like you asked, trying to link him to the vics. He was teaching at Agnes Scott during the summer, and doing research."

"That's when we think he targeted Baldwin and the other woman, the one he raped."

"Baldwin was in summer school, but not in his class."

"He found her somehow. He followed her to the dance club."

"Okay, but that isn't what I called about."

"You found something else?"

"Cohen worked at Agnes Scot last summer."

"At Agnes Scot?" Mick interjected. "That isn't her college."

"She worked as a clerk in the Agnes Scot history department office."

"The history department." Mick gave a low whistle. "If Bradley was doing research there…"

"He was in and out of the department office all the time."

"That's good, but it's still circumstantial. Keep digging. See if anybody can put them together."

Mick dropped the phone and turned to Frank. "Let's go find him."

THIRTY-TWO

Tuesday evening

TWO GIRLS STROLLED from the Chi Zeta house, letting the rear door slam behind them. They peered at the empty patrol car, put their heads together, giggling, and vanished in the direction of the Sigma Nu house.

"Yes," the Professor whispered fiercely, clenching his hands into a double-fisted victory pump.

It was all coming together. He wanted to laugh aloud at the sheer audacity of it. His plan was going to work. He would take Agent Michael O'Shaughnessy's woman right out from under the policemen's noses.

He flicked a glance at the apartment house across the street. The brainless police were concentrating their efforts there, instead of watching their prey and understanding where she'd go to ground. She'd take cover at the sorority house.

For days, he'd thought of nothing but this moment, working different scenarios, until he hit on the perfect approach. Meg's blind spot was her pride—her disdain for men, her drive to show off, to achieve academic acclaim. She'd delivered the seed of her destruction right into his hands. He'd given her an A for her efforts.

He'd planned his own escape long ago: fake ID, tinted contacts, mortgaged the house to the hilt. He regretted having to leave the place, but his treasures were already safe at the lake house. He could stay there a few days and finalize his departure—when he wasn't enjoying himself with Meg.

There was no way the dim-witted cops would find the lake house—unless he decided to tell them. Maybe he'd leave O'Shaughnessy a little message. Let him know where to pick up his girlfriend's body.

He waited, rehearsing his plans for Meg—the approach, the transfer. It was all so risky, but he'd thought of everything—including a way to rub that asshole agent's nose in his failure. He glanced at his watch. His first gift would be delivered soon. He'd give a lot to see the jerk choke on his coffee tomorrow morning when he logged in to e-mail.

Tonight he'd test the digital video camera. If it worked as well as he expected, he'd share the movie with O'Shaughnessy too. The Professor grinned. He was a generous man. He'd give the agent every gratifying moment of Meg's fear, of the beauty of crimson blood on pale, creamy skin. The hysterical note in her voice as she begged...

He shook himself. There was no time for fantasy right now. Stepping from the car, he paused, listening. This small faculty lot was nearly empty, but sometimes a student risked leaving a car overnight, weighing the possible ticket against the proximity to the Greek housing. He stood still, blending into the shadow of a towering hickory. The tree's rock-hard nuts practically guaranteed the shaded spot at the end of the row would be empty. Few people wanted the resulting dents. He smiled. Those risks were so petty compared to what he was going to do.

To what he was *doing*, he corrected.

He inhaled, pushing his awareness into the darkness. Night came early this time of year, but the shadows were his ally tonight. He caught the scent of smoke from what could be an autumn bonfire.

His smile widened. It was a *bon*-fire—a good fire. The

old warehouse had accepted his offering of kerosene and rags, smoldering long enough for him to move away. He'd left as flames crawled along the tinder-dry wood beams and floors.

As predicted, the Clinton cops had pulled one of the patrol cars away from the college. To their limited mindset, the fire was a more pressing concern. He'd dealt with the second patrol car. His gaze wandered to the bushes behind the parking lot.

Effectively dealt with it.

For a moment, he indulged in the beauty of his ploy and the expression on the buzz-cut rookie's face. Darwin had it right—survival of the fittest.

Noise drifted across the parking lot from the Sigma Nu house. The party was heating up. Time to move. Half the Chi Zeta house would be over there, drinking and whoring. The pair who'd just left confirmed that the rear door was unlocked, the alarm unset. None of the girls cared enough about Meg to inconvenience themselves—a detail he'd counted on.

Now he had to get into the downstairs service area undetected. Meg had arrived as expected, carrying her books and laundry basket. She always did her laundry on Tuesday night. She was nothing if not predictable.

THIRTY-THREE

"Hello, Meg."

She jerked, nearly tossing her book into the air, and practically fell off the washing machine.

"Mr. Bradley? What are you doing here?"

Marking her place in her book with a finger, Meg jumped off the machine. The damp warmth of the laundry room, redolent with the odor of Bounce, added to the incongruity of the man's out-of-context appearance. Between Mick and the mean Clinton cop, Detective Martin, she'd gone way beyond paranoid. Whenever anyone startled her, she half-expected to see some degenerate wearing a blinking *I'm a killer* sign.

"The girl at the front desk said you were down here. I was at the ΣAE house, going over some papers with my TA. I thought I'd take the opportunity to stop in and review your paper with you."

"My paper?" *Now?* That was the last thing she expected him to say.

Mr. Bradley removed a folder from his briefcase and placed it on the central laundry folding table. "I wanted to talk to you about your analysis of Aztec tribal trading patterns. I don't know if you're aware that's my specialty."

This is so weird. "I knew you were interested in the Aztecs—all the artifacts in your office." She checked the page number, closed her book and leaned against the washing machine.

"A lifetime collection." He gestured at the folder. "I

can't tell you how pleased I am with your paper. It lines up exactly with research I'm preparing for the symposium in New Mexico."

She moved to the table. "Dr. Faraday's at New Mexico State. I read some of his papers as background."

"Dan Faraday." Mr. Bradley nodded. "I've collaborated with him several times. That's what I wanted to talk to you about—working together. I assume you plan to continue your graduate studies, pursuing an academic career or a curator position with one of the major museums, but when we see this kind of promising research…" He lifted his hands in an expansive gesture. "Well, I'd be remiss if I didn't make the offer."

Meg searched his face. What was he saying? She knew the paper was good, but he thought she had academic potential? In *history?* It sounded like maybe he planned to show her research to Dr. Faraday. "I'm a little confused."

"Forgive me." His hand rose and fell. "I guess I got carried away. As I said, there's a symposium in December, right after exams, at New Mexico State. I've been invited to present, discussing the impact of ritualized warfare on the dissemination of the cultural influence of the Tenochcas."

"My paper covered that." A finger of excitement cut through her. Did he want to include *her* work in his speech?

"Exactly. If you're interested, I'd like you to co-author the monograph that will accompany my presentation. Now—" he held up a hand, "—it'll be a lot of work. Research, document preparation. And, of course, my name gets listed first." He chuckled.

"Would I get to go…?" *New Mexico. Meeting Dr. Faraday. That would be so cool. And my name would be included in the credits. The finance head keeps saying I need to publish more. It's a history paper, but it deals with trade patterns.*

"Absolutely. I'll deliver the address, but I'll introduce you to all the people you should meet. Like I said, Meg, this is really good work." He tapped the folder.

She nearly did a happy two-step right there in the laundry room. Her hard work was paying off in all sorts of ways. Wait until she told Lisa. Financial reality smacked her in the face. Her excitement deflated like a busted inner tube. "Thank you, but I can't go."

Surprise registered in his raised eyebrows. "Why not?"

She sighed, feeling warmth climb her cheeks. "My finances are pretty tight. Airfare, a hotel…" Her voice trailed off as her blush deepened.

Mr. Bradley was shaking his head. "The symposium covers the expenses of the speakers—and their assistants. I'm so used to it, I didn't think to mention it." He waved a dismissive hand. "Of course, you'll earn an additional stipend while you're acting as my research assistant."

A stipend? With more money coming in, she could cut back her hours at the restaurant.

"Now, the section on the expansion of Tenochtitlan by Mocteuzma, is especially good." He opened the folder and extracted her paper. "I'd like you to take a look at this circled section, and see if you can expand it, pull in more of the warfare significance."

Meg took the paper, leaned against the table and started reading. Mr. Bradley crossed to the drink machine and fed in quarters. Vaguely, she heard cans thud into the tray and a pop-top hiss. He returned and placed a Diet Coke at her elbow.

"Thanks," she said, absently taking a sip. "Were you thinking more about the exchange of prisoners for tribute or the impact of road preparation for the armies?"

He gave her an approving smile. "I think we should focus on the second part. You've already started in that direction—it's part of what caught my eye."

She swallowed more soda and placed the can on the table. "I have my research notes in my apartment. I can run over and get them."

"You don't have to do it right now."

"I don't mind." She pushed away from the table. A wave of dizziness washed over her. "Whoa. Moved too fast there. I guess I'm a little excited."

A look of concern crossed Mr. Bradley's face. "It's getting late. Why don't we just talk in general terms for a few minutes and pick a time to get together later this week?"

"We can talk upstairs in the Chapter room. It feels kinda warm down here."

She took a step toward the stairs. The room spun and she grabbed the table, rattling the cans.

"Are you all right, Meg?"

She brought her hand to her head. "I haven't been sleeping well. Maybe I'm coming down with something. I feel dizzy." Her voice sounded strange. Her head felt inflated, like a balloon bouncing along behind her. She took another wobbly step. "Maybe I should go home."

There was an odd expression on Mr. Bradley's face, sort of excited, like he was pleased with something he'd done. The small hairs on the back of Meg's head rose. Her gaze slid from Mr. Bradley to the can of soda. The Professor slipped drugs into the victim's drink. Her gaze returned to her teacher. Several images wavered before her. All wore smug smiles.

The soda. He drugged it.

She blinked.

Time skipped ahead. Mr. Bradley's arm was around her

shoulders. *When did that happen?* She shrugged it off and stepped back. "Stay away from me," she slurred.

"Or what?"

His eyes gleamed with a predatory glint. *How had she missed that?*

"Get away." She wasn't sure she said the words aloud as the room spun. She raised her hands, pushing away. She couldn't tell which of the images was Mr. Bradley.

She blinked.

The world went black.

THIRTY-FOUR

"HE REGISTERED HIS car in his mother's name?" Frank asked.

"Or it's his mother's car," Mick replied. "It's the link we need to pick him up."

"If we can find him." Frank grabbed the phone to get the process started.

The chime of Mick's e-mail interrupted. He glanced at the screen and gave it a double take. TheProfessor@peoplepc.com. The message line was blank.

Mick clicked on the new message. Hopefully the bastard's latest taunt would indicate where he was—or where he was headed.

There was no text, only an attachment. He tapped the mouse again to open it. The file was huge. It opened slowly. A building appeared. Mick recognized it immediately—Meg's apartment building. He already had his cell phone out when the second photo showed a close-up of the second-floor bay window—Meg's window.

"What's the status of the coverage at the target's apartment?" Meg's curtain billowed in the breeze through the open glass. He'd told her to keep the window closed.

Dispatch came back. "We paged Detective Martin. Unit fifteen has been reassigned. Unit eleven is not responding."

The third picture scrolled onto the screen. Meg walked across campus, a brilliant smile on her face. The sun created a halo around her hair. She wore the sweatshirt she'd had on the morning they'd had coffee.

The Professor had added text to the bottom of this photo. "Are you missing something?"

His heart stopped. "Mother of God," he whispered.

Dispatch caught the emotion in his voice. "Do you need assistance, Officer?"

He surged to his feet. "He has her. The Professor has Meg."

Dispatch put Mick on hold. "Frank!" he yelled as he disconnected and redialed. He pointed to the screen while the phone rang. "Get back on the phone with Clinton PD. We need to seal off the roads around campus."

Meg's cell phone rolled into voice mail. Mick mashed the Disconnect button and dialed another number. Meg had mentioned doing her laundry, an idea he'd firmly squelched until she'd told him she wasn't a prisoner and she was going nuts sitting in her apartment.

The girl at the sorority house front desk answered.

"Meg Connelly, please."

"I'm sorry, you have the wrong number."

"She better be in the House." He ground out the words between clenched teeth.

"I haven't seen her today."

"This is Agent O'Shaughnessy." His blood pressure rose faster than his fear. "This is police business. Get her on the phone. *Now!*"

The phone hit the sorority house counter with a clunk. Long minutes passed as Mick paced. Every so often, his eyes strayed to the picture on his computer screen. *Are you missing something?*

Where the hell is she? Where would she go besides the sorority house? He heard Frank murmuring into his phone and glanced in that direction. Frank was scribbling something on a piece of paper.

Damn. Where's the desk girl? Mick paced some more.

The phone rattled, and his knees went weak. He dropped into his chair. "Meg?"

"This is Lisa, Officer O'Shaughnessy. I'm Meg's best friend."

"I remember you," he said.

She hesitated, then plunged ahead. "I can't find Meg." Fear shaded Lisa's voice. "Her books and stuff are in the laundry room, but she's not there."

He frantically tried to recall the layout of the sorority house. "Where's the laundry room?"

"In the basement."

He remembered the hall, the placement of the rooms and doorways. "Are the stairs to the basement by the back door?"

"Yes. Maintenance and all that stuff is down there."

He thought about the lousy security in the sorority house, the inadequate lock, the lack of a decent alarm system. Clinton PD was supposed to compensate for that. With surveillance watching her, Meg should've been safe. One unit had been diverted, but why wasn't the other unit responding? Had the second unit also been diverted, taken another call? Mostly he thought about Meg. "Where could she have gone?"

"She wouldn't have left," Lisa said. "She always stayed downstairs while she did her laundry. She did it every Tuesday night."

Cold dread filled him. *Always.* Stalkers noticed patterns. He forced emotion out of his voice. "Lisa. Listen to me. There are policemen on the way. Don't let anyone near the laundry room or the back door. Don't touch anything. Do you understand?"

He could feel her growing terror. "What is it? What happened?"

"I'll be there as soon as I can."

He hung up the phone. *Oh, God. The Professor has Meg.*

"Let's go." Mick spun out of his chair and grabbed his jacket.

Frank stood directly in front of him. "You're not going."

"Get out of my way, Meyers. He has her. I have to go."

"That's why you aren't going. You're too involved." Concern creased Frank's forehead. "All we know is Meg's not answering her phone. Apparently, she went over to the sorority house, but she could be somewhere in the house besides the laundry room. You know she's going stir-crazy. She could've slipped out. We don't know anything for certain at this point. But you go running off half-cocked and you're a liability."

Frank's cell phone rang. Without moving his eyes from Mick's face, he answered.

To anyone else, Frank's face would be a blank page. Mick knew it was bad news. "What? *What?*"

"Unit eleven, the guy outside, still isn't answering. And before you say anything, there could be any number of reasons. Martin's on his way over there. He's got backup rolling. I'll meet him there. You stay here."

"Like hell." He barely got the words out through his clenched teeth.

"Mick, I swear to God, you show up down there, and I'll personally arrest you. Compton."

Frank gestured to a tan-uniformed rookie. Andrew Compton was the designated thug—twenty-two, high school diploma, no neck and catlike reflexes. Mick didn't stand a chance against him in a wrestling match and knew it.

"Make sure Agent O'Shaughnessy doesn't go to Clinton."

"Yessir."

Mick stormed into the conference room and kicked the closest chair. It crashed off the wall and slammed into the trash can. He swore savagely. He wanted to throw stuff, hit something. "God damn it to hell!"

He wanted to throw up.

He stalked around the room, seething. Finally, he collapsed into a chair and dropped his head into his hands. *Oh, God. The Professor has Meg.*

He tried not to think, but the scenes rotated though his mind. Baldwin, Cohen, Geiger. For one horrible second, he imagined a knife tracing crimson patterns into Meg's flesh and thought he'd explode.

He jumped out of the chair. To hell with Meyers. He couldn't just sit there.

Compton pushed away from the wall. He hadn't heard the rookie enter the room. "I'm sorry, sir. You need to stay here."

He spun and stared unseeing at the maps and notes littering the conference room walls. This was worse than his nightmares. He couldn't wake up and make it go away. He'd never felt so impotent in his life. This was worse than his father's death. At least then, there'd been things he could do.

Emily Geiger's mutilated body flashed before his eyes again. His stomach nearly emptied. His hand rose, covering his mouth. "No." He rejected the vision.

Meg's smart. She knows what the Professor can do. She'll find a way to escape.

The others were smart too, his inner cop voice answered. *And they were dead now.*

Meg knows that, he argued.

She'll be terrified.

Oh, God. The Professor has Meg.

THIRTY-FIVE

"HAVE YOU FOUND her?" Mick hunched over the conference room table, forehead cradled against his hand, phone pressed to his ear. Frank had finally answered his cell phone.

"We're doing everything we can."

It was a stock phrase, and Frank knew it as well as Mick did. It was hollow, what you said when things looked grim. When you knew that even your best efforts weren't likely to matter.

"Everybody's looking for the car," Frank said.

"He could be anywhere by now."

"Every cop in five counties is looking."

"For a phantom." Despair danced in the corner of the room, ready to take center stage.

"Mick…"

"If you say 'trust me,' I'll…I'll…"

"We'll find her."

"How, Frank? How did he get to her?"

Frank hesitated.

Mick's hand tightened around the phone so hard his forearm cramped. "Did Clinton pull the coverage for the fire? Tell me."

"The fire was arson. An old warehouse. The Professor probably set it as a diversion. Unit fifteen was diverted."

"Those ass—"

Frank overrode him. "Eleven stayed put. He's dead."

Mick's rant died on his lips. "Oh, shit. Who was he?"

"A rookie. Apparently he fell for whatever ploy the killer pulled."

A different anger sliced through his pain. There was a special bond among cops. Everyone would look for Meg. It was what they did. But they'd hunt the Professor relentlessly for taking one of theirs. "Tell me he wasn't married."

Please say no, he silently prayed.

"No."

He breathed a sigh of relief. *No widow.* "I'm sorry about the rookie. But I can't focus on that right now." He cleared his throat. "What else? What else do you know?"

"Meg was in the basement, doing her laundry. We found two cans of soda. A tech from the sheriff's department's tested them."

"And?"

"The regular Coke can was wiped clean, but we got two sets off the Diet Coke. We lifted prints in Meg's apartment to use for comparison. She handled the diet can."

"What about Bradley?"

"His were on it too."

"Okay." He took a firm grip on his emotions. "Drugs?"

"Roofies."

"And she's not in the sorority house. Or her office or apartment."

Frank sighed. "No. But we're still looking. She might have gone out…"

Focus on the facts. "How much of the soda did she drink?"

"Not much. As near as we can tell, most of it spilled on the floor."

He knew as well as Frank did that it didn't take much of the drug to incapacitate a woman. Had she realized what was going on? Had she knocked it over on purpose? "Were there any other signs of a struggle? Besides the spilled Coke?" *And my missing girlfriend?*

What happened in that room? He'd have given anything to be there, to see for himself.

Frank didn't answer directly. "I have to go, Mick. I'll call you as soon as I know anything."

THE DARKNESS HAD texture and noise. Woozy and disoriented, Meg reached for the light switch, but her hands wouldn't move. Her shoulders ached. She was stiff and cramped from lying on her side. She shifted, moving awkwardly. Her legs responded sluggishly. Something hard bumped against her knees.

Awareness expanded. She lay in a carpeted box. Music pounded above her head and something sang a monotonous whine below her. Vague smells assaulted her nose— a whiff of exhaust and tire rubber.

The box moved, jarring her, then settled again. She was trapped in a car, she realized with rising terror. Her arms were bound behind her. Her hands were numb. Tape covered her mouth claustrophobically.

Truth dropped like a stone in a black well of panic. She was locked in a killer's trunk. When the car stopped, she would die.

Fear galvanized her. She kicked frantically at the lid. Her chest heaved. She couldn't breathe. The walls were closing in, squeezing air from the box before she could suck it into her lungs. She twisted in terror, thrashing like a crazed animal. The car turned sharply. She slammed against the rear wall. The blow stunned her. Exhausted, she lay panting on the carpet.

She had to regain control. There wasn't time for panic. She had to get out of the trunk.

Lying on her stomach, she raised her hands blindly,

groping for the escape lever. Her shoulders screamed in protest, but she forced her arms higher until she found the lock. Frantically, her fingers fumbled with the mechanism. She identified the parts by touch, the locking device and the retaining bar. Where was the release mechanism?

Her search expanded around the lock, patting the metal lid and fabric liner.

Nothing.

She slumped on the floor, moaning into the tape across her mouth.

There was no safety bar.

THIRTY-SIX

MICK DROPPED THE phone into the cradle. His head sagged onto his hands. *The Professor will keep her alive for a while. He's won. He's in complete control. He can take all the time he wants.*

He stared into the pit of despair. What was the Professor doing to her? Was he already strapping her to a bed, pulling out a knife? Taunting her with it? Stripping off her clothes?

Touching her.

Cutting her.

Gorge rose in Mick's throat, followed by rage.

"No!" He surged to his feet. Striding to the map, he stared at the colored pins. *Where are you, you bastard? Where did you take her?*

Pain overrode his anger. *Where are you, Meg?*

The pins blurred. His shoulders slumped. "I'm sorry, sweetheart," he whispered. "So sorry, I didn't keep you safe."

He sucked in a deep breath. Brutally, he quashed the hopeless thoughts. Despair wasn't going to save Meg. *Focus on finding her. She's smart and resourceful. As long as she's alive, there's a chance.*

He jammed his emotions in a box and closed the lid. *Think like a cop. Do your job.*

He stared at the large-scale map. He found Douglass College and the road behind the Chi Zeta house. His fingers moved outward. Which way would the Professor go? North to the mountains? West into Georgia? South to the lake or coast?

The Newberry County Sheriff Department and the Highway Patrol would saturate the main roads. Sheriff departments from the surrounding counties would coordinate as the manhunt widened. He bracketed the Interstate, US 76 and US 221. They would put the Patrol on those roads and try to contain him.

Not knowing what was going on was killing him. He stalked into the office area and grabbed an ops radio. Compton started to say something, but he subsided under Mick's ferocious glare.

Back in the conference room, he switched to Greenville's tactical command channel. The beneficiary of a Homeland Security upgrade, Greenville Sheriff's had the most sophisticated dispatch system in the Upstate. They were coordinating dispatch for Clinton and the surrounding law enforcement groups.

The communications chatter was constant. As he listened, his grip on the radio tightened. Every cop in five counties, on and off duty, was looking for the Camaro. And here he sat under house arrest.

He focused on the words flowing to Dispatch. The entire network was active. Sheriff's deputies, city cops, a few park rangers and most of SLED were manning roadblocks or crisscrossing the expanding circle around Clinton. He listened, his eyes riveted to the huge map, tracking movements. The further the circle expanded, the more chances the Professor had to slip through the net. The secondary roads weren't fully covered, he realized. That's how the bastard would get past the police.

Use your head. Find them.

The Professor thought he'd pulled it off. He'd snatched

Meg from under their noses. He'd keep her alive for a while. Mick shoved hard as the lid on his mental emotional box slipped. He couldn't think about what the bastard might be doing to her. He shook his head to reinforce the denial. They'd find her first.

Where would he take her? Clinton PD had already searched Bradley's house and found nothing. The Professor needed time. It had to be someplace inside—a house or a cabin. Lake Murray drew his attention. The north shore was less populated than the eastside—too far from Columbia, not as much deep water. His gaze slid west along the shoreline. There'd be plenty of empty weekend cottages. The Department of Natural Resources patrolled the lake. He still had friends there.

Without bothering to see where Compton was, he picked up the phone and punched in a number.

"Yo, Mickie, what's going on up there? We're picking up a lot of chatter."

"We're bird-dogging this asshole who's been cutting up coeds."

"Yeah? Think you got him?"

"Maybe. Listen, I don't have much time. You still over at the lake?"

A new note sounded in the man's voice. "I got three boats out on routine patrol and another one sitting at the dock."

"We think he's heading someplace he can lay up. Can you cruise the north shore? You know the year-round residents. Ask your guys to look for lights at any of the weekend places."

"You want me to call you or Greenville Dispatch if we find something?"

The man wasn't stupid. He'd realized Mick was acting outside official channels. The request should've come through Command.

"Both."

THE SOUND OF the tires changed. They weren't on pavement any longer. Small rocks pinged against the undercarriage. Where were they? Somewhere far from the city. No one would find her now. She was going to die.

Please, God, she silently whispered into the darkness. *Help me.*

"*God helps those who help themselves.*" Her father's words taunted her.

Please, God. Get me out of this and I'll call him. I don't hate him or Mother.

Fear frizzed like a sparkler in the darkness. *Please, I don't want to die. I want to live and love and get married. I want to have children.*

Tears spilled down her face, caught on the edge of the tape.

She'd wasted so much time trying to be perfect, closed off so many emotions—and for what? She hadn't really lived or let herself feel. She'd been so busy protecting herself—keeping everyone at a distance—she'd never looked behind the curtains in her heart. She'd thought if she could earn attention, or maybe it was respect, she'd somehow be worthy of love. That the external trappings would make everything in her life okay.

Staring into the darkness, she acknowledged what mattered. Not fame, not riches, but people. *I want Mick. I love him. He loves me for who I am, in spite of all my flaws.*

The truth brought her rambling litany to an abrupt halt.

Mick would look for her. He would call. He'd check her apartment if she didn't answer the phone.

Hope sputtered to life. *Quit blubbering and do some-*

thing. You aren't dead yet. God helps those who help them-selves, remember?

She just needed to think. To come up with a plan.

It was too loud in the trunk. The music was deafening, distracting. She kicked at the speakers, hoping to knock a wire loose.

Pain surged up her leg.

Instinctively twisting her body, her hands reached blindly for her foot. Probing, she found a warm, wet spot. Blood. Something had cut her foot. The wound throbbed with each movement. She felt a trickle roll toward her heel.

Was this how her life would end? Despair whispered from the blackest corners of the trunk. *Cut, hurt, bleeding?*

No! There *had* to be a way out.

Think, she desperately demanded.

Something cut her. Something on the speaker. Gin-gerly, controlling her rising excitement, she reached for the speaker. The back side of it pulsed under her fingers, but she couldn't find anything sharp. She spread her fin-gers wider, probing the edges. *There.*

Her hand recoiled from the jagged spot. Quickly, she patted the side of the speaker again, seeking the point. The metal deck had been cut for the larger speaker. The ser-rated rim poked into the trunk space.

Stretching awkwardly, she pressed the tape binding her wrists against the protruding metal. Ignoring the burning throb in her shoulders, she sawed at the restraint.

The car jerked into a turn, flinging her across the trunk. Her hand grazed the metal, tearing a gash across her palm. She cried out against the unexpected pain. For a moment, she tucked into a fetal position, waiting for the pain to sub-side. *Hurry,* her logical side urged. *You don't have time to waste.*

She lifted her hands, grasping first the ceiling, then the

speaker. *There*. She found the sharp spot. Frantically, she raked the tape over it and felt the first strands part. She pressed harder.

The tape abruptly separated. Her hands flew apart, striking the wall and the speaker. She slumped on the trunk floor, screaming as circulation returned to her arms and hands. The tape across her mouth limited the sound to a muffled screech.

She didn't have time to nurse her hands or luxuriate in the ability to move. As soon as her fingers responded, she fumbled with the tape around her ankles. Fingers throbbing, she clumsily searched for the end of the restraining tape.

Once her feet were free, she picked at the strip covering her mouth. In one fierce gesture, she ripped it off and flung the strip away.

"Okay," she panted. She could run when he opened the trunk. He wouldn't expect her to be untied.

But he could still overpower her.

She needed a weapon.

THIRTY-SEVEN

MICK STARED AT the huge map of the state and then the larger-scale one of the Midlands. The Professor wouldn't grab Meg and take off without having somewhere to go. The bastard was a planner. The only house in Bradley's name was his residence in Clinton. But that didn't mean it was the only one he owned.

"Compton."

The young man looked up.

"How much computer experience do you have?"

"I do pretty well with programs, but I'm no hacker."

"Come with me. We're going on a records hunt."

"Sir?"

Mick sat at his desk and logged on to his computer. He gestured at Frank's desk. "Log in over there. Bradley's taking her somewhere. Let's start with the obvious." County by county, they searched his name and came up with only the house in Clinton.

Compton caught on quickly. "What if it's in someone else's name?" the rookie asked.

"He put the car in his mother's name. Try that."

Nothing.

"What about his mother's husband?" Compton asked.

That netted them the house in Walterboro and a beach house. Mick lifted the phone and passed the address to Dispatch. Someone at the beach would check the cottage. He rubbed his jaw. There weren't many ways to get to the beach. The Highway Patrol had them covered. The lake or the mountains, he thought again.

Compton was typing away.

"What are you doing?"

"It could be one of his friends, or someone he teaches with. He'd know if one of them had a weekend place. I'm going through Agent Meyers's file, trying the contacts."

"Good idea." Other ownership, he thought. There were other ways to hide it from casual observation. "What if he owns it through a company?"

"How will you find it, if he did?"

"He'd have to register the company." Mick pulled up the Secretary of State's web page and searched the incorporation records. The room was silent except for the clink of keys and an occasional grunt from one of the men.

"Got it!"

His jubilant cry raised Compton's head. "What?"

"Warriors LLC."

"What's that?"

"A limited liability company. Bradley's listed as the managing member." Mick reopened the property records. "Yes! Warriors LLC owns property in Newberry County." He scribbled out the map coordinates and raced for the conference room, Compton on his heels.

The cabin was on the sparsely settled, western section of the lake. Lake Murray was man-made, created in the forties by damming the Saluda River. Anything above the pair of bridges on State Highway 391 was designated the River. The lake split there, meandering up the Big and Little Saluda River channels.

"Let's go," Mick said. "We'll take your car."

The rookie SLED agent was two hundred pounds of immovable determination. His crew cut bristled with sincerity as he planted all five foot, nine inches of his fireplug frame in the doorway. "Agent Meyers said you had to stay here."

"No, Meyers said not to let me go to Clinton," he replied. "We're not going there."

He could see Compton trying to think it through. He wanted to tell the kid that one way or another, he was going. Compton would have to shoot him to stop him. He needed the guy onboard with him, though. "We have a lead that no one else has. There's no one else to follow up on it. It might be just a wild-goose chase."

The young agent hesitated, uncertainty written across his face.

"We can't pull anyone out of Clinton. They need everybody they have down there, trying to find the car. We're just sitting on our asses here, useless as tits on a boar."

He could tell the kid hated missing the manhunt. "Let's check it out," he urged. "If we're wrong, you're still babysitting me and we aren't in anyone's way. If it looks like we're right, we call for backup. We aren't going to go rushing in there. Do you really think I'm gonna do anything to spook this killer? He's got my girlfriend, remember?"

Thoughts were processing slowly through the rookie's brain.

"I want a SWAT team with me when we take him down. Massive force. Tear gas. Stun grenades." He embellished it, painting the biggest, baddest scene he could envision. Compton was actually licking his lips, imagining it.

He kept talking, lying through his teeth as he oozed sincerity. The cabin felt right. It had to be where the Professor had taken her. But Newberry Sheriff's Department wasn't going in there because Mick felt something in his gut. He had to get to that cabin and check it out.

If he was right, if the car was there, he'd take the place apart bare-handed if he had to. They'd call for backup, but he wasn't going to risk Meg's life on how fast some deputy could cover too many miles of back roads. Every second they delayed could be another stroke of a knife across Meg's tender flesh. He suppressed a shudder and concentrated on the kid.

"Taking you to the lake would keep you away from Clinton," Compton said slowly.

He remained silent, trying to breathe normally while the rookie talked himself into disregarding Frank's implied instructions. "They're fanning out, running the highways, setting up roadblocks. They really don't have time to drive out and check some cabin."

Compton picked up his radio and toyed with the Transmit key.

He willed the agent's fingers away from the button. Technically, they should report their position change, but Dispatch had more than enough to do keeping track of all the active units.

Compton twisted the dial, switching to SLED's channel. He identified himself. "I'm moving Agent O'Shaughnessy," he reported. "Keeping him out of the activity in Clinton." He gave the cabin's location.

The SLED coordinator acknowledged and the kid returned his radio to his hip. He'd covered his ass, but he hadn't given the information to anyone who'd tell them to stay put in Greenville.

THE PATROL CAR barreled through the dark at speeds even Mick wouldn't have risked. The lights on the roof rack spun into the night, gone behind them, almost before they registered. Compton had silenced the siren as soon as they cleared the traffic around Greenville.

The kid's hands rested on the steering wheel, moving

confidently, anticipating curves. "Looks like you know these roads," Mick said finally, breaking the silence.

A smile showed in the backwash of the dash lights. "Only thing you need to worry about is a deer jumping out of the woods in front of us."

Compton skidded through a turn, correcting the fishtail, and straightened the heavy patrol car. A plume of dust hung in the air, marking their passage on the dirt road.

"I grew up in McCormick," the rookie said. "There wasn't shit to do but drink beer, chase women and race cars. I can tell you every dirt road inside three counties."

The kid wasn't bragging, merely stating fact. Mick had only the vaguest idea where they were. Rather than take the Interstate, with all the roadblocks and cops who'd send them back to Greenville to cool their heels, they'd blasted down US 25. Once they'd left the highway at Greenwood, the young agent had taken a series of back roads, streaking east toward Lake Murray.

Mick's cell phone buzzed, startling both of the men. He glanced at the display, half-expecting to see Frank's number and to hear the man ordering him back to Greenville. The readout showed a strange number with an 803 area code. Mid-state. "O'Shaughnessy," he said tersely.

"This is Phil Ridley with the Department of Natural Resources. We just ran up the River under the twin bridges. We got headlights up past Sunshine Point."

"We're at…" He glanced at Compton.

"Deadfall Road."

He passed on their location and the cabin's coordinates.

"You're gonna be right on top of that cabin in a couple of minutes. You want backup?"

"We could use it, but if this is our asshole, the last thing we want to do is spook him."

"I hear you. We'll cruise past slow, like we're out fishin'."

Without warning, the dirt road dumped onto Highway 395. "A couple more miles," Compton said. "We'll pick up Hodge Road at Stoney Hill."

Mick leaned forward, as if he could see the cabin from here. *Hang on, Meg. We're coming.*

THIRTY-EIGHT

MEG DESPERATELY GROPED through the darkness, searching the trunk for something, anything, she could use as a weapon. Minutes later, she nearly gave in to renewed despair. She was the only thing in the trunk.

The car slowed and turned. The rear wheel clunked into a pothole and slammed her against the carpet. For a moment, she lay stunned. Then ideas clicked through her mind. Wheels. Tires. Spare tires. Contorting her body, she searched for the spare tire—and the tool kit.

The car stopped.

A noise rumbled under the music. A garage door? The car moved forward and then stopped. The music died. A door opened and slammed, jarring the trunk. Footsteps slapped against a hard surface. They approached the rear of the car.

Meg's heart slammed against her ribs. She had one chance. She had to be ready.

He wouldn't expect her to be untied. He might not expect her to be awake. She had one chance to get away. One chance to live.

She held her breath, waiting for the trunk lid to rise. Her muscles tensed and whimpered at the strain. *Breathe. In and out. One shot.*

Her hands clenched. *One chance.*

The trunk lock clicked. The lid rose slowly. The Professor leaned forward, as if expecting to pull her limp body from the trunk. She surged to her knees. Putting every ounce of her fear and anger into it, she swung at his head.

He recoiled. The tire iron raked across his forehead. Blood spurted and he staggered away from the car. He crouched by the open garage door, hand to his forehead, cursing.

Meg clambered out of the trunk. She sprinted for the door, but the Professor straightened. He sidestepped, arms reaching for her. She spun away from his outstretched hands, back into the garage.

"You shouldn't have hit me, Meg. Now you're just pissing me off." He brushed his hand across his forehead and wiped blood on his trousers.

She held the tire iron like a baseball bat. The cold metal bit into the cut across her palm, but she ignored the pain. "Get away from me."

Barely daring to take her eyes off him, she flicked glances at the garage interior. On the left side, the door into the cabin led only to another trap. A window centered the outside wall on the right, but layers of paint promised it wouldn't open easily. Even as she wondered if she could risk looking behind her for another door, he laughed.

"Only one way out." He edged closer. "Go ahead," he taunted. "Run. I'll hunt you down."

She quickly glanced past him. Lights reflected off water in the distance. A lake? Which one? There were trees. Could she lose him if she made it that far?

He rushed her.

Caught off guard, she swung wildly. He threw up a hand to block the blow. She heard something snap and he cursed. His other hand closed over the end of the rod. The metal slipped in her bloody palm. For a moment, they grappled, then he shoved her. Off balance, they both lost their grip on the tire iron. It clanged onto the concrete floor and flipped under the car.

His hands gripped her arms. Reeling, caught in his embrace, she slammed backward into the car's fender. He fell with her. His weight hammered her like a sledge against an anvil. Pain crashed through her ribs. She couldn't breathe.

His body pressed hers, pinning her to the Camaro. Revulsion shimmied over her nerves as he moved, rubbing himself against her. Suddenly, he drew back. Before she could react, his arm slashed across her chest, smashing her onto the hood. His other hand pressed something hard and cold against the base of her throat.

She froze, barely daring to draw in the air her lungs shrieked for. *This is it. He's going to kill me.*

Please. The word formed in her mind. Not now, not when she finally understood what mattered.

"What shall we do first, Meg?"

The superior smirk, the "I-control-your-destiny" expression, sent a jumble of memories of facing down her father through her mind. Defiance strengthened her resolve. There was only one way to survive a bully. Stand up to him. She wouldn't give this killer the satisfaction of begging.

His arm lifted from her chest. She squirmed, trying to slide away from him.

The blade sliced into her skin. His other hand joined the knife at her throat. "Be still. Don't make me hurt you."

She hardened her expression, waiting, watching for another opportunity.

His fingers tightened around her neck, making it hard to breathe.

The blade moved. She felt a chill as the fabric in her shirt parted. The pain came a heartbeat later. A warm trickle slid between her breasts and puddled against her bra.

"I've wanted your breasts for a while," he said. "Your lover can have your heart." He leaned forward again and fire bloomed in her chest. With a cry of pain, she instinctively smashed her knee toward his groin, but he'd anticipated the move. He twisted and her knee skidded harmlessly across his thigh. His balance shifted with the movement. For a second, the burning pain at her chest released. She whirled to her left, away from him.

"Bitch." He uncoiled and grabbed her arm.

Desperately, she kicked at his legs and broke free.

Gasping for air, she ran to the front of the car and spun to face him. The Professor stood between her and the garage door. He casually rotated something dark and glittery, then laughed. "I can stand here all day. You're awake now, but all I have to do is wait. The next wave of that pill will hit you soon and I can do whatever I want."

Her ribs throbbed in time with her breathing. She pulled the shirt's cut edges together as fear coiled around her. She'd thought she was clear of the drug. *He has to be lying.*

"I've seen all the variations. Sometimes it's only a few seconds of clarity. Others are like Emily and you—aware for a while."

Panic throbbed in the cuts and sent tendrils of horror sliding down her spine. *What had Emily gone through? Everyone knew he'd tortured her.*

She braced herself against the car, denying the terror. She'd made it this far. She wasn't going to give up now.

"You can't escape," he taunted. "I've thought of everything. How to set you up, lure you in—and all of it right under the cops' noses."

He leaned against the door frame and smiled. "It's like a chess game. It takes strategy, thinking—something too few people seem capable of. I plan a series of seemingly insignificant moves, then *poof.*" He flicked his fingers open and closed. "You're mine. And now nobody knows where you are. Nobody's going to save you."

"Mick will," she said defiantly. Ignoring the fire in her ribs and chest, she straightened.

"He doesn't even know you're gone," the Professor scoffed. "I set my message to deliver at six. That's after-hours. He'll have already gone home. He won't know to start looking until tomorrow at the earliest."

Hope flared. The Professor knew nothing about Mick. He'd still be working at six.

"Too bad you never got a phone. A good-night call could've saved you."

He didn't know about the cell phone. When she didn't answer, Mick would know something was wrong.

"Even if he checks his e-mail over the next few days, he'll never find you here."

Next few days? He wasn't going to kill her?

"I see the confusion on your lovely face. Believe me, I intend to enjoy our time together. You've been an enormous nuisance. I've had to change too many of my plans because of you."

He touched his forehead. Blood from the cut trickled down his cheek. "Have you ever tasted blood?"

He raised his hand to his mouth. His tongue slid over the crimson smears on his fingers. "Each person's is unique. I wonder how yours will taste? Sweet? Or spicy with fear?"

His meaning stilled her breathing and drained the blood from her face. Panic froze her. The fire in her chest multiplied, spread in her imagination to other body parts. Just like Emily. He meant to torture her, as long as he could. As long as she stayed alive.

She fought the trembling that started in her legs. She

had to get out of the garage. But she'd lost her weapon. She couldn't get past him without one. *Think,* the rational part of her brain shrieked. There had to be another way— something else she could use. She chanced another look around the small building.

"Meg, Meg." He shook his head, as if disappointed. "I already told you. There is no other exit. It's just you and me and all the time in the world. For me, that is."

There was a pile of gardening tools against the far wall. He'd easily beat her to them if she tried to reach them.

Fool him. Use his expectations. It was her only chance. She knew what it felt like when the drugs hit her. She could fake it.

She swayed, as if the concrete under her feet had suddenly rocked, and reached for the car to steady herself. Head sagging, she leaned heavily on the hood.

"You lose, Meg."

She jerked her head up, shaking it as if to clear her dizziness.

His eyes held a predatory excitement.

"No." She straightened and pretended to lose her balance, staggering a step.

He eased down the left side of the car. "Who knows, maybe you'll enjoy what I've planned. We both know I will."

How close should she let him get? She backed away slowly, stumbling occasionally, until she reached the corner of the Camaro. She stopped and swayed, facing him across the hood.

"We'll let your smug agent friend enjoy it too. I'll send him pictures, each step of the way. Anything that happens to you is really his fault. He couldn't do his job. He expected other people to do everything for him. Men like him are users, Meg. Parasites. Haven't you learned anything? They take the easy way out. You can't depend on him."

She sprinted for the pile of tools. She grabbed the closest handle and kept running. The pile clattered to the floor behind her.

Free of the garage, she spun, looking for the Professor. He was nearly on top of her. Only feet away, he lunged forward, reaching for her.

She swung the handle like a club. The shovel's blade slammed into his face.

He screamed as the metal spade crushed his cheekbone and ripped open a gash. His eyes, which had been locked onto hers in triumphant expectation, went wide with shock.

Reeling backward, his hands cradled his face. Blood streamed down his cheek and neck. Cursing, he stumbled over the tools scattered across the garage entrance.

"God damn you," he roared.

THIRTY-NINE

"KILL THE LIGHTS," Mick ordered.

Compton toggled off the rooftops and the headlights. Without being told, the younger agent slowed and reversed the cruiser into the driveway closest to Bradley's cabin.

The small building stood in a clearing several hundred yards away, at a bend in the road. The front was dark, but a fan of illumination spread from the rear. From this angle, he could see the drive swung past the house and entered from the lakeside. The garage door must still be open, spilling light into the backyard. Another structure, maybe a newer boathouse, sat farther down the drive, closer to the lake.

Cracking the window, he strained to hear. He slashed a finger at the rookie and Compton cut the engine. It took a moment for the silence to fill—water lapping at the shore, insects, light wind ruffling the pine.

He scanned the cabin's windows. Were they dark or blocked by paint or fabric? Was Meg inside? What was Bradley doing to her?

He jerked his thoughts off that track. *Focus.*

He turned his head, taking in the surrounding area. If Meg managed to get away, where would she go? The lake blocked her escape behind the house, the natural flight path she'd take from the open garage. If she ran into the woods, it would be another battle to find her, but the trees would provide good cover as the police moved in.

His cell phone buzzed, vibrating in his pocket. For a

second, he ignored it. It was only a matter of time before Frank figured out what he'd done and ordered him back to Greenville. A quick glance showed the 803 area code and number of the Department of Natural Resources.

"O'Shaughnessy."

Ridley's voice was tense. "We pulled back to the twin bridges. We have two boats inbound. What's your location?"

"Two hundred yards from the target. Agent Compton is with me. He's calling for support from Newberry Sheriff's and alerting SLED."

Mick caught Compton's eye and nodded. The younger agent picked up the ops radio and scrolled the volume. Voices and static filled the car as Compton keyed in, gave their location and requested backup.

Mick crammed a finger into his ear to block the radio chatter. "I see light behind the house. Did you see any activity?"

"We saw a civilian car on Hodges Road. This time of night, this time of year, we'd have noticed it anyway. If this is your guy, we didn't want to get too close and spook him, so we backed off. We kept glasses on the building as long as we could. The car pulled into the garage." He described the driver.

"That's him," Mick said. *Where's Meg?* "You pulled back, when?"

"Maybe two minutes ago."

A lot can happen in two minutes. People can get hurt. People can die.

He closed his eyes and exhaled. *It hasn't happened yet. Figure out how to get her back.*

"Compton?" He quirked an eyebrow at the rookie. "Sheriff's ETA?"

The younger man spoke into the radio. "Confirmed suspect at our location."

Moving his finger off the Transmit button, he answered Mick's question. "Nearest patrol is nine minutes out. Dispatch notified the chain of command."

They were back in the official loop. Sort of. That meant he had minutes before Frank found him.

"The network is diverting in this direction," Compton added, still listening to the radio.

"Okay." Mick returned to the Department of Natural Resources agent. "Cruise in slow." An incoming call beeped in the background. "Let Dispatch know you're here and available."

He clicked to the new call.

"What in the *hell* do you think you're doing?" Frank's voice was low and furious.

"My job."

"I told you—"

"To stay out of Clinton and the manhunt. I did what I'm supposed to do, Meyers. I found Bradley's cabin."

"He doesn't own—"

"Under a corporate name. I played a hunch. I talked Compton into checking it out. We're good on this. It's straight up. Compton's gone by the book every step."

"I don't care—"

"I do. Bradley's here."

"How do you—?"

"Shh." He caught a murmur of voices, muffled by distance and the building. "I hear something."

Two voices. Male and female. Relief drenched him. *She's alive. She's talking, arguing.* The cadence alternated, but he couldn't distinguish the words.

"She's here, Frank. She's alive."

Hang on, Meg. Slow him down. We're here.

"Christ, Mick." Frank continued to swear softly. "You sure?"

"I hear her."

"Don't do anything stupid. We're nearly there."

He had a sudden vision of the cottage surrounded by SWAT, a hostage negotiator, flash bangs and storming the building, but the central image was Bradley swiping a knife across Meg's vulnerable throat as the team burst through the door. "Tell them not to do something stupid, like get her killed."

A clatter rocked the night.

He jerked toward the cottage. A figure burst into the wedge of light behind the garage. Meg! She whirled and swung something like a baseball bat at another figure. A scream split the air.

"Shit."

He dropped the phone and slammed open the door. In two steps he was full-out running. Arms pumping. Feet churning.

Meg. Gotta get there. Now.

"God damn you," Bradley roared. The killer sprang forward, arms outstretched. "You bitch."

Meg dragged her arms back, as if trying to lift the heavy shovel into position, but the killer jerked forward and caught the handle. For a moment, they grappled, then Meg released the tool, turned and ran.

Not that way, Meg. You're trapped. He dodged trees, staggering over a rough spot. His hand reached for his holster and pistol. *Too far. Too far away. Get closer.*

Behind him, he heard the patrol trunk open. *Get the shotgun, Compton. And screw the beanbags. Get ammo.*

The Professor threw the shovel aside and ran after the fleeing woman.

Mick tore across the yard separating the two cottages. "Bradley," he yelled.

The man's figure jumped as if shot, pivoting toward Mick's voice. Meg sprinted ahead, then circled away from the dead end of the lake and dock. The movement brought her closer to Bradley instead of farther away.

"Police. Get down. Now."

The killer laughed. Turning, he angled across the arc of Meg's turn. She pivoted, looking for a way past him. She was trapped between Bradley and the lake, being herded toward the smaller building.

He pounded across the drive. *Closer. Closer.*

"Mick," Meg shrieked.

He tore his gaze from Bradley, shifting sideways. Meg's terrified face glowed in the light from the garage. Feet flying, she changed course again, trying to circle her captor.

Bradley lunged forward. His hands closed around Meg's arm and she screamed.

"Let her go," Mick roared.

The killer jerked her into his chest and spun. His hand whipped to her neck. "Back off," he yelled. "I'll kill her."

Mick didn't pause. Before Bradley could plant his feet and solidify his grip, Mick lunged and slammed into both of them. His hand angled up to shove Bradley's hand from Meg's throat, but the man's fist was moving already, slashing toward him.

Pain lanced across his shoulder. He barely registered it.

They hit the ground, Meg sandwiched between them, in a flurry of arms and legs and bodies. Meg screamed. The men yelled. Everyone hit everything, elbows, fists and knees flashing.

Movement above him registered. *Knife.* A fist rising to strike.

He lashed out and grabbed Bradley's wrist with both hands. A black blade glittered in the available light.

He pushed, forcing the knife into the air, away from all of them. Beneath him, Meg writhed with thrashing limbs, trying to break free. She kicked, using the strength of her legs, but she was hitting him as often as she did Bradley. With a grunt, he released one hand and shoved, pushing her from the melee.

Bradley abruptly twisted, hammering a fist into Mick's exposed ribs, nearly breaking free. "Bastard. I'll kill her. I'll kill all of you."

The knife hovered in front of his face, the sharp tip inches from his eye. He shoved the killer's wrist, forcing the blade aside. His fist slammed into Bradley's already bloody face. Cartilage exploded with a satisfying crunch.

Bradley roared with pain and anger. Arching off the ground, he tried to reverse their positions. His fist battered at Mick, but rage had carried him beyond feeling.

Dimly, he recognized the killer still held the knife. His hand tightened, squeezing the tendons in Bradley wrist until the fingers flopped, useless, and the black blade fell away.

With his other hand, Bradley hammered into his face, his ribs. Knees and feet thrashed.

Blood pounded in Mick's ears. All that registered was Bradley. The Professor, the man who'd threatened Meg, the killer who'd tormented his woman, lay underneath him. Mick's fists pummeled, answering Bradley blow for blow. Rage added power. It seemed endless, a physical volcano of hatred unleashed on the other's body.

"Mick." Meg's voice reached him. "Mick, stop."

Her body floated over them. Her hand tugged at his

shoulder. Mick angled his head, glancing up at her. Another hand wrapped her waist. "Step back."

Compton.

The rookie made no move to end the fight. He simply pulled Meg clear.

Reason seeped into a corner of Mick's mind. Bradley lay limp beneath him. Sirens shrieked in the distance. Mere minutes had passed, but the bloodlust had suspended time.

Bradley moved. He raised defiant fists and battered Mick's ribs in a quick tattoo. Pain flared across his torso.

"Pussy-whipped," the killer taunted. The words tumbled from split, bloody lips in a mangled face. "Can't be a man and finish it."

Mick stared into the man's eyes. Hate shimmied through him in a visceral tangle. Killing Bradley would be easy.

So easy.

The seduction was there. He felt the lure at the same time revulsion flamed through him. Giving in to the compulsion would make him no better than the animal underneath him.

He placed his hands on Bradley's chest and pushed off, deliberately crushing the breath from the other man's lungs. Rising, Mick said, "Get up."

A bloody, pathetic excuse of a human stared up at him, gasping for air. "Go to hell."

Mick planted his hands on his hips and fought to control his breathing and his rage. Forcing his anger aside, he sucked in air. Bradley wasn't worth losing anything over—his career, his beliefs, Meg. The man was nothing.

Compton stepped forward and leveled the shotgun at Bradley. "On your face. Hands on the ground. Above your shoulders."

Bradley spit at them, a bloody mess both agents ignored. Still cursing, the killer rolled onto his stomach.

Mick reached for the cuffs clipped to his belt. Moving forward, he dropped to one knee and slapped the first bracelet around the Professor's wrist. "You're under arrest…"

FORTY

MICK STOOD IN the telephone alcove in the hotel lobby. The receiver buzzed in his ear, but it screened his face—and gave him an excuse to lurk. From the niche, he could see both the elevator bank and the stairs descending from the mezzanine. Meg was staying in the Columbia hotel for both law enforcement's convenience and her own protection. He heard footsteps on the stairs and glanced up.

Black leather pumps appeared on the stairs, connected to a slim pair of ankles. He watched with approval as a long length of leg followed the feet. A simple black skirt cut off the legs at mid-thigh. The fabric moved easily around hips that definitely belonged to a woman.

He ignored the heavy, black brogans and blue serge-clad legs on the far side of the stairs. He already didn't think much of the escort. The cop should've considered that someone could be hidden in this recess.

He hadn't seen Meg since a Newberry sheriff's deputy pried her blanket-draped body out of his arms and took her away for questioning. Since then, it seemed like every cop in South Carolina except him had gotten a chance to ask her about the Professor.

Somebody at SLED apparently wanted him, and any potentially messy entanglements, kept far away from both Meg and the investigation wrap-up. The media—and other assorted lunatics—were going ballistic, angling for a chance at Meg. Hence, the armed escort this morning.

The black skirt nipped into a trim waist, circled by a simple leather belt. The blue silk blouse flowed upward over more curves he couldn't wait to explore. A jacket hung over her far arm. Closer to him, her right hand skimmed the banister.

She'd be completely visible soon. He shifted, so he'd have an unobstructed view of her face. Finally, auburn curls appeared, dancing on her shoulders and around her face. Artful makeup covered the bruises left by Bradley's blows, but he could see the bandage that started at the hollow of her throat.

She noticed his figure first. For just a second, she tensed. Then a brilliant smile erupted and something tightened inside his chest. He could feel the stupid, lovesick grin on his face. There wasn't a thing he could—or wanted to—do about it.

In his peripheral vision, he saw the officer had belatedly noticed him. One arm came up, the other dropped reflexively to the holster on his gun belt. The cop said, "You need to step back, sir," at the same time Meg cried, "Mick!"

She evaded the officer's restraining hand and rushed down the last two steps. Mick caught her in his arms and held on tight. He'd been dreaming about this moment for days—holding her and never letting go.

She relaxed against him with a sigh of happiness and trust that threatened to break his self-control. He felt her heart beat, smelled soap and a subtle scent of citrus and relished the feel of her body against his.

"I've been waiting for this for days." He loved the way she felt in his arms—a perfect fit. If he had any say in it, they'd fit perfectly into each other's lives, as well.

"Thinking about you got me though a lot." Her face

angled to look up at him. "You know, life won't be boring with you around."

Tilting his head, he smiled into her eyes. "It's gonna be a wild ride."

He couldn't wait to start.

* * * * *

ReaderService.com

Manage your account online!

- Review your order history
- Manage your payments
- Update your address

*We've designed
the Harlequin® Reader Service
website just for you.*

Enjoy all the features!

- Reader excerpts from any series
- Respond to mailings and
  special monthly offers
- Discover new series available to you
- Browse the Bonus Bucks catalog
- Share your feedback

Visit us at:
ReaderService.com

RS13